# REFLECTIONS
## OF A
# PILGRIM

*"Now this is eternal life: that they may know you, the only true God, and Jesus Christ, whom you have sent."*

John 17:3

# REFLECTIONS
## OF A
# PILGRIM

## KAMAL BALUJA

2012

Reflections of a Pilgrim by Kamal Baluja – published by the Rev. Dr. Ashish Amos of the Indian Society for Promoting Christian Knowledge (ISPCK), Post Box 1585, 1654, Madarsa Road, Kashmere Gate, Delhi-110006.

Copyright © 2012 by Kamal Baluja

e-mail: kamal_baluja@rediffmail.com

ISBN: 978-81-8465-209-3

Laser typeset by

ISPCK, Post Box 1585, 1654, Madarsa Road, Kashmere Gate, Delhi-110006
• Tel: 23866323

e-mail: ashish@ispck.org.in • ella@ispck.org.in

website: www.ispck.org.in

# Dedications

*This book is dedicated:*

*To my parents who completed 50 years of their marriage this year. We thank God for this blessing. What is most wonderful is that Jesus is now in their lives.*

*To my wife Jane who is a big pillar of support in my life. Without her the troughs would have been much harder to endure.*

*And above all to my Lord and God, Who put this book in my heart and inspired me to things which were beyond me.*

# CONTENTS

**Section III**    *The Disciple*

# PREFACE

*"Blessed are those whose strength is in you,*
*who have set their hearts on pilgrimage."*
Psalm 84:5

**W**e Christians are all pilgrims in this life. Ours is the pilgrimage of faith. The journey starts the day we accept Jesus as our Lord and Saviour; the day we go down on our knees at the foot of the Cross, and exclaim, *"My Lord and my God."* It begins from *that* moment and ends when we finally enter into our rest with God.

However this pilgrimage can well turn into 'a wandering in the desert'; an ordeal the Israelites suffered for forty years roaming in the wilderness (the journey from Egypt to their destination across the Jordan River should have taken them just two weeks!), because they had willfully wandered away from their God and were disobedient to His commands and statutes. We need to be careful that we do not meet the same fate.

The idea of writing a book first came up when I mentioned casually to my wife Jane, that one day I would make a compilation of my writings. That was last year and since being a half-hearted remark, it met its expected fate - it quickly went to the back of the mind. Earlier this year the book idea resurfaced during a discussion with Pastor Vikas Massey (his ministry is serving the Lord amongst the orthodox Hindus in north India), on matters of our faith. He urged me to put my thoughts in the form of a book. I made some polite noises then, but the idea had now been firmly planted and was prodding for action.

After some contemplation and prayer, and also the encouraging support of my wife, I decided to go ahead. I undertook this project as a labor of love – my offering – to God. For whatever shortcomings and jitters of a first time writer that I felt, my thoughts on the Christian faith and spirituality had to be expressed nevertheless; for they might encourage those walking on the same path – my fellow pilgrims – in their growth as disciples of Jesus Christ.

The next thing to be decided was what shape the book should take. Here the thought that had crossed my mind last year became the guiding and decisive factor. I decided to write on diverse subjects; subjects which I considered important and upon which I had often reflected and even wrestled with, and which had a profound impact on my journey of faith; contributing in the process to my development as a disciple of Christ. It is my reflections on these wide ranging subjects that I have put together in the form of a compendium of articles in this book. I feel the readers would relate to them; if not entirely, then hopefully to an extent to make this book relevant and interesting to many. From that perspective this book can be considered as *a primer on Christian faith and discipleship.*

There are 40 topics that I have chosen; each is covered by a chapter. The number could have been less or more, but I settled on 40 as the appropriate; given the number's significance in the Bible. The articles have been grouped into three sections – *The Almighty, The Nazarene, The Disciple* - depending upon the subject. However these sections are not water tight compartments and the string that binds the chapters runs through the entire book.

This book has been for me both a 'burden' as well as a wonderful and blessed experience. I have enjoyed every moment of the time that it took writing this book. It turned out to be a rich theological experience as I went deeper into the Bible; and to my increasing amazement and delight, found that there was a lot that was still new to discover or discover differently or discover more deeply, in the word of God. I found deepening of my faith and my walk with God much closer. The word of God was 'alive and kicking' like never before. It was also a spiritual discovery, as when I wrote on a particular subject, I was perforce moved to introspect; how much of what I was writing applied to my life or was seen in my life. But at the same time I did not allow my shortcomings (as a disciple) to prevent me from writing *what is the ideal for the disciple!* This was not hypocrisy in operation, but an acknowledgment that despite knowing I fell short of the ideal, I still needed to write what God (and what even the world) expects in a disciple of Jesus. I opened with the statement that we are all pilgrims; it was an admission that I too am growing towards the perfection which God wants in every follower of Christ, but at the same time my present imperfect state should not take away from me the goal of the perfect state or disqualify me from writing about it.

The views and the perspective that I have put forth on the subjects covered in this book have been formed over the nearly three decades of my Christian walk. They have been shaped by the sermons and talks of many speakers; the writings of various authors; my own study and reflection on the word of God; *and importantly the insights that God blessed me on these subjects.* And also to quote the great reformist Martin Luther: *"My trials have been my masters in divinity"* (modified to make it more apt to my story). But it could well be that the reader might not agree with all that she finds in this book or the way certain subjects have been dealt with. But these are my views, my perspective, which I have presented in all sincerity and humility. As we know there is but one Absolute Truth; the rest are but *reflections* of that Truth.

This book is meant for all Christians – whether young or mature in their faith. But I believe it will be especially useful for those who are in their formative years as a Christian and even for those who may be testing the waters of Christianity. But it is my hope that all those who pick up this book will get as much enjoyment in reading it as I had in writing it. And I pray it will help you in your pilgrimage - whatever stage you might be in the journey – by giving new or different insights on issues that you yourself may have been reflecting upon. I would invite you to write to me with your opinions, questions, and discussion points. They would be welcome.

Some acknowledgements that I need to make. In my pilgrimage I have been touched and inspired by a number of people; by their lives, words, works, and example. However there are a few I would like to especially mention by name here. Fr. Matthew Padyatty, my economics teacher in high school, in whom I had the first brush with the humility of Christ (that was before I had become a Christian). The late Fr. Christopher Robinson, ex- Bishop of the Diocese of Delhi. He was my godfather at my baptism. His crackling laughter, the twinkle in his eyes, and his child-like enthusiasm, made me wonder if Jesus was like this. And Fr. Amos Rajamoney, who like Bishop Robinson was an inmate of the Cambridge Brotherhood in Delhi. In his work amongst the underprivileged in the slums at the outskirts of Delhi, I saw the compassion of Jesus for the people and the 'social welfare' element in the Lord's teachings. To them and to all others, I acknowledge with much gratitude, their contribution in my development as a disciple of Christ.

Let me conclude with these words of my favorite writer, St. Paul:

*"Finally, brothers, whatever is true, whatever is noble, whatever is right, whatever is pure, whatever is lovely, whatever is admirable - if anything is excellent or praiseworthy - think about such things." (Philippians 4:8)*

Kamal Baluja
A servant of Christ Jesus

# SECTION I

---

# THE ALMIGHTY

*"I am the Alpha and the Omega,"*
*says the Lord God, "who is, and who was,*
*and who is to come, the Almighty."*
*Revelation 1:8*

# Chapter 1

# WHAT IS ALL THIS ABOUT? GOD'S MASTER PLAN

*"Man is God's risk."*

Ever wondered what is all this about? What is God's plan? Why He created all this? Why God created man? And why God took all the trouble and paid such a heavy price to redeem man? To find answers to these questions we must go to the very beginning of the story.

## In the beginning

The Bible starts with creation. The first two chapters of the Book of Genesis record how God created everything – the land, the sky, the seas, the day, the night, the livestock, the wild animals, the birds of the air and *MAN*. Man was His supreme creation; the center piece of His handiwork.

God subjected everything He had created under man. He gave man the keys of the earth and made him the ruler of all that was in it. Why did God do that? Because unlike other creatures that God had created, *He made man in His own image, in His own likeness.*[1] Everything God has created has some likeness to Him; He put in it something of Himself. But it is in man that God's image is seen in its fullest form and that sets apart man from the rest of the beings. That makes man unique!

What does it really mean by, that man is made in the image of God? *'God is spirit'*[2] and man was created as matter. So how are we made in God's likeness? *We are made in the spiritual image of God,* and that really means God gave man of His nature; consciousness, emotions, intellect (also reasoning) and will. And He breathed into him His spirit. The image of God in man is expressed as male and female.

It is this image of God in man which gives man the dignity. And this dignity is for all men; even the lame, the dumb, the deaf, the blind, and those with other handicaps. Each and every person carries in him or her the image of God.

The next question that would be; for what purpose God created man? And why did He create him like Himself - in His own likeness? *God created man to have fellowship with Him.* God made for Himself a family and that is the reason He gave man of Himself, so that man could relate to Him. He made him for His pleasure. God wanted to 'walk' with man and enjoy him. Therefore He took utmost care and love when creating man. For God was creating His family, His children. Our God is a relational God.

## Something went wrong

God is perfect and everything He does is perfect. *Everything He created was good and to His satisfaction.*[3] So what went wrong? Where did the plot go off the intended track? Did God mess up somewhere; some mistake in His planning or execution? Far be from it. That was not the case.

The only thing where we can find 'fault' with the Almighty is, that He gave man the will to decide. To take decisions. *But that was part of giving man His image.* That man should possess volition. He should decide for himself. He could choose to write his own story. He could decide to walk with God or walk away from God. Man could exercise his God given will to obey or disobey God. Amazing isn't it? That God should take such a risk. Of leaving the chance of man walking away from Him, his Creator? Surely man is God's risk.

But that is the point for us to understand. God made man in His love. And love expects a response of love. The response of love has to be free; of one's own volition. Otherwise God could well have made man to be robots or marionettes who would respond to Him in exactly the manner He wanted or programmed them. But would that be love? Love demands a response of love which is not under any pressure or has not been conditioned. Yes God took a risk. He left open the possibility that man may not love Him back. That man may seek an existence outside a relationship with God. This would break God's heart but God had no other choice. If He had to make man in His image, then He had to make him in His full image. There was no half way. He had to give man the will. The will to decide whether to accept Him or reject Him.

This free will in man was what Satan exploited; which he manipulated to result in the Fall of man, and cause a break in the relationship between God and man. Man ate the fruit of the tree of knowledge of good and evil which God had forbidden him to do. He chose to believe the serpent (*'you will not die'*) rather than God (*'you will surely die'*). In doing that he disobeyed God. He showed a lack of trust in God's commands. Man was unfaithful.

The point is not that he ate the fruit of the tree that was forbidden by God - it could have been anything which God may have commanded to check man's love and his obedience to His word – but that man by doing what he did was showing that he wanted to be free from the 'yoke' of God. He wanted to step out from the authority of God. He wanted to decide for himself what was good or bad for him. He wanted to write his own story. He wanted autonomy. This constituted an act of rebellion against God.

And because of that sin came into the world.

How do we define sin? *Sin is to believe that one can have an existence outside of God.* Period! Adam and Eve by falling to the enticement of the serpent ate the fruit, believing that by *getting the knowledge of good and evil they would become like God.*[4] That by eating of this tree they would be able to know what is good for them and that would make it possible for them to live an existence independent of God. This was the lie Satan advocated and the first couple, Adam and Eve, fell for it. It is the same lie, the lie first cast in the Garden of Eden, that Satan has used ever since to entice mankind. That human beings do not need God to tell them what is good or bad. They can live and live well outside God's authority. They need not be dependent on Him.

And because Adam and Eve ate of the fruit of knowledge, they now knew what was good and evil, and because they knew what was good and evil, sin was able to enter the world. The age of innocence was over. *Man now knew.*[5] God's intention was to keep him innocent, away from that knowledge, for his own good. But by that single act of disobedience, man was now knowledgeable about sin and was doomed to combat sin forever.

Sin caused havoc in everything God had created. Man's transgression caused not only his own downfall but the decay of everything that was created. First and foremost sin caused a break in the relationship man enjoyed with his Creator. *He was now awkward and felt conscious of his nakedness.*[6] The nakedness was both physical and spiritual. It was not the open and pure relationship that he used to enjoy with God. He felt uncomfortable to 'walk' with God anymore. That is what sin does. It takes us away from God. It makes us uncomfortable in the light of His presence.

It caused spiritual death as God had warned them: *"you will surely die."* [7] Because of the spiritual death, the image of God in man was marred. The effect of the Fall was now to be borne by all the descendants of Adam. Generation after generation of the human race will have their blood contaminated as a result of the original (Adamic) sin. Man was cursed to be born a sinner. As the psalmist laments, *"Surely I was sinful at birth, sinful from the time my mother conceived me."* [8] Man is destined to inherit the sinful nature.

What are the ravages of sin? Disease, death, decay, incompleteness, degradation of creation. Everything, simply everything, has been affected. It was not like before and would never be like before.

Well it would have been so, if God did not have another plan.

## *God's plan of salvation*

God's plan of salvation is to restore things to their original design, as He had meant them to be. The plan of salvation is that God will redeem for Himself his family. The Bible from Chapter 3 of the Book of Genesis to its last chapter i.e. Chapter 22 of the Book of Revelation, is the story of God bringing back home His children. So desperate is God to reclaim His family that He would go to any length and pay any cost, even the price of His Son, to bring His children home. So much does God love man!

It is said that the Cross was there before the creation of the world. *The Lamb was chosen before the creation of the world.* [9] Well yes he was; in the mind of God. For God could foresee the Fall. That was the chance He took when He gave man the free will. And while God was putting the plan of Creation into effect, He already was finalizing the plan of Redemption! He would need it; He knew that for sure.

He would need it to restore the perfect and pristine relationship He had enjoyed with man, before man decided to go his own way. *But before the relationship could be restored, the image of God in man had to be restored.* He would have to do that Himself. He Himself would have to enter the human race to save the sons and daughters of man. He Himself would have to pay the price for the folly of man. It would be costly, but amazingly to God, it appeared worth it. He loved man and was redeeming him back. Besides there was no other way. A perfect sacrifice had to be made, and God had to give Himself. It took one small act of man - snapping the fruit from the tree - and what all God had to do to restore things back. The restoration is still on.

As part of this plan of salvation, there is the process of Re-Creation under way. The Bible talks of the new earth and the new heaven. American author Philip Yancey calls it the Great Reversal. In his book *Disappointment with God*, he explains this theme in detail.

The Great Reversal (or Re-Creation) commenced with the coming of Jesus Christ. Jesus put into effect the process of Re-Creation. Till then the creation was in a continual and progressive decay; because

7

of the Fall. With the Incarnation, the decay halted and the restoration started.

Now strange it may seem, but God has deemed it fit to involve human beings in this great redemptive process of the restoration of creation. The first creation was completely the work of God and then He handed it over to man to take care of it. Man as we know, instead defiled it by his act of disobedience. Now in the Re-Creation, which has been initiated with Jesus, man has been made a co-worker this time. God has given man the dignity to join Him in this redemptive work. Apostle Paul writes, *"The creation waits in eager expectation for the sons of God to be revealed. For the creation was subjected to frustration, not by it own choice, but by the will of the one who subjected it, in hope that the creation itself will be liberated from its bondage to decay and brought into the glorious freedom of the children of God. We know that the whole creation has been groaning as in the pains of childbirth right up to the present time."*[10]

But for human beings to become co-workers in this divine undertaking, they themselves need to be first restored. They image of God in them has to be made whole again, so that they can become the sons of God. That is where the redeeming work of Jesus on the Cross comes. And once justified (redeemed) they can join him in the mission of the Great Reversal.

And how or in what way can man contribute to the redemption work? *He does so by acts of faith!* Every act of faith on the part of man, contributes one small block, one brick, one little step to God's work of restoration. And why is it so? Well it was an act of unfaith of a man which led to the Fall, and which pushed the creation in a downward spiral of decay. Now the very acts of faith of man will result in the restoration. Faith (rather lack of it) caused the decay, and now God is using the faith in man to redeem things back.

If we are to summarize the message of the Bible, it will go somewhat like this:

*God made man in His own image (spiritual image) so as to have fellowship with Him; man however displayed lack of faith in God and disobeyed His word, as a result of which sin came into the world; sin resulted in spiritual* death which caused the corruption of the image of God in man; Jesus Christ came to restore this image and gave himself as the sacrifice that was needed for this purpose; and because of the redeeming work of Christ, God will one day have His family back and His children will once again walk with Him in the Garden.

The Bible begins and ends with creation. It ends where it began!

1.  Genesis 1:26 (paraphrased)
2.  John 4:24
3.  Genesis 1:31 (paraphrased)
4.  Genesis 3:5 (paraphrased)
5.  Genesis 3:22 (modified)
6.  Genesis 3:10 (paraphrased)
7.  Genesis 2:17
8.  Psalm 51.5
9.  1 Peter 1:19-20 (paraphrased)
10. Romans 8:19-22

# Chapter ~ 2

# THE INCARNATION

*"The Incarnation is God's ultimate act of self-giving."*
— *Philip Yancey*

The Incarnation - God coming as man to live amongst the human race - is perhaps the most profound and amazing revelation of the Christian faith. It is the very cornerstone of our belief.

Incarnation is a profound mystery in terms of what it actually was. God being born as man; amazing! This amazement, this wonder, was expressed by Apostle John when he writes, *"That which was from the beginning, which we have heard, which we have seen with our eyes, which we have looked at and our hands have touched – this we proclaim concerning the Word of life. The life appeared; we have seen it and testify to it, and we proclaim to you the eternal life, which was with the Father and has appeared to us."* [1]

Which we have heard! Which we have seen with our eyes! Which we have looked at! Our hands have touched! God came and lived amongst us! He visited our world! We walked with Him; we supped with Him; we sang with Him; we celebrated the Passover with Him.

Simply mind boggling! Head shaking wonder! No wonder John was amazed when this realization dawned on him, and remained so even many years after the event, when he did write this epistle.

And I also never cease to be amazed by the wonder that is the Incarnation. Not in terms of belief (I have no doubts that it took place) but by the enormity of what it constitutes, what it means. We cannot take it superficially. We have to accord it all the seriousness and respect that it deserves. We have to go to the depths in our understanding of it. It is absolutely an obligation under our faith. Our faith is incomplete without our full understanding and acceptance of what Incarnation means. We have to understand what Christmas really means in a profound sense. We have to fully know what we celebrate every year on the 25th of December. *We have to understand not only what the Incarnation means for us (the human race) but also what it means for God.* We will then, I am sure, be filled with amazement, and like John shake our heads, not in disbelief but in wonder as to what an incredible thing God did.

Philip Yancey writes, *"The Incarnation had meaning for God as well as for us. Human history revolves around not our experience of God, but His experience of us."* Yes and that is what Incarnation is about; *God who is timeless and infinite, condescended at a point in history, to be confined by time and space in a body of flesh and blood.*

*"From a state of being worshipped in heaven to being a baby in Bethlehem"* wrote American writer Max Lucado. That is what the Incarnation meant for God. The King of heaven; the Creator of the world; the Master of the universe; condescended to put on the flesh of a human and put himself on the dissecting table to be examined by human beings. That He was willing to open Himself to close scrutiny by the very beings whom He had created. That was the risk He took in the Incarnation. *"God became earth's mockery to save His children,"* quoting Max Lucado again.

But God had to take that risk. There was no other option. There was no other way He could restore His family. He had tried some other way before. He flooded the earth in the time of Noah and wiped out the entire human race, save the eight who went into the Ark. His intention was to start the human race again with these eight righteous people. But sin was in the human blood. It had defiled the human DNA.

Generations after Noah were also to be born with the sinful nature. It did not work out this way.

The only option remained was to extinguish the human race or to pay the penalty for its sins. To exterminate the sinners or to erase their sins. The penalty for sin had to be paid. God had to be just; it was His nature. He could be no other. His justice demanded punishment. But there was a predicament; He loved man immensely. How could He destroy what He loved? How was He to meet the demand of his justice and the cry of his love? How could He be both just and loving?

The Judge had to take His own judgment upon Himself, so that He could be free to love. To do that He had to be born as man. The perfect offering which was to be given for the atonement of the sins of mankind, had to come from the human race only. He had to take the penalty for man's sins *as a man*. In order to save man, He had to become a man. Any other way would not do. *The Incarnation was an important and integral part of God's plan of salvation.*

For Incarnation to be 'authentic' (it could not be an avatar, which is God appearing as God), God had to be born and live by the rules of this world. The eternal God who knew no boundaries of time and space had to live by the constraints of a human body. Dorothy L. Sayers, English writer and Christian humanist in early twentieth century, writes, *"For whatever reasons God chose to make man as he is – limited and suffering and subject to sorrows and death – He had the honesty and courage to take His own medicine. Whatever game He is playing with His creation, He has kept His own rules and played fair. He can exact nothing from man that He has not exacted from Himself."*

But this was essential; He had to come to earth not as God but as a man. He had to experience all what man experiences. Only then could He be mankind's Savior. *"Jesus came on earth so God could experience all that we experience here,"* said Ron Nikkel, President of Prison Fellowship International.

In a sense the perfect God became 'complete' with His human experience. The Incarnation added to the completeness of the already complete God. Now no man could accuse Him, as once Job did when he asked, *"Do you have eyes of flesh?"* [2] Oh yes! He had eyes of flesh for a time. God could now understand firsthand how humans felt, the struggles they went through, the pain they suffered, the temptations they faced, the death they feared – in fact the entire gamut of human experience. The Incarnation was not only our experience of God but also His experience of humans; at close quarters, as one of them. There is a line from the play Amadeus which goes like this: *"What use, after all, is man, if not to teach God His lessons."* Indeed God learned many lessons by His sojourn on earth.

Another reason for the Incarnation was that God wanted to be seen. The invisible God, God who is spirit, wanted humans to see Him, to experience him in flesh and blood. To know what He was like. Remember what Jesus said to Philip: *"Anyone who has seen me has seen the Father."* [3] Meaning anyone who has known me knows what God is like. John also writes, *"No one has ever seen God, but God the One and Only (Begotten Son), who is at the Father's side, has made Him known."* [4]

*"In becoming man God made it possible for man to see God,"* said Max Lucado. God was no longer appearing to man in a cloud or fire or whirlwind. He no longer appeared only as a shadow or as a thundering voice. He no longer remained only on the top of Mount Sinai. He no longer appeared only to some chosen men, in dreams or visions, or even as one to one in a tent. He now came as a man and that man was called Jesus. And Jesus not only made us understand God better, but also made God understand human beings better.

Between the God *above us* of the ancient times, to the God *in us* of the present, there was once God *with us*. Let us not forget that. Let us ponder over that and ponder deep and long.

*We will be filled with awe!*

1. *1 John 1:1-2*
2. *Job 10:4*
3. *John 14:9*
4. *John 1:18.*

# Chapter ~ 3

# LOVE THAT MYSTIFIES

*"Love consents to all and commands only those who consent.
Love is abdication, God is abdication."*
— *Simone Weil*

Can we ever, ever, understand the love of God? We can try but I
don't think one can fully get to the depth of it. It is unfathomable.

The plain truth is that the infinite God has infinite love for this
creature called man. Why? I don't know. But what I do know is that
He loves us immeasurably and without end. Otherwise how can you
explain His capacity to forgive sins; even our repeated sins? How can
you explain the fact that He was willing to give up even His Son, so
that He may have us, His children, back? How else can you explain
His willingness to leave the heavens and live in this sin infected world?
It was tough for Him to leave His exalted state and dwell in this fallen
world. *"If it costs us a great deal to live in a world like this, we need to
remember that it cost God more,"* wrote Selwyn Hughes, the British writer
of the daily devotional *Every Day with Jesus*.

The truth is - and that is the only explanation possible for all that God was willing to forsake - that God loves us and loves us madly. He is passionate in His love for us and will go to great lengths to express this love, so much so that it may confound and appear crazy.

Paul writing to the church in Ephesus prays that they may, *"....grasp how wide and long and high and deep is the love of Christ, and to know this love that surpasses knowledge ...."* [1] Love that surpasses all knowledge! Yes, it defies the intellect. But it can be experienced. It can be felt. It can also be seen.

This love for humans has come at a great cost to God. It has not been easy. We humans are a stubborn race. We are bent on destroying ourselves - physically and spiritually. We have a high propensity for flirting with sin; risking its consequences. We have an obstinate streak to go away from God; to resist His authority; to disobey Him. And God has had to abdicate much (for a time) – His majesty, His authority, even His throne – to pay the cost for His love for man. God has surrendered much, given up much, for the fallen man.

Philip Yancey comments, *"At the heart of the Gospel is a God who deliberately surrenders to the wild, irresistible power of love."* And in surrendering to this wild, irresistible power of love, God has had to suffer much humiliation and repeated humiliation. Yancey describes it such: *"I marvel at a God who allows Himself to endure such humiliation, only to come back for more."* The more mankind humiliated God by rejecting Him, ignoring Him as if He didn't matter, by spurning His benevolent parenting, by rebelling against His regency; the more God came back in His love to seek the love of mankind. Like a mad lover repeatedly rejected and repeatedly scorned by the object of his affections, but who does not give up, God came back again and again.

God loves all men, without any exception, and in His love He wants all to be saved. The Bible affirms: *"This is good, and pleases God our Saviour, who wants all men to be saved and to come to a knowledge of the truth."* [2] Yes, God's love desires all men to be saved without exception. But sadly not all men respond to His love.

We say God is loving (as a verb) and the love of God (as a noun), but more importantly and more so; *"God is love."* [3] Love is the essence of God. It is His very nature. *It is Him.* He can be none other but love. (The reverse 'love is God' is not true, for not all love is like God's; as some would like to justify their actions or emotions behind this statement).

I confessed earlier that I do not know why God loves man so much. But let me venture a guess. I believe He loves us because we have His image. We, of all creatures, have been made by God in His own image. *God cannot but love His image in us.* That may possibly explain why he cannot give up on man. And the love of God gives man worth. *"Some things are loved because they are worthy; some things are worthy because they are loved"*; quoting from a sermon by Ian Pitt-Watson of Fuller Seminary. Human beings become worthy because God loves them.

*"God loves people because of who God is, not because of who we are,"* says Philip Yancey. We don't have to be perfect or someone special or have special gifts, for God to love us. He loves us as we are. His love is unconditional. *"To love conditionally is against God's nature,"* writes Max Lucado. God loves us as we are. But He loves us too much to let us remain as we are. That is how He is able to separate the sin from the sinner. He loves the sinner but hates the sin. And in love He goes about transforming the sinner, who comes to Him in repentance and faith.

Jesus gave many parables as examples of God's love for sinners and the rejoicing that takes place in heaven over every sinner that is saved. *"God loves each one of us as if there was only one of us to love,"* wrote St. Augustine. The parables of the lost sheep, the lost coin, and the lost son (more famous as the prodigal son) appear in quick succession in Chapter 15 of the Gospel of Luke, and each conveys the importance for God of recovering that *one* sinner. Henri Nouwen, the Catholic priest and Christian writer, describes this wonderfully: *"God rejoices not because the problems of the world have been solved, not because all human pain and suffering have come to an end, nor because thousands of people have been converted and are now praising Him for his goodness. No, God rejoices because one of his children, who was lost, has been found."*

Perhaps no other parable brings out more touchingly the love of God for His lost children, than the story of the prodigal son. Like the father of the wayward younger son in the story, who must have been on the rooftop (perhaps keeping vigil there every day), to have seen his son coming at a distance; God too patiently waits for us with open arms, for us to turn back from our ways and fall into His embrace. The father in the story runs out to meet his son. There is no admonishment for the grief he has inflicted on the father, no scolding for the wealth he has squandered, no berating for the shame he has caused the family; but instead a loving embrace which conveyed that all is forgiven. You are back and that is all that matters. It is THE reason to rejoice and celebrate. My son was lost and now is found. He was (considered) dead and is alive again.

Similarly God wants to embrace each one of us to His bosom, where we can feel the love in His heart. He wants us to repent and come back home. There will be no questions asked; 'how many sins did you commit, how big a sinner you are, why did you not pay heed to my warnings, why did you reject my love, how much you abused the gifts I gave you'; no nothing at all. "*By loving the unlovable, You made me lovable,*" exclaimed Augustine. Everything will be forgiven and forgotten. And of course there will be rejoicing and celebration.

God's love desires a response from man. I would even say such love *moves* a response from us. We cannot but love Him in return. "*We love because He first loved us.*"[4] Our love is in response to God's great love. Our love for God and for one another flows from the love God has loved us with. It is like the moon reflecting the light of the sun.

And God desires love that is of our own free will and voluntary. He will not force us or arm twist us to love Him. He will not bribe us to win our love. He wants to win our hearts by His love and not by beating us into submission. That is not the love He desires. He wants our love as a response to His love. And we are not to love God because of the gifts and talents He gives us (though we must thank Him for them) or for making our lives comfortable or successful. We are not to love Him because we fear Him or are afraid that misfortune will fall on us if we don't love Him. That is not love but appeasement. *We have to love Him for who He is.*

Let us ponder on this beautiful prayer of St. Francis Xavier:-

*"Not because of your promised heaven do I wish to devote my love to you; nor from dread of a much feared hell do I wish to cease from offending you. Even without hope of heaven, I shall love you; and without any fear of hell, I shall fear you. Naught you need give me that I may love you, for even without hoping for the hope that is mine, I shall love you, as love you I do."*

God longs for our love. Love which comes from our own free will. Will we deny Him that?

1. *Ephesians 3:18-19*
2. *1Timothy 2:3-4*
3. *1 John 4:16*
4. *1 John 4:19.*

# Chapter ~ 4

# GRACE THAT AMAZES

*"Amazing grace, how sweet the sound, that saved a wretch like me."*
*- From a popular hymn by John Newton*

God's grace is amazing. It is so amazing that it is even considered unfair by some (erroneously of course). But one thing we can be sure of, it is there for us to receive.

Everyone can receive it. There is no discrimination. No one is barred. It is available for all. It is unconditional and it is free of charge. We don't have to deserve it. We didn't deserve it. God of His own will gave it to us, and it is ours to receive and live in. *Grace is God's initiative.*

The Gospel of Jesus Christ is the gospel of grace. God paying the ransom for us in the sacrifice of His Son. Grace is free indeed; for the receiver. But for the Giver it cost something; well a lot.

How do we define grace? *Grace is God's gift to the undeserving.* Since it is a gift then it is free of cost. And since it is not a reward, we don't have to do anything to deserve or earn it. We have to just accept it. We cannot do anything that will make it increase, and nothing that we do will make it decrease.

Because it is free it becomes difficult for some to accept it. Their reasoning: 'There must be a catch somewhere! How can it come without charge? Surely we must, we have to do something on our part? It can't be that easy. It shouldn't be that easy'. *But it is.*

It is this pride which blocks God's grace. For grace to do its work, we have to receive it. The act of receiving itself can become difficult. *"God gives where He finds empty hands,"* said St. Augustine. You need empty hands to receive God's grace. If your hands are full of yourself, there will be no room for His grace.

*"We cannot find Him unless we know we need Him,"* said Thomas Merton, monk and Christian writer. We have to be aware of our need for God's grace. We have to come to the fountain to drink the water of grace. We have to come to the realization that without God's grace we are nothing and we are lost. We need the lamp of His grace to light our way home. We have to acknowledge that we are sick, that we are sinners, before we can realize the need for the grace of our Savior. Jesus made it clear that he had not come for those who thought of themselves as whole – the self-righteous, the religious - but instead he had come for those who acknowledged their sickness, their brokenness, their incompleteness, and thus their need for help (read grace). We should be in the posture to receive God's grace

Actually it is the poor who are in a better position to receive God's grace. They have the right posture for grace to flow into them. They are aware of their helplessness and their dependence on others. Their status in life is such that they have a humble attitude. They are not ashamed to receive from others. It is easy for God's grace to come to them. Pride will not block it.

And then there are the poor in spirit who are aware of their need for God. Who welcome grace for they know they are lost and can't find their way home without it. They have all the time for God. In the words of Max Lucado, *"God goes to those who have time to hear Him."* Jesus hailed them: *"Blessed are the poor in spirit, for theirs is the kingdom of heaven."* [1] Why? Because aware of their own incompleteness, they are dependent on God's grace and they are not ashamed of it.

God's grace has been accused of being unfair. 'How come God can lump all people into one pot and give His grace to all uniformly? Surely the righteous deserve better (do they mean more grace?).' But we are forgetting grace is free. It is a gift. It belongs to God and He can give to whomever and in whatever measure He wishes. Who are we to object? It is not ours to give. Jesus perhaps knew that such accusations against grace would be leveled one day, and he thus gave the parable of the workers in the vineyard. 'Who are you to tell me, demanded the landowner, how much wages I should give to the workers employed last? It is mine to give. You should be content with what you have received, which is the amount agreed between us'.

And the thief on the cross? He was what we can call a 'death bed' convert. But he was promised paradise. He did not attend the church for even one day, did not evangelize to even one soul, did not give a cup of water to even one thirsty person; but was nevertheless assured of salvation. Only because He knew of his need for grace. He asked for grace. And he received grace. Should we grudge God that?

You cannot be both under law and grace. They are mutually exclusive. It is one or the other. You are either under the law or under grace. You cannot say that I am under grace but at the same time indulge in legalism; follow these rules, observe these rituals, so as to make sure that you attain your salvation. Salvation is not *attained* by us; it is *obtained* by God's grace. And only by God's grace, so that there is no room for self effort. Grace is sufficient. *"There is only one real law - the law of the universe. It may be fulfilled either by way of judgment or by way of grace, but it must be fulfilled one way or the other,"* points out Dorothy L. Sayers.

It is grace which saves us and grace which will carry us through this life. *"My grace is sufficient for you"* [2]; Paul was told by the Lord. And the same is true for us. His grace is sufficient to save and save completely. It is sufficient to take us through all the troubles, all the temptations, all the challenges that we will face in our life on earth. *"Man is born broken. He lives by mending. The grace of God is the glue,"* comments Eugene O'Neill. And this glue which keeps our life together, will keep it together to the very end.

23

Grace covers our inadequacies to meet the requirements of God's love; our failures to keep from sinning, to live Christlike, to meet Gods standards for us. While we are in this body, we will be influenced by the power of sin. Law requires that we be judged (and punished) for even one failure to observe the law. Grace mandates that we be forgiven after confession and repentance. And be forgiven repeatedly. God's grace is not for one time. It remains. That is how grace is able to save and save completely.

If I am sure that I will be forgiven by God again and again, because I am under grace, then let me keep on sinning. Paul could anticipate this devious argument that people would resort to, and makes it clear: *"What shall we say, then? Shall we go on sinning, so that grace may increase? BY NO MEANS* (my capitalization)! *We died to sin; how can we live in it any longer?"* [3] Paul convincingly dismantles the argument that grace promotes sin, or that anyone can use it as a cover or excuse to justify one's sins. If you keep on sinning then it can well be concluded that you never understood God's grace or for that matter you never received God's grace. The result of grace is such that when you receive it you lose the desire to sin. You do not *relish* sin any more. You hate yourself when you sin. You do not want to sin but instead do God's will. That is the work of grace in a person. That is the beauty of grace. However sometimes when you happen to sin or fall into sin, then grace is there to support you and bring you back to God's side.

Having received God's grace, what are we to do? Having tasted His grace, what should be our expected response, beside constant gratefulness to God? We are to be *dispensers* of God's grace to the world. Vessels in which the grace flows in, and then flows out to touch others. C. S. Lewis was clear in his belief that Christianity's unique contribution amongst the world religions was grace. We are known (as Christians) and Jesus is known, by the grace that we show to the world. We, as the Body of Christ (the Church), have to be the conveyors of His grace to those in need. Ralph Reed wrote, *"Every word we say and every action we take should reflect God's grace."* How very true! Grace sets us apart from the world. It distinguishes us as God's children and followers of Christ.

Jesus said, *"Freely you have received, freely give."* [4] You have received grace freely and free from God. Freely and free you must give in turn.

Let me close with another line from that wonderful hymn, *'Amazing Grace'*:

*"It is grace that brought me safe thus far, and grace will lead me home."*

1. *Matthew 5:3*
2. *2 Corinthians 12:9*
3. *Romans 6:1-2*
4. *Matthew 10:8.*

# Chapter ~ 5

# UNDERSTANDING GOD IN THE OLD TESTAMENT

*"I AM WHO I AM."*

How do we understand God? That is, if it is at all possible to fully understand the infinite God. We have the ultimate revelation of God in Jesus and that is more than sufficient for us to know, for the time being at least. We will look at the person of Jesus in a later chapter, but here let us attempt to know more about the God of Israel; the God whom Jesus worshipped.

To know a person we first need to know his or her name. Let us begin with that.

At Mount Horeb (or Sinai), God revealed His name to mankind for the first time. *"I AM WHO I AM (or I WILL BE WHAT I WILL BE)."* [1] Till then He was known to the tribe of Hebrews, as the God of Abraham, Isaac and Jacob. God was now about to free the people of Israel from their bondage in Egypt and make them a nation giving them the land across the Jordan. Moses the leader of the would-be nation wanted the

God of this nation to be known by a name. The people should know who their God is and their enemies also should know who their God is. God obliged. Israel was soon to become a nation. From one man, Abraham, it had grown into a people (Hebrews), and from a people it would now become a nation. God did not take offence that Moses had dared to ask Him His name. It was now time to tell His chosen people about Himself, about His character. Moses was commanded that he should tell the people of Israel that he had been sent by *'I AM'* (*'LORD'*).

The full might of the Almighty comes through in His name. The name conveys in a sense that everything, simply everything, that exists, flows from God who is the Essence. God's majesty, His infiniteness, His timelessness, His omnipotence, is conveyed forcefully in the name that He revealed to Moses. All creation must have bowed down, when they heard the holy name of God from the mouth of God.

I wonder if the words of Jesus: *"I tell you the truth, before Abraham was born, I am,"* [2] had the resonance of God giving His name at Horeb. It conveyed the same sense of the eternal, of timelessness.

Jesus also used the *'I am'* in making his many claims; - *I am the light of the world; I am the gate; I am the way and the truth and the life; I am the good shepherd; I am the bread of life; I am the resurrection and the life;* thereby adding to the name of God his own characteristics, so as to make him (Jesus) more understandable to the people of Israel.

God after revealing His name proceeded to reveal His character to the people of Israel. The young nation was going through the pains of childbirth. It had to know its God. It had to understand its God as to what was His nature. God too *wanted* to be known and understood by His people.

In the Old Testament we find that God revealed the different attributes of His character depending upon the circumstances which existed in the various stages of the development of His people Israel. And He was given a name (a title) befitting the aspect of His character which was revealed at that time and in those circumstances. At one time He was El-Shaddai (God the Enough or God who is sufficient), at another stage Jehovah Jireh (the LORD will provide), at another place it is Jehovah Rophe (the LORD who heals), and then also the well-known Jehovah Rohe (the LORD my shepherd), and many others. By giving Him the different names, the people could relate with God more closely in that particular situation.

What was God in the Old Testament like? We have seen above that His character was revealed in the various names that He was given. But what kind of a person He came across as; and we say this looking back? In the Old Testament God is portrayed in two distinct roles. He comes across as a caring parent (father) and as a jealous lover (husband).

God loves His people Israel. Hadn't He brought them out of Egypt after centuries of bondage? Hadn't He carved out a nation out of a nation; a thing which had been unheard of? Hadn't he promised to lead them to the land across the Jordan? How then can He not but love His people, the children of Israel? They were the apple of His eye amongst all the nations of the earth. *His chosen race!*

But Israel is wayward. Israel is obstinate. It turns to other gods. It is not faithful to Jehovah their God. It does not obey His commands. It does not follow His statutes. While pressing ahead on the journey to the Promised Land, it looks back fondly to its time in Egypt. They have come out of Egypt, but Egypt remains in their hearts. Again and again, like a worried parent, God warns them to return to Him. He pleads with them to turn back to Him. But they would not listen. Like a grieving but helpless parent, who see his child destroying itself, God is filled with anguish over the stubbornness of Israel. *"Return to me and I will return to you,"* [3] He pleads with Israel but to no avail. They are a hard and obstinate ('stiff necked') people. They reject the God who brought them out of Egypt, who gave them the land of other nations; land which they did not have to develop. He accorded them the *'Most Favored Nation'* status but they wanted none of Him. In the wilderness and in the land He gave them, they again and again put God to the test.

But how could He destroy them? *"How can I give you up, Ephraim? How can I hand you over, Israel? .... My heart is changed within me; all my compassion is aroused. I will not carry out my fierce anger, nor will I turn and devastate Ephraim"* [4]; one of the many passages found in the Old

Testament where God reveals the anguish of a 'helpless' father. But Israel is an obdurate child. God mourns to the prophet Jeremiah: *"Yet my people have forgotten me."*[5] God felt offended. God felt hurt. God felt rejected. Israel had deserted Him.

The same anguish, the same helplessness, is to be seen even in Jesus, where he grieves over the impending destruction of Jerusalem: *"O Jerusalem, Jerusalem, you who kill the prophets and those sent to you, how often I have longed to gather your children together, as a hen gathers her chicks under her wings, but you were not willing. Look, you house is left to you desolate. For I tell you, you will not see me again until you say, 'Blessed is he who comes in the name of the Lord'."* [6] Can you feel the pain, the hurt, the poignancy, and the rejection, which comes out in this lament?

At other times, God comes across as a passionate lover and a jealous husband. He is Israel's lover, her husband. But Israel is not a faithful wife. She is a serial adulteress. She takes lover after lover, much to His dismay. His heart is broken at her infidelity. 'How could she prefer anyone else over Him? She was to have but one husband, but one lover. Did I not love her madly? Give her all that she desired? What went wrong?'

But God would not give up on her. He was ready to take her back despite her wantonness. See how quickly God moves from a state of disgust, to pinning after Israel: *"I gave faithless Israel her certificate of divorce and sent her away because of all her adulteries"* [7] and then, *"Return, faithless people, for I am you husband."* [8] God comes across as love sick and one who is determined to make his marriage work. God even takes His prophet Hosea, and uses his marriage as an illustration to drive home the message to Israel; that He loves her and is willing to take her back despite her adulterous ways. But sadly Israel would not relent.

In as many ways as God comes across to His people and reveals His character to them, it establishes one thing very significantly; that God is a person. He is personal and relational. He loves and loves passionately, and He wants to be loved back by the objects of His affection. His name is Jealous. *"Do not worship any other god, for the LORD, whose name is Jealous, is a jealous God."* [9] Our God is a jealous God. He will not share His glory with any other. He will not accept our bowing down to idols or false gods. He alone is God and worthy of our worship and honor and glory.

And our God is perfect. He is to be approached with reverence. He is not to be taken lightly. God does not like to be short changed. He requires that our offerings; whether they be tithes, time, things, and even our own selves; to be perfect. Otherwise they would not be acceptable to Him; as the offering of Cain did not please Him, and as the offering of Ananias and Sapphira caused Him to be angry enough to destroy them. That is why the instructions in the Law of Moses are clear and much repeated; that the animals and birds required to be offered as sacrifice to God, must be perfect and without any defect.

*That is why the Lamb, who took away the sins of the world, had to be perfect and without blemish.*

1.  *Exodus 3:14*
2.  *John 8:58*
3.  *Zechariah 1:3*
4.  *Hosea 11:8-9*
5.  *Jeremiah 2:32, 18:15*
6.  *Matthew 23:37-39*
7.  *Jeremiah 3:8*
8.  *Jeremiah 3:14*
9.  *Exodus 34:14*

# Chapter ~ 6

# OUR SALVATION

*"Salvation is God's business."*

*— Max Lucado*

Salvation is indeed God's business. And He knows His business. Salvation originates from God and is driven by God. Our involvement is only to accept it by faith and to remain in faith. Self salvation does not work. Salvation is from heaven downward, and not earth upward.

*"It is a gift from God and not a gift from man to God,"* says Max Lucado. Therefore we can in no way earn it or attain it. We receive it from God, and we receive it by faith and remain in it by faith. Faith is needed from first to last, for salvation to work.

It is God who works out our salvation from beginning to end. He does it carefully and I would even say slowly. Salvation is a *process* and not a one time event that is over with instantly. For us, the recipients of salvation, it is a journey which we undertake, with God firmly in the driver's seat.

This journey, this process of salvation, is made up of three distinct stages; our justification, our sanctification, and our glorification. One follows the other and in this order. In each phase or part of the process; the effect, the power, and the presence of sin in our lives, also changes.

We will examine the process in detail.

## *Justification*

Salvation begins with our justification, our being made righteous. Righteous (or to be made right) before whom? Before God that is. We have to be made right with God. Sin has made us wrong with God, and we, before anything else, need to be made right with Him again.

And how is that done? God has paid the price for our sins. The Lamb of God has been slain. Jesus has taken upon himself, the punishment for our transgressions (which God's justness demanded), and now God has been freed to forgive mankind. Judgment has fallen on the One who was sinless, so that we sinners can be made righteous before God.

The penalty for sin, which hung upon the human race ever since it first sinned in the Garden of Eden, has been paid for in full, so that we are free from its bondage. This is the first stage of salvation and the rest cannot follow till forgiveness of sins takes place. God cannot do any work in us till we first receive His forgiveness in Christ.

Our part is to receive God's forgiveness. To come to Him in faith and wash ourselves with the blood of Christ, which cleanses us of our sins. We have to repent and confess our sins to God and accept that only in Christ are we saved. *"Salvation is found in no one else, for there is no other name under heaven given to men by which we must be saved."*[1] And that name is Jesus!

We are justified by our faith alone. We are the children of Abraham. He was justified by faith and so are we. *"Consider Abraham: 'He believed God, and it was credits righteousness'. Understand, then, that those who believe are children of Abraham."* [2] We are people of faith.

## *Sanctification*

Sanctification means to be set apart, to be made holy. The second stage of our salvation, the process of making us holy, commences after our conversion. Now that God has washed away our sins and made us righteous, He can do His work in us.

Our baptism, our conversion, is not the end of the journey. In fact, in a sense, it is just the beginning. In baptism we accept Jesus as our Lord and Savior and put faith in his redemptive death on the Cross. We receive the forgiveness which God gives in the blood of His Son. After the first step is over; what then?

Do you ever wonder for what purpose we have been saved? Why God paid such a heavy price to save mankind? Our saving is not an end in itself. It is the step leading to what God has planned for us. *We have been saved so that we can spend eternity with God as His family.*

But in order for us to have fellowship with God it is essential that we be made holy. Why? Because God is holy and no unholy thing or person can come in His presence. Isaiah felt tormented as he became conscious of his un-holiness, when he found himself in the presence of the Almighty, the Holy of Holies, till he was touched by a seraph. The Bible has several verses emphasizing this point. To quote some of them here:- *"Without holiness no one will see the Lord"* [3] and *"For God did not call us to be impure, but to live a holy life"* [4] and *"Be holy because I, the LORD your God, am holy"* [5] and further *"I am the LORD, who makes you holy."* [6]

This is the reason why God does not immediately zip us away to heaven at the point of our conversion. His work in us has to start now. He has to prepare us for our eternity in heaven. To be with Him, we have to be like Him i.e. holy. Our sanctification begins once our justification is done. And He does not inject holiness into us, but refines us slowly, like silver, in the fire of the furnace of life.

The earth has been called the *'vale of soul making'*. The laboratory, where God perfects our soul, through the process of sanctification. *"If you are in Christ you have a perfected soul and a perfected body. His plan is to give you the soul now and the body when you get to heaven"* writes

Max Lucado. God has to prepare our soul to receive the body He will give us at the resurrection. New wine in new bottles!

While on earth we will be God's work in progress. The sanctification continues throughout our lives on earth, and we advance in increasing degree of holiness and perfection. *"For we are God's workmanship, created in Christ Jesus to do good works ....." 7* God's workmanship! His handiwork! God takes pride in His handiwork, for it has been carved out by Him with love and care.

I believe that when Jesus said: *"Do not judge or you too will be judged,"8* he was referring to precisely this; that we, each one of us, are God's work in progress, and are at different levels of holiness. Why should then we judge a person when God is still doing His work in him? Like us that person is still 'incomplete' and not yet perfect. Who can say what the final product will look like? God is quite capable of transforming a hardened sinner into a saint. So instead of judging others, we are called to be tolerant and patient, as God is with us.

What about sin in this phase? Well, we are free from the penalty of sin for it has been paid for. But is it present? Yes. Does it have power over us? Well to varying degrees. As we grow in holiness, as God's work of sanctification takes its effect in us, the power of sin over us diminishes. But it remains nevertheless. We no longer wish to sin or have the desire to sin, but we do fall into sin all the same. While we are in this body and living in this fallen world, our struggles with sin will remain. But we can progressively be victorious over it. The sinful nature we are born with, is still there, battling incessantly with our spiritual nature, for control over us. We can make it dormant and subject it to the spiritual man, but it remains nevertheless; waiting to rear its head again, when it see us dropping our guard or given half the opportunity.

There was only one man, who while he was in this body of flesh, could completely extricate himself from the power of sin. That man: Jesus Christ. The rest only aspire to reach his level of perfection and do achieve so in varying degrees, though never fully.

## Glorification

And we now come to the final stage of the process of salvation - our glorification. This is the culmination of all things. This is the 'reward' stage. We will receive the glory that has been promised. We will be glorified as sons and daughters of God. Having finished the race, we will now receive the crown of life. We will have the glory of Christ and become co-heirs of the inheritance that is his, from God. *"When Christ, who is your life, appears, then you also will appear with him in glory."* [9]

Paul says in the epistle to the Philippians, that God will transform our lowly bodies so that they will be like Christ's body. John in his epistle also gives us the same assurance that we shall be like him, when we see him.

And what about sin? Sin will no longer have any hold over us, for it will not be present. We will be free from both the power and presence of sin. The struggle with our sinful nature will be over. No more will we wrestle with sin. Our sanctification would be complete. We would have reached perfection. We would be ready to spend eternity with God.

*Justification, sanctification, and glorification; God indeed knows His business.*

1.  *Acts 4:12*
2.  *Galatians 3:6-7.*
3.  *Hebrews 12:14*
4.  *1 Thessalonians 4:7*
5.  *Leviticus 19:2*
6.  *Leviticus 22:32*
7.  *Ephesians 2:10*
8.  *Matthew 7:1*
9.  *Colossians 3:4*

# Chapter ~ 7

# THE THIRST FOR THE DIVINE

*"As the deer pants for streams of water,
so my soul pants for you, O God."*

In the soul of each human being is a thirst. The thirst for the Divine; for the living God. We are born with this thirst, this yearning to connect with our Source. This thirst (or one may call it hunger, but irrespective it conveys the paramount need of the soul. Here we shall continue calling it thirst) is only fulfilled when our souls are filled with God. God gave us this thirst and God alone can quench it. *"The soul must long for God in order to be set aflame by God's love; but if the soul cannot yet feel this longing, then it must long for that longing. To long for the longing is also from God,"* wrote Meister Eckhart.

*"You have made us for Yourself, O Lord, and our hearts are restless, until they rest in You,"* said St. Augustine. We will keep wandering and not find our rest till we make God our rest. Do we not identify with the psalmist when he cries out: *"As the deer pants for the streams of water so my soul pants for you, O God. My soul thirsts for God, for the living God.*

*When can I go and meet with God?"* [1] Do we not have the same thirst, the same restlessness, the same yearning, the same burning desire? Do we not feel like Richard Wilbur when he writes, *"I die of thirst, here at the fountainside?"*

This thirst cannot be satisfied by any other thing, for this thirst is not of this world. We can try quenching it but it won't work. We go to the wells of career, success, power, money, status, achievements, hobbies, relationships, sports, alcohol, drugs, sex, religion; these and many others. But none can satisfy. They may appear to satisfy for a while but the thirst surfaces again. It comes back again and again, so that we want more power or more money or more comforts or more sex and so on. The more we attempt to satisfy it, with things other than God, the more we thirst. How can the things of this world quench something which is not of this world? How can the material satisfy the spiritual? How can anything or anyone other than God, satisfy the thirst which has been put in us by God Himself? As Augustine said, *"I call you into my soul, which you prepare to accept you, by the longing that you breathe into it."*

C. S. Lewis wrote, *"If I find in myself desires which nothing in this world can satisfy, the only logical explanation is that I was made for another world."* Yes, we have been made for another world. Our ultimate destiny is the world to come. We are not human beings who have a spiritual experience, but spiritual beings having a human experience. And the thirst in us is not of this world. It is the thirst for the Divine and the Divine is not of this world. Try we might, we cannot satisfy it with anything of this world.

Jesus was referring to this thirst in his encounter with the Samaritan woman at the well. He says to her, *"Everyone who drinks this water* (of the well of Jacob) *will be thirsty again, but whoever drinks the water I give him will never thirst."* [2] Never thirst! Be fully satisfied! Go nowhere else! End of your search, your wandering! Be at rest finally! Only Jesus could give this guarantee. And the invitation, to drink of the water he gives, is not only to the Samaritan woman, but to us all who are thirsty: *"If anyone is thirsty, let him come to me and drink."* [3]

*"O God, you are my God, earnestly I seek you; my soul thirsts for you....."*[4]
Why is the thirst there in our souls in the first place? Why do we ache
for the Divine? Why has God put it there in us, so that we are restless?
Well the answer is there in the question; *so that we are restless.* Man is
made in God's image. The image of God is divine. The divine in us
wants to connect with the Divine who is its Source. Ever since the Fall,
man yearns for God as God yearns for man. The yearning in the two
is for the relationship that they once had. The thirst is there so that we
remain restless in this world, and remain restless till we finally find
our rest in God. This thirst keeps our search for God going, till we
once again connect with Him and have a relationship with Him. This
thirst keeps us conscious of our need for God. Without it we are
spiritually dead. Thomas Merton said, *"We cannot find Him unless we
know we need Him."* And this thirst in us is the evidence of our need for
Him, and it remains in us till we have union with Him. The thirst is
the sign that we are spiritually healthy, for we have the longing for
God.

But it is quite possible for us to harden our hearts and shut the ears
of our souls to the cry for God that resonates within us. Simone Weil
wrote, *"The danger is not lest the soul should doubt whether there is any
bread, but lest, by a lie, it should persuade itself that it is not hungry. It can
only persuade itself of this by lying, for the reality of its hunger is not a belief
but a certainty."* As mentioned we can try to quench this thirst with
worldly things but we will not be successful. We can also choose to
deliberately reject the Fountain of Life whose water will quench this
thirst, and instead drown ourselves with alternates, which sadly will
not serve the purpose.

Referring to the people of Israel, God cries out, *"My people have
committed two sins: They have forsaken me, the spring of living water, and
have dug their own cisterns, broken cisterns that cannot hold water."* [5] We
have to be careful that these words do not apply to us. After a period
of time, if we persist, we can lose our consciousness of this thirst, of
our need for God. How terrible is the state where we don't feel the
need for God in our lives? Where the thirst has not been quenched, but
has died or has been suppressed.

We have considered our thirst for God but does God also have a thirst? Does the Divine also thirst for us? Yes He does and as intensely if not more. On the cross Jesus said, *"I thirst."* [6] Mother Teresa referred to this as the, *"unquenchable thirst of Christ for souls."* The unquenchable thirst! God's thirst is never quenched but always seeks more and more souls to be united with Him. God also wants that the relationship that was ruptured at Eden, be restored again. When man's thirst for God meets God's thirst for man; then communion begins.

*"To him who is thirsty I will give to drink without cost from the spring of the water of life."* [7]

1.  *Psalm 42:1-2*
2.  *John 4:13-14*
3.  *John 7:37*
4.  *Psalm 63:1*
5.  *Jeremiah 2:13*
6.  *John 19:28 (KJV)*
7.  *Revelation 21:6*

# Chapter ~ 8

# JUST LOOK AROUND: FINDING GOD

*"The heavens declare the glory of God;*
*the skies proclaim the work of his hands."*

Just look around you and you will find signs of God everywhere. Everything displays the signature of the Creator. The creation screams the name of its Maker. *"God is like a person who clears his throat while hiding and so gives himself away,"* said Meister Eckhart. The creation gives Him away! You don't have to go far. In every direction that you look, and in every place that you are, you will find the evidence of God in His handiwork. There is no escaping. The stamp of God is too visible to be missed. *"God is wholly present in all creation, in every corner, behind you and before you,"* wrote Martin Luther.

The creation is a witness to God. It is the first missionary of God. Paul writing to the Romans says, *"Since what may be known about God is plain to them, because God has made it plain to them. For since the creation of the world God's invisible qualities – his eternal power and divine nature*

*– have been clearly seen, being understood from what has been made, so that men are without excuse."* [1] No one can complain that God does not give evidence of Himself; of His nature and His power. He does so. And He does so emphatically and loudly. He leaves enough clues around to convince us that our search for Him is not a wild goose chase.

*"The heavens declare the glory of God; the skies proclaim the work of his hands. Day after day they pour forth speech; night after night they display knowledge. There is no speech or language where their voice is not heard. Their voice goes out into all the earth, their words to the ends of the world."* [2] The creation proclaims the work of His hands, it speaks of the glory of God; it is a billboard advertising God the Artist. And it clearly speaks in a language which all men can understand, for it speaks to the hearts and souls of men; *that God is,* and He is majestic in all that He has created. No wonder the psalmist goes gaga over what is on display. He waxes lyrics to the wonder of God's works!

God takes pride in the work of His hands. All that He made gave Him pleasure. He called it good. The account of creation recorded in the first book of the Bible, mentions God surveying His completed work at the end of the sixth day, and found that *'it was very good'*. [3] He then entered His rest on the seventh day. And the subject of God's longest speech in the Bible, which is spread over four chapters (38 to 41) of the Book of Job, is *creation!* God is showing off to Job the magnificent works of His hands. He is impressing Job with the splendour of His creation. Obviously God takes much pleasure in all that He has made and He wants man to also admire and be pleased with His workmanship, and give Him the glory due His name.

But what does man do? He comes up with the theory of the Big Bang which he claims resulted in the formation of the universe. He removes the Creator from the equation. His mind puts more faith in the postulations derived from scientific laws (and there are many ifs, and many assumptions in coming to these conclusions) than in the very obvious. Ask yourselves what is more likely on the probability scale: the universe resulting out of the Big Bang or the work of the Creator God? For me it is no contest; God wins hands down.

So complex is the cosmos, but so much in order that even the skeptics acknowledge that. So many are the laws of the universe, but so well integrated and working in harmony. The design of the universe is flawless; its execution is so meticulous; its running is so orderly. Stand up and applaud the Maker! As the Sunday school song goes – *He has the whole world in His hands.*

The God who made such a universe, with all its magnificent dimensions, also made the creatures that populate the world: - the birds in the sky, the fish in the seas, the animals on the land, and of course man. *Man*; God's prized creation! His supreme work! The psalmist breaks out in amazement, *"When I consider your heavens, the work of your fingers, the moon and the stars, which you have set in place, what is man that you are mindful of him, the son of man that you care for him?"* [4] He cares for man, because man takes the pride of place amongst God's creation. Look at the human body. It is a marvelous piece of work. David writes, *"For you created my inmost being; you knit me together in my mother's womb. I praise you because I am fearfully and wonderfully made; yours works are wonderful, I know that full well."* [5] We are not assembly line products; but each individual has been carefully and lovingly *knit* together by the Maker. Each a masterpiece; carved out with much precision and with close attention to details. A work of genius!

The human body works in a coordinated manner. Each part has an assigned role, and the parts are bound together to make an integrated whole. The parts become complete in and as the body; outside of it they will not be able to function and be useless. *"Men go abroad to wonder at the height of mountains, at the huge waves of the sea, at the long courses of the rivers, at the vast compass of the ocean, at the circular motion of the stars; and they pass by themselves without wondering"* wrote St. Augustine. Man is indeed the supreme creation and he does not have to look beyond himself to know and appreciate the magnificence of the Creator. (To know how amazing the human body is and its parallel with the Body of Christ, I would recommend you the books; *Fearfully and Wonderfully Made, In His Image,* and *The Gift of Pain* - all co-authored by Paul Brand and Philip Yancey).

We ask then if the much debated question - whether man is the result of evolution or there is a mastermind who designed his every detail – is really relevant. It is hard to believe that our origins should be traced back to single cell organisms, which then went through a fascinating journey riddled with many ifs and buts, to evolve into the human specie. And one may ask; why has man stopped evolving? Evolution seems to have come to a dead end. Sorry Mr. Darwin but I don't buy your theory, no matter how well constructed it may be. There are lots of gaps and lots of assumptions in it. For me Eden is simpler and easier to accept, and the belief, that a loving and personal God has created man in His own likeness, is far more credible.

What a paradox it is; the more man increased in knowledge, the more difficult it became for him to believe. Rather it should have become easier. He should have come closer to God as he increasingly made discoveries, understood the laws of the universe, made inventions which helped him to understand matter, and understood the composition and working of the human body. All this understanding should have increased his appreciation and admiration for the genius of God's mind.

Everything should have fallen in place. Faith should have been easier to come. But increasing knowledge only led man to believe that he had figured it all out. They could argue that: 'There is now no need for the invisible God, who anyway cannot be scientifically explained. That belief is for the simpletons. We know everything. We now know that there was no divine hand in the creation of the universe. We now know how man came about. We can clone and recreate animals and one day we will clone the human body.' Knowledge puffs up. Its blinds you in your ignorance. Jesus speaks of this blind knowledge when he quotes Isaiah: *"You will be ever hearing but never understanding; you will be ever seeing but never perceiving. For this people's heart has become calloused; they hardly hear with their ears, and they have closed their eyes."*[6]

But if you have to understand the things of God, if you have to perceive His working, then you must receive His mysteries with childlike wonder. Someone has written, *"God cannot be grasped by the mind. If he could be grasped, He would not be God."* We must accept that we will never get to know everything. We will not have the explanation for each and everything that goes on under the sun. We will not be able reduce every phenomena or wonder in creation to a theory or postulation. We are dealing with an infinite God and His works are too splendid, too complex, and too magnificent, for our minds to understand them fully. We can only be dazzled by them. We have to have that childlike trust and innocence to be surprised and at the same time the willingness to accept.

The stamp of Jesus is found in the structure of the universe, for God created all things through him. John writes, *"Through him all things were made; without him nothing was made that has been made."* [7] The stamp of Jesus, which is found in the Scriptures, is imprinted in the structure of the universe and the same is also imprinted in the human structure. Therefore man can only be in harmony with creation when he follows the way of Jesus. Any other way will lead to chaos.

As it did in the Garden of Eden!

1.  Romans 1:19-20.
2.  Psalm 19:1-4
3.  Genesis 1:31
4.  Psalm 8:3-4.
5.  Psalm 139:13-14.
6.  Matthew 13:14-15
7.  John 1:3

# Chapter ~ 9

# THE FALLEN ANGEL

*"How you have fallen from heaven,*
*O morning star, son of the dawn!"*[1]

The morning star, the son of the dawn, here is referring to our ancient enemy, now known as Satan. He once was an angel, an archangel, and he was then (before his expulsion from the heavens) known as Lucifer, which means the one who brings the light (the light bearer). He was in charge of the important task of arranging the worship of the Holy One. He was responsible for the sanctuary of God in heaven; a guardian cherub covering the place where God's presence was manifested.

So what went wrong? Why was he thrown out of the heavens? What happened that the archangel of the Almighty was banished from His presence and into the darkness? How did Lucifer, the favored celestial creature, become Satan the enemy of God?

We will look at this and also the lessons that the downfall of Lucifer has for us. In a way it is tragic, for the fate which he met, can be that of any of us, if we don't pay heed. And this is the reason that Satan has been included as the subject of a chapter in this book which is primarily about God and His Christ.

Pride comes before downfall; is a warning given many times in the Bible. That is what happened to Lucifer. Pride took hold of him and led him to his destruction. Lucifer, as it is believed, was a beautiful angel with many talents (music being one of them, so considered). It is written about him:

*"You were a model of perfection, full of wisdom and perfect in beauty. You were in Eden, the garden of God; every precious stone adorned you ...... Your settings and mountings were made of gold ..... You were anointed as the guardian cherub, for so I ordained you. You were on the holy mount of God ...... You were blameless in your ways from the day you were created till wickedness was found in you. Through your widespread trade you were filled with violence, and you sinned. So I drove you in disgrace from the mount of God, and I expelled you, O guardian cherub, from among the fiery stones. You heart became proud on account of your beauty, and you corrupted your wisdom because of your splendor. So I threw you to the earth; I made a spectacle of you before kings."* [2]

How did wickedness enter Lucifer? Why did he sin? What was the cause of his rebellion against God? *It was pride.* The perfection of Lucifer had a flaw, and that flaw was pride. His perfection in beauty, his wisdom, his exalted position on the mountain of God as the archangel, resulted in pride springing within him. (Compare his perfection with the perfection of Jesus. There was no flaw in the perfection of Jesus for it was accompanied by humility. And it is this perfection that God wants us to seek).

In his pride Lucifer wanted to be equal to God and perhaps even more than God. He wanted the glory of God to be given to him. He who arranged the worship of the Most High, wanted himself to be worshipped. He desired to be enthroned on the mountain of assembly - Mount Zaphon. He wanted to be like God. Isaiah writes:

*"How you have fallen from heaven, O morning star (Lucifer), son of the dawn! You have been cast down to the earth, you who once laid low the nations! You said in your heart, 'I will ascend to the heaven; I will raise my throne above the stars of God; I will sit enthroned on the mount of the assembly, on*

*the utmost heights of the sacred mountain* (Mount Zaphon). *I will ascend above the tops of the clouds; I will make myself like the Most High'. But you are brought down to the grave, to the depths of the pit."* [3]

Lucifer mobilized a rebellion in heaven against God, and he and the angels who sided with him, were resultantly thrown out of heaven; out of the presence of God. *'He was hurled to the earth, and his angels with him'.* [4] The first sin had been committed; not on earth but in heaven. The sin on earth was to come later and was a consequence of the events in heaven.

Do we detect anything familiar in this story? Haven't we seen it played out many times in the lives of individuals, in every field of human activity? A person gets exalted, is lifted high, everything he touches turns to gold, people admire him, respect him; then pride takes root in him, the person believes he can do anything, get away with anything, people can't do without him, there is no one like him, pride blinds him, puts scales in his eyes, he is a star, he is divine, he is demi-god; and then suddenly comes the fall. The shooting star crashes!

Tragic isn't it? That is the reason God hates pride for He knows what it can do to us and where it can lead us to. And of all the pride, the worst form is the spiritual pride, where you consider you have become a god or equal to God; or where you consider God should be grateful to you because you do Him a favor by serving Him; or where you believe you know better than God, as Lucifer thought he knew better than God in the matter of the human experiment.

While pride caused Lucifer's fall, what could have been the trigger point which led him to rebel against God? At what stage did his pride turn against God? I believe it was when God decided *to create man.* Lucifer saw that now someone else would take his place before God. Now some other being would be the favorite of God and be close to Him. *And that someone had been made by God in His own image!* The angels did not have the image of God in the same way as man. Man would now be the exalted one; more exalted than him (Lucifer). And this was not acceptable to Lucifer. His pride was stoked and he rebelled against God. He attempted to wrest God's authority, power, and glory. From that time on he became the enemy of God.

The stage shifts to the Garden of Eden. Sin which had been first committed in heaven by Lucifer was now repeated on earth. And Satan (by now Lucifer had become Satan, which means the enemy or opposer) used the same emotion to entice man to sin. He fanned the pride, which it seems was dormant but nevertheless there, in man. He told Eve, *"You will not surely die* (implying that God had lied to her). *For God knows that when you eat of it* (the fruit from the tree of knowledge) *your eyes will be opened, and you will be like God, knowing good and evil."* [5] You will be like God! A tempting offer which Eve, and later Adam, found it difficult to refuse. Satan implied in this exchange with Eve, that God did not have their good in mind. God wanted to keep Adam and Eve subjected to Him. He did not want them to rise to their full potential, which was, as Satan alluded to them, to be like God.

Adam and Eve disobeyed God and sin came into the world. They like Lucifer in heaven, rebelled against the authority of God. But why did Satan cause man to sin? What was his objective in bringing down man? Man had become his enemy every since man came between him and God. He had been against the human experiment (in which God for the first time made a being in His own image) and he planned for this experiment to fail. He wanted to show God that man, the creature whom God had placed higher than him, would also disobey Him. That man would exercise his free will in choosing to walk away from God. That the image of God in man could be corrupted by sin. It was Satan's way of retaliating against God, by showing that God had made a mistake when He created man and gave him His image; the image which differentiated man from other beings, even celestial. Satan could not defeat God directly. He was no match. He therefore directed his attack against *the image of God in man*. He became the enemy of man as he was of God.

And ever since he has been the enemy of man and by causing man to fail, by causing the image of God in man to be tarnished, he gains his victories against God. Satan argues with God in this manner: *'You made man in your image. Well see what all he does despite having your image in him. See what sins he commits. See what level of bestiality man can descend to. Admit it God that your experiment has failed. You have failed. Give up* on man. *This is the creature who you love above all? You placed him higher than me, was he worth it? Their sin is no different. If I have paid the penalty for my sin, they too should pay the penalty for their sin. If I have been punished for rebelling against you, they too should be given the same fate. If I am damned they should also be damned. For aren't you supposed to be a just God. Isn't your justice the same for all? Destroy them'.*

I consider that one of the reasons God did not destroy mankind was that He did not want Satan to have his victory. He could not let the human experiment fail. He loved man; loved him too much to give up on him. But He could not let Satan accuse Him of being unjust. God would then have to meet His own demand for justice. He was going to make it work, even if it meant that He Himself had to become part of mankind. To save man, He would become man. God's prestige was at stake.

*"The reason the Son of God appeared was to destroy the devil's work,"* [6] wrote John in the epistle. Because of the Cross, Satan has been unable to get God to condemn mankind, the way he himself has been condemned. He therefore now directs his attack on individual souls and his aim is to take down with him as many as he can. There is a fight between God and Satan over each and every soul; and this would explain why a celebration breaks out in heaven over every soul that is saved! Satan's target is especially the believer; for those who are not on Jesus' side or have rejected the Son of God and embraced the way of evil, he does not have to worry much about. He stands before God, bringing accusations against us (that is why Satan is also known as the Devil which means the accuser or slanderer) for our every sin, our every transgression, our every failure. But we have the cover of the Cross. Our redemption is in the blood of the Lamb, and Jesus stands before God as our advocate, reminding the Father that he has paid the penalty for our sins.

The Bible warns us that: *"For our struggle is not against flesh and blood, but against the rulers, against the authorities, against the powers of this dark world and against the spiritual forces of evil in the heavenly realms."* [7] We have a very powerful and clever adversary (just shut out the image of Satan as that two horned ugly looking creature carrying a pitchfork), who is suave and adept in playing mind games. He uses the weapon of guilt to make the believer's life miserable. He guile runs like this: *'Are you sure your sins are forgiven; this one is too big a sin to be forgiven; God has given up on you for your repeated failures; you have messed it up big time and there is no forgiveness for you'.* The believer drowns in his guilt, in his misery. He is no match against *'the father of lies'*, [8] as what Jesus called Satan. And Satan not only targets our weaknesses and failures, but also our strengths. We have the example of Job, where he attacked Job's strength which was faith and put him through various trials, which took that very faith to a breaking point. Christian walk is not easy and Satan makes sure of that. We have to put on the *'full armor of God'* [9] to repel his attacks. Thankfully God has not left us defenseless.

Another strategy that Satan uses is: he obfuscates the redeeming work of Jesus on the Cross by creating doubts in the minds of non believers and even in the believers. The arguments he deploys are many. Some of them: *'How can one man's death redeem the whole world? Man has to work out his own salvation. Did Jesus really die on the cross? Is the resurrection of Jesus for real? Who rolled the stone from the tomb? All religions of the world are the same, they all lead to God; so does it matter which one you follow? Jesus is not THE way, but A way to the same destination'.* All this leads to confusing the message of the Cross and sows the seeds of doubt. Well the Cross has happened. Jesus died on it and by his death has redeemed mankind. It can't be wished away by Satan. The Cross is a constant reminder of his defeat. Therefore he now goes about diluting its effect. His attempt is to portray an extraordinary act of sacrifice by God as an ordinary one; the most important event in human history as a non-event; so that as many as possible do not accept the salvation that God has for mankind.

Does Satan control the events on earth? Apostle John writes, "*the whole world is under the control of the evil one.*" [10] Jesus called Satan the *'prince of this world'*. [11] And the gospels have the account of Satan tempting Jesus with the offer of all the kingdoms of the world: "*I will give you all their authority and splendour, for it has been given to me, and I can give it to anyone I want to.*" [12] In return he asks Jesus to worship him. I consider that when man sinned, by default he gave the keys of the earth to Satan. God had put man as the ruler over the earth; but one of the consequences of the Fall was that the title deeds of the earth passed to Satan, who then became man's legal sovereign, his ruler. Ever since then, God is wresting man away from Satan's sovereignty. It is not known what are the boundaries of Satan's sovereignty and when does God's *ultimate* sovereignty overrule it. What all the prince of this world can do and what he can't do on earth? What are the limits to Satan's power? These are some questions to which answers are difficult to find.

In a way the story of Lucifer is tragic. But it has lessons for us. We can also fall from our exalted positions, if we are not careful, if we do not pay heed to God's word. Wendy Alec in her book the *Fall of Lucifer* describes a scene between Satan and one of his lieutenants. Satan is in a pensive mood. To his aide's observation that they all are doomed to hell, Satan cries out: *"True hell – true torment is to be banished from the Father's presence."* The agony in his cry can't be missed. One can detect him remembering the time when he was Lucifer, the archangel, and used to live in heaven in the presence of the Most High. He must be wishing for those days to come back. He may have wanted to return to God. But even if he wanted to, he knows that he can't. His darkness, the evil in him, has rendered him incapable to come into God's presence. An ever haunting thought fills up his mind: *'If only he had not rebelled against the Almighty; if only he had repented and sought His forgiveness when he had the chance; he would have still been there in heaven, organising the worship of the Most High'.*

Will this be the fate of sinners who do not repent? *Is this what hell is?* Banished for eternity into darkness; away from the light of God's presence.

What a terrible thought!

1. *Isaiah 14:12*
2. *Ezekiel 28:12-17*
3. *Isaiah 14:12-15*
4. *Revelation 12:9*
5. *Genesis 3:4-5*
6. *1 John 3:8*
7. *Ephesians 6:12*
8. *John 8:44*
9. *Ephesians 6:13*
10. *I John 5:19*
11. *John 12:31 and elsewhere*
12. *Luke 4:6*

# Chapter ~ 10

# THE KINGDOM OF GOD

*"Your kingdom come, your will be done on earth as it is in heaven."* [1]

The Lord's Prayer, recited by millions of Christians every day, has Jesus wishing for God's kingdom to come on earth as it is in heaven. The gospel accounts record Jesus talking about the kingdom of God (or interchangeably as the kingdom of heaven) throughout his public ministry. In fact, if we look closely, this appears to be the main subject of his teachings and sermons. It seemed as if it was his obsession to talk about the kingdom and make references to it whenever he addressed the people.

Jesus oft mentioned the kingdom of God for the simple reason that *it was his mission on earth to establish the kingdom of God.* And he was fulfilling the same zealously. From the very beginning of his public ministry, Jesus started to proclaim the kingdom of God: *"The time has come. The kingdom of God is near. Repent and believe the good news!"* [2] The good news of what? Of the coming of the kingdom of God. Jesus also told his disciples to announce the same, when he sent them out to the towns and cities of Israel: *"As you go, preach this message: 'The kingdom of heaven is near.'"* [3] With the coming of Jesus on earth, God's kingdom started to set in. The wheels of the kingdom were set in motion and they are in motion ever since. The kingdom has not fully set in, as yet, but has been growing every day since then. It will only 'come' in fully, when God's will is fully done. It will happen one day. When, no one knows, but it will surely be established fully; of that we can be certain.

*"The Law and the Prophets were proclaimed until John. Since that time, the good news of the kingdom of God is being preached, and everyone is forcing his way into it,"* [4] explained Jesus. With John the Baptist, the new way to God had been revealed, and everyone who accepted the baptism of repentance laid hold of God's kingdom. The old had gone and the new was being established. The transition point had been marked.

*"My kingdom is not of this world,"* [5] Jesus told Pilate. The kingdom of Jesus, the kingdom of God, is of another world. It is of the spiritual world, it is of heaven, and thus is different from the kingdoms of this world, which are material. Unlike the kingdoms of the world, it is not contained within any boundaries or limits. There is no barbed wire or wall fencing it. It is an invisible kingdom which transcends all the nations (kingdoms) on earth. It happens to be the central focus of God's working on earth. Though it is invisible; its fruits, its influence, its results, are very much visible and tangible.

It was a new kingdom that Jesus was ushering in. Therefore the people needed to be explained the details, the nature, and the essence of this kingdom, so that they could understand its difference from the kingdoms of the world. Jesus set about doing that precisely, using mainly parables, where he drew the analogy to the kingdom of God with the simple things and facts of everyday life, so that the people could easily relate with it. *He used the things of the world, to explain a kingdom which was not of this world.* Let us briefly look at these parables.

The *parable of the mustard seed,* where a small seed grows into a tree that provides shelter to the birds; which shows how God works great things out of little and unimportant ones.

The *parable of the weeds,* where the landowner waits till the harvest before pulling out the weeds that have grown with the wheat sprout, so as not to cause damage to the wheat sprout; which explains why God allows evil to exist, for now, with good in the world.

The *parable of the yeast,* which permeates the entire dough thereby fulfilling its effectiveness; displaying the contagious effect of the kingdom and the stealth with which it spreads.

The two *parables of the hidden treasure and the pearl,* which when a man finds, he is willing to sell everything he has to obtain them; showing how valuable the kingdom of God is considered by those who find it.

The *parable of the net* which explains how God will segregate the righteous from the evil.

The *parable of the unmerciful servant,* who though had himself experienced his master's forgiveness, did not in turn show forgiveness to his fellow servant; providing the teaching that the kingdom of God is as much about giving grace as of receiving God's grace.

The *parable of the workers in the vineyard,* who all got equal wages though had worked for different lengths of time; making it clear that God's grace does not differentiate and it is for Him to give, in whatever measure He chooses.

The *parable of the tenants* of the vineyard who killed the landowner's son; warns us that we cannot take the kingdom of God as our birthright and that it will be taken away from all those who reject the Son.

The *parable of the wedding banquet* illustrates that God will substitute those who do not appreciate His call with those who do welcome receiving His invitation to the banquet, and also prepare well for it.

The *parable of the ten virgins* which warns us to be ever prepared, for the bridegroom can come at any hour; referring to the second coming of Jesus.

The *parable of the talents* shows us that God's gifts and talents to us should not to be wasted, but must be put to good use for His kingdom.

Jesus was concerned that the people should fully understand the essence of this invisible kingdom of God, for there was a strong possibility that they might receive it as another kingdom of the world.

(In fact, as it turned out, this is exactly what happened. The people of Israel mistook Jesus' kingdom as a political one, which they thought he would be establishing by overturning the Roman rule. They believed that the Messiah had come to re-establish the throne of David. This, incidentally, was the main charge levied by the Sanhedrin before Pilate, in seeking the death sentence for Jesus). The people also had to understand the kingdom's value and what was needed to receive it. They had to comprehend the dynamics of its working and the manner in which it grew and expanded.

The way the kingdom advances is best illustrated in the *parable of the growing seed,* where a man scatters the seed (that is sows his good works) everywhere and then just sits back. The seed sprouts and grows and he does not really know what is making it do so (God is silently at work). Then the fruits start appearing which benefit many. Let us consider an example of such a working of God's kingdom in our times. Mother Teresa started her work amongst the destitute on the streets of Calcutta in the late 1940s. When she ministered to the first needy person, that she ever did, did she ever imagine how God would make her work grow? How her ministry - 'Missionaries of Charity'- would one day expand to a global scale? How a small but courageous step by her, would inspire many thousands to follow her footsteps, to show the love of Christ to those who are the neediest of the needy? This is how the kingdom of God grows. Silently, surely, and surprisingly! It just needs a seed to be sown by a heart filled with Christ.

*"The kingdom of God is within you,"* [6] said Jesus. It takes root within us and grows from the inside out. True and lasting transformation only takes place when it is from the inside, because the Holy Spirit resides in the person and it is his power that makes the change. For the person it is a state of being; for those around, it becomes evident in the tangible fruits that he bears as a result. Christian work seen in the service of the lepers, in the orphanages, in the homes for the homeless and for the aged, in the selfless service of the doctors in the hospitals, in the educational institutes for the poor and the handicapped, in the business or profession run according to the teachings of Christ; these and others such, are all tangible and conspicuous signs in this visible world of the invisible kingdom of God and His Son.

Jesus said to his disciples, *"And I confer on you a kingdom, just as my Father conferred one on me."* [7] Not only did Jesus do that, but he also turned over to them his mission to establish the kingdom of God. For three years he had prepared them. He had kept them with him during his ministry; taught them at close quarters; given them exclusive insights to his teaching, his work, his mission. He had groomed them to carry on his work in this world, after he was gone. He had also sent them on trial runs to the different parts of Israel, to preach the good news of the kingdom of God. And when they had returned and reported exuberantly, like little children, as to what all they could do in his name, he had shared their joy and remarked: *"I saw Satan fall like lightning from heaven."* [8] They were on track and the enemy was worried. He was now sure that God's mission, which he had come to accomplish, would continue even after he had left the world. In fact, it would now be able to spread all over the world, for there would be many bodies at work. *"As you sent me into the world, I have sent them into the world,"*[9] said Jesus in prayer. His disciples, and the disciples who would come after them throughout the ages, would become his co-workers in the kingdom. The kingdom of God will thus advance uninterrupted.

The doors of the kingdom of God are open to all, and many will come from all parts of the world and take their places at the great banquet that will be held there. But though the entry to the kingdom is unrestricted, and the invitation is to all and sundry, not all would make it; *"For many are invited, but few are chosen."* [10] Not everyone will enter; *"Not everyone who says to me, 'Lord, Lord,' will enter the kingdom of heaven…,"* [11] said Jesus, cautioning the people against their false sense of righteousness, which could make them complacent that they were sure to enter the kingdom.

Instead the way to the kingdom, as Jesus explains to Nicodemus, is: *"I tell you the truth, no-one can see the kingdom of God unless he is born again."* [12] And goes on to clarify to the bewildered man that by that he meant that you have to be born of the Spirit. Paul is also categorical in stating, *"I declare to you, brothers, that flesh and blood cannot inherit the kingdom of God, nor does the perishable inherit the imperishable."* [13] Spiritual birth is the prerequisite for entering the kingdom of God and it takes place in a person when he accepts Jesus as his Lord and Saviour. Jesus is *THE* gate through which we enter the kingdom of God and the process is our spiritual birth. Only those born of the Spirit, the new man, can be part of this kingdom. It is spelt out clearly.

The kingdom of God has to be received like a little child; with amazement, joy and innocence. *"The kingdom of heaven belongs to such as these,"* [14] Jesus said pointing to the little children. Why is that? For in the kingdom of God the rules of this world are reversed; they are in fact turned upside down. Here the last is the first, the least is considered the greatest, and those who humble themselves are exalted. Things work differently in God's kingdom and it cannot be understood or received with the attitude, thoughts, and stubbornness of an adult. Instead it has to be received with the openness of a child. The kingdom of God won't make sense at all if considered through the eyes of this world, where those who come first are idolized, the powerful and the rich are considered great, and those who occupy high positions are exalted.

For the followers of Christ their citizenship is of the kingdom of God. At the same time we inhabit the material world and are called to be model residents of it. Normally there is a harmonious arrangement between the two; well at least for most of the time. But there could be times when our allegiance to the kingdom of the world and to the kingdom of God would clash. We must then show that our first loyalty is to the kingdom of God. The kingdoms of this world are temporal but the kingdom of God will last forever. It is eternal. So place your bets wisely.

We must make sure that we enter the kingdom of God and remain in it. And also help others to get in there.

*"For many are invited, but few are chosen."*

1.  *Matthew 6:10*
2.   *Mark 1:15*
3.  *Matthew 10:7*
4.  *Luke 16:16*
5.  *John 18:36*
6.  *Luke 17:21*
7.  *Luke 22:29*
8.  *Luke 10:18*
9.  *John 17:18*
10. *Matthew 22:14*
11. *Matthew 7:21*
12. *John 3:3*
13. *1 Corinthians 15:50*
14. *Matthew 19:14*

# SECTION II

# THE NAZARENE

*"God has made this Jesus,
whom you crucified, both Lord and Christ."*

*Acts 2:36*

# Chapter ~ 11

# JESUS OF NAZARETH

*"Jesus is the best picture God ever had taken of himself."*
*- A little boy in Sunday school*

About two thousand years ago God came to earth and joined the human race. He was born in uncommon circumstances and lived his life in an obscure town called Nazareth in the Roman province of Palestine. They called him Jesus - Jesus of Nazareth.

No person in the history of mankind has made more impact than this carpenter from Nazareth. No one has had more books written about him; no one has been the subject of art more than him; no one has had more movies made on his life than him; no one has had more questions raised about him; no one has been more discussed and debated than him; no one has more followers than him; and no one has more detractors than him. He was, presumably, not much educated; engaged in a humble profession; was of modest means; did not have any estate; did not produce any literary masterpiece (the only account of him writing anything is on the ground in Jerusalem with his finger, which must have soon got erased); has no artistic achievement to put him amongst the masters (not counting some innovative furniture designs that he *may* have come up with in his carpentry workshop); he did not marry and so did not leave any descendants who are amongst us today; who died a shameful death; and was buried in a grave donated by somebody.

And yet – and yet, he has attracted more people to him than any other person in history. His following, beginning with a small number while he was living, has grown into a legion spread all over the world. He is a magnet who has drawn multitudes of believers, in all ages, to him and continues to draw even as you read this. He has inspired people to leave their homes, chuck their jobs, give up their wealth; in response to just his two words *'follow me'*. He has been an inspiration for great works of humanity where his stamp of selfless love is firmly imprinted. He has caused many to joyfully suffer trials and persecutions and even martyrdom for his sake. His name is the most recited in the world every day. The more the authorities, hostile to it, have tried to suppress it, the more it has grown and spread. Rulers have come and gone, kingdoms have risen and fallen, ideologies have sprung up and died, but the church he founded on a rock, has remained rock like. He has been loved and hated, admired and reviled, revered and abused; but whatever you may feel about him or consider him to be, you cannot ignore this Jesus of Nazareth. He compels you to take a stand.

How has Jesus invoked such passions in mankind ever since he entered human history? What is in him that attracts us and raises such strong emotions within us – positive or negative? What is it about this man that he moves us to such an extent that someone can comment: *"If anyone proved to me that Christ was outside the truth then I would prefer to remain with Christ than with the truth,"* the Russian writer Fyodor Dostoevsky. And someone else,*"If God is not like Jesus then I do not need that god."* What sublime effect does Jesus have, especially on those who respond to his call and believe in him? How has he changed the overall scheme of things? How has his coming affected the moral universe? What difference has he made in our view of God, in how we relate to the Most High?

Jesus has made God who was considered unapproachable, approachable. He has made God considered aloof and distant, lovable. He has made a faraway God come near us. He has shown who God is. He has showed a new and intimate way of relating with God, of dealing with Him, approaching Him and loving Him. *"Only in seeing his Maker does a man truly become man. For in seeing his Creator, man catches glimpse of what he was intended to be. It is in seeing Jesus that man sees his Source,"* comments Max Lucado. Jesus brought the Creator and the created together in a relationship of love. He set in place a new equation between God and man; the equation of love.

Jesus was a Jew and would have followed the religious rituals, customs, and traditions of the Jewish nation. He was also well versed in the Jewish law; the Law of Moses. He called on the name of Jehovah, the God of the Jews, as any Jew would. But Jehovah was considered to be unapproachable, who appeared to His people only in pillars of cloud and fire. Every year the Jews had to bring their offerings to please Him. His was an image of a strict parent who had given them the Law, which they had to follow in their lives to please Him. Jesus came and put a new face to God. *"Jesus brought the message of mother love to balance the father love of the Old Testament,"* wrote Shusako Endo. Jesus made God complete.

When I was in school, I used to often look (especially if I found the lesson boring) at the cross affixed to the wall above the blackboard. Being a Roman Catholic school there was a cross in every classroom. I used to look at the figure nailed on the cross and wondered - how could a god be so weak that he lets people put him up there? Why did he not get down in an awesome display of power? Why was he wearing a crown of thorns when there should have been a crown of gold on his brow, as it adorns the other gods that I knew of? Being born in the Hindu religion my belief was that gods are meant to be strong and not defenseless; they are supposed to destroy their enemies, in a single blow usually, and not to suffer in their hands. Then why was it, if he was a god at all, that Jesus made such a pathetic sight; an antithesis of all that we expect from a god. Despite these honest but somewhat mocking thoughts and the troubled questions that I had, I could not help but be drawn to the cross. There was something in that broken and wounded figure that was mesmerizing.

Little did I know, not realizing then, that I had raised some fundamental questions of the mystery of God in Christ, the answers to which I would get later in my life after I had accepted Jesus. *"The other gods were strong, but Thou wast weak; they rode but Thou didst stumble to a throne; but to our wounds only God's wounds can speak and not a god has wounds but Thou alone,"* wrote Edward Shilitio, which most perfectly explains the 'weak' God that we Christians follow. I believe that this remains the stumbling block for many people. Jesus was too much like us for the Jews of his time and for people later to accept as God. He was too human to be God. We make our gods in the image we want; strong, powerful, a regent, adorned in splendor, and flashing his might when provoked. We could never think of a god like Jesus. Walter Wink writes, *"If Jesus had never lived, we would not have been able to invent him."* That is true and for this VERY reason alone we can conclude that Jesus was a real person who lived in history. If we had invented him then we would have made him just like the other gods; gods that we invent as per our taste and liking.

What do you say of a god who walked with us; talked with us like any other person; took his meals when hungry; as an infant suckled at his mother's breast; as a child held his father's hand; when growing up played tricks on his friends; felt excited to attend the festivities in the village; asked questions to the village rabbi during the lessons on the Torah – the law he himself had authored; looked forward to his annual visit to the temple in Jerusalem; was serious in going about his heavenly Father's business but at the same time diligently learned the craft of his earthly father; who cried out in pain when the blade use to accidentally nick his finger while at work; who must have sweat and got tired after working long hours on the shop floor; who was happy to find faith even as small as a mustard seed; who was saddened by all the suffering in the world, knowing this was not as per the original plan; who wept at the sight of death, seeing the havoc sin had caused; who faced the pain of rejection by his own people, his nation and even his close friends; who was filled with fear at the prospects of his suffering on the cross, on what would be his last day on this planet; who therefore pleaded for some concession (*'take this cup away'*) from the One who alone could have given him, but did not receive any; who endured the injustice of being subjected to farcical trials by the Jewish and Roman authorities; who suffered the indignity of his beard being pulled, his face being spat, his body being pummeled with blows; who underwent the humiliation of being led in a procession to the place of his execution, burdened with his own execution tool; whose death became a public spectacle, with more number of people mocking and jeering than those who wept and beat their breasts; who felt abandoned even by his own Father, and at a time when he needed Him most; who died and was laid in a borrowed tomb, with a Roman guard outside to make double sure that he was not a cause of trouble even in death!

What do you make of such a god? Do we need such a god? Do we need such a 'human' god? Gods are supposed to be - well gods. Never seen or will see one like him. Imposter or really what he claimed to be? Paul writes in the letter to the Corinthians: *"But we preach Christ crucified: a stumbling block to Jews and foolishness to Gentiles, but to those whom God has called, ... Christ the power of God and the wisdom of God."* [1]

Who really was Jesus; the Son of God or the Son of Man as he preferred calling himself?

Deity or human? God or man? *Well he was both.* He was God living on this planet as one of the human specie. As a man he lived within the constraints and limitations of the body of flesh and blood. He got no concessions, no dispensations, and no special powers to make life easy for him. He lived on earth within the rules of the earth. God made no special favors for him; he could draw on no privileges to make his life easier in this sin infected world. Rather in his life he faced the most difficult conditions and circumstances which a man can be subjected to. The perfect one learned perfection in the human body through trials and sufferings. The Book of Hebrews vividly describes the route the Son of God had to take while he was the Son of Man; the route to perfection through suffering. God made no exceptions for Himself when he was Jesus of Nazareth. He played it fair; by the rules of the game. *"Whatever game He is playing with His creation, He has kept His own rules and played fair. He can exact nothing from man that He has not exacted from Himself"* wrote Dorothy L. Sayers, underlining the humanity of Jesus.

Sometimes I wonder why Jesus had to be born poor. Why did God not choose a higher station in society and be born into a wealthy and powerful family? Wouldn't it have been easier for him to influence the people if he was to be born the son of a rich and influential member of the Sanhedrin, rather than the son of a poor carpenter? Would he then have not secured an edge in his public ministry and be received well by the important sections of the society; that is by those that mattered? Would he then have not ridden into Jerusalem on a horse, instead of a donkey, with all the pomp and grandeur of an important leader?

Well Jesus would not have been Jesus if he had taken any other position to be born into this world. The message of Jesus would have got lost in the trappings of the high and mighty. Much of his teaching would have sounded hypocritical, and in fact we might well ask - would his teaching have been the same then? How would it have appeared if a finely clothed and well-manicured Jesus, with opulence exuding out of him, had given the Sermon on the Mount? How convincing would have the words, *"blessed are the meek, the poor, those who mourn,"* sounded then? Jesus would have sounded similar to most of the present day politicians when giving their speeches to the poor. Jesus would have been no different.

Jesus was a man of the masses. A crowd puller. He was 'one of us' for the crowd. A rabbi whom they could approach. A teacher who simplified the Law for them. Jesus attracted people from all strata of the society. His warmth was like a magnet to them. There were no barriers he erected between himself and the people. People found him approachable and he never discriminated against anyone because of race, gender, profession, or position in society. Rather he 'leaned' towards the weak and the poor. The kingdom he was propagating was open to all the rejects of the society. He was willing to associate with all and sundry and even those the religious leaders shunned; tax collectors, fishermen, women, soldiers, lepers, prostitutes, Samaritans, Gentiles..... . He was not shy to be known as their friend.

Unlike the religious leaders of his time, Jesus did not have a 'stiff upper lip' and did not overwhelm the people; with his righteousness acting as a curtain between them. He was the teacher from Nazareth that one need not be afraid to get close to, who was not out of bounds like the other religious teachers. Would Jesus have attracted people, the way he did, if he did not have the appearance of an ordinary man? Sure his 'officials' would have guaranteed a big crowd at his rallies, but then he would not have been approachable to the multitudes. He would have not been the darling of the crowd. The connect with the 'sinners' would have been missing.

But God had to identify with the poorest, the weakest, the helpless, and the oppressed amongst His people. He had to be born as one. If the message of the Messiah had to make any impact on the people, it had to come from the one who was humble amongst them. To reach the hearts of the people the message had to come from the heart of the messenger. The messenger had to be seen as one of them – an ordinary guy, a man with no 'connections'. The power of Jesus had to come from his persona and not from any external means, for it to have a lasting impact. The appeal of Jesus had to be in his charisma and not in any official position, so that his influence could be wide reaching. The authority of Jesus had to be innate and not external or of this world, so as to draw a willing response from the person. This is the reason the message of Jesus carries the same weight, the same conviction today, as it did two thousand years ago. The message did outlive the messenger.

*"I do not ask the wounded person how he feels; I myself became the wounded person"* wrote Walt Whitman. God made Jesus wounded. *'A bruised reed'* [2] as Isaiah describes him. The reason God condescended to live amongst humans was to experience the *identification;* identification with living in the worst of human conditions, with the worst of indignities suffered by man, with the worst of pain that man can inflict on another, and with the worst of death that a man can die of. Jesus of Nazareth was born in the most abject and unreceptive circumstances (it is ironical that there was no proper room for the one who fills the universe to be born). He led a hard life as the son of a

carpenter and as a grown up took up the profession of his father. He was rejected by his nation, his family, his friends (one of them even playing an active role in his arrest). His trials were a charade that made a mockery of what was supposed to be the most advanced and just legal system in the world at that time. He was flogged till his back was raw meat; he was beaten black and blue; he suffered indignities as a prisoner; he had nails driven through his hands and feet right into the wood; he was put up for public display in the company of two criminals; he suffered the most excruciating, mind numbing pain for six hours; till death finally came as a welcome relief to his torment.

What a miserable life. What a horrific death. Is this the one who will give us salvation? We worship this god? Yes we worship *THIS* God, and precisely for this very reason. We can worship no other. No one moves our heart like this God. For no other god went through all what our God in Jesus did. No person can ever make the accusation that God does not know what it feels to be rejected; what it feels to be poor; what it feels to be weak; what it feels to be a victim of injustice, to be imprisoned, to be tortured, and to die a gruesome death. God has gone through all this, in the worst possible way, to the worst possible extent. No human can ever say that he has suffered more than what God did. God subjected Himself to the worst that a man can go through – in life and in death.

Jesus was both the Son of Man and the Son of God. Though while on earth he used the former title more often; let there be no mistake that he is God. God on earth. *"The Son is the radiance of God's glory and the exact representation of His being..."* [3] and, *"For in Christ all the fullness of the Deity lives in bodily form"* [4]; are two of the many verses in the Bible which underline his divinity. In Jesus we have the full and final revelation of God. His claims, such as; *"I and the Father are one"* [5] and *"Anyone who has seen me has seen the Father"* [6], are affirmations that there is absolutely no difference between him and the Father. They are of the same essence.

God lived as a man at a point of time in human history. He was born, he lived, he died, he rose again, and he finally ascended into heaven. The tiny planet earth has a special place in God's universe. It is the *'visited'* planet. God came down and lived amongst its inhabitants for a time.

*And he was known as Jesus - Jesus of Nazareth.*

1.  *1 Corinthians 1:23-24*
2.  *Isaiah 42:3*
3.  *Hebrews 1:3*
4.  *Colossians 2:9*
5.  *John 10:30*
6.  *John 14:9*

# Chapter ~ 12

# THE SUFFERING MESSIAH

*"Did not the Christ have to suffer these things and then enter his glory?"* [1]

They got it wrong. They all got it wrong. His people, his nation, the chief priests and the elders, the crowd, even his disciples who were also his close friends and confidants, his family with the sole exception of his mother, who also would not have imagined the extent of the sufferings he would go through. They all got him wrong. He had not come to be their ruler but a suffering servant.

Jesus Christ came into the world to suffer. There was no other way for him. For the path to redemption was to be through suffering, culminating in the Cross. It had been written so in the Scriptures. The Messiah to come was to be the Suffering Messiah.

The prophets of old were absolutely clear what kind of Messiah was to come. The Christ of God would partake of the sufferings of this world, when he would be a part of this world. Isaiah in particular is descriptive of this Messiah: *"He was despised and rejected by men, a man of sorrows, and familiar with suffering. Like one from whom men hide their faces he was despised, and we esteemed him not. Surely he took up our infirmities and carried our sorrows, yet we considered him stricken by God, smitten by him, and afflicted."* [2]

Certainly not a prophecy that comforts. Not a Messiah one would eagerly wait for centuries. The prophets of God were known to give it straight. They did not sugar coat what the LORD told them to prophesy. See how the prophecy in this chapter (Isaiah 53) is fulfilled in the life of Jesus. For centuries the people of Israel were waiting for the Messiah, their King to come, who would establish his reign over the nation. They would diligently scrutinise the Scriptures for the signs that would tell them of his coming. And yet they missed him! They did not recognize the Messiah in Jesus of Nazareth. For Jesus did not fit with their idea, their conception, of what their Messiah would be; a political leader who would ascend the throne of David and whose rule would bring back the golden period of Israel that was there during the time of David and Solomon. This Jesus did not fit the bill.

*"If you, even you, had only known on this day what would bring you peace – but now it is hidden from you eyes ..., because you did not recognize the time of God's coming to you"* [3]; Jesus weeps over Jerusalem knowing the fate that was going to befall it. And thus even though all the prophecies of the Messiah given in the Scriptures were fulfilled in Jesus, he was rejected by his people. *How could they recognize the Messiah in him when they were looking for a different Messiah?* They were expecting an emancipator from the Roman rule and not a savior for their sins; they were wishing for a Messiah who would lead an invincible army against their enemies and not someone who would ask them to love their enemies and offer the other cheek; they wanted a king who would set his kingdom here and now and not a dreamer who was preaching the kingdom of God that was to come. They rejected him and not only rejected him but they made sure that he got the punishment due to him for daring to raise their hopes, even if briefly, that the time had come for God, silent for ages now, to finally deliver His people. *"He was in the world and though the world was made through him, the world did not recognize him. He came to that which was his own, but his own did not receive him."* [4] This is the irony of Jesus who is God incarnate.

Why did the Messiah have to suffer? Why did Jesus have to be *'a man of sorrows and familiar with suffering'*? Why couldn't the Messiah be in his *first coming* what we (Christians) expect him to be in his *second coming* (which would be the *first coming* as per the belief of the Jews)? The victorious Lord of lords and King of kings, who will establish his long reign on earth and defeat Satan and his armies. Why was the route to redemption to be through the thorns of suffering and not in a blaze of glory? Why was evil to be overcome by weakness and not by power? God in His wisdom chose to restore the fallen world this way – the way of suffering. For good to triumph over evil it had to suffer in the hands of evil. That was the *ONLY* way possible to save mankind. Any other option would have been the annihilation and replacement of the world and not its redemption.

Jesus Christ suffered in more than one ways. That God chose to send His Son to dwell in this sin infected world amongst fallen humans was in itself a suffering. He who was pure and sinless had to live amidst the muck and mire of sin. And while he lived on earth he suffered seeing the decay and havoc around him which was the result of the evil prevalent in the world. The misery caused by disease and death, the groans of the creation, and all other wages of sin, grieved the Son of God. This was not the way it had been planned. This was not how it was supposed to be. God had seen that everything He had created was good. Man was supposed to enjoy God's creation and live in joyful abundance. How wrong things had gone. History had moved off the intended track. The world had turned out different from its original design. But that was why he was here on earth; *to restore things to their original state.* But for that he had to go through suffering.

Another reason for the Messiah to be subjected to suffering was to make him the perfect offering. The offering for the sins of mankind had to be perfect. God's justice had to be met and it was to be only by way of a perfect offering. The Lamb of God had to be without blemish. In the Book of Hebrews we find written: *"In bringing many sons to glory, it was fitting that God, for whom and through whom everything exists, should make the author of their salvation perfect through suffering"* [5] and also, *"During the days of Jesus' life on earth, he offered up prayers and petitions with loud cries and tears to the one who could save him from death, and he was heard because of his reverent submission."* [6] Jesus suffered not only on the cross and the night before his execution but he also faced sufferings throughout his life. God did not spare him. He learned obedience by the trials he faced. He attained perfection by the sufferings he went through.

Perfection for the Son of God? Wasn't he perfect already? Isn't God perfect? Well yes He is. *But in his human body, as the Son of Man, he had to attain perfection.* The atoning sacrifice for the sins of mankind had to be from the human specie itself. But there was no one found perfect in the human race, not even one; for all men are born with the sinful nature resulting from the Fall. No one could be the perfect offering that was required.

Therefore God Himself had to be born as man. Jesus was *begotten not made, created not reproduced;* and thus he did not have the nature which was contaminated by the original sin of man. *He was the Second Adam.* But he was still human. He was not like human but human; the Son of Man. He was exposed to the same trials, the same allure, the same temptations, and the same wickedness that each and every human being faces, living in this fallen planet. He had to achieve perfection in this sin infected world. He did not have any divine help and did not count on his supernatural powers to overcome the evil. He had to do so as a man and in the human state achieve the perfection that was required to be *THE* offering that would redeem mankind for God. *"Although he was a son, he learned obedience from what he suffered and once made perfect, he became the source of eternal salvation for all who obey him."* [7]

Another justification for Christ's sufferings was that he could identify with his brothers - us. He had to experience all that we experience; pain, rejection, failure, loneliness, being misunderstood, trials and temptations. He needed to have the complete human experience so as to be the perfect high priest representing mankind before his Father. Isaiah speaks of the Messiah's role as the intercessor before God: *"After the suffering of his soul he will see the light of life and be satisfied; by his knowledge my righteous servant will justify many and he will bear their iniquities. Therefore I will give him a portion among the great, and he will divide the spoils with the strong, because he poured out his life unto death, and was numbered with the transgressors. For he bore the sin of many, and made intercession for the transgressors."* [8]

Jesus could understand our emotions, our dejections, our failures, our weaknesses only if he himself had gone through them when he was a man. He could only then empathize with his brothers and could intercede for them; which he has been doing so ever since he laid down his life. *"For this reason he had to be made like his brothers in every way, in order that he might become a merciful and faithful high priest in service to God, and that he might make atonement for the sins of the people. Because he himself suffered when he was tempted, he is able to help those who are being tempted."* [9] And for good measure it is further affirmed: *"For we do not have a high priest who is unable to sympathise with our weaknesses, but we have one who has been tempted in every way, just as we are – yet was without sin."* [10] Jesus is both the sacrifice and the high priest!

And what about the suffering Jesus experienced in his last hours on earth? There was the physical suffering; the draining out in the garden of Gethsemane, the flogging, the blows, the beard being pulled by the soldiers, the exhausted and broken body made to carry the cross to the execution spot on the hill, the shooting pain of the nails being hammered into his hands and feet, the excruciating pain of the dislocated shoulders as he hung on the cross, the writhing body which pushed up gasping for air to fill the screaming lungs. Isaiah had seen this horrific sight: *"But he was pierced for our transgressions, he was crushed for our iniquities; the punishment that brought us peace was upon him and by his wounds we are healed. We all, like sheep, have gone astray, each of us has turned to his own way; and the LORD has laid on him the iniquity of us all."* [11]

And above all that, and more than anything else, the spiritual suffering he underwent for a period on the cross, when the full weight of the sins of the world fell on him and God did not seem to be there by his side when that happened. God appeared to have abandoned him, forsaken him, leaving him alone in his darkest hour; to face the full brunt of the punishment.

In life and in death, God gave his Son no relief but gave him sufferings without measure. Not once did Jesus use the supernatural powers that were at his disposal to lessen his suffering but willed himself to take the full measure of them. Even at his crucifixion he refused the drink of wine and gall offered to him to dull his senses to the pain that he would suffer on the cross. He had to suffer fully and in all consciousness, the punishment his Father had set for him.

And even today Christ suffers. He suffers with every heart that is broken; he suffers with every parent that loses a child; he suffers in the pain of every patient battling sickness; he suffers when a home is broken; he suffers with the one being persecuted and those under the yoke of oppression of their fellow human beings; he suffers every time when evil has its way and good is forsaken. His suffering hasn't ended. It continues. He suffers with us in our every situation. God does not offer explanation for suffering in this world. He enters our suffering. And He can do so because He has gone through the same in Jesus. Looked through the prism of Jesus' life and suffering, all the suffering in this world takes on a different perspective, and hope springs anew that one day God will restore the world in which suffering will be found no more.

In choosing the path that He did for the Messiah, God laid the pattern for his followers. Because of the example of its founder, suffering became integral to the Christian faith. *"The blood of Christians is the seed of Christianity"* wrote Tertullian. Suffering assumed a new dimension in the New Testament times, where in fact it appears to be welcomed by the disciples of Jesus, as a thanksgiving that they had been counted worthy to suffer like their Master. Jesus had called it a blessing: *"Blessed are you when people insult you, persecute you and falsely say all kinds of evil against you because of me."* [12] Their reward in heaven was assured.

Apostle Peter considered it a matter of rejoicing to share in the sufferings of Christ: *"But rejoice that you participate in the sufferings of Christ, so that you maybe overjoyed when his glory is revealed."* [13] And makes it clear that the call to discipleship included suffering: *"To this you were called, because Christ suffered for you, leaving you an example that you should follow in his steps."* [14] Paul held out the promise that we are: *"...heirs of God and co-heirs with Christ, if indeed we share in his sufferings in order that we may also share in his glory."* [15] Christianity was thus built on the suffering and martyrdom of countless followers of Christ who had showed them the way of suffering. It has proven to be a lasting foundation.

And so we need not be ashamed of the sufferings of Christ. Like Paul who said, *"but we preach Christ crucified....,"* [16] let us also boldly and proudly proclaim the Suffering Messiah. Philip Yancey wrote, *"Jesus gives God a face and that face is streaked with tears."*

Yes, tears that roll down for us!

1. *Luke 24:26*
2. *Isaiah 53:3-4*
3. *Luke 19:42,44*
4. *John 1:10-11*
5. *Hebrews 2:10*
6. *Hebrews 5:7*
7. *Hebrews 5:8-9*
8. *Isaiah 53:11-12*
9. *Hebrews 2:17-18*
10. *Hebrews 4:15*
11. *Isaiah 53:5-6*
12. *Matthew 5:11*
13. *1 Peter 4:13*
14. *1 Peter 2:21*
15. *Romans 8:17*
16. *1 Corinthians 1:23*

# Chapter ~ 13

# THE SERMON ON THE MOUNT

*"Jesus made the law impossible for anyone to keep and
then charged us to keep it."*

*– Philip Yancey*

The Sermon on the Mount is astounding. Given on a hill (now called
the Mount of Beatitudes) overlooking the Sea of Galilee, the Sermon
is the heart of Jesus' teaching. To understand Jesus one must understand
the message he brought and the Sermon is at the core of his message.

The Sermon contains the golden rules for Christian living. It is
considered to be the Charter of Christianity. No sermon or speech in
the history of mankind has been (or will be) so powerful, so impacting,
so amazing, so moving, and so disconcerting as the Sermon on the
Mount. Jesus in the teachings of the Sermon turned the rules of the
world upside down. It was a contrarian message that he was giving
which he knew would provoke those who were listening; shock them
of their understanding of God's law and what God wants of them. The
Sermon shocks even now.

Jesus was giving a new interpretation of the Law that the Jews had possessed for more than twelve centuries, which they recited and memorized diligently, and which they also failed to follow conscientiously, ever since the time it was given to Moses. It was a different interpretation, for Jesus stretched the existing laws to the extreme. It was also the right interpretation for Jesus alone could tell them how God had intended His laws to be received and how they were to be followed in letter and spirit. He could because he was the Author of the Law which the Israelites had been given in the wilderness.

The Sermon on the Mount, which has been covered in detail in the Gospel of Matthew, has not failed to fascinate me every time that I have read it. The message contained therein pierces right through to the soul. For it is the message of truth; and no matter how stretched and extreme and radical it may be, you know it is the truth. You know Jesus is making impossible demands of you, but you also know that he wants you to accept them and fulfill them. You simply cannot accept Jesus without accepting that he meant every word that he said in the Sermon. He was serious and he was not speaking in vain. He was not giving a sermon to win a popularity contest. He was giving the truth for which he had come into this world. He was speaking the truth that he had received from his Father. *"My teaching is not my own. It comes from him who sent me,"* [1] he had said. Even then his message was rejected by many for truth is difficult to accept; truth is hard and demanding.

The teaching of Jesus is central to his ministry and the Sermon on the Mount is the heart of his teaching. Jesus came to establish God's kingdom; the foundation of which was to be laid on the golden rules of the Sermon. This is how things would be from now onwards and his followers are expected to live by these rules in this world, so as to be prepared for living in his kingdom. These are the principles which we are to follow and which will prepare us for eternity with God.

Many people during the time of Jesus found his teaching to be offensive and thus they rejected it. It is so even now. Commands like, *'Love your enemies and pray for those who persecute you'*, [2] are hard to accept and even more difficult to follow. The normal human reaction is to hit back and get even with those who hurt you. Our natural instinct is not to love but to crush our enemies. And here is this rabbi from Galilee talking of loving our enemies! Israel was under Roman occupation at the time of Jesus and was subjected to atrocities and oppression at the hands of their foreign ruler. Love them? This was atrocious. No wonder many who would have heard the Sermon must have found it offensive.

And the commands on prayer, fasting, and good deeds for example, appeared to be particularly aimed at the Pharisees and the teachers of the law. These must have delighted the crowd but surely would not have won him many friends amongst the religious leaders of his time. Not only was this man giving some radical views on the Law and not thinking twice of 'breaking' it at every opportunity, but he was also ridiculing them in his teaching. How could then the Sermon find acceptance amongst this influential segment of the Jewish society?

The Sermon begins with the beautiful sayings; the Beatitudes which mean supreme blessedness or happiness. In them Jesus reverses the norms of the world. The rich, the powerful, the strong, the proud are not the favored ones, as per Jesus. Instead the weak and the defenseless, the poor and the hungry, the oppressed and the mourning, the sick and the dependent, the meek and the humble, are the blessed ones before God. How can it be? How can these be God's favorites? Those that are neglected and considered inconsequential, the 'have nots' of the world, are to consider themselves blessed? Was Jesus fooling the people; dangling out promises to them so as to get a following? Or has the world got the pecking order of the lucky people all wrong - right from the beginning?

In a way the poor and other disadvantaged are indeed blessed. God, *'and there is no favoritism with Him'*, [3] does however appear to have a bend towards the underdogs - towards those whom the world does not back. Remember David facing the giant Goliath or Israel battling the stronger armies of the nations they displaced in the Promised Land or Moses confronting the mighty Pharaoh. The poor, the weak, the oppressed are blessed because they have the right posture, the posture of dependence, to receive God's grace. They have no shame in receiving and thus God's grace can flow to them unhindered.

Unfortunately the rich, the strong, the powerful do not have the posture which is conducive to welcome God's grace. *"It is easier for the camel to go through the eye of a needle than for a rich man to enter the kingdom of God,"* [4] said Jesus. They are steeped in their arrogance and self dependence. They are blinded by their power, riches, and self-righteousness.

An interesting point comes up; should we stop works of charity, whether individually or collectively as a church, because the poor are the blessed ones of God? If they are blessed let them continue to remain so? Why lift them up from their state? Are then the social and medical programmes of the church, in a paradoxical way, contravening the teaching of Jesus? Well no, this is not the case. Those who are more fortunate than the others, when they extend love and help to the needy, it becomes a blessing for both the receiver and the giver. Grace abounds. God provides the giver the opportunity to be blessed as he is the dispenser of His grace; and the receiver to be blessed as he is the recipient for God on earth. The teaching of Jesus where he says that whatever you do for one of them (the least among you), you do it for me, points to the fact that the poor, the weak, the needy are God's nominated receivers on earth. You want to do something for God, do it for them. You give to them, consider given to Jesus. Mother Teresa once explained a typical day in the Missionaries of Charity: *"In the morning we pray to Jesus and then go out to look for him."* Look where? In the streets of Calcutta. Find in whom? In the destitute, in the sick, in the dying.

Jesus embodied the blessed ones of the Beatitudes. The Son of Man was born poor and lived a hard life. His life was marked with suffering. He was weak (in the worldly sense) and a man of sorrows. He was afflicted and oppressed. He therefore had affinity with those in similar positions; the poor, the social outcasts, the oppressed. He freely moved with them and even went to their homes. No wonder he reserved God's blessings for the disadvantaged of the world.

The Sermon on the Mount is not legalism in another form. It did not replace the existing Law but gave a new (and the right) reading of the law. Jesus made it clear that, *"Do not think that I have come to abolish*

*the Law or the Prophets; I have not come to abolish them but to fulfill them.*"[5]
Jesus in establishing the new covenant made the law of the stone tablets,
the law of the heart. What the LORD had promised through the prophet
Jeremiah now came to fulfillment:

"This is the covenant that I will make with the house of Israel after
that time," declares the LORD. "I will put my law in their minds and
write it on their hearts. I will be their God, and they will be my people.
No longer will a man teach his neighbour, or a man his brother, saying,
'Know the LORD,' because they will all know me, from the least of
them to the greatest," declares the LORD. [6]

The time had come for the law to be written on the hearts of men.
To move from the scrolls and stone tablets to the tablets of the heart.
The law external so far, was now to be internalised. The equation was
to be direct between God and every man. And that could be possible
because only God knows the hearts of men. In the light of this change,
we can understand the rules given in the Sermon, which are otherwise
perplexing. Jesus was now able to stretch the commands in the Law
from an external act to an internal one – the feelings and thoughts
within a man. For instance an act of adultery now extended to, "*Anyone
who looks at a woman lustfully has already committed adultery with her in
his heart*" [7]; and murder from a physical destruction of someone and
thus liable for judgment to, "*Anyone who is angry with his brother will
be subject to judgment.*" [8] So according to this change, now even emotions
of hatred and anger would be equated with the act of murder. No
criminal law of any country in the world goes to such an extreme. For
they cannot. How can you know what is in a man's heart; how will a
system find out if he is lusting after a woman or hates someone to the
point of imagining murdering him? Only God knows the heart and is
able to judge the people by the law of the heart.

The Sermon on the Mount gave the law of the heart and in doing
that fulfilled the Law that was already in existence; by giving it the
right perspective and its original intent. Now all pretensions of men
could be found out, all hypocrisy laid bare, and all deceit could be
caught; simply because it was now a matter of the heart and God who
is the Judge knows the heart. Therefore the warning from Jesus that,

*"Unless your righteousness surpasses that of the Pharisees and the teachers of the law, you will certainly not enter the kingdom of heaven."* [9] That is our righteousness should not be limited to rituals and externals, which was what the Pharisees had reduced their observance of the law to, but should flow from keeping the intent of the law.

The Sermon on the Mount contains the call for perfection. It calls us to be perfect just as God is perfect. Jesus exhorted the people, *"Be perfect, therefore, as your heavenly Father is perfect."* [10] Why did Jesus 'toughen' the law for us? As it is the Jews had consistently failed to observe the existing Law of Moses. Why did Jesus have to stretch the same law to extremities and then charge us to keep it? We can understand this when we are to consider that the standards given in the Sermon on the Mount are meant not only to apply to us, but they are God's moral standards which also apply to Him. They reveal His character and nature. God operates by these rules and by the same rules He wants us to live; so that we may be perfect like Him.

At the same time Christ knew that no one, not even the most ardent of saints, would be able to live fully by these standards. Somewhere, sometime you would fall short. But this does not take away from the command that we have to be perfect as God is perfect. *"The New Testament teaches no such thing as a Judeo- Christian ethic. It commands conversion and then this, 'Be perfect as your heavenly Father is perfect'"* wrote Jacques Ellul. This is the end game; the end of the race is our perfection. And what is amazing is that God should want us to match Him in perfection. Not less. The perfection which He requires us to attain is to be equal to His.

Christ knew that his law could be turned legalistic and could result in comparative evaluation of morality by the people. 'I am a better Christian than that fellow in my church for I give more tithes; or thank God I am not an adulteress like her but just a simple cheat (implying a far lesser sinner); or that God must be holding me in higher esteem than him for I go to church every week'. Such and other such 'justifications' could abound. The Sermon on the Mount is however a great leveler as it brings all types, kinds, and degree of sinners to the same level. For the end goal of these golden rules is to make us perfect like our Father and no one, simply no one, can claim to be so. If under the old Law one could say 'that all have sinned and fall short of the glory of God', then under the new Law we can say with equal justification 'that no one is perfect as God is perfect.' Relative perfection does not hold good where absolute perfection is the command and goal. We are all work in progress.

But in order that we do not fret over our inadequacy to meet the perfection that is required of us, God provides us the support of His grace. Grace covers the gap between our level of perfection at any time and that which is required in us. The standards given in the Sermon on the Mount could not be lowered because they were God's standards of holiness, but grace is given where we fall short of these standards. God does not want us to despair of our failure to meet these standards as long as we keep striving towards that goal of 'perfect' perfection. *"To search your imperfection is itself perfection,"* said St. Augustine.

Leo Tolstoy, the famous Russian author, was tormented throughout his life by his failure to meet the golden rules of the Sermon on the Mount. He had to finally concede that: *"The test of observance of Christ's teachings is our consciousness of our failure to attain an ideal perfection. The degree to which we draw near this perfection cannot be seen; all we can see is the extent of our deviation."*

Blessed are those who strive for this perfection!

1. *John 7:16*
2. *Matthew 5:44*
3. *Ephesians 6:9*
4. *Matthew 19:24*
5. *Matthew 5:17*
6. *Jeremiah 31:33-34*
7. *Matthew 5:28*
8. *Matthew 5:22*
9. *Matthew 5:20*
10. *Matthew 5:48*

# Chapter ~ 14

# "I AM THE RESURRECTION AND THE LIFE"

*"God has to be God in the face of death. If not, he is not God anywhere."*
— Max Lucado

Of all the claims Jesus made of himself – I am the light of the world; I am the bread of life; I am the good shepherd; I am the way and the truth and the life; and many others - none is more incredible, none is more forceful, and none is more giving hope than the one: *"I am the resurrection and the life."* [1] The words hit you with a powerful impact. They give rise either to a sense of exhilaration or to a sense of disbelief. It is either the claim of the Saviour or the claim of a mad man.

It was a claim which was made with authority. It was spoken in strength. It was a clarion call given with conviction. It was a challenge that was given on the enemy turf.

Let us understand the setting where this call was made. It was the setting of death; the death of Lazarus. And Lazarus had been dead for four days and buried in his tomb. Why did Jesus not come to Bethany when he received the news that Lazarus was sick? Why did he delay his departure and waited for Lazarus to die? Well it can be said that Jesus wanted God's glory to be revealed in a more magnificent way if Lazarus was to be raised from the dead rather than being healed from his sickness. But there are two other accounts in the gospels of Jesus raising the dead - the widow's son in Nain and the synagogue ruler's daughter. So what was so special about the raising of Lazarus other than that he was Jesus' friend and his sisters were dear to the Lord? What was different in this case (compared to the other two) that it is recorded in such detail by the gospel writer?

The setting of Lazarus' death was the stage for a bigger drama; a cosmic battle. Jesus had intentionally waited for Lazarus to die. He was going to use his death to confront the enemy - Satan. And the singular thing which comes out of this event is the claim of Jesus: *"I am the resurrection and the life."* Note he did not make this claim in the four walls of a room; in a closed setting with his disciples over a meal, where Jesus while dipping the bread in the soup says, "By the way I am the resurrection and the life." The stage had to be bigger and the occasion had to be just right for Jesus to make this claim; for it was no ordinary claim. He makes the claim in public, within the pall of gloom that has set in where death has recently taken place, in the parlour of death where the grief caused by death is still raw. In the home turf of the enemy where death's presence is at its strongest, Jesus comes and mocks death!

*"I am the resurrection and the life."* It was here in this statement that Jesus challenges death and Satan, who forever has used the sting of death to terrify human beings. In the enemy stronghold he was mocking the most powerful weapon of the enemy. The statement was to be the battle cry for the showdown that would soon take place at Calvary. With it the countdown to that combat had begun. Satan had been taunted in his own territory and Jesus had declared that even death had no mastery over him and importantly would soon be losing its grip of fear over mankind. Jesus was holding death in contempt. Standing eye ball to eye ball with death, he was scoffing at it. And death blinked first. It gave up Lazarus, as we find later in the account.

When sin came into the world, due to the Fall, much else also came as a result of it; - sickness, decay, suffering and *death*. Death is the sword that hangs over every man right from the time he is born, that he would have to face it one day. And Satan has used this absolute certainty of death as his most potent tool to put fear in mankind. It is mentioned in Hebrews: *"who all their lives were held in slavery by their fear of death."* [2] It is not the fear of death in itself; it is the uncertainty of what will happen next. Is my death the finality? Is that the end of me? Will I be nothing once I am gone? Is that the final lights off? Curtains forever? Or is there something....? It is the most important question that haunts man. And in Jesus it is answered.

In this claim Jesus was giving the answer that mankind has always been seeking. With his claim he was in fact saying: 'I am the final solution to your final problem; I am the ultimate answer to your ultimate dilemma; and I am the only hope of your worst fear. *I AM THE RESURRECTION ......* ' Jesus was not claiming here that he will bring about the resurrection (that he will for us all), but he was claiming here that *the resurrection was him!* He was pointing out that the event of resurrection was in him! 'Martha you are talking of your brother rising up in the resurrection that will happen on the last day, look the Resurrection is standing here in front of you.'

But this claim of Jesus would have been just a claim if he himself had not risen from the dead and become the Resurrection. He had to defeat his own death and be resurrected, in order to hold out the hope to mankind. His rising from the dead he had predicted well in advance of the event and thus he could make that emphatic claim at the tomb side in Bethany; that he is the Resurrection.

Jesus in his own resurrection became the Resurrection for mankind; a promise that death is not the end of the story. There is much more and much anew. There is renewal, there is revival. In the resurrection of Jesus, God holds out this hope to mankind; that what He did in His Son, He will one day reproduce on a cosmic scale, in all of us. And we will have new, resurrected bodies. Jesus was the firstfruits. We will follow. As Paul writes, *"For since death came through a man, the resurrection of the dead comes also through a man. For as in Adam all die, so in Christ all will be made alive. But each in his own turn: Christ, the firstfruits; then, when he comes, those who belong to him."* [3]

Jesus said, *"I am the resurrection and the life. He who believes in me will live, even though he dies, and whoever lives and believes in me will never die."* [4] When he had thus made this claim he asks Martha a question, a question of faith. He also asks the same question to each one of us:

*"Do you believe this?"* [5]

1. *John 11:25*
2. *Hebrews 2:15*
3. *1 Corinthians 15:21-23*
4. *John 11:25-26*
5. *John 11:26*

# Chapter ~ 15

# TEMPTATION IN THE DESERT

*"Then Jesus was led by the Spirit into the desert
to be tempted by the devil."* [1]

The Temptation of Jesus in the desert is the hinge moment of his life on earth. It is the pivotal point of his mission. The outcome would reveal who actually Jesus was; a man or God masquerading as a man. It would also determine what powers he had and how he would be using them, which would define the very nature of his public ministry.

This was probably the first showdown on earth between Satan and the Son of God, who was facing him as *a man*; a fact which Satan was to find out in the course of the duel. Like two gladiators they squared off against each other in a combat whose outcome would not only have implications for this world but would also have far reaching cosmic ramifications. On one side was Satan, strong and confident for he was in his territory (he was the ruler of the world, wasn't he?) and on the other side was Jesus, weakened by his fasting and the harshness of his sojourn in the desert, but ready to face the enemy's assault. The Son of Man had the odds stacked against him. The battle was crucial for both the adversaries for it would define many things.

Let us first see when this event took place in Jesus' life. Jesus had come out of his home from Nazareth to be baptized by John. It marked the end of his private life; of a life lived in obscurity for thirty years as a carpenter in a small village in Galilee. The time for him to come into his public ministry must have been set by God and he must have received THE signal from God that his mission was to begin. The time of preparation and wait was to be over.

But before he was to actually commence his public ministry he had to go through the initiation necessary to determine whether he was ready for his mission. At his baptism the Holy Spirit descended on him in the bodily form of a dove. The Spirit remained in him then onwards. And what is the first thing which the Spirit does or makes him do after his baptism? The Spirit leads him to the desert to be tempted by the devil. *"Then Jesus was led by the Spirit into the desert."* Mark's gospel brings out more forcefully the compelling nature of this act: *"At once the Spirit sent him out into the desert ...."* [2]; as if Jesus was commanded to do so; as if this was pre-decided and Jesus had no choice but to accept its inevitability. This showdown with the old adversary at the commencement of his ministry was important for it would impact the showdown that would take place at Calvary at the end of his ministry. It was so critical that it had to be positioned at the very beginning; for it was to determine whether Jesus was up to the task or not.

For Satan this faceoff was important in a way for he would find out who actually Jesus was; *was he really man or pretending to be one.* To what extent Jesus would be operating within the rules of this world or will he use the divine powers (another point to be discovered was what all powers he had!) at his disposal to attend to his needs or alleviate the pains that he felt as a man or protect himself from dangers that were to threaten him mortally. It was important for Satan to know whom he was dealing with because the Incarnation had taken him by surprise. It had been a raid in his territory and posed a mystery for him. Know your enemies before you take them on; Satan was thinking on these safe lines.

For God this showdown was equally important. That is why it was planned to take place at this juncture; a prefixed entry in the calendar of the life of Jesus. An appointment set well in advance. It would reveal if Jesus had become perfect, *as a man,* by the trials and sufferings which he had been subjected to during the thirty years of preparation that he underwent, when he lived as an ordinary man in Nazareth. Whether *"he had learned obedience from what he suffered,"* [3] and whether he would be *"obedient to death – even death on a cross."* [4] Had he achieved the perfection needed to *"become the source of eternal salvation"* [5] for mankind? He had to be subjected to the tests to establish this truth of the Incarnation. All this had to be known and known before he actually stepped into his mission field. For much was at stake. The fate of mankind was at stake. God's reputation was at stake. Before the Lamb of God was to be sent to his death, it had to be seen whether he was without blemish and thus fit to be sacrificed for the sins of the world. It had to be seen whether the Son of God had truly become the Son of Man, in the very essence.

The showdown was a sparring match where the two combatants sized each other up. Jesus was on trial. He was the one facing the tests; the temptations. But the fate of this encounter was equally vital for both the duelist. It would turn out to be the forerunner of the Big One that was to come in about three years. The battle lines were being drawn.

We can rightly consider that the temptations that Jesus faced in the desert were more than the three which have been described in the gospels. It would also be correct to understand his temptation to be spread over the entire period that he was in the desert and not limited to what he faced at the end of the forty days of his fasting. We will focus on the three which have been covered in the gospel accounts.

The three temptations were essentially with one intent. Satan was creating situations where Jesus would be forced to reveal his hand; to show his powers. He was luring him with a short cut and a speedy way to fulfill his mission. And that path did not have the Cross in it. In short, the devil was showing Jesus a way which was not filled with pain and suffering. It was to be the way of the all-powerful, conquering

Messiah whom the people were expecting and would have accepted with awe and open arms; rather than the way of the weak, suffering Messiah whom God had sent and who would be rejected by those to whom he had been sent. The difference was to be in the Messiah, Jesus would turn out to be; one who would dazzle the people by his power and force their loyalty and obedience by coercion and enticement or one who would win the people over by love and sacrifice and make them to love and follow him of their own free will. This was to be the difference. This was to be unwrapped and seen in this trial by temptations that Jesus faced in the desert.

The first temptation was expectedly aimed at the physical state of Jesus, feebled after forty days of fasting. *"If you are the Son of God, tell these stones to become bread."* [6] 'Well that should be easy for you. First tend to your hunger, address your own immediate need'. But actually it was not the hunger of Jesus that Satan was interested in. He was alluding a way to Jesus for winning the crowds, for controlling the people. Feed them! The Messiah should be able to provide food security to the people; quite like the food stamps distributed by the communist governments and the food incentives (5 kilo rice!) with which the politicians lure the people during election time. The Messiah should win the hearts of his people by their stomachs; by satisfying their basic need. Mind you this was a sound advice for Israel at the time of Jesus had heaps of poor people who would have had trouble making their ends meet. They would have jumped at such a deal. A leader who can provide them with their daily ration, like God who provided their forefathers with manna everyday in the desert, would have been easily accepted as King and Deity. Jesus would have quickly ascended to the top of the popularity charts and remained there forever. We want this Messiah!

Jesus refused. Not only to turn the stones into bread for himself but also at the attempt to turn the Messiah into a magician dishing out miracles by the minute. He instead pointed out that the physical needs of a person are subjugated to his spiritual needs: *"Man does not live on bread alone, but on every word that comes from the mouth of God."* [7] Jesus had the power to produce bread as Satan had prompted him, and indeed he would later do precisely that and feed the multitude on two different occasions recorded in the gospels. But in the instances that he did give the people food to eat, it was because of the exigency of the situation. Jesus' concern for the people following him is seen when he says, *"I have compassion for these people; they have already been with me three days and have nothing to eat. I do not want to send them away hungry, or they may collapse on the way."* [8] And in the other instance where it was already getting late and they were in a remote place; by implication that it would not be possible for the crowd to source food easily at this hour. Thus in both the cases his miraculous intervention in providing food to the people was justified.

But he did not use his powers to provide food on a regular basis, so that it became the major draw for people to come to his gatherings or be the reason for following him. Rather he wanted them to come to him because he was the *'bread of life'* and eat the spiritual food that he gave them. With that he ended this matter decisively with Satan.

*"If you are the Son of God throw yourself down."* [9] That is from the highest point of the temple where the devil had taken him. What was in this second temptation? We must note that in this (and also in the first) temptation, Satan addressed him as the Son of God. He was provoking him to use his divine powers; in the first to satisfy his bodily cravings and in the second to save himself from bodily harm. He was inciting him to reveal in his body of a man, his true essence which was God. 'The angels will lift you in their hands and break your fall. You are God; you will not fall like ordinary mortals'. But Jesus did not yield to this temptation. His reply was straight, *"Do not put the Lord your God to the test."* [10] God is not to be tested. He is God. His power is not to be put on trial.

And this was the pattern which we later see in Jesus' life when he underwent suffering and injustice. He refused to 'reveal' himself and show the people who he really was. At his arrest, he confessed he could have called to his Father and He would have at once sent twelve legions of angels to battle for him. But he did not. And on the Cross he was taunted by the jeering crowd: *"Come down from the cross, if you are the Son of God"* [11] (it has the same ring as Satan's challenge in the desert).

He could have come down for he had the power to do so. But he didn't. He didn't then in the desert, he didn't at his arrest, and he didn't also at the cross. Having resisted this temptation once in the desert, he was able to resist the same on the occasions that it raised its head later.

In the third temptation, Satan now uses a different tactic. The failure of the first two temptations had convinced him that Jesus will not use his divine powers either to meet his physical need or save himself from physical danger. From another angle it could be inferred that Jesus would also not use his powers to attract or impress the people. So now Satan tempts him with something of his own, something which was Satan's to give. This time his appeal is to the Son of Man. He shows Jesus ALL the kingdoms of the world and makes the offer: *"I will give you all their authority and splendor, for it has been given to me, and I can give it to anyone I want to. So if you worship me, it will all be yours."* [12] Here was an offer which could not be refused, so thought Satan. He was prepared to give away his kingdoms, his domain to the Son of Man, if only to derail him from his mission. Jesus dismissed the offer saying, *"Worship the Lord your God and serve him only."* [13] Only God is to be worshiped. The idea that any other but God is worthy of worship was offensive and to be rejected outright.

At this rebuke the devil was finished with tempting Jesus and left him *'until an opportune time'*. [14] Though Jesus was the victor in this duel in so much as having withstood everything that Satan had thrown at him, but Satan did not go away empty handed. He had done his evaluation of the powers of Jesus and where and to what purpose Jesus would be using them. Satan had collected enough material to devise his game plan and future strategies, which he would use against Jesus at the opportune time or times.

There are three things which stand out in this account of the temptation of Jesus in the desert. Firstly, he resists the temptations thrown at him by the devil, by quoting the Scriptures. His reply to all the three temptations includes the words; *'It is written'*. Jesus is showing to us that the only way temptations can be faced and Satan's schemes defeated is by taking recourse in the word of God. He cannot be defeated by fine arguments and logic. Remember he is the *father of lies* and a master of this game. We are no match for him if we use human means to resist him. We need divine weapons. We have to take the *"sword of the Spirit, which is the word of God,"* [15] as Paul advises us to do so.

Secondly, right through the event in the desert, what comes out strongly is the restraint shown by Jesus. Restraint was seen in the very fact that Jesus allowed himself to go through these temptations. He could have resolved the issue once for all by destroying the tempter. Then there would have been no need for the Cross. History would have wrapped up there and then. But that would not have been the way God had planned out the salvation of mankind. If God had to do it that way, then there would have been no need for Him to send His Son into the world. No need for the Incarnation. There would have been no showdown in the desert, for Satan would have been destroyed long ago. There would have been no need for the salvation of mankind to be put through this slow, painful, and long process. But evil had to be destroyed and God had to win the love of man without taking away his free will - his right to love or not to love God in return, his right to accept or reject God. That choice God had given to man at his creation and that choice was to remain.

And restraint was a trait which was to be seen throughout Jesus' life. *"Beginning with Temptation, Jesus showed a reluctance to bend the rules of the earth,"* observes Philip Yancey. He showed much restraint, as mentioned earlier, during his arrest and also while hanging on the cross. Restraint was also seen in his trial before the Sanhedrin when witness after witness levied false accusations against him but he did not defend himself. Restraint was shown by him when facing Pilate's boast that he had the power to release him or crucify him. The only statement he made to clear Pilate of this delusion was: *"You would have no power over me if it were not given to you from above."* [16] The restraint at the Stone Pavement standing next to Pilate's judgment seat; when the treacherous crowd who had seen his miracles, who had heard his teaching, who had welcomed him to Jerusalem with palm branches and hosannas just five days ago, was now baying for his blood and choosing amnesty for the murderer Barabbas instead. Restraint was seen when he was spit at, when his beard was pulled, when his forehead was clamped with a tight crown of thorns, when blows were rained on his face, and when his back was whipped to pulp.

Restraint was shown by Jesus even earlier in his ministry when the swelling crowd, fascinated by the rabbi from Galilee, who taught with authority, healed the sick, and performed astonishing miracles, forcefully wanted to crown him king. Instead he withdrew and would have none of it. Restraint was seen in his refusal to dish out miracles on demand for he did not wish his ministry to be reduced to that of a magician. So concerned was he of the crowd's fascination for signs, that many a time he even cautioned those whom he had healed privately not to publicize that he was behind the act. And when the Pharisees and other religious leaders demanded signs from him as proof of his being the Messiah, he refused to oblige; though if he had done so they would have likely welcomed him to be a member of the Sanhedrin. When his disciples wanted to call fire from heaven to destroy the Samaritan village which would not receive him, he rebuked them for suggesting this wanton display of strength. His was not to compel belief or impose himself on anyone, but to find a willing faith. Many times he must have restrained himself to be the Messiah that the people wanted but instead chose to remain the Messiah that he was sent to be. Many a times the Lord of lords must have wanted to lord it over others but instead chose to be the servant of all.

It was the restraint which Jesus showed at the Temptation that prepared him to show the same later. But restraint in fact has been the nature of God. Fyodor Dostoyevsky in his novel *The Brothers Karamazov* calls it: *"the miracle of restraint."* We want miracles from God. We ask for signs and wonders, which will convince us of His power; even provide proof of His existence. But the most amazing miracle which God performs is the miracle of restraint, and it is ongoing. Evidence of it has been seen right from the Old Testament days, in God's dealing with His people Israel. How many times He forgave them, how many chances He gave them to mend their ways, how many times he relented and did not bring upon them the punishment He had declared that He would do so, and how many times He restored His relationship with them. God truly showed Himself to be 'slow to anger and abounding in love and faithfulness'.

And even now in His dealings with the human race, God shows incredible restraint. He has not wiped out mankind though it has fallen to abysmal depths (it would have been easier to destroy it rather than redeem it); He lets evil to still exist (and some would say even flourish) in this world, letting it to run its full course; He allows His name to be tarnished for all that ills this planet – disease, sickness, plague, earthquakes, floods, pestilences; He is even blamed for all the injustices that man has to suffer at the hands of another man (Holocaust being the case in point); He shows restraint at the slow pace at which His Kingdom advances. In all this He has shown restraint, waiting for His restoration work to come to completion. And the same restraint was also seen in the earthly life of His Son.

Thirdly, in a profound way the Temptation in the desert prepared Jesus for his most severe trial: the Garden of Gethsemane, where he was the weakest and most vulnerable. There too he was tempted to take the other way to fulfill his mission; a way much easier and without pain, a way which did not have to go through the Cross. The temptation which came to him when he was setting out on his mission, came back again, more strongly, when he was at the concluding stage of his mission. But just as he overcame it in the desert, he was able to overcome that temptation in the garden. We can even say that because he overcame it in the desert of Judea, he was able to overcome it again in the Garden of Gethsemane. The Temptation in the desert was the precursor to a more potent visitation later; as the final attempt of Satan to avert the showdown at Calvary the next day.

The temptations that Jesus faced in the desert are not unique. In one form or the other we also are lured by the same. John in his epistle, groups the unhealthy desires into three: *"the cravings of sinful man, the lust of his eyes and the boasting of what he has and does....."* [17] The temptations that we face are principally aimed at these desires. The temptations that Jesus faced in the desert can also be understood similarly. The temptation of food – fulfilling the cravings of hunger (the lust of the flesh); the vision of the kingdoms and authority of the world – which one covets and longs to possess (the lust of the eyes); the prodding to jump from the high point of the temple – boasting of who he really is and what he can do (the pride of life).

We find ourselves, in this world and in this flesh, visited by the same temptations. But like our Lord are we able to stand up against them and defeat them? Or do we give in and are overcome by them? Paul gives us the assurance: *"God is faithful; he will not let you be tempted beyond what you can bear. But when you are tempted, he will also provide a way out so that you can stand up under it."* [18] Which means that the temptations that come our way, are the temptations that we can stand up to; even though we might be stretched fully. And the devil gives up after some time when he fails to make a breakthrough. James writes, *"Resist the devil, and he will flee from you."* [19]

Jesus resisted the devil in the desert and the devil eventually left him, seeing that he was unbreakable.

It was round one to Jesus!

1.  Matthew 4:1
2.  Mark 1:12
3.  Hebrew 5:8 (modified)
4.  Philippians 2:8
5.  Hebrew 5:9 (modified)
6.  Matthew 4:3
7.  Matthew 4:4 (Deuteronomy 8:3)
8.  Matthew 15:32
9.  Matthew 4:6
10. Matthew 4:7 (Deuteronomy 6:16)
11. Matthew 27:40
12. Luke 4:6-7
13. Luke 4:8 (Deuteronomy 6:13)
14. Luke 4:13
15. Ephesians 6:17
16. John 19:11
17. 1 John 2:16
18. 1 Corinthians 10:13
19. James 4:7

# Chapter ~ 16

# AGONY IN THE GARDEN

*"Father, if you are willing, take this cup from me ...."* [1]

It was the cool of a typical spring night. The shadows were slowly lengthening. The olive grove on the mount facing the Kidron Valley was bathed silver with moonlight. There was a deep quiet engulfing the place, broken only by the rustle of the leaves as a light breeze caressed the trees. Despite the pleasantness of the evening, one could not escape noticing the eerie calm which had set in, as if in anticipation of the tragic events which would soon be unfolding in the vicinity. It was the calm before a big storm.

Figures could be seen in three different places in the olive garden. A group of eight men were sleeping under a bunch of trees. Further down there was a smaller group of three men, also fast asleep. And even further down, a stone's throw distance away, there was a solitary figure. He was prostrate – his face to the ground. But he was not sleeping. Sleep was far from his eyes this night. He was wrestling with the strongest temptation of his life, which was trying to pierce through in his moment of weakness and defeat the purpose for which he had come into this world. The figure was that of one Jesus of Nazareth.

If one were to go closer to the figure, one would hear his murmured prayers. One would also detect the beseeching note in his voice, which threw out haltingly, his entreaties to his *Abba*, Father. He lifts his face and you cannot but see the pained look on it; which is mirroring the acute struggle in his soul. His was a face of a man in deep anguish. His eyes, which were otherwise serene at all times, looked terrified now. He pounded on the ground; he clawed at the stray grass; his legs thrashed aimlessly; sobs escaped his mouth; he was sweating profusely and his sweat was like drops of blood falling on the ground. Clearly he was a man going through an intense tortuous strain; whose internal agony was manifesting in his outward physical struggles.

*God was never more God than when he became man, and Jesus was never more a man than here at the Garden of Gethsemane.* He had been feeling distressed and troubled throughout the evening. His soul was *"overwhelmed with sorrow to the point of death,"* [2] as he had confided earlier to his disciples when they had just come to the Garden. Here he felt weak like he had never felt before in his life. Here he felt temptation, never before as strong; temptation to change the rules and take a short cut. An easier path for achieving the goal of Redemption, a path which does not go through the Cross! He was 'negotiating' such possibility with his Father. He could have chosen to do his own will, but he wanted his Father to agree to a different course. He was pleading with Him in prayer, to the One for whom all things were possible, to provide a different way instead. His spirit was willing but his flesh was weakening. He knew his mission, it had been with him ever single moment of his life. His spirit was committed to fulfilling it. But his flesh trembled as he looked ahead, at what lay in store for him, starting from the point of his arrest which would take place in this very garden, this very night. Even now as he prayed a group of soldiers and officials from the chief priests, led by his friend and betrayer Judas, would be making their way across the Kidron Valley.

He was shaking; shaking with fear of the lashes that will fall on his back, the blows that will be struck on his face, the nails that will be driven into his hands and feet, and the cross on which he will be hung to die. And his soul was also shaking with dread; dread of the moment when the sins of the world will fall on him, the Lamb of God. The break that will be caused in the perfect union between him and the Father, as he makes the atonement for the sins of mankind. Will he be forsaken by God? Will he be abandoned by his Father? Will he have to go through it all alone, till death would finally relieve him of his sufferings? He was pleading with his Father to give him a different way. He was ready to be sacrificed but please could his pain – physical and spiritual – be lessened, if he was to take a path other than the Cross.

But despite his frantic pleas, his Father would not budge. God who had heard his each and every prayer, and who was pleased with him calling him His beloved Son, did not answer this one. This was the first and only time he was praying for himself; the prayers he had offered, the miracles he had done, were all for others. Still the Father refused him.

Yes all things were possible for His Father, but the way of the Cross was a must. For it was the ONLY WAY for the salvation of mankind. How could God then show him another way? The Cross was there at the creation of the world. *"The Cross was drawn in the original blueprint. It was written into the script. The moment the forbidden fruit touched the lips of Eve, the shadow of the Cross appeared on the horizon,"* says Max Lucado. How then could it be removed now? And Jesus, even while he was pleading with his Father, knew that it would not be taken away. His prayers were going to be futile. He had to walk on the way of the Cross. *"But I, when I am lifted up from the earth, will draw all men to myself,"*[3] he had declared earlier, well knowing the death that will be his. *The Son of Man had to be lifted up, just as Moses had lifted up the snake in the desert.* [4]

Having been renewed in spirit, having received strengthening of his faith, which had momentarily wavered, he felt the peace and calm that he was so used to, return to him. His struggles had come to an end. The face which had been so strained, now finally relaxed. The stress lifted up from him along with despair. He nodded in acceptance to his Father and said a few words in concluding his prayer. He gets up determined and walks towards his sleeping disciples. Time for action had come. The last train of events of his life would soon be commencing. He was no longer afraid of facing them. He was in control.

*"The Messiah was not going to save the world by miraculous, Band Aid interventions. Rather it was going to be saved by means of a deeper, darker, left handed mystery, at the center of which lay his own death,"* wrote Robert Farrar Capon. Jesus knew this too well. *'It was for this very reason that he had come to this hour'.* [5] His faith, though it had weakened for a short time, ultimately stood against the attack of the enemy. The temptation was strong, but he did not give in. He struggled with God, but at the end yielded to His will. Thank God that he did! That Jesus triumphed over his last temptation. Otherwise mankind would have had to wait for another Saviour to come.

Faith has it two gardens of testing. Two men went on trial. In the Garden of Eden, Adam's faith failed. He fell to temptation. The result was the fall of man and mankind was doomed. Paradise was lost. In the Garden of Gethsemane, Jesus' faith held. He triumphed over temptation. The result eventually led to the salvation of mankind. Paradise was regained. However it appears ironical that the reward for obeying God's will would have been life for Adam, but for Jesus it was his death. That seemingly 'unfairness' of God is understood when we see that the death of Jesus meant life for mankind. Really lot was at stake at both Eden and Gethsemane.

Like Jesus, we also have 'Garden of Gethsemane' type situations in our lives. They can come more than once. It is when our faith is under attack. We can see that the road ahead would be a tough one; we know that God would be seeking a heavy cost from us if we are to walk on that road. We hesitate. We struggle. We pray. But the only reply we get is the reply we do not want, the reply that we dread. Should we turn back or continue walking? Should we deny Jesus or deny ourselves? Should we say no to God, even apostatize, or should we accept His will, no matter what the cost? Strange it may seem but our decisions do matter to God, to His scheme of things. Our choice will make a difference, just as Jesus' choice made THE difference to the history of mankind. Did Jesus have a choice in the Garden of Gethsemane? Yes he sure had. He could have done his own will or subject his will to the Father's will. He chose to do the latter. He did finally say in conclusion of his prayer:-

*"......yet not my will, but yours be done."* [6]

Do we say the same when we face that choice in our gardens of Gethsemane?

1.  *Luke 22:42*
2.  *Matthew 26:38*
3.  *John 12:32*
4.  *John 3:14 (paraphrased)*
5.  *John 12:27 (paraphrased)*
6.  *Luke 22:42*

# Chapter ~ 17

# THE CRY OF DESOLATION

*"Eloi, Eloi, lama sabachthani?"* [1]

It was dark which was unusual for that time of the day. In fact darkness had descended over the land three hours ago at noon (the sixth hour), when the sun should have been at its peak. As if the elements had to dress up according to the solemnity of the proceedings that were being witnessed on a hill aptly named Golgotha - The Place of the Skull. Here three figures were hanging on their individual crosses. The middle cross was that of God's Son.

*"My God, My God, why have you forsaken me?"* [2] A shrill cry rendered the air and appeared to hang there. It startled the crowd that was gathered at the hill, watching the macabre spectacle of life slowly ebbing out of the tormented bodies of the two robbers and *THAT MAN*, who pretended to be the Messiah, in a gruesome death on the cross. The cry came from the one who had the written charge placed above his head: *'THIS IS JESUS, THE KING OF THE JEWS'.* [3] They were surprised to hear him cry out so loud for they thought that by now, after nearly six

excruciating hours on the cross, there would be no strength left in him to speak audibly let alone make this heart wrenching appeal.

Some thought that he was crying out for rescue to Elijah, their great prophet of old. Some even had pity on him and offered him a concoction of wine vinegar, which they put on a sponge at the end of a long stick to reach his mouth. The priests and those who were well versed in the Jewish holy books shook their heads. Even now, even when dying on the cross, this man was obstinately quoting the Scriptures. Wasn't this verse from a psalm of David? Amazing! What was this dying man trying to prove; that King David had predicted this hour a thousand years ago? That his crucifixion was no accident but an event which had been foretold long ago?

The cry pierced the heart of God. The Father had wept seeing the broken body of His Son writhing in intense pain. And now this haunting wail! He knew what Jesus was going through. This was the cry of desolation, of someone abandoned by his very own. It was a cry of grief, of loneliness, of wretchedness. The Father's heart broke in thousand pieces. He longed for His Son as much as His Son longed for Him. He wanted to hold him, to give him the assurance of His presence.

Was Jesus *really* abandoned by God on the cross? Or did it *seem* to Jesus that his Father was not with him in his worst hour? Beliefs are divided on this. But it does not matter which was the case. The fact is that for the one and only time there appeared to be a chasm in the perfect unity of the Trinity. The Son felt all alone and he was crying for his Father whom he loved, and who in turn loved him immensely. But where was God when he needed Him the most? He appeared to have left him like all others.

What had caused Jesus to feel this abandonment? *SIN.* The sins of mankind were falling upon the head of the Saviour. He was cleansing the human race of its sins, taking upon himself the punishment due to us all. He was winning our pardon from God. He was meeting the demands of justice of a just God. He was paying the price of love of a loving God. He was making it *possible* for God to be both loving and just; to love the sinner while punishing the sin. And it was not going to be easy for Jesus. He well knew that, "*God could not save man without killing His Son,"* as Max Lucado puts it. His soul had shuddered during the time of his agony in Gethsemane the night before. It was precisely because he knew what lay ahead; the pain, the suffering and above all the abandonment. He would somehow bear his physical sufferings. But his spiritual sufferings, the horrors of which he had foreseen, would be unbearable for his Father would not be there by his side.

But that is what the wages of sin are; separation from God. Spiritual death! *And he, who knew no sin, when he became sin for us, experienced the full punishment of our sin.* He was separated from his Father. And for how long did the separation last? It was likely for the three hours when darkness descended over the whole land - from the sixth to the ninth hour (that is from noon to three in the afternoon). During this period of darkness *God was struggling with God.*

The desolation ended soon after the cry. With another loud cry Jesus gave up his spirit into his Father's hands. *'It is finished.'* [4] His work for which he had come to earth was accomplished. The Cross which was there in his Father's mind at the creation of the world had now become an event in history. The Cross had moved into reality. And the Cross will soon become the symbol of hope, victory, and reverence for those who will put their faith in the one who had died on it.

It was for this reason that the Lamb of God was not sacrificed within the four walls of an execution chamber but out in the open, in full public view. Jesus had to defeat the enemy in the open. He had to disarm the forces of evil and darkness before all to see. Paul writes, *"And having disarmed the powers and authorities, he made a public spectacle of them, triumphing over them by the cross."* [5] Triumphing over them by the cross! The Cross a symbol of victory and not defeat! Jesus was put up as spectacle for the public but instead he made a public spectacle of his enemies! The Cross shattered the long accepted notion of weak victims and strong heroes. Here the victim was to prove the victor and the weak would turn out to be the hero. That was to come soon. *"Jesus planned his own sacrifice. He was born crucified,"* writes Max Lucado. Yes Jesus planned it all. And he pulled it off!

We have times when we feel abandoned by God, just as Jesus did on the Cross. At those times, we do also cry out, *'My God, my God, why have you forsaken me'*. Take heart, God is near us though He may appear to be far away. We may not feel His presence but He is there with us in our periods of 'forsakenness'; just as He was with His Son at the Cross. The dark night of loneliness, of abandonment, of desolation, does surely end and we do then experience the joy and light of the Easter morn.

For we have this promise from God; *"Never will I leave you; never will I forsake you."* [6] And Jesus, who well knows what it is to feel abandoned, has himself given us this assurance:

*"And surely I am with you always, to the very end of the age."* [7]

1. *Matthew 27:46*
2. *Matthew 27:46*
3. *Matthew 27:37*
4. *John 19:30*
5. *Colossians 2:15*
6. *Hebrews 13:5 (Deuteronomy 31:6)*
7. *Matthew 28:20*

# Chapter ~ 18

# RESURRECTION: THE GAME CHANGER

*"Where O death is thy victory? Where O death is thy sting?"* [1]

At dawn on the first day of the week (the day after the Sabbath), a group of women made their way to a newly laid tomb. As they hurried through the garden, their hearts were heavy laden with grief over the death of their beloved master two days ago. They were carrying spices with them to anoint his body as per the Jewish custom. Their minds were however occupied with the more immediate task that would be facing them when they would arrive there. There was a large stone rolled at the entrance to the tomb and they would have to overcome this obstacle to reach the object of their early morning mission.

They reached the tomb and what they saw gave rise to mixed emotions in them. The stone had been rolled away and the entrance to the tomb was exposed! They were both relieved as well as terrified at that sight. Their problem had been removed but at the same time they wondered as to who could have rolled the stone. Who had come to the tomb before them? Fearfully they entered the tomb not knowing what awaited them. What they beheld was the most significant sight in the human history; for it was a sight which would eventually turn out to be the harbinger of hope and promise. *The tomb was empty!*

Little did these women know when they beheld the sight of the empty tomb, that things would never be the same again for them. In fact things would never be the same again for anyone. A new dawn had broken in the history of mankind. The game had changed. Man would not be the same.

What had happened? Who had removed the body? I wonder if a tiny thought, even fleetingly, came to any of those who witnessed the empty tomb (first the women and then Peter and John), that the impossible may have occurred; *that Jesus had risen.* I doubt it. The disciples were in no state of mind to anticipate such an event. It was only when he *appeared* to them did they understand the meaning of the empty tomb. He had risen. He had risen just as he had said he would, on the third day. Just as it had been written about him in the Scripture. They now would recall that when he was with them, he had many a time told them so, that he would rise from the dead, but they had not truly believed him or perhaps did not really comprehend what he was saying. *"Destroy this temple, and I will raise it again in three days,"*[2] Jesus had challenged. They like all others had understood that to mean the temple built by Herod, the imposing structure in Jerusalem, which was their holiest place of worship. That he was talking of the temple of his body, it would dawn to them now.

These realizations must have slowly come to the disciples as they encountered the risen Lord in a series of his appearances over the next forty days, amidst different settings. Their Rabbi, their Master, was now their Lord and God. Now they knew and in turn could preach with conviction that he was not some dreamer who had made big claims about himself while he was alive. *He was what he had said he was.* His resurrection had settled that conclusively. If he can be true on this most important claim, then he was to be believed on all others, on everything that he had said. *"Indeed his teachings were so entwined with his person that many of his words could not have outlived him, the grand claims would have died with him on the cross. It took the Resurrection to turn the Proclaimer of the truth into the one proclaimed,"* wrote Philip Yancey.

What if Jesus had not risen from the dead? What if the women had found the stone intact and the body of Jesus lying in the tomb just as they had laid him after his death on the cross? Well, then we would not have celebrated the Friday he was crucified as the Good Friday (and of course there would have been no Easter to celebrate). The Friday would have been observed, if at all, as a day of mourning; a black day. It would have been called the *Black Friday*. It would have been a day when a righteous man who gave a new meaning to the old Law of Moses; when a good teacher who taught the message of love and forgiveness; when a compassionate healer who cured many who were sick even on the Sabbath; when a Jewish prophet (and this one coming after an interval of 400 years) who talked of the coming of the kingdom of God; when a son of man who was born of Mary and Joseph but addressed God endearingly as his *Abba* and taught others to do the same; was brutally executed in the worst form of death that can be given to man. It would have been a day when evil had triumphed, once more, over good.

If it had been so, then Christianity would not have spread to different parts of the world; the way it started doing soon after the death of its founder. Take out the Resurrection from the Christian faith and you are taking the promise out of it. It would not have grown to the faith that *it is*. It would have at best remained a Jewish sect, localized mainly in the province of Galilee. It would have been confined to just a movement centered on a carpenter, who had spread the message of love and compassion in Israel. Jesus would have been considered, at best, a prophet, who had Messianic ambitions but with no army or organized group of followers to either present a serious challenge to the Jewish priestly establishment or provide real hope to a people groaning under the iron rule of the Romans. His execution under Pontius Pilate would have been considered a bad end to a good man. But then history is full of such tragic endings. Jesus of Nazareth would have been just a footnote in history. Long forgotten and with a handful of people to count as his followers.

But Jesus is far from forgotten. He is not a footnote in history. He is the central character of the human history. In fact history revolves around him. Even the secular world takes his birth as the dividing point in the calendar of history; as BC (Before Christ) and AD (Anno Domini - in the year of our Lord). And this has been so because of that one event; his resurrection. He came back from the dead as was promised by him. Because of that he could rightfully claim to be the Messiah. Mary's son proved to be God's Son. The Son of Man was shown as the Son of God. To be revered and not just remembered. To be worshipped as a Deity and not just respected as a good leader. To be called Lord and not just Master.

His resurrection would change many lives, of those who had seen him in flesh and of those who came after him but still experienced him as the Living Saviour. Of all the arguments supporting the Resurrection, the most convincing is the transformation which took place in his disciples after they had witnessed the risen Lord. From a bunch of frightened men who had fled their master's side at the time of his arrest, who (most of them) must have watched him dying on the cross from a safe distance, who hid in the city after his death from fear of the authorities; these same men underwent a complete change after they encountered the resurrected Christ. *They were now convinced that their Lord was who he had claimed he was.* They now believed every word that he had spoken to them. They were ready to follow every command that he had given them. The Resurrection was the game changer.

A change took place in them (change is a mild word, it was more of a complete makeover), and this change was to be inflamed by the power they were to receive on Pentecost. The disciples were no longer afraid of the authorities or of any other. They knew Jesus was living and with them, and they continued to believe so even when he ascended to heaven. They were now ready to suffer, and suffer gladly. They would now die, and die willingly. Who dies for a dead man? No, but they were ready to die for their living Lord. Would they have spread his message so zealously and so boldly if they knew they were proclaiming a dead man? Would they have suffered martyrdom (and most of them did), if Jesus had not risen but remained buried in a tomb in a garden near the place of his execution? No they would not have, but instead would have very likely returned to their homes, back to their old lives, with the memories of Jesus as the only leftovers of their time spent with him.

But that was not to be. Being changed they would now go out to change the world. They would be thrown into an enterprise which would build up into a massive scale (and is still growing) and against which even the gates of Hades have not been able to stand. They would have thrust upon them the mantle of Jesus and the mission which he had started on earth; the mission of establishing the kingdom of God, for which sake they would now become fishers of men. They would now fearlessly proclaim the Proclaimer of the good news. They were convinced that in doing so they would be spreading the truth about the *One* who was the Way and the Truth and the Life.

The Resurrection is the turning point of history. It evidences that good will eventually win over evil, that life will ultimately be restored over death. That death will not have its victory, that grave will not swallow the dead. If Good Friday is the most crucial day in the history of mankind, then Easter is the most defining. Sin was defeated by Jesus on the Cross but the bugle was sounded only on the day of Resurrection; for it was only on that day that the victory was sealed. What Jesus accomplished on the Cross was only known in his Resurrection. We live on the other side of Easter and our faith thus sees through the prism of the resurrected Christ. Things look much clearer from here and I must say a lot happier.

What does the Resurrection mean to us? What is the promise or promises held out in the resurrection of Jesus Christ? How has it changed things?

Firstly, it signifies victory over death. Death has lost its aura of fear over those who believe. Death has lost its finality. We now know it is an impostor. In fact it is even to be welcomed. As Paul writes, *"For to me, to live is Christ and to die is gain."* [3] For to die is to be with the Lord; free from living in this fallen world. By being free from the fear of death and looking forward to the world to come, man acquires a different perspective towards living in this world. Death has been vanquished by the resurrection of Jesus. It will now be destroyed once for all. Paul writes, *"The last enemy to be destroyed is death"*[4] and the Book of Revelation describes how the 'death' of death will take place: *"Then death and Hades were thrown into the lake of fire."* [5]

Secondly, the Resurrection is a promise that what God has done in one body, Jesus Christ, He will replicate on a larger scale one day. He did it once and He will do it again. We also will be resurrected and will have new bodies. God will give us exalted bodies like Jesus and *"will transform our lowly bodies so that they will be like his glorious body."* [6] Christ was the first fruits and God will add us to him. The bodies we will receive shall be imperishable, immortal, and uncorrupted by sin and illness. It will be a spiritual body, prepared to inherit the kingdom of God. This is God's plan for us and we have the resurrected Christ as an assurance to hold on in faith; that some day the promise will find fulfillment.

Thirdly, the Resurrection holds the message of hope that in the end good will triumph over evil. That God, who has been accused by many of being indifferent or even powerless to exterminate evil from this world, is restoring the world to its original sinless state. And if He could transform the darkest deed of evil ever done i.e. the Cross of His Son, into the glorious promise of Resurrection; He will surely use all things, good or bad, for His redemptive purposes. *"God did not abolish the fact of evil: He transformed it. He did not stop the crucifixion: He rose from the dead,"* wrote Dorothy Sayers. This is the way God works; not completely sweeping away everything but using everything to fulfill His ultimate purpose, which is the redemption of the world. He will surely mend this broken world. He will make everything new. When that will see completion is not known. But it is certain to happen and we have the Resurrection as a proof and hope.

Mankind is presently in *'Easter Saturday'*. We are in the state of waiting. Waiting for the day when God will bring to fulfillment all that He has promised in the resurrection of His Son, Jesus Christ.

It is just a matter of time.

1. *1 Corinthians 15:55 (Hosea 13:14)*
2. *John 2:19*
3. *Philippians 1:21*
4. *1 Corinthians 15:26*
5. *Revelation 20:14*
6. *Philippians 3:21*

# Chapter ~ 19

# A TALE OF TWO DISCIPLES: JUDAS ISCARIOT

*"I know those I have chosen."* [1]

Jesus had a close circle of disciples who were known as the Twelve. They were privy to some of the deeper and closed door teachings of the Master. He spoke in parables to the people but in private explained them to these disciples. And within this group there was an inner circle of three; Peter, John and James, who were present with him at his Transfiguration and were also those whom he took with him a distance away from the rest in the Garden of Gethsemane, with the hope of their support at the time of his distress.

Two of these twelve disciples deserve a closer look, for the reason that they both betrayed Jesus. These two are Judas and Peter. However if we study the gospels for the conduct of the other disciples, we find they fare no better. They also must have disappointed Jesus many a times during their association with him. All left him when he was arrested. There is no record that any one of his disciples accompanied him to the midnight trial before the Sanhedrin or before Pilate. Probably Judas went back with the company of soldiers who had arrested Jesus at Gethsemane. But he had his own reasons; the same that had led him to the act of selling out his Master. But the fact is that none of the disciples were arrested along with Jesus, which is quite surprising for if Jesus was leading an insurrection or a revolt or posed a danger to the authorities, they could be charged as his accomplices and put to trial along with him. Jesus had been left alone to his fate. *'The shepherd had been struck and the sheep of the flock had been scattered,'* [2] as foretold in the Scriptures.

Perhaps where all the disciples had let Jesus down was that they did not fully understand him, fully grasp as to *who he really was.* They did not understand the reason for which he had come, the mission of his coming to earth. They did not tie up the Old Testament prophesies with this Jesus of Nazareth, who they had followed around Israel for three years. To their credit they believed that he was the Messiah, but they understood him to be the political and kingly Messiah who had been long awaited by the Jewish nation. They understood his kingdom to be that of the world, which then meant that he would be overthrowing the Roman government in Jerusalem and establish the throne of David in its place.

Given the human weaknesses of the disciples, and there are many instances of such in the gospels (to their credit these have been kept in the accounts), they must have already started dreaming of their positions and roles in the Messianic kingdom which Jesus was expected to usher in soon. Recall Peter's consternation that Jesus should speak otherwise concerning his suffering and death, which was not in consonance to their expectations of and from him (he of course received a stinging rebuke from Jesus for this). And remember the instance when the mother of John and James requested Jesus for special positions for her sons in his kingdom. That his kingdom will be of the other world and that the prophecies in the Scriptures pointed to the sufferings of the Messiah, all these made full sense to them only after his death and resurrection and not before. They failed to connect the dots.

Let us focus on the changing behaviour of the disciples during the arrest of Jesus. When the arresting party arrived at the Garden of Gethsemane looking for Jesus, the disciples who were sleeping, and must have woken up with a rude jolt, quickly sized the situation and were prepared to give a fight. Peter even drew out his sword. They were ready to fight for the Messiah. But then they saw that the same Messiah was not retaliating with any action that could be remotely considered as offensive, but instead was conceding docilely to his arrest. There was no show of any divine sign, no manifestation of any supernatural power, but instead a plea to his disciples to lay down their arms. Their leader had meekly surrendered to his enemies. They must have been perplexed and were not sure how to respond next. Resultantly, after the initial bravado, they ran away from the scene lest they also be arrested along with Jesus. They were now more concerned of their own safety than the safety of their Master. For them their dreams of the last three years, of impending political power, had been dashed. It was more or less over, they must have sadly thought, as they ran away.

So why highlight the case of Judas and Peter in particular? All disciples in varying degree had shown lack of faith and commitment to the Lord. Why then single out Judas and Peter?    Judas, because perhaps there is another side to his story, one which is less incriminating and damning one.   And Peter, because he was different from any of the disciples. A man of a highly volatile nature, he was also the first one to take up any challenge. An impulsive character and a simpleton in many ways, his sole desire was to impress upon his Lord that he was his best disciple or at least the most eager and the most daring one. But it was because their betrayal of Jesus took highly visible and extreme dimensions, that we take these two for our study.

Both Judas and Peter were with Jesus during his public ministry and in a sense were not only his disciples but also his friends. They had known him from close quarters; Peter perhaps the more as he was part of the inner circle of Jesus. They shared rare and precious moments with Jesus and had 'handled the Word with their hands'. Yet both let him down badly. Judas betrayed him by handing him over to the chief priests and elders, and Peter betrayed him by denying that he ever knew him, when faced with danger to his own person. I would consider Peter's act also as betrayal of Jesus though it has been leniently labelled as denial in the church history. But whatever name we may give to it, at the core it remains a betrayal; make no mistake about it. Peter had forsaken his Lord. He denied his association with him, lying his way out of trouble on three different occasions, on the night that Jesus was facing his many trials. The acts of Judas and Peter were betrayal of the trust that the Lord had bestowed on them (and other disciples) and we can only differentiate between them in terms of their relative impact.

Another reason why we need to study the acts of betrayal of these two, and also the motives behind why they did what they did, is to learn our lessons from them. They impart us lessons in our own humanity and if we are to do some honest soul searching, we will find the numerous occasions in our lives when we have betrayed the Lord. The many times we have denied him, or forsaken him, or have not stood by or for him. There is a Peter and a Judas in each one of us; so let us not rush to haul these two disciples on the coals.

In this chapter we will take the story of Judas and in the next that of Peter.

## Judas

*"I tell you the truth, one of you is going to betray me."* [3]

Is Judas one of the most misconstrued characters of the Bible? Have we rushed to paint him as a monster, even the devil himself? Is there another side, one much more balanced, to the story of Judas? Does he deserve a fairer judgement in Christian history? Is he entitled to grace like we all are?

Judas was very likely a learned man, perhaps even a scholar. He was the only disciple among the Twelve who was from Judea. He, like the others, had been selected by Jesus to be part of the group of his twelve disciples. And Jesus had made the selection after a night of intense praying. Had he made an error in picking Judas as his disciple? Or do we bring in here the element of pre-knowledge but not predetermination on the part of God? But then Jesus had come to die and Judas' act was in fulfilment of the prophecy about the Messiah: *"He who shares my bread has lifted up his heel against me."* [4] So why fault Judas? I know when we discuss this subject we are walking on very difficult and delicate theological grounds. No one can address these matters with absolute certainty. We can only speculate and give our views, different though they could be.

Why did Judas agree to hand over Jesus to the Jews i.e. to the chief priests and elders of the Sanhedrin? And why did they need his assistance at all? They could have arrested Jesus any time for he was preaching openly and even inside the temple. One reason could be that if it had been done in the open and during the daytime, the chief priests feared the possibility of riots breaking out, for the people were behind Jesus, at least at that time. It was the Passover week and Jerusalem was filled with many people who had come to the holy city from their native places. Any overt action against Jesus would have been risky and would have incited the people against the Jewish religious leaders.

So any action against Jesus that they were to plan, had to be on the sly and in the stealth of the night, and in Judas they found a willing accomplice. He agreed to guide them to the place where Jesus was to be found at that time of the night. In the quiet of the night and away from the spotlight of the people, Jesus would be arrested. That was the plan. Everything would be executed surreptitiously, and by the time the news of the arrest would spread amongst the crowd, which would be in the morning, it would be too late for any possible resistance. Things would be well in control of the authorities by the time the crowd came to know of the deed. Covert deeds are best done in the cloak of the darkness. And Jesus did say to the arresting party: *"But this is your hour – when darkness reigns."* [5]

Another way in which Judas would be serving the purpose of the chief priests was that they could now claim that it was one of his own disciples who had given him up and who had even led them to his arrest. This would make their charge of sedition against Jesus much more 'legitimate'. Their scheming brains would have considered this (Judas coming to them) a master stroke of luck which had fallen in their laps, and which had made possible their goal of getting rid of this troublesome rabbi from Galilee.

What about Judas? What was his motive in going to the chief priests and personally leading the armed crowd to Jesus? Did he anticipate Jesus would be arrested; that it was an arrest party that he was leading to his Lord? Had he given up on his Master? Was he giving over Jesus to the authorities or did he have some other intent which had made him take part in this event? Did he do it for money (it has been mentioned elsewhere that he used to dip into the group's purse as he was the treasurer)? But if money was the motivation and the thirty silver coins was the price of his betrayal, then why did he attempt to return the money back to the chief priests after he came to know that they had tricked him into their plot, and that Jesus had been arrested (and not escorted) and would be put on trial by the Sanhedrin.

It was not to be a meeting organised, as Judas might have believed so, for the chief priests and Jesus to sort out their differences, and where Jesus would impress upon them all, that he was indeed the Messiah who was to come. It was to be a gathering for sure, but not where Jesus would be accepted and crowned as the King of the Jews; instead it would be a kangaroo court where he would stand on trial and finally be declared a heretic under the Jewish law and an insurrectionist under the Roman law (so as to make his execution possible). That hit Judas hard. He had led Jesus to his death. For him the thirty silver coins were now blood money. He threw them in the temple and hung himself.

Let us back up a little and understand the plausible motives for Judas' action. He was a scholar and perhaps amongst all the disciples was the most conversant with the prophecies of the Messiah in the Scripture. These prophecies he saw fulfilling in Jesus. The crowds were mesmerised by this teacher from Galilee, who performed many miracles; multiplying the bread, healing the sick, opening the eyes of the blind, and even raising the dead. And when he preached on matters of the Law, he spoke with such authority and also simplicity. The people were ready to crown him the Messiah, their King. He had just to give the signal and the crown would be his. Just a few days back, at the beginning of the Passover week, he had made a triumphal entry into the city of Jerusalem. People had laid palm branches for him and sung hosannas, as if welcoming a king. Judas noticed all these events concerning his Lord with growing exhilaration. The moment had arrived for Jesus to ascend to the throne of Israel.

But his Master was a strange man. He slipped away from the adulation of the crowd. He was reluctant to be declared the Messiah in public, though privately and to a select few, he had admitted that he was the one to come. Further he certainly was not on the best of terms with the Sanhedrin and the Jewish leaders, some of who in fact were supportive of him in private. This group had to be on his side if Jesus was to be accepted and crowned the Messiah. But Jesus rather than reaching out to them was actually bent on antagonising them. He had his confrontations with them on many occasions. He had rebuked them for their shallow rituals and superficial righteousness. He had even blasted them calling them *'brood of vipers'* [6] and *'whitewashed tombs.'*[7] Though this delighted the ordinary folks but it certainly caused the chiefs priests and the elders to lose face in public. Thus not surprisingly they viewed Jesus as their enemy, and there was even a buzz that the religious leaders were planning to do away with Jesus.

But before the matter came to head, Judas could see that he had a role to play in getting the two sides together, to talk to each other away from the glare of the people. He knew Jesus would not agree to his plan and meet the Jewish leadership in secret, so there was no option but to force the situation upon Jesus. If Jesus would not go to them of his own will, then steps needed to be taken where he would be taken to them. It was imperative that Jesus had the dialogue with these influential leaders of the society. There was no way he could come to the throne without the support of the Jewish leaders. Jesus had to explain his plan, his mission to them, in a face to face meeting, and convince them so that they would give their support to him.

This was the way Judas was thinking. Put Jesus in the corner and force upon him to reveal himself as the Messiah, to the people who mattered. And if he was not able to prove that he was the Messiah; well then, that settles the matter the other way. Then there would be no need to follow him. Either way things had to be set in motion and had to be settled once for all. And he (Judas) would be the catalyst for that.

Was Jesus aware of what was going on in the mind of Judas? Well Jesus made a statement at the Passover meal, which indicates such, when he told Judas: *"What you are about to do, do quickly."* [8] Judas must have taken this as some sort of a signal to go ahead with what he had planned. He took it as consent from Jesus. And when Judas came to Gethsemane with the armed group, his first gesture was to kiss his Lord. It must have been only when Jesus remarked, *"Judas, are you betraying the Son of Man with a kiss,"* [9] that Judas must have sensed that something was not right, and that he and Jesus were not on the same page. His Lord was calling his effort (to promote him) as *'betrayal'*!

And the ways things turned out subsequently, it indeed set in Judas that he had actually betrayed his Master. Things were to go out of control quickly, and did not transpire the way Judas was expecting. Jesus was being tried like a criminal. This was not what had been arranged with the chief priest and the elders; this was not the way they were supposed to treat Jesus. The horrors of what he had done must have hit Judas with a big force. He went to the chief priests and tried to scrap the deal by attempting to give back their money. But it was too late. Like a fool he had played into their hands and they now had no use of him. They were going to deal with Jesus, just as they had intended all along.

Where had Judas gone wrong? That he wanted Jesus to be the Messiah they all believed him to be, they all wanted him to be? If we look at the gospels carefully, we will see that not a single disciple really and fully understood the mission of Jesus. Not one of them understood that the kingdom he was referring to was not of this world. Judas went a step further than the others. He wanted to force Jesus to act. He wanted to draw up the agenda for Jesus. He acted upon what he believed Jesus should be doing. In that he was really putting God to the test. Jesus had faced a similar situation in the desert where he was tempted by Satan to show his hand. He was challenged to throw himself down from the highest point of the temple, and as is written in the Scriptures, the angels would come and arrest his fall; thus revealing him to be the Son of God. A similar *fait accompli* situation was attempted to be created by Judas. Bring Jesus face to face with the Jewish leaders and force him to reveal his identity. As in the desert before, even this time around, Jesus did not fall for it. *"Do not put the Lord your God to the test,"* [10] was his answer to Satan then, and it remained his line in this situation too. You do not draw up God's agenda.

We are also susceptible to make the same mistake. We try to pin God into a corner: 'Do this and I will believe in You; if You are God Almighty then give me this; God You have to show me Your power'; are some of the ways that we try to push God into the desired action. But God cannot be excited or instigated or bribed or forced into action. He has His own game plan; His own rules with which He governs; and His own timetable to act. There is no more Jesus to be handed over to the authorities, but he can still be betrayed, in numerous ways, by his followers. And when we do so, spare a thought also for Judas, whose very name became synonymous with betrayal.

Was Judas forgiven? Who knows? But we know that God can forgive the worst of sinners. On the cross Jesus prayed to his Father to forgive his executioners, *for they did not know what they were doing.* We ask the question was Judas fully knowing what he was doing? Did he realise at that time, the diabolical plot of the Jewish leaders, and how his own role in it, would ultimately lead Jesus to his death? If he had known such, then would he have done what he did? He was Jesus' disciple and friend and not his enemy, so as to desire his death. If he was disillusioned with the teachings of Jesus or did not agree with his approach, he could have simply parted company with him. He may have considered his act to be for the good of the Lord, but it actually turned out to be the act which caused the most tragic betrayal in history.

Judas was filled with remorse for his act, when the full implications of it were clear to him. Some people would say he did not repent like Peter; therefore he did not receive the Lord's forgiveness. How do we know that? How do we know that he did not repent? And there is a thin line between remorse and repentance. Remorse should normally lead to repentance. It is the first step in the process of repentance. How can we say with certainty that Judas took only the first step? Maybe he went the full way and received God's forgiveness.

Jesus did say: *"The Son of Man will go just as it is written about him. But woe to that man who betrays the Son of Man! It would be better for him if he had not been born."* [11] Indeed this is a curse, and a heavy one, which hangs over Judas for all time; that he would be known as the one who betrayed Jesus. He had let down his friend. He had handed over his Master to the enemies. If only he could reverse what had been done. The burden was too heavy upon his soul. He was suffocating. The only relief for him would be death. And that is what he proceeded to do.

Perhaps if he had not ended his life and lived sufficient enough, he may have given the Lord the chance to work his grace in his embittered and grieving heart. He may have even been reinstated by the risen Christ, just as Peter was. This is just a thought.

In this article I have attempted to paint an alternate picture of Judas. I may be completely wrong. He may well have acted deviously and knowingly sided with the enemies of Jesus to get rid of him. But as I said earlier no one can know for certain.

I just gave Judas some benefit of doubt.

1.   John 13:18
2.   Matthew 26:31 (modified) (quoting Zechariah 13:7)
3.   John 13:21
4.   John 13:18 (quoting Psalm 41:9)
5.   Luke 22:53
6.   Matthew 23:33
7.   Matthew 23:27
8.   John 13:27
9.   Luke 22:48
10.  Matthew 4:7
11.  Matthew 26:24

# Chapter ~ 20

# A TALE OF TWO DISCIPLES: SIMON PETER

*"And when you have turned back, strengthen your brothers."* [1]

**W**e look at the most interesting of the disciples of Jesus; Simon also known as Peter. The gospels give more details of this disciple than any other. Simon was the brother of Andrew, and both were part of the select group of Twelve. They were fishermen by profession, from the town of Capernaum, and plied their trade in the Sea of Galilee. It was Andrew who was first called by Jesus. Subsequently Andrew introduced his brother Simon to the Lord, and Jesus gave him the name Cephas (Aramaic of Peter which is Greek, both meaning *'rock'*). Eventually Peter proved to be the rock which Jesus had predicted he would be.

But Peter was most unlike a rock when Jesus found him. He was of a colourful and unpredictable temperament that was likely prone to flashes of anger and vitriol. He carried these traits throughout his time with Jesus; till his fall. That episode would change him completely.

But we will come to that later. Peter was impulsive by nature and often did not think much before reacting. But he had zeal in abundance. It was this zeal which stood out and was both a blessing and a bane for him. The Lord was impressed by this character trait of Peter; it only needed to be harnessed and channelized into working for the kingdom of God.

Another side of Peter which endeared him to the Lord was his heart. His heart was right with God. Very likely, as a fisherman, he must have carried out his profession with little care for scruples. But the Lord was not looking at such misdemeanours or faults. In essence Peter's heart was what Jesus wanted in a disciple. Eager to please, receptive, and having a child like quality. This is what God looks for. God's grace is able to change such a heart. God wants it. In this respect Peter's character was similar to that of the biblical giant David. Their hearts were seeking to please their Lord all the time.

Peter when called by Jesus to follow him did not think twice before 'chucking his job'. He had been promised by Jesus of a more important job description; *'fishers of men'*. Peter did not doubt the Lord, but left everything behind and went after him. His decision, like that of the other disciples, was a big leap of faith. Jesus was relatively unknown then. He had just begun his mission. To put your trust in a stranger, an itinerant rabbi from Nazareth, called for some great courage and a heart for big risk taking.

We will take up some important events in Peter's association with Jesus, which will reflect upon his character and give us some understanding as to what lead to his denial (betrayal I maintain) of Jesus; how the change took place in him and what are the lessons that we can take away from these accounts.

The first event that we will consider, illustrates the fickleness of Peter's faith. The disciples were in a boat on the Sea of Galilee. Jesus had sent them ahead to the other side of the lake. It was the fourth watch of the night when they saw Jesus walking on the lake towards the boat. The disciples thought that it was a ghost that was approaching them and cried out in fear. Jesus reassured them that it was he. Then Peter, the ever zealous, wanted to walk on water too, just like Jesus.

Jesus agreed and asked him to come to him and Peter started walking on the water towards Jesus. Midway he began having doubts and wondered what he was doing ON the lake. He was walking on water! He became conscious of the howling winds around him and was afraid. And the moment he became afraid he began to sink. He cried out to Jesus to save him and the Lord caught hold of him. Instead of receiving praise from the Lord for his faith, Peter was chided for the lack of it.

What had happened? Why did Peter fall prey to his doubts, even after starting off well? The answer is simple - *he took his eyes of Jesus.* He started off with great zeal, was thrilled to be doing the impossible (the Lord must have enjoyed Peter's expression of wonder while he was walking on the water), and then was suddenly scared as to what he was doing! This is the pattern we find in our faith many times. We start off with great enthusiasm and on the way we encounter winds of peril. As long as we keep our eyes on the Lord we keep going. But the moment we start looking around at the obstacles and dangers that are on the way, we begin to sink. We becoming immobilised with fear. That is what happened to Peter, but this episode has lessons for us all to take.

Another striking incident is Peter's confession of Christ. Jesus inquired of his disciples who the people believed he was. After hearing them tell different accounts, he then directed the same question to them: *"But what about you? Who do you say I am?"* [2] What Jesus was actually saying was: 'That I expect a more insightful answer from you. You have the benefit of knowing me closely. So surely your reply would be more informed'. Peter as usual was the first off the block and the reply he gave is the cornerstone of the Christian faith, and is forever etched with the story of Peter (along with his denial).

Peter answered, *"You are the Christ, the Son of the living God."* [3] This was the confessional statement of faith and filled Jesus with immense joy. He proceeded then to bless Simon Peter and declare that it was on this rock that he will build his church on earth. What did Jesus mean by: *'on this rock I will build my church'*? [4] What was he referring to by the *'rock'*? Was the rock Simon Peter or was the rock *the statement* made by Peter; his confession of Christ – *'You are the Christ, the Son of the living God'?* Was this profound statement, which contained the acknowledgement of the real identity of Jesus, to be the foundation on which the church was to be built? It is open to interpretation. But clearly this statement by Peter, and I think he spoke on behalf of all the disciples, filled the Lord with much hope for his disciples.

But soon after his exaltation by the Lord, Peter received a stinging rebuke from Jesus: *"Get behind me, Satan!"* [5] This incident is recorded immediately after the above and could have well followed one after the other. Jesus then proceeded to tell his disciples of his suffering and death in Jerusalem and his being raised on the third day. Having heard Peter (and others) confess who he was, Jesus now considered them ready (mature enough) to hear the more serious things concerning him. But Peter would have none of it. The Messiah does not get handed over to his enemies and be killed by them. Why was Jesus speaking in such a strange way? He should be talking of victories and triumphs and not sufferings and death. The Master should stop such talk. It affects the morale of everyone. So he takes Jesus aside and reprimands him. Jesus reacts by tearing into him. He calls him Satan and rebukes him for his lack of understanding of the ways of God. Peter must have slinked away; dazed as to what had hit him.

Reading these two incidents together, we can see how on one hand our confession of faith pleases God. And if that faith is founded on the truth and confessed without reservation, it brings immense joy to God. The second is this clear message - do not lay the ways for God, but rather understand His ways, strange though they may seem sometimes.

*"I tell you the truth, this very night, before the cock crows, you will disown me three times."* [6]

How are we to describe the denial of Peter? Shocking, but not unexpected, given his unsteady nature and the past instances of his fickleness. Let us now look closely at the sequence of events which led to the denial. The disciples were having the Passover meal with their Lord. Little did they know, at that time, that this will be their last supper with him. The events that were to follow, would take place at a head spinning pace and with heart rendering impact. Jesus throws a bombshell at the dinner table, that one of them will betray him. There is commotion amongst the disciples. Once it became clear that it was Judas who was to be the betrayer, some calm returns to the gathering, but the disciples would have continued to remain in a troubled frame of mind. Something was going on behind the scenes. Something that was to happen soon. Their Master knew of it, but had yet to confide in them.

Then Jesus drops the second bombshell, much more stunning then the first. He tells them that this very night the shepherd (he) would be struck and the sheep (they) would be scattered. What were they to make of that? Was everything going to end in an instant, in a whimper? They were dumbfounded. Peter expectedly was the first to speak out. He professed his loyalty to Jesus, vowing that all may fall away, but he would not. And he will lay down his life for him. *'Lay down his life'*; Jesus should have appreciated that but he knew better and said to Peter, *"Will you really lay down your life for me? I tell you the truth, before the cock crows, you will disown me three times."* [7] This must have hurt Peter. The question was direct and all knowing. His Master had expressed disbelief in his claim. In Matthew's gospel account it is added *'this very night'* conveying that the betrayal would be soon. One will not have to go beyond this night for Peter's tall claims to be grounded.

And it happened just as Jesus had said it would. Peter followed, at a distance, the arresting party which had taken Jesus away from the Garden of Gethsemane. Waiting outside in the courtyard of the house of Caiaphas the high priest, while inside Jesus was facing the Sanhedrin; Peter was identified on three different occasions, as being part of the group with Jesus. His Galilean accent had given him away. On all these three occasions, Peter denied he knew Jesus. He disowned Jesus in these very words: *"I don't know the man!"* [8] You don't know that man Peter? The one whom you called Lord and Master? The one whom you confessed was the Christ, the Son of the living God? One for whom you left everything you had and were, and followed him for three years? One to whom you had said, just a few hours ago, *"Even if I have to die with you, I will never disown you."* [9] And so soon, at the first threat to yourself, you have denied him! O Peter! Peter! What have you done?

The cock crows. The Lord looks at Peter with a gaze which pierces his heart. The deed has been done. Peter breaks down and weeps bitterly. He has betrayed the one whom he had vowed to follow always and even die for. The Lord was right about him. How shallow was his love for him; it had turned out. Peter must have despised himself, as he found himself shorn off all the bluster and bravado he had. The real Peter had been discovered and he hated the picture of what he saw of himself. And that piercing look of the Lord! He did not detect any expression of *'I told you so'* in it, but a deep hurt and sadness of one suffering the betrayal of a close and dear one. At the hour when Jesus needed all the support he could have, his chief disciple had been found wanting. He was more concerned in saving his own hide, then to provide any comfort to his Lord, in the hour of his need.

What does the betrayal of Peter amount to? Have we really tried to gauge the gravity of it? For Peter, since he left his home in Capernaum three years ago, Jesus had constituted his family. His life was centred on Jesus. And to betray him was to betray himself, his own identity. It is the same as someone betraying his mother or father or wife or children. Giving them up to save his own life. But it went beyond that. Jesus was his Lord. The one in whom he had put his faith and for whom he had left his life in Capernaum. And the Lord trusted him. He had let down that trust. How could he, Peter, of all the disciples, do that? Peter despised himself. That face he saw of himself was unknown to him and he found it to be very despicable.

Aren't we like Peter? We make tall claims of what we can do for the Lord, how much we love him and that we can even die for him. But we are relying on our strength, which will be shown for what it is, when the time comes to stand for and by the Lord, in our beliefs. We can be found wanting. And this is why this 'puncturing' of Peter was necessary? If Peter was to do the works for which Jesus had chosen him, the self-dependence in Peter had to be removed first and replaced with dependence on God. The 'I will do this or that for you, Lord' had to be replaced with 'what do you want to do through me Lord'. If Peter continued to look at himself, it would not have been possible for him to be the 'rock' which the Lord wanted him to be and had planned him to be. He had to fall before the Lord could raise him. He had to be broken down before he was to be reinstated as a person that God wanted him to be. For Peter it was the moment of his transformation. If to pinpoint the exact moment, it was when Jesus looked at him after his third denial.

It is the same in our case. God can work his transformation in us only after first breaking our dependence on ourselves, on our 'I'. Once that is done and we find ourselves in weakness and brokenness, God will come and strengthen us. Dependent on Him and Him alone, we would be able to do things beyond ourselves; things that we never could imagine could be achieved by us. For Peter the reinstatement came and came soon.

*Simon, Simon, Satan has asked to sift you as wheat. But I have prayed for you, Simon, that your faith may not fail. And when you have turned back, strengthen your brothers."* [10]

Jesus had now risen from the grave and had appeared several times to his disciples. As per his command they had gone ahead of him to Galilee. One morning they went fishing in the Sea of Galilee. There they encountered Jesus. After an astonishing catch, under the direction of a person on the shore, they experienced what is known as the *'Tyranny of Familiarity'*. It was then they discovered that the person on the shore was Jesus. And Simon Peter, as impetuous as ever, jumped into the waters and swam to the shore. When the rest arrived in the boat, along with the fantastic catch, they had breakfast with Jesus. When they had eaten the drama began.

*"Simon son of John, do you truly love me more than these?"* [11] This was the first question which Jesus asked and it was exploring what Peter had always prided himself on, that he loved Jesus more than the other disciples. Peter replied meekly in the affirmative. But his answer was not to confirm that he loved more than others (how could he make such a claim now?) but simple an affirmation of his love. No comparisons with others. Good the first lesson had been learnt.

*"Simon son of John, do you truly love me?"* [12] The second time and this one a more probing question. The Lord was closing in. No more

comparisons but this time the emphasis was on the word *'truly'* as if questioning the genuineness of his love. Peter was sinking more and more with shame. He just repeated his reply, again affirming his love.

*"Simon son of John, do you love me?"* [13] The third and final time, and the question which was the knockout punch. Simon Peter was shattered. He didn't know where to hide. He wished the ground would open up and swallow him. This question was the straightest and the most hurtful. The Lord was questioning his *very* love. *Whether he loved him at all!* Peter couldn't stand this; that his Lord should question the fact that he loved him at all. Flashes of the night when he had denied Jesus played on the screen of his mind. The Lord could not be faulted for asking this question. Peter had done nothing to retain his trust. He answered in a small voice: *"Lord, you know all things; you know that I love you."* [14] See how the emphasis shifts from Peter himself to the Lord. *'I love you but I have really lost the right to claim so. I used to boast once but all my boasting has proved to be nought. You know better. You decide if I love you'*; Peter appeared to be saying.

Three times denial. Three times reinstatement. Three questions, which were progressively going deeper and deeper. Peter must have been an emotional wreck at the end of it. But this is what Jesus wanted. Already for many days, Peter had been living in the hell of his betrayal of the Lord. He must have repented like he had never repented before. He must not have been able to see Jesus in the eye after the resurrected Christ started appearing to them. His act of denial was coming in between him and the Lord. Will it ever remain so? Not if left to the Lord. Peter had to be picked up from the ground.

Along with these questions and answers, side by side the reinstatement of Peter was going on. Feed my lambs after the first reply; take care of my sheep after the second; feed my sheep after the third and final. Peter was being restored to the position of leadership. He who was grovelling by then and must have felt unworthy of any calling, was being called by the Lord to lead the disciples. He who had failed the trust of the Lord, was being trusted with the leadership of the group. It was an anointing where Peter was being declared the leader after Jesus. But now, he would not be the brash, arrogant, and abrasive Peter. It was a mature, humble, and chastened Peter whom Jesus finally lifted up. Jesus had marked Peter for leadership and he ultimately brought that to fulfilment. But he made Peter a leader like himself; a servant leader.

One thing which stands out for me, is that the gospel writers have included the accounts of the disciples which do not show them in good light; their foolishness, lack of faith, personal ambitions, shortcomings, doubts, failings, and even betrayals. All have been recorded. Nothing has been hushed up or doctored. Instead they appear to have been highlighted to portray the disciples as what they really were; essentially flawed human beings. And therefore it brings to the fore more strongly, the transformation that Jesus brought in them, and subsequently used them for great works for the kingdom of God. This makes the gospels even more authentic accounts of Jesus and his men.

What amazes (and impresses) me, is the kind of people God selects for His work. He does not necessarily pick up the strongest, the most brilliant, the well-learned, and the rich and influential. He can do his work through the lowest of the lowest; the least likely candidates in the list if prepared by the standards of this world. All God needs is a willing and teachable heart. The rest, just leave it to Him. He will mould the person and make him suitable for the task that He has for him. The apostles are a case in point. They were not the best of men which Israel had to offer at that time. Most of them belonged to the bottom strata of the society. Not many were well learned. Most of them had professions which were not something to be proud of. Yet for Jesus they were good enough. He would polish them over the three years he was going to be with them, so that when the time came for him to leave, they would be ready to take over his mission.

In the case of Simon Peter, the rough fisherman from Galilee, he would become one of the founding fathers of the Church and the first bishop of the church in Rome. Amazing what God can do, where He can take us! How he can transform base metal into gold! We look for miracles and signs on the outward, but I believe the biggest miracle of God, is the transformation He can bring in men and women and do magnificent things through them; things which are way beyond their normal human capacity.

The lessons for us, from the life of Peter, are quite encouraging. First, as explained above, if we leave ourselves in God's hands, then God can achieve much through us. He can change our lives, our personalities, completely. And being transformed, we can become the instruments of his purposes on earth. We all know of the frail lady who lived in Calcutta in the last century. She allowed herself to be the instrument of God, and just see the magnitude of God's work through her. She will be canonised one day as a saint by the Vatican, and we will call her then: *Saint Teresa of Calcutta*. This is just one example. There are many, many more in Christian history.

Secondly we can take heart that despite our betrayal (s) of the Lord (and is there anyone who has not betrayed the Lord at some point?), we have the assurance of his forgiveness and reinstatement, just like it happened to Peter. But just like Peter we would need to repent first.

I have titled the accounts of Judas and Peter as, *'A tale of two disciples'*. Theirs are two stories, each with a different ending, but actually both have the same theme; the theme of betrayal. It is *a tale of betrayal* of the Lord, separately by two of his disciples; Judas and Peter.

*"Lord, why can't I follow you now? I will lay down my life for you,"* [15] Peter had asked Jesus at the Passover meal. He did not lay down his life that night; that night he was to betray him. But he did get to follow the Lord to death, as he had stated, and as the Lord had said he would do so later. About thirty years afterwards, Peter's wish was fulfilled. Tradition has it that he was crucified (upside down) and buried in Rome at the place where now stands St. Peter's Basilica, one of the holiest shrines of Christendom.

*"Men of Israel, listen to this: Jesus of Nazareth was a man accredited by God to you ........"* [16] A man is speaking fearlessly and passionately to a large crowd in a public place in the city of Jerusalem. Who is this man?

*Simon Peter, son of Jonah, formerly a fisherman in Capernaum, now beginning his life as a fisher of men, in service of his Lord and Master Jesus.*

1. *Luke 22:32*
2. *Matthew 16:15*
3. *Matthew 16:16.*
4. *Matthew 16:18*
5. *Matthew 16:23*
6. *Matthew 26:34*
7. *John 13:38*
8. *Matthew 26:72*
9. *Matthew 26:35*
10. *Luke 22:31-32.*
11. *John 21:15*
12. *John 21:16*
13. *John 21:17*
14. *John 21:17*
15. *John 13:37*
16. *Acts 2:22*

# Chapter ~ 21

# THE LORD'S SUPPER: THE MYSTICAL UNION

*"This is my body given for you; do this in remembrance of me."* [1]

**W**hen I go to the church for the Sunday morning service, I am filled with excitement, and a sense of anticipation grips me. I know I will be having a meeting that I do eagerly look forward to every time, though I have had it now countless number of times. The meeting is with someone special. It is a standing invitation, a rain check which I can encash again and again, though on certain days and occasions. I sit through the service waiting for *that* moment, and when the priest invites the congregation to come forward and participate in the Lord's Supper, the moment does finally arrive. I get up and move towards the altar in a line along with my fellow worshippers.

The line moves slowly as no one is in a hurry to get it done with. There is no jostling or jumping, which you might expect in a queue for some other purpose. Everyone is aware of and respects the enormity of the event. For me this is the high point of the Sunday service and it is well worth the weekly wait (sometimes longer). I am going to meet my Lord. I am going to meet Jesus of Nazareth. A mystical union with the Lord will take place, as I *receive* the bread and wine of the sacrament, and *take* it in me as his body and blood. In *that* moment when faith combines with the act of consuming, the *union* takes place.

Flash back to about two thousand years ago. It is the Passover meal which Jesus is having with his disciples. Jesus takes the bread, breaks it, and gives to his disciples saying, *"Take and eat; this is my body given for you, do this in remembrance of me."* [2] He then takes the cup of wine, gives thanks, and passes it to his disciples saying, *"Drink from it, all of you. This is my blood of the new covenant, which is poured out for many for the forgiveness of sins."* [3] Jesus was having, what is now well known as the Last Supper with his disciples, and during this meal he was instituting a sacrament which he asked his disciples to follow, *in remembrance of him.* This has been established as one of the holiest sacraments of the church, and is known as the Lord's Supper or the Holy Eucharist or the Holy Communion.

Jesus through this act was symbolizing the establishment of the New Covenant. A day later the body would be broken and the blood would flow; as the price for the sins of mankind is paid for. Today, this evening, the symbolic enactment of that actual sacrifice was being carried out by Jesus, and the disciples (and subsequently the church through them) were being entrusted with the perpetual observance of this sacrament, in remembrance of the Lord. In remembrance of his blood that flowed and his body that was broken, to put into effect the new order of things. It is an act symbolizing that we are under the New Covenant, which Christ established by his death on the Cross.

Why did Jesus resort to such dramatic symbolism of his sacrificial death? Why was this act so important that it had to be done a day before his death, so that it will be etched in the disciples' memories? How is taking of the wine and the bread to be understood (by faith) to be taking his blood and body? The New Testament would come into effect the next day when his body and blood will actually be given up in a sacrificial death; then why the establishment of this symbolic act the evening before?

This enactment, which was willed by the Lord to become a sacramental re-enactment, is an important part of the Christian faith, because it is done in remembrance of Jesus, and of his sacrificial death, and the covenant that he resultantly established with his death. It was important for the disciples of that generation to remember this, and not only to remember, but to also commemorate and celebrate it as often as they could. And additionally, when this ritual became part of the church sacraments and tradition, then the disciples who would come afterwards, those who had not seen the Lord in flesh and blood, would proclaim by this, that Jesus was no myth or legend but a *real* person. That they would acknowledge that God once came to earth and made his dwelling amongst men. That they also, in some mystical way, *will be joined with the historical Christ; the Jesus of Nazareth.* That they also would be privileged, through this way, to experience the Incarnation.

*"For whenever you eat this bread and drink this cup, you proclaim the Lord's death until he comes,"* [4] writes St. Paul. When we take part in the Lord's Supper, we are proclaiming his death. Enjoined to his death is his rising from the grave. Besides, in proclaiming one's death, you are also proclaiming that the person was born. So by taking part in this one sacrament we are proclaiming (and celebrating) at the same time; the birth, the death, and the resurrection of Jesus. Thus every Sunday becomes a Christmas, a Good Friday and an Easter; if you can accept this. In short we are commemorating and participating in the very INCARNATION, every time we take part in the Holy Communion.

Now we can see why this sacrament is so important and the privilege it provides to the disciples who came afterwards. We can thus understand why the Lord made it a point to establish this. He was very particular that it be followed by his disciples and also by those who would not see him in the earthily body. That this act would be an act of remembrance of him.  Remember what the resurrected Christ said to Thomas: *"Because you have seen me, you have believed; blessed are those who have not seen and yet have believed."* [5] This is the way the Lord still 'connects' physically with all his disciples. This is the way they can still 'see' and experience the Lord. By taking part in the

Eucharist, they can be part of his Incarnation. They too can feel his humanity when they take the bread and wine of the sacrament, as the body and blood of Christ who once walked the earth.

In this mystical union of Christ with the believer, at the time of the Communion; not only the disciple experiences the Incarnation, but the Incarnation is expanded and multiplied. Christ takes on the flesh of the disciple and experiences the Incarnation through him. The totality of the experience is a communion of the Son of Man with the sons of men. Jesus joins his flesh with me and experiences my earthly life, and I experience his earthly life (i.e. his humanity) of two thousand years ago.

It was not just only during the Last Supper that Jesus talked of eating his flesh and drinking his blood. He earlier referred to himself as the 'bread of life'. [6] In one of the discourses, given earlier in his ministry, we hear him say: *"I tell you the truth, unless you eat the flesh of the Son of Man and drink his blood, you have no life in you. Whoever eats my flesh and drinks my blood has eternal life, and I will raise him up at the last day. For my flesh is real food and my blood is real drink. Whoever eats my flesh and drinks my blood remains in me, and I in him. Just as the living Father sent me and I live because of the Father, so the one who feeds on me will live because of me. This is the bread that came down from heaven. Your forefathers ate manna and died, but he who feeds on this bread will live forever."* [7]

This is part of a much longer discourse which Jesus gave in the synagogue in Capernaum. The people hearing him must have been puzzled at his words and coming at the heels of the miracle of the feeding of the five thousand, they must have wondered what Jesus was referring to and what type of food was he talking about. They would rather that he gave them the bread of this life with which they could satisfy their physical hunger, rather than the *Bread of Life* that he was offering to them when referring to himself. For Jesus was giving them *spiritual bread*, the living bread from heaven, which by taking they would never hunger (spiritually) again. And he was that living bread of heaven. Even now these words of Jesus are considered pretty heavy and are also prone to be misunderstood (or deliberately misinterpreted) by people of other faiths, who accuse the Christians of cannibalism, for they are asked to feed on the flesh and blood of their Lord.

While Jesus did mean that we spiritually feed on him, so that we may remain in him; the physical expression of this gratification is seen in the Lord's Supper. Here the spiritual meets the material. The natural (the bread and wine of the sacrament) is converted into the supernatural (the body and blood of Jesus) by the faith of the communicant.

Jeremiah had written about the New Covenant which God will establish: *"The time is coming, when I will make a new covenant with the house of Israel and with the house of Judah. ......This is the covenant that I will make with the house of Israel after that time, I will put my law in their minds and write it on their hearts. I will be their God, and they will be my people."* [8] The New Covenant, which God established in the blood of Jesus Christ, is written on our hearts and not on stone tablets, as it was with the earlier Law. The word of God has been internalized i.e. in the hearts and minds of the believers. John in the gospel writes that, *"The Word became flesh."* [9] And Jesus sets in the new covenant at the Last Supper, by asking his disciples to eat his body (the bread) and drink his blood (the wine). Do you see the connection sewn together in these truths?

So the next time you go for the Holy Communion, do ponder in your heart, when taking the bread and wine of the sacrament, that what you are taking is the body and blood of the Lord Jesus Christ, which he gave for the forgiveness of our sins; and that by this act of consumption, you are acknowledging the New Covenant that he established by his death, and under which you are. Having done this, you will find yourself in a union with Christ; wherein you will experience the Incarnation and Christ will experience your earthly life.

*"I am the living bread that came down from heaven. If anyone eats of this bread, he will live for ever."* [10]

1. *Luke 22:19*
2. *Combining Matthew 26:26 and Luke 22:19*
3. *Matthew 26:27-28*
4. *1 Corinthians 11:26*
5. *John 20:29.*
6. *John 6:35, 6:48*
7. *John 6:53-58*
8. *Jeremiah 31:31-33*
9. *John 1:14*
10. *John 6:51*

# Chapter ~ 22

# ABUNDANT LIFE: LIFE TO THE FULL

*"I have come that they may have life, and have it to the full."* [1]

This is one of the promises held out by Jesus to all those who come to him. To all who will follow him. The promise of a fulfilling life; of life lived abundantly; of life which is overflowing; of life which is satisfying and complete; of life which is special, extraordinary and different. Different from the drudgery, the emptiness, the monotony, the superficiality, and even in some cases the excesses of the life, which this world has to offer. The promise has to be there, of a life or *a way of life*, which is fundamentally, qualitatively, and substantially different from the worldly options that are there, in order for us to be attracted to the call of Jesus. St. Irenaeus has said, *"The glory of God is a fully alive human being."* Jesus in his promise of abundant life wishes to make us exactly that.

This promise from Jesus comes in the passage where he is referring to himself as the Good Shepherd. And we are the sheep. So if we follow the good shepherd he will lead us to the pastures where we will enjoy this abundant life. He also refers to himself as the only true Gate through which the sheep must enter in order to come to the pasture of abundance. I quote here that wonderful and soothing psalm: *"The Lord is my shepherd, I shall not be in want. He makes me lie down in green pastures, he leads me besides quiet waters, he restores my soul ......."* [2] What David wrote of the LORD in this psalm, a thousand years earlier; Jesus later explained in detail the shepherding trait of God, and the life to which He leads his sheep. *Jehovah Rohe!*

So what is this life Jesus was referring to when he said: *"I have come that they may have life."* He appeared to be stating one of the reasons of his coming into this world. To give us the *real* thing. That all our other experiences are shallow and incomplete compared to the life Jesus has to give us. Like the water which he gives is different and like the bread that he gives is different, this life which he promises is also different. It is far superior, and nothing that the world can give will come anywhere near it. And this life is durable and permanent. It will not be changing but will be for ours for eternity. It shall be *eternal* life but it will start here and now on earth. We get to have a taste of heaven on earth. *We will be given a bit of heaven, to go to heaven in.* And in fact this is very much needed by the disciple. Otherwise the struggles, the challenges, the trials, and the battles of a Christian life can be overwhelming. The promise to the disciple is not just of the heavenly life to come, but also of the taste of the same, to carry him through this earthly life. It is not a milestone waiting for us in future, but the wings which will carry us to our future life in heaven.

But some people tend to take this promise wrongly. For them, Jesus is offering his disciples material abundance and prosperity in this life. And some do follow Jesus with this intent and expectation. They will be disappointed for that is not what Jesus meant. His *'abundant'* life is not the same as what is defined by the standards and the value system of this world. His offer is of a *spiritual life* of abundance, which will begin here on earth and last for eternity. So if you are following Jesus with the purpose of an *abundant worldly life*, you are in for a big shock.

Did Jesus mean what he said? About giving us this life to the full, life which will be overflowing?

Then how does one understand his seemingly conflicting words: *"In this world you will have trouble"* [3]; warning the disciples what to expect going forward. And elsewhere he gives details of what trouble they would face: *"Then you will be handed over to be persecuted and put to death, and you will be hated by all nations because of me."* [4] How is the abundant life congruous, or even possible to have, with such troubles in one's life: rejection and hostility of the world, beatings and other persecutions, and even threats of death? If you look at the lives of the apostles and other disciples, they did indeed face all these hardships in their lives and many of them even received martyrdom. And this has been true with all the saints of Christ. Their lives have not been easy but instead have been filled with tension, strife, and trials of all kinds. The church has no saint of comfort that the world knows of.

Even the prophets and other biblical figures, whom God chose for His purpose, had lives full of trouble and hardship. Their lives from the time of their calling changed; changed for the worse from the worldly point of view. Abraham was asked to leave his father's household and make a journey to a distant land; where soon after his arrival he encountered a severe famine. Moses had to cope with the scoffs and threats of Pharaoh and the taunts and rebellion of his own people, while he got on with the job of delivering Israel from Egypt and leading them to the Promised Land. David, after he was anointed king of Israel, had to hide in the caves in the Judean desert for many years, as Saul, the reigning king, sought his blood. Jeremiah lived in the constant danger of being killed by the Jews for making prophecies that they were not pleased to hear because they spoke of the desolation of the land. Elijah fled from the wrath of Jezebel, after he had the prophets of Baal slaughtered, and was much distressed over his troubles. Hosea faced the shame of his community for taking a wife who slept around with other men (not the marital bliss that he had hoped for), just so that the LORD could make a point to His people through this marriage.

And a few examples from the New Testament: John the Baptist lived a harsh life in the desert, eating locusts and wild honey, and wearing clothes made of camel hair, and he was even considered to have a demon by the Pharisees and the religious leaders. Paul gives us a vivid account of the hardships and dangers that he faced on account of Christ, and on top of that carried a thorn in his flesh, which was not removed despite his pleadings to the Lord. Stephen gave a powerful testimony for Jesus before the Sanhedrin, but received the same judgment as his Master; being stoned to death to become the first Christian martyr. And I am sure the other disciples would have their own list of trials and woes that they endured. *Hardly the abundant life which had been promised?* Andrew Greeley writes, *"If one wishes to eliminate uncertainty, tension, confusion, and disorder from one's life, then there is no point in getting mixed up either with Yahweh or with Jesus of Nazareth."* I am certain, this is not what many churches and evangelists would like to preach.

But ask these giants of faith, whose names are given above and also others who suffered similarly, whether they would like to exchange their lives for something else. I am sure the answer from each one of them would be an emphatic *NO*. They were living with and for God. They were in a different zone where the tribulations and worries of this world were of no consequence to them. The reason they could stoically face all the suffering that they went through was *because of the abundant life they had,* that had been given to them by God. This abundant life was both their solace against the troubles that they faced in this world, as also their hope of the life to come. When Jesus said, *"In this world you will have trouble,"* he added to it, *"But take heart! I have overcome the world."* [5] This is the key. Because Jesus has overcome the world (something accomplished; in the past tense) we his disciples can also overcome the world. And how? By having the abundant life that Jesus gives to us. That life is impregnable to the pressures from without. This is the quality and characteristic of this life; that despite all the storms around us, our lives are unshakeable. We are moored on the rock called Christ.

The life, the abundant life, which Jesus gives us, *is his own life!* That is the secret of living. *To live the life that Jesus lived on earth.* And he invites us to take hold of the life which *is truly life.* This is what he meant when he said: *"I am the way and the truth and the life."* [6] He is the model. He is the pattern for our abundant life. Was he materially rich? No. Was he powerful (from worldly point of view)? No. Did he belong to an influential family? No. Did he hold any position of status? No. But he had abundant life and it is the same life that he offers to us. *Abundant life is Christ living in us.* And we his disciples can live the life Christ once lived on earth. That is we can have the same experience, the same taste of life, that Christ had, and *this is what abundant life is.* Even in this fallen world and in a body which is prone to sin, Christ makes it possible for us to have the quality of life which is eternal. But for that we need to take hold of it. We need to walk behind the Shepherd. We need to walk through the Gate which is Christ.

To a question from Jesus whether they (the Twelve) also wanted to leave him (like some of the disciples had), Simon Peter answered: *"Lord, to whom shall we go? You have the words of eternal life."* [7]

Jesus not only has the words of eternal life, but he also gives us this eternal life - here and now on earth.

1. *John 10:10*
2. *Psalm 23*
3. *John 16:33*
4. *Matthew 24:9*
5. *John 16:33*
6. *John 14:6*
7. *John 6:68*

# Chapter ~ 23

# BORN AGAIN:
# THE NEW CREATION

*"You must be born again."* [1]

The man sitting in front of Jesus was an old, venerated leader of Israel. A member of the Jewish ruling council and a Pharisee by sect, he had come in the cloak of the night to have a discussion with Jesus. He could not be seen during the daytime, and in a public place, interacting with *this* rabbi. Jesus had not yet been 'recognized' by the religious council as one of them. So any open liaison with him was not advisable; at least at this stage.

But Nicodemus was intrigued by this teacher from Galilee, and curiosity had brought him to Jesus, despite the risks involved. He could see that Jesus was fast becoming the crowd's favorite religious leader. People were drawn by magnet to his preaching, which sometimes though bordered on the radical. His teaching was definitely different and in some ways even revolutionary. His message was new, though there appeared to be a ring of the old in it. He was not scrapping the

Law of Moses; he had made it clear, but instead appeared to be giving it a new meaning, a new perspective (or was it actually *the real and the original* perspective which they, the Jewish leaders, had not seen?). And he was often talking of the kingdom of God. This was a new teaching. Nicodemus *had* to engage him, one to one, and learn further what he had to say of the deeper things of their faith, which only a religious leader like him (Nicodemus) would be able to comprehend. So this covert visit was well in order.

Nicodemus made some careful opening remarks, sufficient to convey to Jesus that this visitor was an admirer of his. Jesus however went straight to the point, expecting this secretive visit from Nicodemus to be a short one, and what he said must have made the old leader's jaw drop to the ground: *"I tell you the truth, no-one can see the kingdom of God unless he is born again."* [2] What Jesus was telling him was this: 'Nicodemus, the righteousness by law, which you Pharisees pride yourself of, will not be able to make you enter the kingdom of God'. But Nicodemus held on valiantly and asked: *"How can a man be born when he is old? Surely he cannot enter a second time into his mother's womb to be born!"* [3] Jesus brushed aside his protestation. 'You got it wrong Nicodemus but at least my statement got you thinking. Now you are ready to hear me explain one of the deep but essential tenets of the new deal that I am bringing in'.

*"I tell you the truth, no-one can enter the kingdom of God unless he is born of water and the Spirit. Flesh gives birth to flesh, but the Spirit gives birth to spirit."* [4] This is it! The new birth Jesus was talking of was a spiritual and not a physical birth. 'You don't have to enter your mother's womb to be born again. Second time round you need to be born of the Spirit. Does that explain, Nicodemus'?

The old leader persisted in his objections and received a mild rebuke from Jesus. Jesus then proceeded to explain to him further on spiritual matters, and at the end of the session Nicodemus must have left a satisfied man, even though dazed by some of the things he had heard from Jesus. The visit was worth it. Light was dawning on this teacher of Israel. He went away into the night, more in awe of Jesus than when he had come.

You must be born again. Simple enough! And this time of the Spirit. You need a spiritual birth to be able to enter into the kingdom of God. In his conversation with Nicodemus, Jesus laid out one of the most mystifying secrets of the Christian faith. Born again! New birth! New creation! All sufficient to confound anyone, as Nicodemus was. But this is one of the unshakeable truths of our faith. And it has the air of non-negotiability to it. God cannot do his work in us without this new birth taking place first. He cannot make us Christlike without us being born again. God has accepted us as we are because He loves us. But He loves us too much to let us remain as we are. But He will start His work in us only once we are born of the Spirit. No new birth, no new creation. No new creation, no new life. Period!

But for the new birth to take place the old has to die. We have to die to be born again. *"Therefore, if anyone is in Christ, he is a new creation; the old has gone, the new has come!"* [5] This is the basic truth. The old self has to disappear for the new self to appear. But at the same time our new birth is *a process.* Just as our dying is continuous, our birth also stretches. The new self keeps forming. As the old decreases (dies) in us the new increases (takes birth) in us.

But while our new birth may continue even unto the end of our lives, it has a distinct starting point. A cut off point when the old starts dying and the new starts appearing. *And that is our baptism.* Our spiritual baptism – the day, the moment, when we accept Jesus as our Lord and Saviour, and the Holy Spirit enters in us, and gives us the new birth. This may or may not coincide with our public baptism, where we confess our faith in Jesus before the whole world. Paul writes in Romans, *"Or don't you know that all of us who were baptized into Christ Jesus were baptized into his death? We were therefore buried with him through baptism into death in order that, just as Christ was raised from the dead through the glory of the Father, we too may live a new life."* [6] And in Colossians, *"Having been buried with him in baptism and raised with him through your faith in the power of God, who raised him from the dead."* [7]

What an excellent portrayal is seen in the ritual of baptism, of what happens spiritually in a believer. The believer when he submerges into the water, is symbolically dying with Jesus and being buried with him.

When he emerges out of the water he is being raised into a new life, as Christ was raised from the dead. He is a new man now. The old was left behind in the water. He is born again!

Born again into a life with Christ. Christ will live through us. Paul explains, *"I have been crucified with Christ and I no longer live, but Christ lives in me."* [8] The new man is Christ living in us. The new man is no longer under the law but under grace. The New Covenant which Jesus put in place is applied to him. And when God sees the new creation, He sees Christ, as Paul says, *"For all of you who were baptized into Christ have clothed yourself with Christ"* [9] and *"For you died, and your life is now hidden with Christ in God."* [10] We are cloaked with the righteousness of Christ. When God sees us, He does not see us, but Christ. And thus there is no condemnation for the new man. He is under grace.

As a new man, everything is different: our lives, our perspectives, our attitudes, our behavior, and even our thinking undergo a change. *"We have the mind of Christ,"* [11] as the new creation and everything is filtered through the prism of what would the Lord do, think, act or react in a situation. We are admonished, to consciously and willfully, *"To put off your old self, which is being corrupted by its deceitful desires; to be made new in the attitude of your minds; and to put on the new self, created to be like God in true righteousness and holiness."* [12]

As a new creation, we are the new 'specie' which flows from the Second Adam, Jesus Christ. We have been injected with the DNA of Christ (the genetic code of God), as one writer puts it. We now have the imperishable Seed, which is Christ. Apostle Peter writes, *"For you have been born again, not of perishable seed, but of imperishable...."* [13] As his brothers and sisters we are one with Christ and members of God's family. And therefore now:

*"None of us lives to himself alone and none of us dies to himself alone. If we live, we live to the Lord; and if we die, we die to the Lord. So, whether we live or die, we belong to the Lord."* [14]

1.  *John 3:7*
2.  *John 3:3*
3.  *John 3:4*
4.  *John 3:5-6*
5.  *2 Corinthians 5:17*
6.  *Romans 6:3-4*
7.  *Colossians 2:12*
8.  *Galatians 2:20*
9.  *Galatians 3:27*
10. *Colossians 3:3*
11. *1 Corinthians 2:16*
12. *Ephesians 4:22-24.*
13. *1 Peter 1:23*
14. *Romans 14:7-8*

# Chapter ~ 24

# CHRIST THE SERVANT: THE VIRTUE OF HUMILITY

*"The Son of Man did not come to be served, but to serve."* [1]

Jesus Christ is Lord and God. But Jesus came *as a servant* when he came to earth. *"Here is my servant, whom I uphold, my chosen one in whom I delight."* [2] When he comes the second time, he will come as the Lord of all, *for that is who he is.* Before we are to experience Christ as the Lord, we need to experience Christ as the servant. Let us do that.

We once again turn to the Passover meal, the Last Supper which our Lord had with his disciples, the evening before his death on the cross. At the very initial stages of the meal, Jesus does an unusual thing. I am convinced that he had not done this before, for it took the disciples by surprise. They saw their Lord get up from the supper table, take off his outer garments, and wrap a towel around his waist. He then proceeded to wash his disciples' feet, with the water he had poured in a basin, and then dried them with the towel he had wrapped around his waist. Peter being Peter, of course had to react differently. He first protested vehemently – how could the Master be doing such a thing? Washing their feet? But when he saw that Jesus was determined to carry out the act, he asked for the full treatment; he asked him not to stop at just his feet but also to wash his hands and head. Typical Peter!

The disciples did not understand why Jesus did what he did. They must have been confused and mystified as to what was the meaning of this act; but having been with Jesus for about three years now, they must have been used to such strange and baffling acts of their Master. He would have a reason for it, as he had for everything that he said or did. And Jesus himself said, when persuading Peter to let him do to him what he had done to other disciples, that: *"You do not realise now what I am doing, but later you will understand."* [3]

Why did Jesus wash his disciples' feet? What point was he conveying to them (and to us) by this act? Why did he do this lowly act which is really the job of a servant - to wrap a towel around the waist and wash the feet of his master and guests when they come from outside? Why was this so important that it had to be done on the night before he was to die (Jesus knew this but his disciples didn't), along with the many important things that he would be telling his disciples in the discourse over the meal and through the evening? What was so important a message that it could not be conveyed just verbally, but had to be dramatized, so as to leave a lasting impression?

Jesus proceeded to explain his actions, when he sat down at the table again, having completed washing their feet and putting back his clothes: *"Do you understand what I have done for you? You call me 'Teacher' and 'Lord', and rightly so, for that is what I am. Now that I, your Lord and Teacher, have washed your feet, you also should wash one another's feet. I have set you an example that you should do as I have done for you."* [4] My dear disciples, my friends and brothers you have to be servants of each other. You should serve one another in love. What you have seen your Master do, you should be ready and willing to do, for, *"I tell you the truth, no servant is greater than his master, nor is a messenger greater than the one who sent him. Now that you know these things, you will be blessed if you do them."* [5]

The message had been given and it was loud and clear. Jesus was laying down the basic principle of functioning in the kingdom of God. And this principle is diagrammatically opposite of how the world operates: *"You know that the rulers of the Gentiles lord it over them, and their high officials exercise authority over them. Not so with you. Instead, whoever wants to become great among you must be your servant, and whoever wants to be first must be your slave."* [6] The rules of the world are turned upside down in the kingdom of God. Here, in this world that we live in, you are known by how many servants you have, how many people are under your control and command. No one wishes to be a servant. It is considered a lowly undertaking. But if you want to be great in Jesus's kingdom, then you have to be a servant; just like he was. Not lording it over others, but serving others. *In God's kingdom the way up, is down.*

Jesus could see the trouble that loomed in the future for his group of disciples. There could likely be a tussle amongst them for the leadership position, after he was gone. Following the pattern of this world, there could be a succession struggle that is often to be seen in kingdoms, in governments, in corporations, or even in families. He could see that the disciples had already thought of the positions they would be holding in his kingdom. The mother of James and John had come to him (likely at their behest), seeking the seats adjacent to his, in his kingdom. Already Peter was behaving as the leader of the group (next to Jesus), and considered himself as his chief disciple and right hand man. Their fascination for positions of power and status was worldly. In his absence it would lead to power plays and factionalism, and eventually to the breakup of the group. And that would be the end of his mission, which they, the disciples, were to be given to carry forward.

It had to be strongly impressed upon the disciples that the rules of the game were different in the kingdom of God. Here the least is the greatest. *"The greatest among you will be your servant."* [7] Here you don't lord over others, but you serve. And you serve Christlike. You serve willingly, because you know that your Lord came as a servant; he came to serve. And therefore so must you. This is the central part of being his disciple. This is what it means to be the disciple of Jesus – to serve. So the 'wrapping of towel and washing of feet' act became of dire importance to press this teaching home. Jesus knew that time was running out for him; therefore the message had to be given in a dramatic way so as to leave a lasting impression. Something that the disciples would never forget and would be an example for them to emulate. When Jesus was performing this act, what was his posture? He must be stooping and possibly be even on his knees. *The Master kneeling!* That sight would be forever imprinted in the minds of the disciples.

What it means to be a servant? We will get our cue from this passage from the letter to the Philippians, where Paul gives a wonderful description of the Incarnation: *"Your attitude should be the same as that of Christ Jesus: Who, being in very nature God, did not consider equality with God something to be grasped, but made himself nothing, taking the very nature of a servant, being made in human likeness. And being found in appearance as a man, he humbled himself and became obedient to death – even death on a cross!"* [8] It is the *attitude!* The attitude should be that of a servant. No matter what position or station you occupy in life – all won't be servants by profession – it is the attitude which makes you like a servant. And if you have that attitude; no work is too low for you, no degree of stooping will break your back, and no amount of kneeling will graze your knees. You will have the desire to serve without reservations.

Christ was not a servant in the literal sense. He came to serve and therefore he took the nature of a servant. And because of that he could leave his heavenly throne and be counted as one of his creations - man. In fact the principle here is that those who are secure, those who are well aware of their own status and position and therefore do not need to flash it around, are the ones who can be true servants. They don't have a point to prove. They know their worth. John writes, just before Jesus got down to the act of washing his disciples' feet, that, *"Jesus knew that the Father had put all things under his power, and that he had come from God and was returning to God."* [9] Jesus knew his greatness and therefore proceeded to be the least.

Being a servant is not a part time job that we can do for some time and switch off for the rest of the time. It is also not a mask that we wear, where we pretend to be servant-like in our behavior. Nor is it done to impress others. The focus is on the attitude. The attitude should become servant-like. We should take on the 'nature' of a servant just as Christ did. And what is it about being a servant that is so important, that Christ wanted to instill it deep in his disciples? Being a servant is a humbling experience. Nothing can better teach us humility than being a servant. *And humility is a must to become Christlike.* It is a trait required in our character for the Spirit to produce his fruit in us. God cannot work in a heart which is not humble. For only a humble heart is a teachable heart. Humility is required to enter the kingdom of God. *"I tell you the truth, anyone who will not receive the kingdom of God like a little child will never enter it,"* [10] Jesus had said holding a child as an example of the innocence and humbleness that he seeks in his disciples. And you can best learn humility by being a servant.

Humility is a virtue which God searches intently in man. There are many verses in the Bible, which stress the need for a humble heart, and how important it is to God. God detests a proud heart and delights in a humble heart. The LORD says, *"I live in a high and holy place, but also with him who is contrite and lowly in spirit."* [11] God can take His residence only in a heart which is humble. For a humble heart is the heart which welcomes Him, which opens its door for His grace to enter, where His word can take root and produce its fruit, where the Holy Spirit can make his temple.

But being humble does not mean that you have to mop the floor (figuratively). It does not mean that you have to be a whip dog. There is a difference between humility and humiliation. Humility is looking at oneself through God's eyes. Then you would get the right perspective of yourself. It is not remaining bowed down but standing as tall as you can, and realizing that you still fall short of *that figure* on the Cross. It is not thinking any less of yourself, but thinking of yourself less. It is, though not being a servant, but having the attitude of a servant, and be willing to do (joyfully) what a servant would do. It is occupying the lowest seat, so that you may well be invited to take the best seat in the house; and if you are not asked, then so be it.

Humility is when a chord strikes in your heart every time you hear these words of the Lord: *"Blessed are the meek, for they will inherit the earth."* [12] These words, strange though they may appear, make perfect sense to you. Humility is when you realize that the sacrifice that God desires has no monetary value but is still precious, for it is the sacrifice of, *'a broken and contrite heart'.* [13] Humility is when you finally accept that you cannot be a servant of God unless you first become a servant of men. That in being the latter you become the former. Humility is when you finally stumble upon that the key to success and happiness in God's kingdom is found in these words of Jesus: *"For whoever exalts himself will be humbled, and whoever humbles himself will be exalted."* [14]

Ever thought of what if God was not humble in the manner He has dealt with and continues to deal with mankind? Well then many things would have been completely different and we can begin listing those. But one thing we can be sure of; there would have been no Incarnation then. *For the very act of God coming in flesh and blood to this world, was in itself an act of humility.*

Or let us suppose that if Jesus was not humble. Would he have been acceptable to us then? Would he have been approachable then to the masses who followed him everywhere? That quality in him which attracted people from all walks of life (and still does), would have been missing. That Jesus who melts our hearts would not have been there. We would have had a different Jesus and not the one who called, to one and all: *"Take my yoke upon you and learn from me, for I am gentle and humble in heart, and you will find rest for your souls."* [15]

So if we humans would not like a God who is proud and haughty, and we also do not like the proud and arrogant amongst us; then any wonder that God does not like proud men but seeks the humble and contrite?

Do you wish to be *'gentle and humble in heart'*, like the Lord was? And do you wish to be a servant, like the Lord was?

Then rejoice the kingdom of God is near you!

1. *Matthew 20:28*
2. *Isaiah 42:1*
3. *John 13:7*
4. *John 13:12-15*
5. *John 13:16-17*
6. *Matthew 20:25-27.*
7. *Matthew 23:11*
8. *Philippians 2:5-8*
9. *John 13:3*
10. *Mark 10:15*
11. *Isaiah 57:15*
12. *Matthew 5:5*
13. *Psalm 51:17*
14. *Matthew 23:12*
15. *Matthew 11:29*

# Chapter ~ 25

# THE EMPOWERING:
# THE PENTECOSTAL EXPERIENCE

*"And I will ask the Father, and he will give you another Counsellor to be with you for ever – the Spirit of truth."* [1]

In the famous Upper Room discourse, Jesus' last discourse and the lengthiest one (that is recorded), which he gave to his disciples the night before his death, he covered many vital issues. These were those which Jesus considered important for the disciples, in preparing them for life without him, which was soon to be a reality. One of the subjects he covered was that of the Holy Spirit. It was important at that time that the Third Person of the Triune Godhead be made known to the disciples; who he is, what is his nature, what is his role, and what he will do when he comes.

In the above verse our attention is drawn to the words, *'another'* and *'for ever'*. Jesus mentioned that on his request the Father will give *another* Counsellor to them. The first one was Jesus himself. But he was going. So the disciples would need another Counsellor to fill in for

Jesus. And this Counsellor will be with them *forever,* unlike Jesus who was to be for a limited period of time. Jesus being God incarnate as a man, would have at best had the life span of a human being i.e. if his life had not been cut short by his sacrificial death at age thirty three. The Counsellor to be sent in his place, being a spirit, would not be confined to a human body and would thus be free from the constraints of time and space. He will be with the disciples forever, and not only with the disciples living at the time of Jesus but those to come after. Jesus was heralding the *age of the Holy Spirit,* which continues even today and is the age in which we live.

"*I will not leave you as orphans,*" [2] Jesus told his disciples. The imparting of the Holy Spirit was not an afterthought or incidental. It was an important part of the original plan. Jesus was comforting his disciples knowingly. He was assuring them that whether he was with them or not, they will always have a Comforter and Counsellor, the Holy Spirit. The difference will be that instead of God being *with* them, as it was now, they will have God *in* them in the future.

And what will the Counsellor do? "*But the Counsellor, the Holy Spirit, whom the Father will send in my name, will teach you all things and will remind you of everything I have said to you.*" [3] That is an important ministry of the Spirit. Jesus must have surely said many things to his disciples and they certainly were not taking any written notes of his sermons and sayings. The Spirit would keep the Word alive in their hearts and in their minds. And further, "*When the Counsellor comes, whom I will send to you from the Father, the Spirit of truth who goes out from the Father, he will testify about me.*" [4] The Holy Spirit will confirm to the disciples all they have known from and about Jesus; and through the disciples, the Spirit will testify to the world about Jesus.

There was a lot Jesus had to still tell his disciples, a lot that had yet to be revealed. But he knew that it was not possible for him to do so entirely during his time with them (besides the disciples would have not been able to absorb so much) and thus all further revelations were turned over to the Spirit, which in fact continue even to this date. "*I have much more to say to you, more than you can now bear. But when he, the Spirit of truth, comes, he will guide you into all truth.*" [5] Jesus appeared to be saying here that what I have told you (the disciples) is sufficient for now, sufficient to take you through. The rest (and there is much more of the truth that is yet to be revealed), I will leave it to the Holy Spirit to impart to you gradually.

Thus the disciples received sufficient information from the Lord about the Holy Spirit, who they were to expect when Jesus had left. I am not sure how much attention or importance, the disciples were giving to all they were hearing about the Holy Spirit from Jesus. Did they from that moment on, or from the time of the death of Jesus, or from the time of his ascension, started willfully and eagerly expecting the Holy Spirit, the Counsellor promised by Jesus? Or were they still expecting (and hoping) that Jesus would return; rather than be expecting the Spirit? Jesus had to tell them clearly that, *"Do not leave Jerusalem, but wait for the gift my Father promised, which you have heard me speak about. For John baptized with water, but in a few days you will be baptized with the Holy Spirit."* [6] But still the disciples' minds were on immediate things, the things of the world, and they even inquired with Jesus whether he at this time was going to restore the kingdom to Israel. Jesus brushed aside their query and again directed their attention to the coming of the Spirit: *"But you will receive power when the Holy Spirit comes on you; and you will be my witnesses in Jerusalem, and in all Judea, and Samaria, and to the ends of the earth."* [7] He was explaining to them what they were to do and also the geographical reach of their mission. The power that would be needed by them to do this work, that empowering will come from the Holy Spirit.

So whether they were consciously waiting for the promised Holy Spirit or not; when the Spirit finally came, the manner of his appearing must have shaken them to the bones. It was the day of Pentecost, the Harvest Festival celebrated by the Jews, when the Holy Spirit came upon them and took his residence in them. That day they were baptized with the Holy Spirit, as Jesus had told them they would. That day the Church was formed; the Body of Christ on earth came into being.

What was the effect on the disciples when they were filled with the Holy Spirit? They became changed persons. They were now empowered. The power of the Spirit was in them. The same power which was in Jesus was now in the disciples. *"You will do even greater things than these,"* [8] (than what I have done) Jesus had declared to his awe struck disciples, because he knew they would be given the same Spirit one day. The mice would become tigers! And their roar would be heard in all corners of the world. Those who hid in fear of the Jewish authorities would now openly and fearlessly challenge their authority.

The Pentecost – the coming of the Holy Spirit - is an important event in the history and formation of the Church. The *'Great Commission'*[9] had been given to the disciples by the Lord. This day the power was being supplied to them to fulfill that task. *They needed the power of the Spirit to accomplish the mission of Christ in the world.* The Resurrection had convinced them of who Jesus was; the Messiah, the Son of God. They now believed that all that he had claimed about himself was indeed the truth. The Pentecostal experience started them on the mission. The Resurrection testified to them of the Word; the Pentecostal experience unleashed them to testify about the Word to all people. The Resurrection was in a sense more for Jesus, to validate the truth about him. The Pentecostal experience was more for the disciples, to set them out on the mission they had been entrusted by the Lord. The Resurrection *convinced* them; the Pentecostal experience *fired* them up.

*"But I tell you the truth: It is for your good that I am going away. Unless I go away, the Counsellor will not come to you; but if I go, I will send him to you."* [10] The Holy Spirit, in a sense, was waiting for Jesus to leave the world before he came to the disciples. The Spirit was in Jesus and unless Jesus went from this world i.e. left his earthly body, the Spirit would not be 'released'. That is what Jesus meant when he said that his leaving was in a way good for the disciples, because now they would be able to receive the Holy Spirit. No work would have been possible by the disciples unless they had the Holy Spirit. In fact this is true even of now; no Christian enterprise or work is possible without the power of the Spirit. If the Holy Spirit is not present in the worker(s), then that work is just a worldly enterprise and not contributing to the kingdom of God.

With the Holy Spirit coming and residing in the disciples, and the same act will be repeated with the disciples to come thereafter, a very profound thing had taken place. The Incarnation, in a way, had been expanded. God's dwelling was now not in one body (in Jesus), but from the time of *that* Pentecost day, in many persons. The Incarnation had spread and God's work here on earth would now be done by His Body, the Church. *"Christ was himself but one and lived and died but once; but the Holy Ghost makes of every Christian another Christ, an After Christ; lives a million lives in every age,"* wrote George Manley Hopkins. And this is the mystery. *Christ in us!* Christ living through the ages, in and through the lives of all those who would believe and follow him; all those who would be called by His name. Christ has thus lived in all centuries and in all ages, even after his time on earth as Jesus.

Jesus Christ had come to earth at a specific time and place in history. He did much during his short life, but it could never be enough for the purpose that he had come to earth; to establish the kingdom of God. He knew that he would lay the foundations of the kingdom during his life time and also set its wheels in motion, but it would take much longer before it was fully established. So he had to prepare people (his disciples) who would carry forward his mission, and not only continue with it, but also spread it to every part of the globe and for the ages to come; till the appointed time of wrapping up all things would arrive.

Thus it was necessary that one day he would hand over his mission to the Church. For this reason Jesus had to die and return to the Father, so that the Church could take his place. *"I tell you the truth, unless a grain of wheat falls to the ground and dies, it remains only a single seed. But if it dies, it produces many seeds."* [11] Jesus had pointed out clearly, in this, that the kingdom of God would need the workers to be multiplied. But for the Church to carry forward the mission, it had to receive the same power that resided in Jesus during his time on earth, the power of the Holy Spirit. And that is what happened on the day of Pentecost when the Holy Spirit was poured into the disciples.

Whatever the Church does on earth is on behalf of God. It is God's work. It therefore becomes binding upon God. And here lies the risk. For all the suffering, the wars, the oppression, the injustices that we see in this world; if we are bound to ask where God is in all these, then basically we should be directing this question to the Church. Where is the Church in all these situations and causes? Is it raising its voice? Is it supporting the victims or is it silent? And on the positive side, the relief work during the times of natural and man-made disasters, the work for the emancipation of the needy and the underprivileged, bringing the word of God to those who are unreached, healing those who suffer in body or spirit, and other such acts of compassion; all these are reflection of Christ working in our midst. And we the foot soldiers, who are entrusted by God to be his representatives on earth, are taking part as co-workers in the Restoration of the world; the work which God has been doing ever since the Fall took place.

The same Holy Spirit comes and resides in every person who put his faith in Jesus and calls him Lord and Saviour. Every believer is baptized with the Holy Spirit and gets the same 'Pentecostal' experience as the first disciples did, though it may not be as dramatic. The Incarnation keeps spreading. God finds new bodies to make his dwelling in. The Spirit keeps working in wondrous and diverse ways. We can talk of the gifts of the Holy Spirit, and the fruit of the Holy Spirit, and the other wonderful changes that the Spirit brings in us, as we remain in a relationship with God. But it is not the intent of this article to cover all that. Its main purpose was to show at what point the Spirit started his work in the disciples of Jesus; at what point the Church of Christ began on earth.

The Spirit is still at work. The age of the Third Person of the Godhead continues. And for us who have believed and thus received the Holy Spirit, we have these reassuring words of St. Paul:

*"Having believed you were marked in him with a seal, the promised Holy Spirit, who is a deposit guaranteeing our inheritance until the redemption of those who are God's possession – to the praise of his glory."* [12]

1. *John 14:16-17*
2. *John 14:18*
3. *John 14:26*
4. *John 15:26*
5. *John 16:12 -13*
6. *Acts 1:4-5*
7. *Acts 1:8*
8. *John 14:12(modified)*
9. *Matthew 28:19-20*
10. *John 16:7*
11. *John 12:24*
12. *Ephesians 1:13-14*

# SECTION III

# THE DISCIPLE

*"We are therefore Christ's ambassadors,
as though God were making his appeal through us."*
*2 Corinthians 5:20*

# Chapter ~ 26

# THE COST OF DISCIPLESHIP: IN DYING WE LIVE

*"If anyone would come after me, he must deny himself and take up his cross and follow me."* [1]

**W**e have seen that the way to take hold of the abundant life, which Jesus promises to all his disciples, is to follow the Good Shepherd and to go through the Gate that is Jesus. That is the only way - *The Way* - to receive the abundant life, which Jesus himself had and which he gives to us. But what does following Jesus involve? What is the cost of being his disciple?

The above verse gives it straight. Jesus created no smoke screens. He laid out no mirages. He spelt it out in clear, unequivocal, and even frightening terms, what it meant to follow him, what it meant to be his disciple. So that no one can say that he was misled, that he was deceived, and that this was only in the fine print. As Philip Yancey puts it, the above is the least manipulative invitation *ever given*. 'All are warned beforehand. I am not putting wool in anyone's eyes. I am not leading anyone down the garden path. Come in with your eyes wide open'.

*"For whoever wants to save his life will lose it, but whoever loses his life for me will find it."* [2] Jesus spells it out plainly that the way to abundant life is by losing your life - the life that you now have. 'How can you receive the life I have to give you, unless you let go (die) of the life you are leading and holding on to?' Like so many other things Jesus said, which were shocking and puzzling to hear, this too must have been hard on the ears of the people. These words shock and puzzle many even now. But in fact this one verse, this saying of Jesus, holds the secret to Christian life. It has to be the main credo of those who wish to follow the Lord. And whoever has understood, accepted, and lived this teaching of Jesus, has really known and followed the Lord. It all boils down to this – *in dying we live.* The teachings of Jesus can be reduced to this one verse. Nothing less and nothing more. Accept it and you have understood his life and his message.

There is more: *"If anyone comes to me and does not hate his father and mother, his wife and children, his brothers and sisters – yes, even his own life – he cannot be my disciple. And anyone who does not carry his cross and follow me cannot be my disciple."* [3] I would understand Jesus to have meant by this, that anyone who puts some else (even that be his close family members; his near and dear ones) *before* him, is not fit to be his disciple or cannot be an effective disciple. For somewhere he would be compromised. I can guess that many would have turned away when they heard this call, considering it to be too heavy a cost to bear. But Jesus had said something even more startling here. *You have to even hate your life (i.e. your existing life).* For unless you hate it, you will not let go of it, and then how will you obtain the abundant life that Jesus has to give you? You will be following Jesus and looking back to the life you have left behind, that you once had. That way you will end up with having nothing. You have to deny yourself the life you have been used to and all that which makes you up; the lifestyle, the habits, the temperament, your nature. Unless you do that, God cannot reconstruct a new life in you. A life which is the life of Jesus in you.

*"Christianity has always insisted that the cross we bear precedes the crown we wear. To be a Christian one must take up his cross with all its difficulties and agonizing and tension packed content and carry it until that very cross leaves its mark upon us and redeems us to that more excellent way which*

*comes only through suffering,"* wrote Martin Luther King. And William Penn puts it this way: *"No pain no palm, no thorns no throne, no gall no glory, no cross no crown."* Both spell out clearly that the cross is important and even requisite in the disciple's life. For each disciple the cross is different. Each has his or her *own* cross to carry that is unique.

The cross on our back can be of financial constraints or even impoverishment; persecution or discrimination at home or at workplace or in the community; threats, beatings, fear of death, from the zealots of other faith; a series of failures or missed opportunities in life leading to low self-esteem and depression; loneliness, rejection or non-recognition of one's work, talent, or even intentions; fall from a position of strength resulting in loss of status or wealth or both; a terminal or prolonged sickness, a major disease, or a physical handicap, to self or to someone close; divorce, broken relationship, or death of a loved one; temptations of lust, of earlier addictions, of material gains. These and many such could be your cross. It could be one or more of these burdens which may comprise the cross that you have to carry for a period of time or for your entire life.

Despite the 'variety of crosses' that the believers may have to take up to follow Jesus, the one thing common for all the believers, is the yoke that is around our neck. The yoke is the same for all of us. The yoke is that of Jesus. Hear his call: *"Come to me, all you who are weary and burdened, and I will give you rest. Take my yoke upon you and learn from me, for I am gentle and humble in heart, and you will find rest for your souls. For my yoke is easy and my burden is light."* [4] The yoke of Jesus is the yoke of self denial and suffering. Interestingly all those who come to Jesus to take his yoke are those who are weary, tired, and burdened of their life in this world. They need rest, and despite the yoke of Jesus calling for denial of self and involving suffering, it is still easy to carry and its burden is light, *because Jesus is carrying the yoke along with us.*

But denying oneself is not easy. *You have to die every day.* You have to deny yourself of all that you are. You have to deny yourself of all that comes in between you and your carrying your cross. Whatever that be: relationship, career, wealth, status and all that you may consider to be your very life; you have to put to 'death'. The rich man, who came to Jesus, was asked by Jesus to forsake his riches and follow him, so that he may have eternal life. But he could not do so. He could not deny himself his riches. He could not die to his lifestyle of luxury and material abundance. Therefore he could not receive the *abundant life* which Jesus was calling him to.

So it can be with us. We believe a particular thing is so important for our life that it becomes an idol. To forsake it would mean forfeiting one's existence. We thus cling on to it ever so strongly. Actually we then end up in a state where we do not hold the idol but the idol holds us. The truth is that we would have to die to the idol(s) in our life, to have the life that Jesus would give us.

Christian life is a life of denial and not gratification. It is a life of self-sacrifice and not self-fulfillment. It is a life of service and not pleasure seeking. *It is a life of dying to self so that we may live for others.* In this we are following the footsteps of our Master. Jesus has walked this path before us and is now an example for us. He denied himself and left his heavenly riches; and died every day in living in this sinful world, in being unrecognized as God with us, in being rejected by his own nation, in being expelled by the people of his town, in being considered crazy by his own family members, in being abandoned by his disciples. I wonder how many times Jesus had to carry his cross, before he carried it to Calvary; how many times he had to die, before he gave up his breath on the Cross.

But the promise of life is there besides the suffering and 'death'. Paul writes, *"If we died with him, we will also live with him,"* [5] and further, *"We always carry around in our body the death of Jesus, so that the life of Jesus may also be revealed in our body. For we who are alive are always being given over to death for Jesus' sake, so that his life may be revealed in our mortal body,"* [6] and also, *"For just as the sufferings of Christ flow over into our lives, so also through Christ our comfort overflows."* [7] But life only comes after death; we start living only in dying; abundant life only comes after losing our present (worldly) life; comfort of Christ comes in our lives only after we have mourned.

Apostle John in his epistle writes, *"This is how we know what love is: Jesus Christ laid down his life for us. And we ought to lay down our lives for our brothers."* [8] Quite similar is what Jesus had said: *"Love each other as I have loved you. Greater love has no-one than this, that he lay down his life for his friends."* [9] Here dying does not necessarily mean physical death (though if needed then one must be prepared to accept even physical death, as Christ did for us). Death here, in these verses, also means that one denies himself, so as to live for others. That one puts the interests and concerns of others before his own. And in this is fulfilled what Jesus taught: *"For whoever wants to save his life will lose it, but whoever loses his life for me will find it."*

Dying, and dying daily, is a vital part of Christian life, because this way we experience Christ growing in us and his power increasingly working through us. *"He must increase, but I must decrease,"* [10] is how John the Baptist had put it. His increase is only possible if we decrease in ourselves. And that is by way of our daily death.

The profound truth is that we *have* to experience the sufferings of Christ. And through our individual crosses we can indeed experience the *Cross of Christ*. There is *"the fellowship of sharing in his sufferings,"*[11] as Paul puts it in his letter to the Philippians. If we do not experience that, then how will we ever know, what and how much Christ suffered, and the extent of his sacrifice for us? How will we know him at all? To know Christ is to know him crucified. As Paul said, *"we preach Christ crucified."* [12] The principle is pretty straightforward: the disciple has to go the way of the Master. When the call comes from the Master to *'follow me'*, the call is to walk behind him irrespective of the path on which he is walking. We have to keep our sights focused on the figure of Jesus walking ahead of us, rather than be diverted to the perils that the path may hold.

There is a story about St. Francis of Assisi. One day he was walking down the road and he was crying aloud as he went. On being asked by the people as to why he was crying, he replied, *"I am crying for the passion of Christ."*

Do you also cry for the passion i.e. the sufferings of Christ? If yes, then rejoice; you are dying daily.

1.  *Matthew 16:24*
2.  *Matthew 16:25*
3.  *Luke 14:26-27*
4.  *Matthew 11:28-30*
5.  *2 Timothy 2:11*
6.  *2 Corinthians 4:10-11*
7.  *2 Corinthians 1:5*
8.  *1 John 3:16.*
9.  *John 15:12-13.*
10. *John 3:30 (NKJV)*
11. *Philippians 3:10*
12. *1 Corinthians 1:23*

# Chapter ~ 27

# FORGIVENESS: GRACE ABOUNDS

*"Be kind and compassionate to one another, forgiving each other, just as in Christ God forgave you."* [1]

Peter comes up to Jesus and asks him a straightforward question: *"Lord, how many times shall I forgive my brother when he sins against me?"* [2] Before Jesus could reply, he follows up with another question by way of suggesting an answer to the first: *"Up to seven times?"* [3] Peter considers that this should please the Lord. Seven times is over doing it.

Jesus answered, *"I tell you, not seven times, but seventy-seven times."* [4] Peter's elation is short lived. The Lord's reply, as most of the times, catches him on the wrong foot. Some versions of the Bible state Jesus having said 'seventy times seven' instead of seventy seven times. That makes it 490 times! Jesus might as well have said unlimited times. *Actually he meant unlimited times.* You must forgive without keeping a count. Forgive as many times as your brother sins against you. And why so? Because there is no limit to God's forgiveness. So there has to be no limit to our forgiveness. *"Forgive as the Lord forgave you."* [5] Do we remember how many times our sins have been forgiven by God? And for the same sin which we repeatedly keep doing? We have lost count, haven't we? Do we keep the score – the number of times God forgives us? No. Then in the same measure God expects us not to keep the score when we forgive our brother. *"For with the measure you use, it will be measured to you."* [6]

But forgiveness is not easy to come by. We find it difficult to forgive. I will be the first one to admit that I struggle in giving forgiveness. I wish I could forgive more than what I do, but this is the truth. Seventy times seven or whatever number Jesus meant is far off; I sometimes do find it hard to forgive even once. But no excuse will do. God not just wants or expects us to show forgiveness, but *commands* that we forgive one another. It is not optional. It is an *absolute* in God's kingdom, of which we all, who have faith in his Son, are citizens. We have to forgive. Why?

Why God wants us to forgive? *We have to forgive so as to experience God's forgiveness.* Let me explain how it works. We have been forgiven in Christ; all our sins have been washed away. God has accepted us once for all. That is done with. But we have to *experience* God's forgiveness, more so for the sins that we keep committing, even after our accepting Christ. And how can we do that? It is by forgiving one another. In the very act of our forgiving, we experience God's forgiveness. *And we feel how God feels when He forgives us!* Amazing that God should give us this way to feel like Him. Do we want to miss that? Do we not want to take hold of God's forgiveness?

Forgiveness is no more God's problem after Calvary. His forgiveness is always there. His arms are always open. His heart is always ready to embrace us. Forgiveness has become our problem now; both in terms of receiving it from God and in terms of giving it to others. *And in the act of forgiving we experience both.* We not only receive His forgiveness but also feel how He feels when He forgives us.

Forgiveness is an act of love. It is an act of mercy. And we are called to be merciful: *"Be merciful, just as your Father is merciful,"* [7] Jesus had said this in the context of loving our enemies. Mercy is God's character trait, and our Father wants us to show the same trait. One of the blessedness spoken by the Lord is to do with mercy and forgiveness: *"Blessed are the merciful, for they will be shown mercy."* [8] The sequence is quite clear. We have to show mercy first. We have to be merciful to expect mercy from God. *"Forgive, and you will be forgiven."*[9] It shows the same sequence again. First forgive and then you will be forgiven.

Why it is that God has made his mercy, his forgiveness, conditional and subject to our first showing mercy and forgiveness? Well one simple explanation is that we cannot and should not expect from God what we ourselves can't give to others. But a deeper explanation is that God wants us to experience not only his forgiveness but also experience how He feels when He forgives us. And this is His way of making sure that we do that. The Lord's Prayer states: *"Forgive us our sins, as we have forgiven those who sin against us."* [10] And Jesus goes on to explain: *"For if you forgive men when they sin against you, your heavenly Father will also forgive you. But if you do not forgive men their sins, your Father will not forgive your sins."* [11] God is merciful and God has forgiven us; but the dynamics of laying hold of His forgiveness is laid out in these verses.

What if we don't forgive? Then there will remain a 'distance' between you and the other person. There will be a friction zone and tension between the two of you. The heart will not be at peace if there remain open wounds. And you will also not be at peace with God. The tension between you and your brother in such situations will spill over in your relationship with God. You will be restless, unless of course you have hardened your heart. And that is the reason Jesus exhorts you to be reconciled with your brother before you go to the altar, or in other words before you worship: *"Therefore, if you are offering your gift at the altar and there remember that your brother has something against you, leave your gift there in front of the altar. First go and be reconciled to your brother; then come and offer your gift."* [12] And also: *"And when you stand praying, if you hold anything against anyone, forgive him, so that your Father in heaven may forgive you your sins."* [13] The message is quite clear here; you cannot possibly have a right relationship with God without first making right the relationship with your brother.

Forgiveness breaks the chain of 'un-grace' or hatred. The world is caught in the web of settling scores, getting even, and in 'an-eye-for-an-eye' syndrome. The only thing which can break this cycle, is grace expressed in forgiveness (which is a form of love in action). As followers of Christ, we are required by God to be 'dispensers' of His grace in this world; that grace which washed away our sins and made us acceptable to Him. We are now to relay it and spread it around. If we don't do that, we break the chain, and then the question arises: Do we feel forgiven? Have we tasted God's grace?

Remember the parable of the unmerciful servant. The servant was forgiven a huge debt by his master as he was not able to pay it back. After being forgiven he goes out and encounters a fellow servant who owed him a small debt. The servant, who has been forgiven the large debt, now demands the payment of his money from the fellow servant, failing which he has him thrown into the prison until he could pay the debt. Did the servant who was forgiven a huge debt, show mercy in turn to the one who owed him a small debt? No. Having tasted grace, should his heart have not been filled (rather overflowing) with grace, to give out the same to his debtors? We of course know what the master did when he came to know of the actions of the ungrateful and unmerciful servant.

Mother Teresa once said: *"Be kind and merciful. Let no one ever come to you without coming away better and happier. Be the living expression of God's kindness."* I underline that as Christians we are called upon to dispense God's grace in this world. That is our hallmark. That is the distinguishing mark of the Church of Christ. That is how the world should see us – dispensers of God's grace in this hate filled, battle scarred, callous, and selfish world. We have received grace from above and we must spread it around. *"Freely you have received, freely give."* [14]

But as said before forgiveness is not easy to come by. We find it hard to forgive those who have hurt us or have done us wrong. But forgive we must. We are called to forgive as explained above in detail. But how do we do that? How do we go about forgiving our brothers, our friends, and even our enemies? If we hold on to the following things we may find it easier to forgive.

First of all we must remember that we will never be called upon to forgive anyone more than what God has forgiven us. *"You will never be called upon to give anyone more grace than God has already given you,"* wrote Max Lucado in his fascinating book *'In the Grip of Grace'* (A must read for all who want to explore the topic of grace in depth. Another book that I would strongly recommend is *'What's so Amazing about Grace?'* by Philip Yancey). We cannot even start comparing. It is the same equation as in the parable of the servant recounted earlier. What God has forgiven us is the huge debt of the servant in the parable. And what we are called to forgive in turn are minor or small debts in comparison. We can choose to be merciful or go the way of the servant in not showing mercy to others; when we ourselves have been forgiven much. *"The key to forgiving others is to quit focusing on what they did to you and start focusing on what God did for you,"* quoting Max Lucado again.

The second thing we must remember is that the other person – the one who has sinned against us – is also made *in the image of God.* That the image of our heavenly Father is also in him. Are we still going to be angry or be unmerciful or carry resentment, against a brother in whom we see the image of God?

And the third thing to remember is that when we forgive, we set free two persons; the one whom we forgive, and the other one is *ourselves.* We free ourselves from the prison of hatred that we find ourselves in, when we don't forgive. Being caged in hatred, we find its poison slowly spreading and eating our inside, till it has fully destroyed our spiritual lives. We have to break this circle of hatred and set free others and ourselves. Jesus broke it right there on the Cross. He cried, *"Father, forgive them, for they do not know what they are doing."* [15] He didn't carry his hurt, the wrong done to him, to the grave. He not just paid the penalty for our sins, but also forgave us (i.e. the whole mankind and not just those who were directly responsible for putting him to death) for what we did to him.

At the end let me quote from the much loved prayer of St. Francis of Assisi:

*"For it is in giving that we receive, it is in pardoning that we are pardoned, it is in dying that we are born again to eternal life."*

1. *Ephesians 4:32*
2. *Matthew 18:21*
3. *Matthew 18:21*
4. *Matthew 18:22*
5. *Colossians 3:13*
6. *Luke 6:38*
7. *Luke 6:36*
8. *Matthew 5:7*
9. *Luke 6:37*
10. *Matthew 6:12 (NLT)*
11. *Matthew 6:14-15*
12. *Matthew 5:23-24*
13. *Mark 11:25*
14. *Matthew 10:8*
15. *Luke 23:34*

# Chapter ~ 28

# "GO AND SIN NO MORE": THE BATTLE WITHIN

*"I do not understand what I do.*
*For what I want to do I do not do, but what I hate I do."* [1]

**J**esus when he had saved the woman, who had been caught for adultery, from death by stoning, asked her if anyone remained there who condemned her of her act of sin (well her sinful life). The woman replied that there was no-one. Jesus then said these words to her in parting: *"Neither do I. Go and sin no more."* [2]

These words of exhortation that the Lord gave to the woman, he also imparts to us, at our own individual turning point; our point of conversion, our point of becoming a Christian, our point of becoming his disciple. *'Go and sin no more,'* is what is expected from us. But the reality is different. In the opening verse we see the predicament of Paul, as he struggled with sin, which was ever present and which still exerted its power over his body of flesh (read chapter seven of the Book of Romans to get a full description of this intense struggle). In this we empathize with Paul. We carry on within us the same struggle, the same war with our sinful nature; that nature which veers constantly towards the desires of the flesh. Sometimes we are overwhelmed by these desires and we give in and sin.

Why do we do what we do not want to do and do not do what we want or should do? Why do we still struggle with sin even after becoming a Christian – in fact I would say the struggles start or are intensified when we accept Christ. Why is it that at some moments we are full of grace and love and at some moments we behave like a fiend? Why is it that the same lips which sing praise to God one moment, hurl curses and swear words at our 'neighbor'? Why is it knowing that a particular act may not be pleasing to God, we still end up doing it? Why is it that on some occasions we use this body, *'a temple of the Holy Spirit',*[3] in acts which are unholy? I can go on but the cold fact is, that having accepted Christ we do not transition into a state of sinless bliss. Can we at all attain a sinless state? We will look at this later.

But first let us look at the working of God's grace. We have to understand the problem of sin at two levels or in two stages. Firstly as regards the 'generic' sin of which the whole world stands condemned of: *"For all have sinned and fall short of the glory of God."* [4] It is a sweeping condemnation. All mankind has been condemned. There is no exception and not a single one born of flesh is excluded, other than of course Jesus, who was without sin in the flesh. ALL stand condemned, but ALL (i.e. those who accept) also stand justified, by the redemptive grace of God in Jesus Christ. Only in Jesus the forgiveness of sins has been given to mankind and we are saved from condemnation. The other level of sin or sinning is that which we continue to commit even after accepting the forgiveness of God in Christ. It is this post conversion sinning, that we will be covering here.

Apostle John was categorical that: *"If we claim to be without sin, we deceive ourselves and the truth is not in us."* [5] Someone has stated that the world is classified into two categories of people. In the first category are those who admit they are sinners and in the second category are those who do not admit they are sinners. But it remains that ALL are sinners. I will venture to sub-classify the first category into those who know they are sinners and have accepted God's forgiveness in Christ, and those who while they acknowledge they are sinners, are yet to know or accept Christ as their Saviour. Of course accepting your sinfulness is the first step towards accepting God's grace. *"It is not the healthy who need a doctor, but the sick. I have not come to call the righteous, but sinners,"* [6] declared Jesus. Those who do not acknowledge their sinful state, or have their own form of righteousness, do not feel the need for or can accept the Saviour Christ. Christ cannot heal them of their sickness. *"The worst thing about being a sinner is that one has to live with perpetual sickness,"* wrote Cynndylan Jones, the Welsh preacher.

Before we look at the problem of why we sin, let us first see what sin does. What is its effect on the spiritual life of a disciple? We should accept as a basic truth that ultimately *all* sin constitutes sinning against God. David sinned against Uriah the Hittite, the murdered husband of Bathsheba, with whom he had committed adultery; but acknowledged that it was ultimately a sin against God. He cried out: *"Against you, you only, have I sinned ..... "* [7] in a psalm which is perhaps David's most heartfelt because it was written with a broken, contrite, and repentant heart. When we sin against a person, we are actually sinning against the *image of God* in that person, which is tantamount to sinning against God. That is why all God's laws – whether positively stated or those which are negative (Thou shalt not ...) – have been given to preserve the dignity of His image in man.

When we sin, we not only break God's law, but also His heart. We are figuratively – when we sin – turning our backs to Him; rejecting His love for us and His concern for what is good and bad for us. And this hurts God and causes Him much grief. The relationship is broken. We are restless. God is restless. And this restlessness remains till the relationship is restored once again. We lose the joy of salvation. The Holy Spirit, whom we have ignored and grieved when we sin, though does not leave us, but withdraws. We do not feel God's presence anymore. Listen to the words of David from the same psalm; they would appear to you as if it is your heart that is crying out: *"Do not cast me from your presence or take your Holy Spirit from me. Restore to me the joy of your salvation and grant me a willing spirit, to sustain me."* [8]

Sin weakens the voice and the power of the Holy Spirit within us. It gives the devil a foothold in us; who then attacks us with the weapons of guilt (you have let God down) and failure (you cannot keep God's commandments; you do not really love Him). The result is a weakened disciple, and a spiritual life that limps. Actually in a way we hand over victory to Satan, who can then mock God that here is another of your child who is still continuing in his sinful ways. Do we want to keep giving Satan his victories?

*"Blessed are the pure in heart, for they will see God,"* [9] is one of the blessedness promised by Jesus. And David cries over the uncleanness of his heart which has been caused by sin. Some portions of that wonderful psalm again: *"Wash away all my iniquity and cleanse me from my sin. Cleanse me with hyssop, and I shall be clean; wash me, and I shall be whiter than snow. Create in me a pure heart, O God, and renew a steadfast spirit within me."* [10] Francois Mauriac wrote, *"Impurity separates us from God....... purity is the condition for a higher love – for a possession superior to all possessions: that of God."*

Why do we sin? Why after accepting God's forgiveness and having been justified, we still commit acts of sin or trespass? Why do we fall short of God's standards, when we know what He expects from us? The answer lies in the fact that while we have been justified and are considered righteous, once we accepted that the death of Christ has paid the penalty for our sins, we still have to undergo sanctification and that too to its fullest extent. That is we are in the process of being made holy, of being made Christlike. The sanctification process is underway and will carry on in us till the very end of our life.

To put it differently; let us look at this from the aspect of the 3 Ps of sin - penalty, power, and presence. The penalty for our sins (both past and future) has been paid for by Jesus. We only have to take hold of the forgiveness God has given in him. The power of sin remains throughout our earthly life; while we are in this body of flesh, which is to say while we have the sinful nature. The power of sin diminishes as we increasingly become Christlike. The work of transformation or making us holy is that of the Holy Spirit. We all are presently in this stage. Then finally the presence of sin; while we are in this corrupted and fallen world we will always experience the presence of sin. That will disappear only when we have been glorified; which will be when we finally have our dwelling with God. Taking the example of Christ to illustrate the point; sin had no power over him, but he felt the presence of sin while he was in this world.

So currently we remain subject to the power of sin. How much power ultimately sin has over us, depends on our level of holiness or in other words our level of spiritual development; how much Christ has developed in us. So depending on that, will be our level of susceptibility to sin. The more Christ develops in us, the stronger we will be in resisting temptations that we will face in different circumstances and situations.

The sinful nature, with which we were born, remains present in us even after we become a Christian. This sinful nature is at warfare with our spiritual nature. The *old* man constantly clashes with the *new* man. Therefore we can never be completely free from the power of sin. No saint, no matter how big a one, can claim that he or she has become free from the power of sin or has not fallen into sin at one time or the other. The only difference between a saint and another saint is in their level of saintliness (godliness or holiness), which then determines how much power sin has on them. *"It is the saints who have the sense of sin, the sense of sin is the measure of soul's awareness of God,"* wrote Father Daniel Lou.

Please note that God will not make us 'sin-free' with a wave of His hand. But He will give us power, the power of the Holy Spirit in us, to face up to the power of sin, and overcome it. Without this power we have no hope. Of our own strength we cannot overcome sin. We are impotent to subject sin to our control. We have to take hold of this power, which God gives us, to fight *'against the powers of this dark world and against the spiritual forces of evil in the heavenly realms'* [11]. In fact it is my firm belief that the believer is specially marked for attack by the devil and his legions; and the more we grow in Christ the stronger the attacks become, as if to test our level of development in Christ. This appears to be part and parcel of what we can expect when we become Christians. Charles Peguy wrote, *"No one is so competent a witness to the substance of Christianity as the sinner; no one except perhaps the saint."*

So given the state that we are in, that is subjected to the power of sin; where do we stand in our faith? Are we to be perennially 'disabled' Christians, always struggling with sin, which is ever present and which does not relent in appealing to our degenerate nature? Where is our hope? Where is the victorious life which we are supposed to lead in Christ? While Paul describes at length (in chapter seven of the epistle to the Romans) the inner struggles of the believer against sin, he does however end with a note of hope: *"What a wretched man I am! Who will rescue me from this body of death? Thanks be to God – through Jesus Christ our Lord!"* [12] He then gives a thumping statement in the next chapter: *"Therefore, there is now no condemnation for those who are in Christ Jesus, because through Christ Jesus the law of the Spirit of life set me free from the law of sin and death."* [13] What has happened to make things different? To give this hope?

Grace has been introduced and it changes the whole scheme of things. Paul explains how: *"For what the law was powerless to do in that it was weakened by the sinful nature, God did by sending his own Son in the likeness of sinful man to be a sin offering."* [14] God provided the way out of the dilemma. By giving us grace, He provided the way for us to be righteous. Read on: *"And so he condemned sin in sinful man, in order that the righteous requirements of the law might be fully met in us, who do not live according to the sinful nature but according to the Spirit."* [15] That is Paul at his brilliant best!

So we need not despair. No need for sin to beat us down and make us lead a deflated life as Christians. As Paul stresses, *"But if Christ is in you, your body is dead because of sin, yet your spirit is alive because of righteousness."* [16] And also, *"In the same way, count yourself dead to sin but alive to God in Christ Jesus."* [17] This is possible because God did not move us from one form of legalism to another, so that we would continue to remain occupied keeping count of our sins or the number of times that we broke the law. No, rather He has moved us under His grace and therefore we need not engage in book keeping any longer; for God Himself does not do any book keeping of our sins. *"For sin shall not be your master, because you are not under law, but under grace."*[18] And should we sin we have this confidence that our intercessor is always at work. John writes, *"But if anybody does sin, we have one who speaks to the Father in our defense – Jesus Christ, the Righteous One."* [19] And the Father listens to him because: *"For this reason he had to be made like his brothers in every way, in order that he might become a merciful and faithful high priest in service to God, and that he might make atonement for the sins of the people. Because he himself suffered when he was tempted, he is able to help those who are being tempted."*[20]

With a mediator of such tremendous credentials, ever standing before God, we can expect God to always accept the intercessions that he makes on our behalf; which might somewhat run on these lines: *'Father please forgive Kamal this very sin. Though I do not condone it but I emphathise with his struggles against temptation, knowing fully well how weak is the flesh that he is wearing. I myself did not give in when I had a body like his, but I can see that Kamal has yielded and given in. But please remember that I have made atonement for his sins – this one included. So please forgive him, merciful Father'.* God, the righteous and merciful Judge, would not be able to turn down such an appeal from His Son. Therefore Paul would not let his failures, his sins, rule him out of the race: *"Forgetting what is behind and straining towards what is ahead, I press on towards the goal to win the prize for which God has called me heavenwards in Christ Jesus."* [21]

And so must you. Satan will try his best to see that you self disqualify yourself, and bow out of the race; weighed down by your sins. Or he will see that you limp and are not a robust Christian, in service of God. Do not let this happen. For this is not the way God would want it. Remember you are under His grace and not the law.

We have seen that a believer can fall to sin even after his conversion, for he is still in the tent of flesh and living in a fallen world, where the decadence caused by sin is widely prevalent. We have also seen that the believer is justified by God's grace; and once justified, he is no longer under the law of sin, but lives under grace. We have also seen that when he does sin, there is Jesus our high priest before God, who intercedes on his behalf; and his mediation is effective and protective. So when all things are in our favor, *should we not go on sinning?* Should we not go on a rampage; for it appears that we have been given the licence to sin? Let us lie, steal, hate, indulge in slander, covet our brother's possessions, and what not. Even the 'higher' sins we can commit with impunity, because we are under grace and will surely receive God's forgiveness, as our standing mediator (Jesus) will bail us out.

This is a dangerous situation and has been described by Philip Yancey as *'the scandal of grace'*. Grace becomes scandalous for it appears that it is open to abuse. Paul puts the question: *"Shall we go on sinning, so that grace may increase?"* [22] Well if my sinning results in God's grace to be all the more evident or operative, then in fact I am doing a service to God by continuing to sin. If Christ's name is glorified because of my sinning, then should I not carry on with it?

BY NO MEANS! Paul appears to shout these three words from the rooftop, and they emphatically attack any misconception that we may form of God's grace. Yes grace has the potential of being abused; but only a warped mind can twist God's grace in this manner. We can even conclude that perhaps that person has not tasted God's grace at all. To his own question: *"Shall we go on sinning, so that grace may increase,"* Paul replies, *"By no means! We died to sin; how can we live in it any longer."* [23]

To Paul it is inconceivable that the one who has tasted God's grace, the one who has been forgiven, would carry on sinning or would persist in his sinful ways. The reality is that you no longer want to carry on sinning. You no longer relish or enjoy sinning. Sin is not a habit any more. You find it repelling, should you sin. The Holy Spirit is in you and he convicts you and makes you conscious of sin. He will not leave you at peace when you sin, but fill you with remorse. You will not be at rest till you repent and seek God's forgiveness. You will be restless till your relationship with God is restored and you feel His presence once again. John writes in his epistle: *"No-one who lives in him keeps on sinning,"* [24] and, *"No-one who is born of God will continue to sin, because God's seed remains in him; he cannot go on sinning, because he has been born of God."* [25] This is the wonder of grace and this is how grace scores over the law.

Through the law we came to know what sin is. We became conscious of sin. Sin came to be recognized as sin. To put it simply, sin became sin. But other than pointing to what sin is, the law did not give us the power against sin. In fact it worked the other way round. The law fanned our sinful nature. Now knowing what sin is, we had all kinds of desire in us to commit sin. The law was powerless to produce in us the desire not to sin. It only gave us direction of what was right and wrong.

Grace on the other hand, produces in us, because of our gratitude for receiving forgiveness, every intention not to sin; and thus please God, who has loved us and given us the forgiveness. What law could not do, grace has achieved. We no longer want to sin. The heart changes and the transformed person wishes to live a sinless life, emulating his Lord Jesus, so as to please God. He wants to use the parts of his body, not as instruments of wickedness (which was the case earlier), but as instruments of righteousness, and thereby bring glory to God. With the Holy Spirit making his dwelling in him at his conversion, he can no longer use his body for sinful acts without causing grief to the Spirit and bringing dishonor to God. *"Do you not know that your body is a temple of the Holy Spirit, who is in you, whom you have received from God? ......... Therefore honor God with your body."* [26] That person is now part of the Body of Christ and must live his life as Jesus did. *"Whoever claims to live in him must walk as Jesus did."* [27]

The word of God has enough warnings for the charlatans, the imposters, the pretenders. *"If we deliberately keep on sinning after we have received the knowledge of the truth, no sacrifice for sins is left."* [28] Note the word *deliberately.* And the writer of the Book of Hebrews points out that in that case (of those who deliberately sin), they are trampling the Son of God under foot and judgment awaits them. Peter warns that: *"Live as free men, but do not use your freedom as a cover-up for evil; live as servants of God."* [29] The point is, while God is merciful and forgives us when we sin; He at the same time comes down hard on those who are abusing or misusing His grace to cover up their sinful ways and acts. You cannot expect to fool God who searches and knows the hearts of men. Hypocrisy and shamming stand exposed before Him.

We can gain victory over our sinful nature. While we will never be completely free of it, we can subject it under our control. This is possible by a conscious act on our part. An act of will, which has to be constantly applied. *"Those who live according to the sinful nature have their minds set on what that nature desires; but those who live in accordance with the Spirit have their minds set on what the Spirit desires."* [30] We have to will ourselves to let the Spirit take control. The surrender has to be both in general and also specific to every situation we face; where we can fall into sin. *"You, however, are controlled not by the sinful nature but by the Spirit, if the Spirit of God lives in you."* [31] It is our willingness and the power of the Spirit which will give us the victory. *"But if by the Spirit you put to death the misdeeds of the body, you will live, because those who are led by the Spirit of God are sons of God."* [32] Controlled by the Spirit, led by the Spirit, mind set on what the Spirit desires; this is the key to a truly Christian life. Live as a 'free' man.

And should we sin, then we must confess our sin before God; and Christ's atonement will apply to that act of sin. And then move ahead, as Paul chose to do and advises us to do, having the confidence that:

*"He has removed our sins as far from us as the east is from the west."*[33]

1.  Romans 7:15
2.  John 8:11 (NLT)
3.  1 Corinthians 6:19
4.  Romans 3:23.
5.  1 John 1: 8.
6.  Mark 2:17.
7.  Psalm 51:4
8.  Psalm 51:11-12
9.  Matthew 5:8
10. Psalm 51:2,7,10
11. Ephesians 6:12
12. Romans 7:24-25
13. Romans 8:1-2.
14. Romans 8:3.
15. Romans 8:3-4.
16. Romans 8:10
17. Romans 6:11.
18. Romans 6:14.
19. 1 John 2:1.
20. Hebrews 2:17-18.
21. Philippians 3:13-14
22. Romans 6:1.
23. Romans 6:2.
24. 1 John 3 :6
25. 1 John 3:9.
26. 1 Corinthians 6:19-20.
27. 1 John 2:6
28. Hebrews 10:26.
29. 1 Peter 2:16.
30. Romans 8:5
31. Romans 8:9
32. Romans 8:13-14.
33. Psalm 103:12 (NLT)

# Chapter ~ 29

# PERSPECTIVE OF ETERNITY

*"He has also set eternity in the hearts of men."* [1]

God has put eternity in our hearts. Man was meant to spend eternity with God and not a finite life on earth. *"Surely God would not have created such a being as man to exist only for a day! No, no, man was made for immortality,"* wrote Abraham Lincoln. Therefore the longing for eternity is carried in our hearts. But do we conduct ourselves as if we are eternal beings or do we limit our vision and our perspective to our lives on this planet? The big question is do we live here in this world with an eye on our future life in the world to come?

Paul said, *"If only for this life we have hope in Christ, we are to be pitied more than all men."* [2] Paul had the perspective of eternity, and thus he could take all his sufferings with one eye upon his eternal life with God, that he knew would be his someday. In fact take out the eternity or eternal life from Christianity and the faith will fall flat. The very tenets and foundation on which the Christian faith is based upon, point to the world that is to come. The end game of God's plan is our eternal lives with Him. Without this hope, one cannot and will not be able to bear the struggles and demands of being a Christian. The cross would be too heavy to bear. As a matter of fact the cross would be meaningless to bear.

The Bible is replete with references to the eternal life, the other world, heaven, the resurrected bodies; leaving us without any doubt that this present world will be replaced by a world which will last forever. That God is making everything new, which would be enduring. That the end game of Creation and Redemption is to bring back home God's children (His family). When Jesus said, *"In my Father's house are many rooms ...... I am going there to prepare a place for you,"* [3] he was talking precisely of our eternal home where we will dwell with God.

Sometimes we humans are given glimpse of the 'other' side i.e. of the world which will not perish. The curtain between the natural (material) and the supernatural (spiritual) worlds is lifted, giving us a peep into what is going on behind, on the other side. Jesus' resurrection is one solid and convincing proof of the eternal world, where *'God is making everything new'*[4] for us. *"The world and its desires pass away....."* [5] wrote John with reference to the present world. But the world which will come, will last forever. It will be for eternity. There will be nothing in it which will be temporal. Everything will be everlasting – creation, resurrected humans, and of course the presence of God. It will be Eden once again, but this time it will be for permanence; for there will be no evil present to cause its fall, decay, or corruption.

We were not made for this world. We have been originally designed for a different world. We are just sojourning here on earth. We are passing through. The earth is a staging ground and not meant to be our eternal home. We are foreigners on this planet and *'our citizenship is in heaven'* [6]. Jesus said of the believers (his followers) that: *"They are not of the world, even as I am not of it."* [7] His disciples must always be conscious of this fact, that like their Lord, they are in this world but not of it. They must be aware that they are destined for another world, and this awareness must be instilled deep in their hearts, so that they *'do not love the world or anything in the world.'* [8]

The Book of Hebrews gives us a star lineup of biblical heroes who lived by faith, and says: *"They admitted that they were aliens and strangers on earth. Instead, they were longing for a better country – a heavenly one."*[9] And because they knew they were aliens and strangers 'visiting' this planet for a while, they could endure the sufferings and hardships that they were subjected to in their lifetimes. Peter speaks in the same way: *"Dear friends, I urge you, as aliens and strangers in the world ....."* [10] Aliens, strangers, visitors, foreigners; this is how the believer is referred to, and this is how the believer should conduct himself during his time in this world. An ever present consciousness that I am not of this world, that I am just passing through. That my eternal home is my destination. And because this world is not our home (some have likened it to a stay in a hotel), we will be restless while we are here. Nothing in this world will be able to satisfy us, in a lasting or fulfilling way. C.S. Lewis concluded: *"If I find in myself desires which nothing in this world can satisfy; the only logical explanation is that I was made for another world."* He was right on the mark!

It is not that the Christian does not believe in heaven or in the spiritual world or in the life to come; he would not be truly a Christian if he did not believe so. For then he would be questioning the resurrection of Christ, which is the essential tenet of the Christian faith and in fact the VERY pillar on which the faith stands. Paul was categorical: *"If there is no resurrection of the dead, then not even Christ has been raised. And if Christ has not been raised, our preaching is useless and so is our faith."* [11] We can turn this around. It is *because* we believe that Christ has been resurrected, do we have belief that we also will be resurrected and have eternal life. But here this belief is not being questioned. It is taken that a Christian (a true one) has this belief. What is being questioned is; whether he carries in him the perspective of eternity. A sense of being here but not belonging here. That strong and ever present consciousness of his eternal home and life; which impacts and even defines his thoughts, words, action, and conduct in his life in this world.

Having an eternal perspective is necessary because it gives us the right perspective of things in this material world. It is the right perspective because it is the perspective of Jesus. It shapes our life while we are on earth and we lead a life which Jesus did. The words of Jesus make sense only when we understand them keeping eternity in view. *'Blessed are the meek, blessed are the poor, blessed are those who mourn, and the other Beatitudes'*; have meaning only when we look at them from the eternal prism (otherwise as we see in this world, not the meek but the powerful inherit the earth). *'The first will be last and the last first, the greatest will be your servant, in losing your life you will save it'*; these principles do not work on earth, but only in heaven they will. *'Give up your riches on earth and store up for yourselves riches in heaven'*; will only be acceptable to the one who is looking at a life beyond this world.

Christians have been accused at times of being too much other worldly, of being too much preoccupied with heaven; to the extent of neglecting their earthly lives and responsibilities. We are in a sense blamed for living too much in the future and chasing mirages. In some cases this accusation may be valid as some Christians do really go 'overboard'; but what is more of a fact is that most Christians in the present times do not have the sense of eternity. Having an eternal perspective and living good and responsible lives on earth are not mutually exclusive. In fact I would even say that it makes us more responsible and conscientious residents of this world. Dr. W. E. Sangster wrote, *"You will work with zest and skill and thoroughness in all that concerns the outworkings of God's purpose on this earth, and you will work the better, because by faith you have the perfect end always in view."* The right balance is to live as good denizens of this world but with our eyes expectantly set on eternity and always remembering that: *"We live by faith, not by sight."* [12]

Having an eternal perspective does not mean that we will have no plans, ambitions, or aspirations in this world. We will have all these but we will subject them to God's will. To illustrate:- a career oriented Christian will not indulge in tricks, or in back stabbing, or in 'dog eats dog' machinations, to climb the corporate ladder; a business man will not use 'whatever means it takes' to promote his business; a government servant, though having many opportunities and seeing it rampant around him, but still will not take bribes. These are a few examples where people, because of their eternal perspective, understand and apply these words of Jesus: *"What good is it for a man to gain the whole world, yet forfeit his soul?"* [13] They wisely decide to save their soul which is eternal, rather than gain the world or the things of this world, which are temporal and will pass away. So aren't they living the more principled and better lives? Yes they are, and if all the people started living with this perspective, wouldn't the world be a better place. Heaven on earth! But that is foolish to expect.

Having an eternal perspective also helps you to cope stoically with the sufferings in your life and be an example for those around you. It gives you a better understanding of suffering, and the will to endure it and persevere, because you know that it will not last forever. *"From heaven the most miserable life will look like one bad night in an inconvenient hotel,"* wrote the mystic Teresa of Avila. You see a meaning in your trials and hardships and the pain and grief that you have to go through because of them. The focus shifts from 'why' to 'what for' or 'for what end' you are suffering, and you realise that your sufferings are not meaningless but have a purpose. *"For our light and momentary troubles are achieving for us an eternal glory that far outweighs them all."* [14] And because of this Christians with eternal perspective, are more likely to face their sufferings with dignity, calm, and resoluteness. They know their Lord suffered and faced his sufferings in the same manner. You also are not disillusioned when you see the suffering around you in this world. You know that one day God will wipe out all suffering, all ills, all wickedness, all injustice, all crying, all mourning, and all pain. *"He will wipe every tear from their eyes."* [15]

Knowing, like Jesus did, *'that he had come from God and was returning to God'* [16], we also would return to our eternal home; we must see to it that we do not get too 'comfortable' living in this world. *"Don't you know that friendship with the world means enmity against God? Therefore, anyone who chooses to be a friend of the world becomes an enemy of God."* [17] We must live good and godly lives while we are in this world; but let us not attempt to recreate heaven here on earth. It will never be. Heaven will be only in heaven. And that is our home and not earth. So don't get cozy here. Consider your sojourn on earth as a pilgrimage, which can well turn into a wandering in the desert as the case with the

Israelites, if we do not live here as per God's commands and wishes. Paul warns us of the same: *"Therefore we are always confident and know that as long as we are at home in the body we are away from the Lord."* [18] So don't get too comfortable in the body and with this world but rather groan inwardly like Paul: *"Meanwhile we groan, longing to be clothed with our heavenly dwelling ....."* [19]

Keep groaning till you arrive there.

1. *Ecclesiastes 3:11*
2. *1 Corinthians 15:19.*
3. *John 14:2.*
4. *Revelations 21:5 (modified)*
5. *1 John 2:17*
6. *Philippians 3:20.*
7. *John 17:16.*
8. *1 John 2:15*
9. *Hebrews 11:13,16*
10. *1 Peter 2:11.*
11. *1 Corinthians 15:13-14.*
12. *2 Corinthians 5:7*
13. *Mark 8:36.*
14. *2 Corinthians 4:17.*
15. *Revelations 21:4.*
16. *John 13:3*
17. *James 4:4*
18. *2 Corinthians 5:6.*
19. *2 Corinthians 5:2*

# Chapter ~ 30

# FAITH: GOD'S DELIGHT

*"However, when the Son of Man comes, will he find faith on the earth?"* [1]

**O**f all the things that God seeks in man, faith is what He values the most. Our salvation depends on God's grace and our faith, from start to finish. That is why the supreme thing, which God looks for in man, is faith. Faith is a precious commodity which God seeks; for He needs faith to work in and through the person. It is the one thing which stands out amongst all character traits in a believer. The heroes of the Bible were all men and women of faith. If you want to endear yourself to God, and wish to be counted in the galaxy of the giants of God, then you need to be a person of faith; because as the Scriptures say: *"And without faith it is impossible to please God."* [2] Our fight is the fight of faith, is what Paul exhorts: *"Fight the good fight of the faith."* [3] God delights in faith.

When Paul writes of the greater gifts, that we must aspire to receive from God, faith is listed as one of the three such; the other two being love and hope. Paul then proceeds to extol the virtues of love in that famous chapter of the first book of Corinthians, and concludes decisively that the greatest of the three (*faith, hope, and love*), is love. That may well be. I consider love is indeed the greatest in man's equation with man; however when it comes to man's equation with God, it is faith which is paramount. The other two are also important but the very basis, the very foundation of our relationship with God, is faith. That is the starting point and that remains the building blocks of our relation with God. But faith and love are not mutually exclusive; both need to be found in the believer. As Paul says, *"The only thing that counts is faith expressing itself through love."* [4] Paul is underlining here that faith and love go hand in hand. Faith in God expressed in love for one another.

What is faith? What is involved in faith? What are the different kinds of faith? What is the type of faith that pleases God the most? Why should we have faith? Why it matters so much to God?

A very appealing definition of faith that I find is by Philip Yancey, who writes, *"Faith means believing in advance, what will make sense only in reverse."* Other writers have penned something similar and to quote a few: *"Faith is the deliberate confidence in the character of God whose ways you may not understand at the time,"* by Oswald Chambers, and Voltaire writes, *"Faith consists in believing when it is beyond the power of reason to believe."* The one thing being underlined by all is that faith requires trust and obedience without full knowledge. As Paul writes, *"Now we see but a poor reflection as in a mirror; then we shall see face to face. Now I know in part; then I shall know fully, even as I am fully known."* [5] That is what faith is. That is the intrinsic quality of faith; the core and the heart of faith. When you don't have all the information, when the picture is only partially seen by you, when the view that you see is hazy, when there are many variables that cause uncertainty, when there are many ifs and buts; but yet you still believe, you still put your trust in God. That is faith.

You see God has revealed just enough of Himself - His nature, His character, His power - for us to believe in Him. But He has left room for faith; which then becomes a conscious decision or a willful act on the part of man. What has been revealed is *"too much to deny and too little to be sure"*- to quote Pascal. If everything was crystal clear, if everything was absolutely certain; then where is the room for faith?

Where is the need for faith then? *Then all will believe.* Believing will come easy, and in fact become mechanical and move out of the realm of human will. *"God gives us just enough to seek him, and never enough to fully find him. To do more would be to inhibit our freedom, and our freedom is very dear to God,"* wrote Ron Hansen. Based on all that we see and all that has been revealed by God and about God, we *will* ourselves to have faith. Paul is clear that, *"We live by faith, not by sight"* [6] and *"But hope that is seen is no hope at all."* [7] Faith has to allow room for doubt otherwise it is not faith; it is *certainty* then. We put our faith in what is not known or not seen, basis what we know or see. Faith is not belief without proof, but trust without reservation. The Book of Hebrews puts it wonderfully: *"Now faith is being sure of what we hope for and certain of what we do not see."* [8]

It is wrong to consider that the opposite of faith is doubt. It is not doubt, but fear. Fear drives away faith. *"You block your dreams when you allow your fear to grow bigger than your faith,"* said Mary Morrissey. Doubt coexists with faith. Having doubts is not an indication of the absence of faith. *"Doubt is the skeleton in the closet of faith,"* says Yancey. Doubt spurs faith, and the struggle with doubt makes faith grow. *"Doubt is merely the seed of faith, a sign that the faith is alive, and ready to grow,"* wrote Kathleen Norris. So if we have faith and we have honest doubts; then these doubts can be used to grow the faith. Again the principle, much used by God, applies here too: The negative is used to further the positive. In the process of resolving the doubts, we would find that our faith, when we come out of the struggle, has grown stronger. God is not angry with the doubts that we may have; it is the lack of faith which disappoints Him. *"Without somehow destroying me in the process, how could God reveal Himself in a way that would leave no room for doubt? If there were no room for doubt, there would be no room for me,"* is how Frederick Buechner explains it. Better to have faith with doubts, than no faith at all.

Another thing about faith is that it is not a compulsion. God does not bully us into a corner, so that we have no choice but to have faith in Him. Like love (for God) is voluntary on our part; faith too is an act of will, as pointed out earlier. Faith has in itself the intrinsic option of 'not to have faith.' It allows the possibility of rejection. If it did not, then it would not be faith but a compulsion and a 'conditioned' response. God must give man the possibility of not to believe in Him, to reject Him. Only then faith that comes is like a sweet aroma to Him. A response under force or pressure is not what God wants. Beginning with Adam and Eve, God has given man the option of 'walking out' on Him.

There are three elements of faith. In fact these are the pillars on which faith stands. They are: *trust, patience, and hope.*

You have to trust God to put your faith in Him. Faith involves trust, not certainty. You have to trust that He is what He claims He is. You have to trust in the constancy of His nature; in the might of His power; in the solidness of His character. You have to also trust that He knows what He is doing; that all things are under His control; that there is nothing that is happening in your life which He has not allowed. You also have to trust that He has your good in His heart; that all things will work for the good of those who trust in the Lord; that He will even use your mistakes, your failures, the evil and injustice that may have be done to you, for His redemptive purposes.

You have to keep the trust despite all indicators being adverse and circumstances going against you. You have to trust when there may be nothing that may encourage you to trust. You hold on to trust even when nothing makes sense. *You trust because it is God who you are called to trust.* Remember Abraham; he trusted that God would provide the animal for the sacrifice: *"God Himself will provide the lamb for the burnt offering, my son."* [9] And God did! And Jesus; it was an act of supreme trust in the Garden of Gethsemane, when after an intense struggle, he willed himself to drink the cup which the Father wanted him to.

Patience is vital for faith. It keeps it going. God has His own time table. He will bring about things only as per His timeline. We are called upon to, *"Be still before the LORD and wait patiently for Him."* [10] You have to be patient and persevere in faith. Remember David; he had to wait for a number of years after his anointing by Prophet Samuel, before he would become king of Israel and only after Saul had been killed in battle. And in the meantime he had to hide from King Saul on numerous occasions, with his life hanging on a thread. This was not what he had bargained for; hiding in the caves of the Judean desert. But he was patient. He knew what the LORD had promised would be fulfilled one day; and that is the reason he did not eliminate Saul on the occasions he had the chance. David would rather wait for the Lord to bring about the change in the kingship at His appointed time.

And Abraham? He had to wait a number of years before God's promise of an offspring to him would be fulfilled. He kept his patience. Jesus waited patiently for thirty years, in the nondescript town of Nazareth, for the signal from above for beginning his mission. Adel Bestavros said, *"Patience with others is love, patience with self is hope, and patience with God is faith."* And there are enough verses in the Bible encouraging us to have patience, to persevere, to just hold on. *"Let us hold unswervingly to the hope we profess, for He who promised is faithful"*[11] and *"So do not throw away your confidence; it will be richly rewarded."*[12] These are just two such verses calling for patience. God will work as per His timeline and not ours. We have to go through the period of waiting (I consider this waiting to be even mandatory in God's scheme of things) and persevere; not by fretting and lamenting, but *"with an upward look and trustful silence,"* as recommended by Selwyn Hughes.

Hope. Hope is what sustains us. Without hope the soul will wither. Hope in the goodness, fairness, and justness of the One in whom we have put our trust. Hope that He will not allow things to continue longer than what is necessary for Him to work out His purposes for us in a painful situation. Hope that no matter how hopeless the situation becomes, God can engineer a radical turnaround, as He did in the case of: the three men put in the fiery furnace by King Nebuchadnezzar; Joseph who faced a bleak future in the Egyptian prison; the people of Israel under slavery in Egypt; David facing Goliath in battle; and what more hopeless than Jesus lying dead in a tomb. Hope that things will work out; that God will ensure that ultimately they work out, and work out for the better. Hope that there would be light at the end of the dark tunnel in which we find ourselves. Hope that there will be a rainbow at the end of the deluge of troubles that have beset us. Hope in the fulfillment of ALL the promises God has made in Jesus. And the ultimate hope that one day we will be in the presence of God and live with Him for eternity.

Abraham and Sarah held on to the hope of God fulfilling His promise of an offspring to them, even though they were well advanced in years; and finally Isaac was born to them at ages 100 and 90 respectively. David kept his hopes alive to be the king of Israel, even under distressing circumstances; and he finally did ascend to the throne. And Jesus put his hope in his Father when he cried, *"Father, into your hands I commit my spirit,"* [13] that God would not let death have victory over him; and we know what happened on the third day - Jesus rose from the dead.

Trust! Patience! Hope! All three are the vital ingredients that go in faith in equal measure. And to cement them and also to sustain them, we need the power of prayer. It is prayer which keeps the trust going, patience bearable, and hope refreshing. It is prayer which provides the nourishment to faith and keeps it alive. We will cover the subject of prayer in a later chapter.

What are the kinds of faith that we find or more importantly, God finds in man? There are many ways in which we can differentiate, but I consider that faith is essentially of two types. The first is *conditional* faith where we are essentially negotiating with God. It runs like this: 'God *if* you do this then I will do that (believe you or worship you or obey you or put my faith in you) or God *if* you can do this then do it (here we are throwing it back to God and basically telling Him that if He considers He has the power to deliver, then let Him do it)'. There is *IF* in this faith.

I am sure God is not much pleased with such faith. You don't negotiate with God. And also you do not put God to the test. Why should He be put in a situation, where He has to pass with flying colors, for you to accept that He is God and that He is capable of doing what you want? Jesus had rebuked the devil with these words of the Scriptures: *"It is also written: Do not put the Lord your God to the test."* [14] We are insulting God when we do that. It is humiliating for Him that the created should test and judge the Creator. Unfortunately people with such faith tend to do exactly that. They treat God as genie who will fulfill their every wish, a magician who will do his tricks on demand, an ATM machine that will dispense all the life's pleasure for the asking. And if God does not oblige, then He is no God. He can be discarded. He is not worthy to put one's faith in.

I believe God does accommodate such a faith in 'young' Christians and new believers. He understands that they have just begun their walk with Him. They have not tasted His power much. They do not fully understand His nature. They are yet to sufficiently know His ways. Their faith is still in the infancy stage and may not be able to stomach rejections and disappointments. God thus 'obliges' their prayer requests and desires. He carries them to adulthood. However this phase is not forever and as a matter of fact does not last long. God then wants us to become 'adult' Christians and our faith to develop, so that we can have a mature relationship with Him, in which He expects us to handle every type of response from Him.

And we now come to the other type of faith. This is *bedrock* faith; faith which has been matured by many trials and testing and even sufferings. This is a faith which is unshakeable because it has already been shaken to the roots, but has stood firm. This is a faith which has been brought many times to the breaking point, but has not broken. This is a faith which has gone through the furnace of testing many times, but has not melted, and on the contrary has come out strengthened. This is the faith which has grit its teeth, clenched its fists, dug its heels, and says: 'I will take whatever is thrown at me but will not give up'; just like a boxer in the ring who is taking a lot of pounding, but again and again comes back from the ropes or picks himself up from the floor.

It is a faith which says of God: *"Though He slay me, yet will I hope in Him."* [15] Instead of IF there is THOUGH in this faith. From conditional it becomes *'come-what-may'*. The focus here shifts from God to the faith. God is not put to test, but faith is subject to testing. *This is the faith which delights God.* This is the faith which God can use for His glory, for He knows that this is the faith which has stood the test of time and the test of trials and hardships, and will stand so in future.

The story of Job in the Bible is the story of faith. His faith proved itself to be a *'though'* faith. Job, unknown to him, became the subject of a cosmic wager between God and Satan. Under this wager his faith was to be tested; whether it was a conditional faith, where Job had faith in God because of all what God had given him in life *or* whether it was a faith which will remain even when all the things he had were taken away from him. It was to prove whether Job had faith in God for no other reason *but that He is God*. Satan alleged that it was the former. Take away all his earthly possessions and Job's faith will collapse; Satan was confident.

Well as we know poor Job was stripped of everything; his wealth, his children, his health. Overnight he was reduced to nothing and must have been subjected to much shame and ridicule besides undergoing immense misery and suffering. *BUT* Job kept his faith. His faith in God, in the goodness of God, did not waver. He did not rebel against God. He accepted whatever afflictions that he had to suffer. All he wanted from God was a vindication of his name; that it was not because he had sinned, as his friends were alleging, that these calamities had come upon him. At the end he indeed stood vindicated and God was much pleased with Job's faith. His faith had made God win the wager.

Like Job, would we still keep our faith in God even *though* He may appear to be silent and unresponsive to our prayers; even *though* our world may come crumbling down; even *though* God may appear to be indifferent to our sufferings and may even appear to have caused them? Would we still believe in God? Would we still believe in the goodness and fairness of God? Would we be able to say, *"I know, O LORD, that your laws are righteous, and in faithfulness you have afflicted me?"* [16] Would we still believe that there has to be a reason, a purpose for which God has allowed us to suffer such, and that God knows best what is for my good? Would we join the psalmist in saying, *"It was good for me to be afflicted so that I might learn your decrees?"* [17]

Faith is easy to come by when the going is good; but when the going gets tough, it comes difficult. In fact it is seen that faith is difficult to come by when it is most needed. But it is the crisis in life (and even in our relationship with God), that matures our faith and can make it rock like. And bedrock faith is self-feeding! The more you hold firm, the stronger the faith becomes; the stronger the faith becomes, the more you hold firm. You then develop a view similar to what Stanley Baldwin expressed when he said, *"I am one of those who would sink with faith than to swim without it."*

Is faith a gift from God or is it completely a cultivated response of human will? It is both. As we saw in the first book of Corinthians, Paul wants us to desire the greater gifts from God, of which faith is one. Elsewhere he talks of, *"the measure of faith God has given you."* [18] And in listing down the gifts of the Spirit, Paul includes faith as one of them: *"to another faith by the same Spirit."* [19] Let us understand how faith can be both a gift from above and a self-willed response.

The core, the base, the starting point, has to be the *faith in us*. God will not give us faith so that we can believe in Him, or take the first steps towards Him. That has to come from us. God will only build on something which He finds in us; and the principle (which He often applies) seen here is: *"Whoever has will be given more; whoever does not have, even what he has will be taken from him."* [20] If you have faith, God will give you more faith. He will build on your faith. He will give you faith because you have shown faith. You know the value of faith and will appreciate receiving the gift of faith. At times when your faith appears shaky, when it comes under heavy attack, this gift of faith from God will supply what your faith is lacking. Resultantly a higher level of faith is developed in you. Remember that *'the author and perfecter of our faith'* [21], is Jesus.

Why does faith matter? Why faith is so important? Why God desires faith in us? These we will look at in the next chapter. We close here with this quote by Samuel Butler:-

*"You can do very little with faith, but you can do nothing without it."*

Perhaps this statement was meant for the skeptics and the fence sitters. But the believer, he can do a lot with faith.

*Rather God can do a lot with faith!*

1. *Luke 18:8*
2. *Hebrews 11:6*
3. *1Timothy 6:12*
4. *Galatians 5:6.*
5. *1 Corinthians 13:12.*
6. *2 Corinthians 5:7*
7. *Romans 8:24*
8. *Hebrews 11:1*
9. *Genesis 22:8.*
10. *Psalm 37:7.*
11. *Hebrews 10:23*
12. *Hebrews 10:35*
13. *Luke 23:46*
14. *Matthew 4:7*
15. *Job 13:15*
16. *Psalm 119:75.*
17. *Psalm 119:71*
18. *Romans 12:3.*
19. *I Corinthians 12:9.*
20. *Mark 4:25*
21. *Hebrews 12:2*

# Chapter ~ 31

# BELIEVING IS SEEING:
# THE MIRACLE OF FAITH

*"Faith does not spring from the miracle but the miracle from faith."*
*- Fyodor Dostoevsky*

In the previous chapter we discussed the subject of faith in detail. But the fundamental questions remain: Why is faith needed? Why is it important? Why it matters to God? We will consider them now.

God needs faith (in man) to do his work in and through him. Without faith, man cannot be an instrument of Divine purpose and intent. Every work of God can be considered to be a miracle. We, in this material world, consider a supernatural intervention to be a miracle. But for God it is an act like any (of His). Max Lucado underlines that, *"In fact the normality of and not the uniqueness of God's miracles cause them to be staggering. The frequency of the miracles blinds us to their beauty."*

All the works of God that we see around are miracles. But we nevertheless clamor for the Divine intervention that will be startling and a convincing expression of the extraordinary; thus setting it apart from the routine and the usual. We then call them miracles or signs and wonders, and they often become the precondition for our belief. 'If we see then we will believe'; is the perspective that we form. From God's perspective however, it is the reverse which holds: 'If you believe then you will see'. God is laying down His terms: 'If you have faith then you will see my works, my wonders, my miracles'. *"Some things have to be believed to be seen,"* wrote Ralph Hodgson. Believing is God's precondition for action on His part.

How much faith God seeks in us? What is the minimum we should have, which is needed by Him to work something out? Well *'as small as a mustard seed'* [1] would be sufficient for God to even move mountains. God doesn't ask much, though if there is more than a *'mustard seed'*, it would be very much welcomed by Him. The point here is that even a little faith is sufficient; but there should be something at least. There must be some faith for God to do His work in a situation.

The gospels are full of references to faith and accounts of faith; highlighting its importance in God's scheme of things. Jesus stressed much on faith; he applauded where he found faith, but he rued the lack of faith that he often encountered. And he was able to do his miracles where he found faith. In fact he made it a point to shift the focus from himself, the performer of the miracle, to the faith of the one requesting the miracle. *It became miracle of faith.*

He sought that people should believe in him not just because of the miracles he performed, and therefore he was often perturbed that the people should be insistent in their demand for signs and wonders. He rebuked them: *"Unless you people see miraculous signs and wonders, you will never believe."* [2] He was concerned that the focus of the people was more on his giving them miracles, rather than on his words, which were the 'bread of life' and the 'living water' that he was giving them. He did not want miracles to be the mainstay or the focal point of his ministry. That is why he used to deliberately underplay them (he told those he healed in private not to disclose who had done the act and he used to often withdraw after performing a miracle) and shifted the focus from himself to the faith of the person, as being responsible for the miracle.

But wherever or when he found faith, Jesus was delighted. It did not matter how much it was; the very presence of faith was appreciated by him. And if he found a faith that was extraordinary, he used to make it a point to praise it openly and even marveled at it. There are some remarkable accounts in the gospels of Jesus encountering faith in persons and performing his miracle as a response to it. Let us look at a few of them that are the most striking.

The one which stands out is the account of the centurion in Capernaum, whose servant lay paralyzed (another account indicates that he was in fact on his death bed) at his home. He comes to Jesus for help. Now here is a Gentile coming to the Jewish Messiah for help; an interesting situation and that could have well crossed the mind of Jesus. The Romans were ruling the Jewish nation and had subjected the people to much hardship and suffering. The Jews would have nothing to do with them and the very sight of this senior Roman soldier coming to him for help would have appeared strange to Jesus and also to those gathered there. Am sure the people, especially the Pharisees and the priests among them, would have keenly waited to see how Jesus would respond to the request from the centurion.

But Jesus was more interested in the faith of the man and his love for his servant, which had caused him to take this bold step of coming to Jesus. Jesus offered to go with him to his home and heal the servant. But the response the centurion gave, stumped him. From what the centurion said it became clear that he had great faith in the power of Jesus. He understood that for a Jew (and that too a religious leader) to come to the home of a Gentile (and a high ranking one for that) would be scandalous and 'unclean'. He believed that Jesus could perform the healing from there itself! And if Jesus was to say the word, he (Jesus) need not ascertain whether the healing had taken place or not; it would certainly take place for Jesus was a man of authority! Absolutely stunning! No wonder Jesus was astonished.

Do you see what the situation has developed into? A Roman official, a man of authority himself, believes that Jesus (a Jew and hence a subject of Rome) has the authority to perform a long distance healing and he need not even have to go and verify it, for it would be done! What was the response of Jesus to this? He was amazed at this show of faith. The centurion's words would have pleased him no end, and before everyone gathered there, he said of the centurion: *"I tell you the truth; I have not found anyone in Israel with such great faith."* [3] The centurion's faith was rewarded. Jesus did as he requested him to. Jesus assured him, *"Go! It will be done just as you believed it would."* [4] Just as you believed! These are the catch words. And the servant was healed at that very hour. Miracle of faith!

And then there was this Canaanite woman whom Jesus encountered in the region of Tyre and Sidon. The woman was persistent in her request that Jesus free her daughter from demon possession. The Lord tested her patience and perseverance. He first told her that his mission (his healing) was only amongst his people – the people of Israel. The woman persisted. She would not take no for an answer. Jesus then attempted to dissuade her by telling her that it would be wrong for him to take what belongs to the Jews and give it to other people. The woman's reply touches him: *"Yes, Lord, but even the dogs eat the crumbs that fall from their masters' table."* [5] What she meant was that she is not seeking to take away the right of the Jews to the Messiah's largesse; she would be happy with only the crumbs, the leftovers, of his mercy and grace. Jesus yielded to the woman's faith and said to her, *"Woman, you have great faith! Your request is granted."*[6] The lesson here is; don't give up in faith but persevere. Sometimes God tests our faith in this way; to see how desperate and persistent we are in our request. Miracle of faith!

Now we come to the faith of the father whose son was possessed by an evil spirit. Jesus accompanied by Peter, James, and John, was coming down the mountain. The three disciples were in a dazed state. They had a short while earlier witnessed the transfiguration of Jesus on the top of the mountain. They had beheld him in his glory, talking to the patriarchs of old – Moses and Elijah. Coming down they came upon the rest of the disciples and a large crowd which had gathered around them. They found that the center of attraction was a man who had brought his son to the disciples to rid him of the evil spirit that possessed him. The disciples had been unable to do so. So now it fell on Jesus.

The boy's father, discouraged by the disciples' failure to drive out the evil spirit, says to Jesus, *"... if you can do anything, take pity on us and help us."* [7] This was not good enough. There was faith but it was the faith of a fence sitter, the faith of a tester. What the man meant was: 'your disciples have been unable to help my son, but let us now see if you can'. Jesus said to him, *"'If you can'? Everything is possible for him who believes."* [8] The emphasis is on the words, *'if you can'*. Jesus needed to see faith which was full, unadulterated, and unconditional, before he did the healing. The man moved quickly from being a skeptic to an unabashed convert. *"I do believe; help me overcome my unbelief!"* [9] Now was the right posture; sincere, humble, and pleading. Jesus could work with that. He healed the man's son and the evil spirit left him. Miracle of faith!

We now come to the amazing account of the woman who had been subject to bleeding for a long time (it was likely the menstrual bleeding). She must have led a difficult life carrying this affliction. Besides the suffering from her bleeding, she would have faced ostracism by her community and family from many social settings. She must have been forbidden to enter the temple and likely even barred from the kitchen at home. With this condition she very likely would not have borne any children; if at all she was married. The social stigma must have dogged her cruelly.

This is the woman, whom no one could heal of her long suffering affliction, who dares to touch the edge of Jesus' cloak, so that she could be healed. Why did she not go openly to Jesus and request him for healing? Obviously this woman lacked confidence to make social contact, with her status as an outcast. She was afraid that she would driven away and not allowed to meet Jesus. So she must have thought: 'if I touch only his clothing, touch just his cloak, that would be enough to heal me and Jesus and the crowd would not even know what had happened'. What faith, woman! And when she touched him she was immediately healed. *Her faith had extracted the healing from Jesus!*

Jesus came to a halt. He wanted to know who had touched him. It was not an accidental touch or brush of the crowd around him, but a deliberate act, for he had felt the power go out from him. I believe the Lord could have left it unexposed. He was hurrying to the house of Jairus to heal his daughter and this diversion could have been avoided. But he chose to bring it out in the open. And for good reason. The woman's faith had to be made known to the people around. The woman when seeing that she would not remain un-discovered came and fell at his feet and owned up that she was the one who had touched him, narrating the reason for her covert act. She was probably fearing at this time that her 'stolen' healing would be taken back. Jesus then said these reassuring words to her, *"Daughter, your faith has healed you. Go in peace."* [10] 'Don't be afraid, the healing is now yours for sure, for it is your faith which has won you the healing'. Mark the words: *your faith has healed you!* Once again the spotlight is trained on the faith of the person. Miracle of faith!

The same words, *'Your faith has healed you'*, Jesus said to Bartimaeus in Jericho when he had healed him of his blindness. And this has been the pattern. God searches those who come to Him with their requests and petitions; do they have faith - even as small as a mustard seed? At Lazarus' tomb, just before calling the dead man out, Jesus remarks to Martha, *"Did I not tell you that if you believed, you would see the glory of God?"* [11] The principle then is clear: Believe and you would see. Miracles need the soil of faith to sprout. They cannot where there is barrenness of faith.

What makes pilgrimage sites holy or places where people believe that their wishes will be fulfilled? God is everywhere, isn't He? So what is so special about these sites that makes hordes of people to come there to offer their petitions? What makes these places special is faith; faith of the believers which rises collectively as an acceptable and pleasing aroma to God. The presence of faith is so strong and pervasive in these places.

Believing can lead us to see God's miracles and His signs and wonders. But miracles, by themselves, need not necessarily lead to faith, or to a faith that will last. And that is why Jesus, though had the use for miracles, for they served their purpose in his ministry, did still downplay them; because the faith that would be forged as a result would be 'miracle' dependent. It would require periodic dose of miracles to keep it going. Miracles can serve the purpose of awakening faith. But that faith has to be supplemented (and soon enough) with the knowledge of the One who is behind the miracles and also a close relationship with Him, for it to develop into a solid faith. If not, then it will collapse soon.

Miracles alone will not lead to bedrock faith because we are relying only on our sight and not on our heart and mind. When we base our belief mainly on seeing, we are basing it on the works (miracles) of God; on what He does and not who He is. When we stop seeing i.e. when the miracles dry up, or God does not act as we want Him to or are used to Him to act, then faith crumbles; for it is a faith whose foundation is weak. When we believe in God, that is put our faith in the person of God, then usually that faith comes from inside us (we don't 'see' God, do we?); and that faith has a solid foundation because it is based on *who God is*. That is why Jesus calls them blessed who would believe in him though they have not seen him: *"Blessed are those who have not seen and yet have believed."* [12]

We need to stress the point that miracles need not guarantee faith. If it was so, then all who saw Jesus doing his miracles would have come to believe in him. There would have been no exceptions. Everyone would have become his disciple. But speaking in the temple area, Jesus says to the Jews there: *"The miracles I do in my Father's name speak for me, but you do not believe...."* [13] Jesus did enough miracles to cause faith to generate in all the people of his time. But not all believed as we know. Especially the Pharisees and the religious leaders of his time; they did not believe basis the miracles he performed, that he was the awaited Messiah. *'Even after Jesus had done all these miraculous signs in their presence, they still would not believe in him'.* [14] We find that the miracles in fact increased the chief priests' hostility towards Jesus, as they were making him highly popular with the people. They alleged that his power to drive out evil spirits from possessed people came from Beelzebub! Jesus encountered this hostility on many occasions and did even ask them: *"I have shown you many great miracles from the Father. For which of these do you stone me?"* [15]

In a meeting of the Sanhedrin, after the stupendous miracle of the raising of Lazarus from the dead, the matter of his miracles was brought up. The priests contended: *"What are we accomplishing? Here is this man performing many miraculous signs. If we let him go on like this, everyone will believe in him......"* [16] It was in this very meeting that it was decided that one man (Jesus) had to be sacrificed to save the nation. The chief priests planned to kill Lazarus too; for after all he was a walking proof of the miracle that had been performed and was attracting large crowds because of that. In fact it looks like that this miracle was the proverbial straw that broke the camel's back, as far as the rulers of the people and the chief priests were concerned. The miracles of Jesus did not produce faith in them but jealousy and insecurity as they considered him a threat to the established religious order of the day, which they presided over. Their hearts were hardened, and Jesus saw coming true in them what Isaiah had prophesied long ago: *"You will be ever hearing but never understanding; you will be ever seeing but never perceiving. For this people's heart has become calloused; they hardly hear with their ears, and they have closed their eyes. Otherwise they might see with their eyes, hear with their ears, understand with their hearts and turn, and I would heal them."* [17]

We can also understand the disappointment that Jesus may have felt with the faith that he found in his own disciples. In fact where faith should have been easy to come by; it turned out to be lacking or missing. The disciples had close encounters with the teachings and works of Jesus. He was their Master and they lived and moved with him during his earthly ministry. Of all the people, faith should have come easy to them and in abundance. Yet many a times Jesus was left exasperated for he did not find the faith in the disciples that he expected or desired. He once even chided Peter: *"You of little faith, why did you doubt?"* [18] Strangely the kind of faith he wanted in his disciples, only came about after he had left the world and not when he was with them. In his home town too he did not find much faith (a prophet without honor in his own home!) and therefore he could not do any miracles in Nazareth, except for some cases of healing. *'And he was amazed at their lack of faith'.* [19]

So pestered was Jesus with people's demand for miracles and for signs and wonders from heaven, and so saddened was he that they should put so much emphasis on them for believing, that he had to tell them: *"A wicked and adulterous generation looks for a miraculous sign, but none will be given it except the sign of Jonah"* [20]; referring here to the three days that he will remain in the belly of death and then be resurrected. *That would be the ultimate sign.* If you can accept that, then accept; for he knew that no amount of signs can produce in us the faith that God wants.

In fact why only accuse the generation of Jesus' time. Throughout the Bible we find ample proof that miracles do not result in faith. Take the case of the Israelites; would they have ever rebelled against their God, if miracles and signs were sufficient to produce faith and loyalty? They had ample display of God's power; the plagues in Egypt including the plague of the first born; God leading them out of the land of slavery – out of mighty Egypt; God parting the sea so that they could cross on its dry bed and escape Pharaoh's army; the provisions during their time in the desert – the manna from the sky and the water from the rock; the defeat of armies, stronger than they, whom they encountered in the wilderness; and the very fact that they survived as a nation wandering forty years in the desert. And above all, the presence of God in their midst; as the pillar of cloud by day and the pillar of fire by night, which went before them during their journey in the desert. And once they arrived at the Promised Land, the rout of their enemies. It was the LORD who won them their victories and gave them the rich and fertile land over there. All this should have produced in them a faith which would have been everlasting. But what do we find? Israel had difficulty remaining faithful to their God for much long. It was rebellious and disobedient; putting God to the test again and again.

Even with us. If we reflect on our lives, we will see how much God has done for us, and we will also see the direct evidences of His working (miracles) in many situations. But unfortunately we all cannot claim to have a rock like faith that pleases God. We forget over time and then we ask for more evidence of His power and His love. We also, obdurate that we are, repeatedly put God to the test. We want to see and see more to keep our faith going. But faith comes from within, as Jesus so strongly established. *"A sign is not the same thing as proof; a sign is merely a marker for someone who is looking in the right direction,"* writes Philip Yancey. Faith has to come from within to be enduring. If we are looking for miracles so that we may believe, we would be disappointed. If we believe, the miracles will add to that belief.

We have seen how our faith can enable God to intervene in particular situations in our life. But is that all what faith does? Is that why it is important? Does it have any other impact? Does the faith of an individual matter in the wider scheme of things, or at the cosmic level? *Well yes it does.* God's uses our faith (the faith of individuals), to do his redemptive work. With faith we can contribute as co-workers with Him in the restoration of creation. My faith counts! Each and every man's faith is important in the bigger picture of things. It makes God win his battles. It was the lack of faith which Adam and Eve displayed, which made God lose the battle in Eden. Now my every act of faith makes God win that battle. The small acts of faith add up and contribute to the Restoration. God will use the faith in us to restore everything: to turn evil into good, defeat into victory, death into resurrected life.

We touched upon the story of Job in the last chapter. By holding on to his faith, by trusting in the goodness of God in the face of all the calamities that befell him, he won the battle for God. It was his faith which did it. It was Abraham's faith which did not wilt over the many years of waiting that won God the battle. It was the dance of David before the ark like a mad man and also his repentance when convicted of his sin with Bathsheba that won God the battle. It was Jesus who by suffering the Cross won God the *ultimate* battle. And we too in our daily lives, in our small ways, can give God His victories. Faith matters. *It surely does.*

We will end reflecting on these words of Thomas Merton: *"We receive enlightenment only in proportion as we give ourselves more and more completely to God by humble submission and love. We do not first see, then act; we act, then see. And that is why the man, who waits to see clearly, before he will believe, never starts on the journey."*

So believe and start on the journey - the journey of faith. And you will surely see!

1.  Matthew 17:20
2.  John 4:48.
3.  Matthew 8:10
4.  Matthew 8:13
5.  Matthew 15:27
6.  Matthew 15:28.
7.  Mark 9:22
8.  Mark 9:23
9.  Mark 9:24
10. Luke 8:48
11. John 11:40
12. John 20:29
13. John 10:25-26
14. John 12:37
15. John 10:32.
16. John 11:47-48.
17. Matthew 13:14-15
18. Matthew 14:31
19. Mark 6:6.
20. Matthew 16:4.

# Chapter ~ 32

# PRAYER:
# THE BREATH OF THE SOUL

*"Prayer unlocks the power of God in our lives."*

The above sentence perhaps brings out the most important aspect of prayer in a Christian life. Prayer is the key which when properly turned, unleashes God's power in a believer. It opens the gates of heaven, and the treasuries of God's mercy and grace are there for the believer to take. Prayer is the instrument which when properly tuned, plays the divine music in our life. A Christian life without prayer will not last long. *Prayer is the breath of the soul* without which the soul would be sickly and eventually wither away. Without prayer the soul would remain isolated from its Source and will not survive.

We have the example of our Lord before us. Jesus spent long hours in prayer. He used to withdraw from the crowds, even from his own disciples, and spend time in isolation praying. Did he need to pray? What did he pray about? Well the gospels mention what, for the prayers that he made before his disciples and the crowd. And the prayer in the

Garden of Gethsemane, though made in isolation, has some parts of it made known to us. But what about the prayers where it is only recorded that, *'he went up on a mountainside by himself to pray'*? This must have happened many times, when Jesus would go to solitary places to spend time with his Father in prayer. *God praying to God!* What would he be praying then? What was the need for the Son of God to pray at all?

Well the Son of God was also the Son of Man, and the Son of Man needed his power from God. Jesus in the body of a man was constantly tapping the resources of God. Sometimes he might well have been seeking guidance from the Father, regarding the next steps that he needed to take in his mission. Sometimes after the performing of a miracle (for instance feeding of the multitude), he may have gone to his Father so as to keep pride in check and Satan at bay. Sometimes he went to the Father with petitions before a miracle was to be performed. Sometimes he went for the strengthening of his spirit when it appeared to be waning in the face of the trials and temptations that he had to face on earth. It is written in the Book of Hebrews: *'During the days of Jesus' life on earth, he offered up prayers and petitions with loud cries and tears to the one who could save him from death, and he was heard because of his reverent submission'* [1]. If the Son of Man had to do that, so must we.

For each and every reason that Jesus prayed to God, the same holds true for us. We have to tap the power of God; the resources that He wants to give us. *"Ask and it will be given to you; seek and you will find; knock and the door will be opened to you,"* [2] said the Lord. When we realize and accept our total dependence on God, prayer will come fast and easy. Prayer gets us up close and personal with God. Prayer gives us a sense of oneness with Him. And the closer we get in our relationship with God, the more we find ourselves praying. It is like a circle. We just have to get into it. Besides prayer is also a means of self-discovery. C.S. Lewis wrote: *"Prayer is taking part in the process of being deeply known."* Our prayers often tell us (and others) how much we have grown as a Christian; the level of spiritual maturity that we have reached. This discovery is important in our pilgrimage before the Lord.

A question which many do ask is: 'why should we pray when God knows everything that we need, when he knows the desires of our hearts'? Jesus said, *"… for your Father knows what you need before you ask Him."* [3] Then why does God wants us to pray and why is prayer so important for our spiritual health? Well God wants us to pray despite His being all knowing. God likes us to pray. It is like communicating with anyone. It is the means of our getting in touch with Him. God wants us to keep the channel of communication with Him vibrant and alive. We are His children. Don't you parents feel good when your children come up to you with their requests (sometimes even when you know in advance what they want)? It makes you feel good that your child has approached you. It makes you feel – well a parent! It is the same with God. It gives Him pleasure to see us coming to Him and putting forth our prayers and petitions. And He loves to see that look of surprised joy that breaks out on our face, when we receive what we have prayed for. He takes pleasure in our pleasure.

How much should we pray? Well the answer to that would be – as much as our soul needs. We cannot quantify our prayers. There is no maximum and no minimum here. We cannot define any limits. It differs from person to person. For Isaac Bashevis Singer it was quite simple. He said, *"I pray only when I am in trouble; but I am in trouble all the time, so I pray all the time."* The Bible encourages us to: *'pray in the Spirit on all occasions'.* [4] The soul should be in a constant state of communion with its Maker. And there is no time or place for prayer. The spirit is free to break into prayer anytime and anywhere; besides one's scheduled times of prayer. But care should be exercised that we do not make a show of it (draw unnecessary attention to ourselves) if we are in public places. And we must also not reduce our prayers to babbling. We are dealing with an intelligent God who wants us to communicate with Him passionately but coherently. It is not the length of the prayer that impresses Him but whether it comes from the heart of the person. So don't deliberately stretch your prayers, more than what is needed, thinking that the excess of words would impress God or induce Him to action.

These simple guidelines of prayer our Lord included in his Sermon on the Mount. He also gave us an example of *how* we should pray. It came in the form of the Lord's Prayer. It is simple but beautiful in its structure and content. We start the prayer by calling on the Father and acknowledging His holiness; then we go on to what is the prime work of God now and which was the mission of Jesus when he came – that His Kingdom come on earth and His will be obeyed in heaven and on earth; we then remember God as the provider of our daily needs; we acknowledge the need for forgiveness of our sins and also forgiving others of theirs; we accept that the evil is lurking to entice us and we need God's help to save us from our temptations; and finally we close with voicing that God's supremacy is for eternity. Jesus wanted us to pray in this way - in the form and simplicity of the Lord's Prayer. He was giving us the prototype for our prayers so that they would be like incense at the altar of God; giving out an aroma pleasing to Him.

What are the kinds of prayer that we offer to God? We engage in various types of prayer but depending on the situation, the phase of our life, and the level of maturity that we have in our Christian walk, one kind of prayer may be more dominant than the others. We look at the main forms of prayer.

## Petitions and requests

We will never get tired asking of God. And we should not, for God doesn't mind. It is *what* we ask for that is important. Folded hands and bend knees, is the posture which portrays our dependence on Him. A humble and contrite heart in prayer, is an offering pleasing to God; and an acknowledgement that we are nothing without Him and can do nothing without Him. Augustine prayed, *"I can do nothing without You."* Pat came God's reply: *"And I will do nothing without you."* The Lord is happy to receive our petitions and requests and is pleased to give us those which He knows are for our good and are as per His will. *"If you, then, though you are evil, know how to give good gifts to your children, how much more will your Father in heaven give good gifts to those who ask Him!"* [5] So bring your petitions - for your needs and the needs of others (our intercessions) - before God and He will be pleased to look at them.

And it can be anything: your problems, your fears, your inadequacies, your material requirements, your aspirations. Bring them to the Lord in prayer and wait on Him.

But don't get stuck to the 'need' prayers. Let not your prayers be reduced to just drawing out the shopping list from your pocket. There is much more to prayer than presenting to God your requests and petitions.

Prayers (verbal) can also be in the form of thanksgiving and praise and could be part of a structured worship, in prayer groups, and individually.

## Meditation

I consider meditation to be a form of prayer. We go deeper in our minds and hearts to search the mind and heart of God. Through deep reflection, we seek to understand and be enlightened to what God may be saying or revealing to us in a verse or passage of the Bible, or in a vision or dream, or through a sign that He may have given us. Here we listen and God speaks; and we wait for light to flood our souls, for realization to dawn in our consciousness, for illumination to break forth so that we may see. This requires a state of intense concentration, calm, and attention. And preferably one has to be alone, as God may speak in a whisper to reveal His will.

## Communion

In its transcendent form prayer is communion. Communion between God and us. Mother Teresa was once asked by an interviewer, as to what she prays about in her time of prayer with God. She replied, *"I listen."* The interviewer followed up with another question: *"And what does God say to you?"* She replied, *"He listens."* This is what communion is! Neither you have to talk to God, as in prayer (requests, petitions) nor God has to talk to you, as in meditation. Henri Nouwen also found that prayer for him had primarily become a time of listening in the later stages of his life. *"The real 'work' of prayer is to become silent and listen to the voice that says good things about me,"* he said. You just savour

239

the very presence of God and fill your soul with Him. *"Be still, and know that I am God."* [6] It is a mystical experience where we are consumed by Him, by His very being. Here we seek the face of God and not His hand. We do not seek what He can give us, but who He is.

Let us also consider the role of fasting. What is the usefulness of fasting in prayer? Does it contribute to our prayers? Prayer and fasting can be done separately but if prayer is accompanied by fasting, it heightens the receptivity of the senses to the presence of God and to His voice. It makes us spiritually in a more conducive state to approach and commune with God. After the healing of the boy with evil spirit, Jesus was asked by his disciples as to why they couldn't drive out the spirit from the boy. They had made the initial attempts, when Jesus was up on the mountain with Peter, James, and John (the Transfiguration), but were unsuccessful. Jesus replied, *"This kind can come out only by prayer and fasting"* [7]; thus underlining the importance of fasting in a Christian life.

And let us not forget that even the Holy Spirit prays for us, of things that we may not even be aware of. *"We do not know what we ought to pray for, but the Spirit himself intercedes for us with groans that words cannot express. And He who searches our hearts knows the mind of the Spirit, because the Spirit intercedes for the saints in accordance with God's will."* [8] We are mercifully in safe hands (and many pair of them). An intercessor on earth, another intercessor in heaven before the throne of God, and a Father who is kind and forgiving - and giving.

A dilemma for me, and I believe for many others who lead a prayerful life, is: when to stop praying about a particular thing and when to persist in prayer. It is a tight rope walk for the dividing line is pretty fine. This has challenged many. Many a times we do not receive what we have been praying for over a considerable period of time. Should we continue praying about it or should we drop it? Perhaps the Lord has already given us the answer and we are not seeing it because it is not the one that we wanted or expected. Or the Lord maybe testing our faith, to see if we will persevere. How do we discern what is the right way to go forward in such situations?

First of all we need to accept that not all our prayers will be answered the way we want. James puts it like this: *"When you ask, you do not receive, because you ask with wrong motives, that you may spend what you get on your pleasures."* [9] What we ask for is important. Is it as per God's will, His character, His ways? Do we disappoint God, even shame Him, by what we ask for in prayer? Jesus said, *"I tell you the truth, my Father will give you whatever you ask in my name."* [10] Well then, what will you ask in Jesus' name? And what will you NOT ask in Jesus's name? Think about it and the closer you come to Jesus, you will be able to make a better call on this.

And it might be that even though we may be praying for the right things, we may not be tapping God to the extent we can and should. A writer has said, *"Prayer is taking hold of God's utmost willingness."* Are we really 'stretching' God? Or do we stop short? Max Lucado believes that: *"Our problem is not so much that God doesn't give us what we hope for, as it is that we don't know the right thing for which to hope."* The Bible says: *"Delight yourself in the LORD and He will give you the desires of your heart."* [11] How about tapping God for the *desires of His heart for you*?

It is also true that some of our prayers will not be answered where they are not in line with God's ultimate plan and purpose for our life. Jesus' prayer in the Garden of Gethsemane was not answered. The cup was not taken away from him. He had to come in line with God's will. There may be nothing wrong in what we may be praying for, but remember God has the big picture and our full life before Him. He is in a better position to take the call. *"You have to wonder if God's most merciful act is His refusal to answer some of our prayers"* – Lucado again. Well we might not know, but what we may be asking for, may really not be for our good.

And what about God's silences? When does the period of silence become long enough? Does His silence mean that the answer is NO or that He wants us to continue praying? Jesus encouraged us to, *'always pray and not give up'*, [12] and then recited the parable of the widow who kept coming to the judge till he was fed up with her and gave her the justice that she was seeking. On the other hand we must know when to stop. This is the dilemma! The only solution is to have a closer and closer walk with God and that will increase our discernment in this matter. *"Faithful servants have a way of knowing answered prayer when they see it and way of not giving up when they don't"* - in the words of Max Lucado. That is the only way out!

Prayer is both a defense shield and a weapon of attack. The Christian must have it in his arsenal. As James said:

*"The prayer of a righteous man is powerful and effective."* [13]

1.  *Hebrews 5:7*
2.  *Matthew 7:7*
3.  *Matthew 6:8*
4.  *Ephesians 6:18*
5.  *Matthew 7:11*
6.  *Psalm 46:10*
7.  *Mark 9:29*
8.  *Romans 8:26-27*
9.  *James 4:3*
10. *John 16:23*
11. *Psalm 37:4*
12. *Luke 18:1*
13. *James 5:16*

# Chapter ~ 33

# TRUE RICHES

*"Again I tell you, it is easier for a camel to go through the eye of a needle than for a rich man to enter the kingdom of God."* [1]

**B**y the *'eye of a needle'* that is mentioned in this verse, some scholars are of the view that Jesus was likely referring to the opening in the wall of Jerusalem, through which the camels of the returning merchants used to enter the city, after the main gates had been closed at dusk. The opening was so small that the camels had to pass through by crawling on their knees. It was a hard task for the camel and also for the owner of the animal in getting it to passage through that opening. Well the point that Jesus was making to the people was (irrespective whether he was referring to the opening in the wall or not); that if you consider it tough for a camel to go through the 'eye of a needle', then know this, that it is much tougher for a rich man to enter the kingdom of God. Jesus was underlining here the high degree of difficulty and the 'disadvantage' of the rich man in getting to God's kingdom.

Is God against riches i.e. worldly wealth? Was Jesus being prejudiced against the rich when he made this statement? Remember he said this after the rich young man had rejected his invitation to give away all his riches and follow him. I do not believe God is against riches or rich people. But He definitely wants us to have the right perspective and the right attitude towards our earthly possessions. Because our possessions are a trap; they can easily and quickly consume us and create a chasm between us and our true riches, which is God Himself. If our possessions start possessing us then we are in trouble. If our riches become our master than we have a problem. Riches or wealth is a good servant but a bad master. Jesus made it clear: *"You cannot serve both God and Money."* [2] The word to note is *'serve'*. Jesus did not say you cannot *have* both God and money. It is which of the two you make your master, that will have an important bearing on your life.

God is not despising the rich when He gives them the many warnings that we find in the Scriptures. Rather He is cautioning them in love that they need to be more careful; for riches can easily lead them away from Him. It is love that comes out not loathing, in these warnings. When and how can one's riches become dangerous? Riches can lead us to all sorts of immoral habits and indulgences. Having our needs satisfied, we spend the surplus that we have on our wants. And there is no end to wants. It is directly related to your surplus money. Wants is a leviathan whose appetite is never satisfied. In fact the more you feed it, the more it demands. You 'invent' wants. That is where greed comes. That is where the 'Jones Effect' comes, where you are measuring yourself against others (your friends, neighbors, your social circle) as regards your possessions. It becomes a rat race and the emphasis shifts from *who you are to what you have.* You are consumed by your possessions. Your possessions make you. You identify your worth as a person with the things you have, and thus you want more and more of them, so as to increase your perceived worth. It becomes an insatiable hunger.

The danger is that your possessions will become the idol that occupies the central place of your life, replacing God. Jesus said: *"Watch out! Be on your guard against all kinds of greed; a man's life does not consist in the abundance of his possessions."* [3] You are so full of the waters from the wells that you have been drinking from, that you do not drink the water of life that God has to give. This is the danger of riches.

Paul tells Timothy: *"For the love of money is a root of all kinds of evil."*[4] Again it is to be noted that it is not money per se that is dangerous, but the *love* of money. It is the obsession with it; the obsession of acquiring money and creating wealth. It becomes your preoccupation which can make you resort to immoral and unscrupulous means. And once you have acquired it; it can then lead you to evil ways for spending it. The temptation to do evil comes easily. You plunge yourself into all kinds of evil ways and habits, and they then take you away from God. This is what God has against money. That the strong lure of it can easily make you fall in love with it, and that is when your spiritual ruin and destruction takes place. It is the love for, and the wrongful use of money, that leads to one's downfall and to the insensitivity of the soul and the hardness of the heart towards godly things. Therefore the warning in the Scripture is loud and clear: *'Keep your lives free from the love of money and be content with what you have'.* [5]

However the biggest danger of money is that it can easily lead to pride. Pride in one's own capabilities, independence, and sufficiency. As long as we consider money and wealth to be a gift from God and which, like all other gifts from Him, has to be used for His glory, we will remain grounded. But that is not easy. Some element of pride comes with wealth. You are proud that your hands have created such material riches. You boast and become arrogant; even treating other people with contempt for you consider them inferior to you. And pride blocks the grace of God. Your self-sufficiency and independence leads you to believe that you can do without God; that you are not dependent on Him for anything. You become a god of your own world, of your own empire. There is no room for God in your life. Philip Yancey wrote: *"We lean on God out of our need, not out of our surplus."* The problem with the rich man, which unfortunately he is blind to, is that he considers that he has no need for God; that he is sufficient to meet his own needs. He loses his dependence on God. That is the danger of riches which God is warning us of.

It is again to be stressed that God is not against riches. In fact money is needed to buy the material things of this world, which are essential for our physical existence. But it is the love of money and our obsessive pursuit of it (no matter what the cost!) that is unacceptable to Him. He wants us to have the *right attitude* towards riches. What is that attitude?

Firstly, we have to treat riches as a gift from God and us as its stewards. We must accept that there is only one Giver and all others are debtors. If we have this approach, then we will accordingly use our wealth for the purposes and advancement of God's Kingdom, and not to splurge on ourselves. We have to be *'rich towards God'*. [6] Also if we consider it as a gift from God, then there will be no boasting. If we have to boast we will then boast only in the Lord as the Scripture says: *"Let him who boasts boast in the Lord."* [7] There will be no grounds for pride and we will have the right attitude towards those who are less fortunate than us. We will be sensitive to their needs, rather than be preoccupied with our wants. We will then not be comfortable possessing two cloaks, when we know our brother has none.

Someone has said, and rightly so: *"Make as much wealth as you can, and give away as much wealth as you can."* To this I will add: create your wealth by godly means and principles, and its creation should not become an obsession for you. Keep always before you what Jesus said: *"What good is it for a man to gain the whole world, yet forfeit his soul?"* [8] As for distributing your wealth, there is no limit. From tithes (ten percent), which should be taken as the minimum, to an undefined upper figure, you can decide for yourself as the Lord may guide you. Remember the gospel story of the widow who put in two very small copper coins in the temple treasury. Jesus considered her offering to be more valuable in God's sight than the large sum of money that the rich put in the offering box. For she gave out of her poverty (all that she had!), while the rich made their offerings from their surpluses. She denied herself to give to God. And that Jesus found commendable.

So be prepared to listen to your heart. God can even ask of us, as He asked of the rich young man, *"Go, sell everything you have and give to the poor......,"* [9] if that is His will for us. Will we disappoint Him like that rich man or will we respond to Him, the way the first disciples did? The call to the first disciples involved in their giving up everything to follow Jesus. They went through with it and so did many after them. I have a beautiful picture of St. Francis of Assisi, in which, with his one foot on the globe he is clinging to Christ on the Cross; and the Saviour has dropped one arm from the Cross, and is holding Francis. The picture says it all. I treasure it.

In the worship service every Sunday, we recite these words: 'all things come from you and of your own do we give you'. If you consider God as the owner of your wealth and you only the steward, then do not worry, He will guide you as to how much you must keep for yourself and how much you must use for His Kingdom. But be honest in this and listen to your conscious carefully. Remember the fate of Ananias and Sapphira, who should have given all the money to the apostles from the sales proceed of their property, but kept some part of it discreetly for themselves. God does not like being short changed.

How do we further God's kingdom by our riches? We do so by investing in it. Jesus advises us: *"I tell you, use worldly wealth to gain friends for yourselves, so that when it is gone, you will be welcomed into eternal dwellings."* [10] Gain friends by helping your brother in need, by providing for others, by using your wealth wisely for creating the means of livelihood for the poor. And when you would finally arrive at heaven, you will find a big reception waiting for you. All those whose lives you had touched in this world, will be waiting to welcome you. You will have eternal friends.

We humans have the innate need for securing our future. That is why we engage in long term planning, where the investment of today will provide the returns in the future. If we consider our future to be heaven, if that is where we will be spending eternity, then should we not listen more carefully to Jesus, as we would to our personal financial adviser? He advises: *"But store up for yourselves treasures in heaven, where moth and rust do not destroy, and where thieves do not break in and steal."*[11] That is invest in the treasure that will last forever.

The good that you do on earth is storing up rewards for you in heaven. There your wealth is absolutely safe. No need for taking out an insurance on it. Whatever you are doing for God's kingdom on earth, is earning you reward points that are encashable in heaven. Put your deposits in the bank called *The All Saints Bank,* which has only one branch and that is in heaven. Make use of your time on earth to build your future life in your eternal home. If your wealth can assist you in this, all the much better. Remember it all boils down to the heart and the words of Jesus resound: *"For where your treasure is, there your heart will be also."* [12] And Christ is your treasure, your very riches. He is there above, seated at the right hand of God. Invest in Christ; invest in his kingdom. The returns will be mind boggling.

*"You shall not covet....,"* [13] is the only commandment (of the Ten which God gave to Moses on Sinai), which is internal. And this commandment in a way is a precursor to the full blown dispensation of the internal laws by Jesus in the Sermon on the Mount, about thirteen hundred years later. Why are we forbidden to covet? To covet is a sign of greed and envy. You have your own, but you are not satisfied and desire what the other has. It also conveys that you are not happy with God, with what He has given you, and consider that He has been unfair to you in your share of worldly riches and material things. That is why you covet and are envious of what others possess. The Bible warns us of this: *"Do not be overawed when a man grows rich, when the splendour of his house increases ..... ."* [14] Remember that we are all poor in the eyes of our Lord. Earthly riches are a matter of relative comparisons. Spiritual riches are what count before God.

Jesus was born poor. He did not have worldly riches. *"For you know the grace of our Lord Jesus Christ, that though he was rich, yet for your sakes he became poor, so that you through his poverty might become rich."* [15] Jesus by coming and living as a poor man, wanted to highlight that a relationship with God is independent of a man's financial status; that earthly riches do not count for a man to have a rich spiritual life. He thus intentionally chose to identify himself with the poor.

You will do well to pay heed to these words of the psalmist:

*"Though your riches increase, do not set your heart on them."* [16]

Pay heed and you will be safe.

1.  Matthew 19:24
2.  Matthew 6:24
3.  Luke 12:15
4.  1Timothy 6:10
5.  Hebrews 13:5
6.  Luke 12:21
7.  2 Corinthians 10:17 (quoting Jeremiah 9:24)
8.  Mark 8:36
9.  Mark 10:21
10. Luke 16:9
11. Matthew 6:20
12. Matthew 6:21.
13. Exodus 20:17
14. Psalm 49:16
15. 2 Corinthians 8:9
16. Psalm 62:10

# Chapter ~ 34

# DARK NIGHT OF THE SOUL

*"Do not cast me from your presence..."* [1]

I first came upon the phrase *'dark night of the soul'* in an article in Time magazine (issue of 3 September 2007). The article was on a book (though not a review) which had recently come out - *Mother Teresa: Come Be My Light*. The book was a compilation of, till then, unpublished letters of Mother Teresa; her correspondence with her confessors and spiritual mentors. Mother had wished the letters to be destroyed after her death, but the Vatican thought otherwise. So ten years after her death these private letters were made public in the form of this book.

The letters revealed a startling fact of the spiritual life of Mother Teresa who is known by the title: *'Saint of the Gutters'*. For nearly half a century (from 1948 to her death in 1997), she did not experience the presence of God in her life, except for a brief period of five weeks in 1959. She was tormented by a state of perpetual darkness and emptiness in her soul, wherein she felt bereft of the joy of her spouse, Jesus Christ. For 50 long years, this highly popular and admired saint did not feel the presence of God and of His Christ in her life. Incredible!

This came as a shocker to many (including me who holds Mother Teresa as the nearest to Christ that we will get to see in this age), for her life and work had been closely interlinked with her faith. It was at Christ's behest (she had heard Christ speaking to her) that she had left the 'comfortable' life of a nun of the community of Loreto Sisters, to work amongst the most destitute of the society – the poor, the sick, the dying, the rejected, the abandoned. God's hand was clearly to be seen in the way her work and organization, the Missionaries of Charity, had spread worldwide; growing from a single woman's calling to a large enterprise of dedicated individuals willing to follow in her footsteps, in self-giving service to the 'poorest of the poor' in this world. That a saint like Mother Teresa should experience such 'abandonment' by God, and for such an extensive length of time (perhaps the longest known), was hard to believe. One cannot but wonder how she could have endured such a long spell of spiritual barrenness and still carry on her work, and without any outward sign of the turmoil in her soul!

This intrigued me no end. Further reading in this matter revealed that this 'darkness' has been experienced by many saints, even by those considered to be spiritual masters, throughout the history of the Christian faith. The phrase *'dark night of the soul'* was coined by St. John of the Cross, the sixteenth century mystic. It refers to a phase in the saint's life (we all are saints), which is characterized by spiritual dryness, darkness, loneliness, and a seeming abandonment by God. It is a spiritually fallow period, where one does not sense the presence of God and may even have bouts of doubting His very existence. You do not feel the love of God in your life. You feel forsaken by Him and all your prayers, pleas, and entreaties appear to meet a deafening silence. God seems to have hardened His heart towards you and appears to be callous, indifferent, and even hostile.

In any other crisis that you undergo, you can lean on God for support. But where or whom to go to in this case? It is a period of extreme suffering where you do not have God to comfort you. You lose *'the joy of salvation'*. [2] Gerald Manley Hopkins prayed: *"God, though to Thee our psalm we raise, no answering voice comes from the skies; to Thee the trembling sinner prays, but no forgiving voice replies; our prayer seems lost in desert ways, our hymn in the vast silence dies."* You experience hell, when you are going through it!

Henry Nouwen wanted the absence of God (besides His presence), to be witnessed to by the Church, calling it *'the ministry of absence'*; so that the people may be aware and prepared for this phase of the Christian faith. For all saints, at one point or the other, do experience this period of darkness; though it may differ in severity, in duration, and even in the number of times it may happen in one's life. We can even say that the closer the saint is in his walk with God, the intensity of the dark night is likely to be more severe. *"The 'hiddenness' of God perhaps presses most painfully on those who are in another way nearest to Him, and therefore God Himself, made man, will of all men be by God most forsaken,"* wrote C.S. Lewis. The reference here of course is to Jesus. Did Jesus experience this dark night on the Cross, when he felt abandoned by God, so that a cry escaped from him: *"My God, my God, why have you forsaken me?"* [3] I believe so. Jesus did experience the dark night, possibly for three (out of six) hours of his suffering on the Cross, when the darkness had set in on the land; symbolizing the darkness that had descended on his soul.

This phase seems invariably to be part of the spiritual ministry of a saint; a thorn that is in his side to torment him. Philip Yancey believes: *"As God entrusts us with more responsibility, the hardships may increase as well. Feelings of abandonment intensify, any sense of the presence of God fades, and temptations and doubts multiply."* So the nearer you get to God and the more you love Him; the more you can expect the attacks of doubts and temptations to increase and hardships to multiply. Why is it so? As we grow in Christ, we become more and more threatening to Satan, and therefore his attacks targeting us and our faith intensify. Also God considers us strong and mature to 'handle' more and to be moved to the front lines of the spiritual warfare. Christian walk is not easy, and it becomes increasingly difficult as we advance in faith.

Why does a saint go through this testing period of darkness? Is it a period of crisis in faith, a *'darkness without faith'*; or is it a period of *'darkness within faith'*, which is a necessary part of every Christian journey, for it results in spiritual growth and purification of the soul?

Philip Yancey writes, *"Faith can survive period of darkness but only if we cling to it in the midst of darkness."* Is that why this period comes? As the ultimate and supreme test of faith; where you must cling on to your faith in God, despite not finding Him anywhere near you? *"The prayers offered in the state of dryness are those that please Him most. When a human, no longer desiring, but still intending, to do His will, looks around in the universe from which every trace of Him seems to have vanished, and asks why he has been forsaken, and still obeys,"* wrote C. S. Lewis. You don't feel the presence of God, yet you continue in your faith; as we see in the case of Mother Teresa. Despite her intense and persisting spiritual struggle, she displayed a calm and serene exterior, and was steadfast in her belief and work. It was not hypocrisy; but the evidence of a faith that had held out, even when the object of her faith was missing.

Another reason for this dark night is that God intends it to be an antidote to pride. It is this tension which keeps us grounded, especially in cases where God is doing (or intends to do) great works through us. In the case of Mother Teresa, her dark night started around about the time (in 1948) when she began her work amongst the destitute on the streets of Calcutta. This was perhaps God's way of keeping her pride in check, which could easily have raised its head, considering the magnitude of her task, the global recognition that she received, and the many awards that she was feted with including the Noble Peace prize. For God does not want us to go Satan's way, which pride, especially spiritual pride, can lead us to. And He uses various means to keep this pride in check. Paul had his *'thorn in my flesh'* [4] to live with, and he accepted that it was there to prevent him from becoming conceited. The dark night is also one such way; and in that it can be considered as a divine gift to our faith, even though it may lead us into the spiritual desert for a period of intense agony.

While this may be one of the worst forms of suffering, we can rejoice that by undergoing it we are sharing in the Passion of our Lord on the Cross. We can feel the abandonment, the forsakenness, which he felt for those hours on the Cross. In this experience, we are one with Christ and this fact instills an element of blessedness in this ordeal. But nevertheless ordeal it is.

Does God really abandon us when we are going through this dark night or is it that we perceive a sense of abandonment? Is God actually not present or do we lose the sense of His presence? Is this spiritual suffering caused by the real absence of God or just our feeling that He is absent? If we believe in God's promise that: *"Never will I leave you; never will I forsake you,"* [5] and in David's questioning that: *"Where can I go from your Spirit? Where can I flee from your presence?"* [6]; then I do not believe God abandons us even for a little while but that He is always present, in our every situation. How can the omnipresent God, who fills everything in everyway, be shutout from any situation? The darkness is definitely the darkness of our not being able to sense His presence. But He is surely there. The period of *'absent presence'* of God is an extremely testing and hard time for the saint; for the faith comes under attack from within.

However it brings out a fundamental truth: that faith cannot be a product of, or based on, just our feelings. *'Feeling' God is not the only proof of His being there.* The will and the intellect have also to go in the experience, along with feelings, to make the totality of our faith. In fact during the dark night, when we do not feel God's presence, it is our will which has to take over and be the dominant factor in our faith; for faith to survive. We have to will to hold on to our faith. We have to will to keep our trust in God; that God is, and even though I may not feel His presence, He is there with me. It is not a show in make believe but evidence of an enduring faith. C.S. Lewis commented, *"Faith is the art of holding on to things your reason once accepted, despite your changing moods."*

When going through your own dark night, just remember these words of James Howell: *"God comes at last when we think He is farthest off."* When we lose all hope, when despair is setting in, when the darkness of the dark night becomes unbearable, when the pain of loneliness becomes too overwhelming, when the dryness in the spirit is crushing; then hold on to these words. And also to these words of Tony Campolo; they will surely provide you comfort:

*"They (the disciples) had learned that when God seems most distant he may be the closest of all, when God looks most powerless he may be most*

*powerful, when God looks most dead he may be coming back to life. They had learned never to count God out."*

The disciples learned that. Jesus on the Cross knew that. Many saints have discovered that. We also will do well to hold on to that.

For after the dark night of the soul, there is the light of the Easter morning.

1.   Psalm 51:11
2.   Psalm 51:12
3.   Matthew 27:46
4.   2 Corinthians 12:7
5.   Hebrews 13:5 (Deuteronomy 31:6)
6.   Psalm 139:7

# Chapter ~ 35

# CALLED TO LOVE

*"But the greatest of these is love."* [1]

The gospel of Jesus Christ is the gospel of love. Of God loving mankind so much that He gave His Son for it. The gospel is also of the transformation of men and women into a new creation in Christ, where they reflect his attributes. One such attribute is *love*. Love towards God and love towards one another, for the entire humanity. Love that is to be seen in everything that we do. There is nothing that we are to do that should not be done in love. If anything is not done in love, then it becomes meaningless. Paul states this emphatically in the famous thirteenth chapter of his first epistle to the Corinthians. On the other hand if with love we are to give even a cup of water to a thirsty man, we are giving it to Christ. Love changes the dimension of our every act.

The call to love is binding. It is not an option that we have, for love defines a Christian, and is the first and the most important thing that anyone will see in us. If there is no love, then people won't see Christ in us. Love is the mark of Christ that we carry and should be clearly visible to the whole world. *"In the world Christians are a colony of the true home,"* said Dietrich Bonhoeffer. By showing the love of Christ, we give a glimpse to this world, of the world which is to come.

There are two important points that we need to note in our understanding of love. Firstly, that the Christian faith is relational. It is as much of belonging as it is of believing. There is no saint in isolation in Christianity. Rather sainthood is verified only in a social setting. *"Christianity is not the religion of doing our best or a religion of effort. The key word is union. It is not a set of rules but relationship,"* wrote Derek Prince. We have relationship with God (vertical) and relationships with others (horizontal). And both these relationships, vertical and horizontal, require the expression of love.

We love God because we are commanded to love Him above all, and with all that we have. *"Love the Lord your God with all your heart and with all your soul and with all your mind and with all your strength."* [2] Love is the obeisance of the created for his Creator. It is the reason for our existence; we were created to love Him. But we also love God for no other reason than that He loves us. *"We love because He first loved us."*[3] We love God with the overflow of His love in our hearts! He is the initiator. He has started the circle of love. We have to just keep it going and see that there is no break in it or that the flow does not stop.

The other relationship which we have is with one another; the people in our lives. Here we will distinguish between those who are our brothers and sisters i.e. fellow believers in Christ, and those who are our neighbors. As per the definition of neighbor given to us by Jesus in the story of the Good Samaritan, this would then include everyone. Everyone in this world is my neighbor. The distinction in our love for our brother and for our neighbor (which we shall be touching upon later in this chapter), be what it be, the essence of the command to love does not change. We have to love the other person because he has in him (like us) the image of God. If we cannot love the image of God that we see, how can we claim that we love God? The reverse would also hold true: If we love God, we will also love His image in each and every human being, without any exception. Dorothy Day said, *"I really only love God as much as I love the person I love the least."* This is how you can judge your love for God.

John highlights this point very strongly in his epistle: *"No one has ever seen God; but if we love one another, God lives in us and His love is made complete in us"* [4]; and further, *"If anyone says, 'I love God', yet hates his brother, he is a liar. For anyone who does not love his brother, whom he has seen, cannot love God, whom he has not seen. ..... Whoever loves God must also love his brother."* [5] And the love that we give to the other person again springs from the love of God in us. Love comes from God and we have to only distribute the same from the overflow in our hearts.

The second point we need to note is that love is supreme for *'love is the fulfillment of the law'.* [6] All the commands of God which govern our relationship with one another have the underlying concern and objective of upholding the dignity of God's image in the other person. And when we love the other person, that is the image of God in him; we are automatically fulfilling the requirements of the law. As Paul writes, *"Let no debt remain outstanding, except the continuing debt to love another, for he who loves his fellow man has fulfilled the law."* [7] If we look at the commands and teachings of Christ, we will find that the principle underlying all of them is: *Love one another.* This is the *'law of Christ'.* [8] All other laws and commands are flowing out of it and are fulfilled in the fulfillment of this one command.

The beauty of love is that it encompasses in itself grace and forgiveness. Love can forgive all, can give all. In fact grace and forgiveness are only possible where there is love. Peter writes, *"Above all, love each other deeply, because love covers over a multitude of sins."* [9] This is the manner in which God loves us. He covers all our mistakes, all our sins, all our foolishness, all our rebellions. And this is how we are to love. If we do, then streams of grace and forgiveness will flow out from us. This is the reason the Scripture places so much importance on love and is full of teachings about it. God wants us to have love and have it in abundance.

We need to understand that love, that is Christian love, is not just an emotion. It transcends feelings and is not subject to our likes and dislikes. Christ did not command: "you must *like* one another." The command was to love and love can be found (Christian love that is) even where you may not like a person or be in a disagreement with him or simply cannot get along with him. You are to still show him the love of Christ. It is not hypocrisy but the essence of this love. Jesus did not like all the people that he encountered in his time. He railed against the Pharisees (calling them white washed tombs), the money changers (they were labeled thieves), and the religious leaders who were full of their legalistic righteousness (he warned them of their spiritual hypocrisy). Though he disliked them, yet he loved them to the extent of asking for forgiveness for them on the cross ('*Father, forgive them, for they do not know what they are doing*', [10] was meant to include all those who were directly or indirectly responsible for his death).

Just for a moment consider if God was to deal with us only as per His likes and dislikes, then where would we be. We would not have seen the love that made Him sacrifice His Son. And among humans, let us take the case of St. Francis of Assisi, as just one example of this love: even though he found the leprous beggar, whom he had encountered on the road, repulsive to touch, he still put his hands in the hands of the leper, so that the leper would also be touched by love – the love of Christ. Francis willed himself to show love and love made him overcome his repulsion. Christian love works as such.

The love of God that is in us, and that flows out from us, is not about feelings. It is about will, about obedience, and about our actions. In this, it is unlike the love of the world. This love (godly love) is the most exalted form of love, in which even if we may not like a person or find him detestable, YET we are to love him. For Christ does love him and we therefore must show him the love of Christ, who is our Master. And even for those who are our enemies or whom we consider our enemies, the command of our Lord is clear: "*Love your enemies and pray for those who persecute you.*" [11] This will not be easy. This form of love is difficult to come by and will require the overruling of emotions by the will many a times. But nevertheless God has called us to take hold of this love. "*To love a person means to see him as God intended him to be,*" said Fyodor Dostoevsky and that is only possible when we love as God loves; that is looking right through the muck that clings to the person and see the pristine creation that the Maker had made.

One way our faith is expressed is love. Paul says, *"The only thing that counts is faith expressing itself through love."* [12] In the gospels we find three calls of love being made. They require an increasing response of love from us. The demand gets progressively harder.

The first call of love we find in the Sermon on the Mount where Jesus says, *"So in everything, do to others what you would have them do to you, for this sums up the Law and the Prophets."* [13] In this, our love is largely reactive or subject to the expectations that we might have of what we want the other person to do to us. So in a sense and compared to the other two (that we shall see) it is limiting and we might even say defensive.

The second call of love is in what James calls the 'Royal Law', [14] referring to the Old Testament command of: *'Love your neighbor as yourself'*. [15] Jesus testified to the importance of this commandment by putting it right there at the top, next to the greatest commandment. On being queried by a teacher of the law as to which is the greatest commandment in the Law, Jesus answered: *"'Love the Lord your God with all your heart and with all your soul and with all your mind'. This is the first and greatest commandment. And the second is like it: 'Love your neighbor as yourself'. All the Law and the Prophets hang on these two commandments."* [16]

The teacher had asked for one commandment, that is to be considered the greatest, but Jesus in reply gave him two; implying that these two go together. Though, *'Love the Lord your God ..."* would rank the number one in terms of being greatest or in importance, but the second, *'Love your neighbor ...'* is LIKE IT, as Jesus said. In fact the second one is the corollary to the first. And Jesus did underline that the entire Scripture boiled down to the fulfillment of these two commandments. Paul emphasized the same point when he wrote, *"....and whatever other commandment there may be, are summed up in this one rule: 'Love your neighbor as yourself'. Love does no harm to its neighbor. Therefore love is the fulfillment of the law."* [17] The relational aspect of our faith comes out clearly in this teaching of Jesus. You cannot love God and not love your neighbor. Both the commandments go hand in hand.

Let us try to understand this commandment. It starts with the premise that one loves oneself. If we don't then there is a problem. We are either suffering from a low self-esteem or are angry with ourselves. But normally it is in the human nature to love oneself. Rather the problem is seen more often in the excess love that we have for ourselves, leading to narcissism and even self-worship. But it is the 'healthy' love of the self that this commandment is referring to, and anyone who loves himself does not desire his own harm. It is the love of the self which makes us forgive ourselves when we commit a wrong, or a mistake, or a sin. It is only because of this love that we are able to distinguish between ourselves (the person) and the actions that we commit, and thus can forgive ourselves. We are patient, and even absolving, of our own weaknesses and shortcomings. And we definitely desire good things for ourselves.

The commandment works on this very principle. If we apply to others all that we apply to ourselves, and consider the other person no different from ourselves in terms of the treatment he deserves, then we will love him as ourselves. The commandment seeks to elevate the love one has for the other (neighbor) to the level of one's love for oneself. For example: If we intentionally cannot cause harm to ourselves, then likewise we cannot harm or desire harm to our neighbor. All commandments are thus fulfilled by the same working. God showed us a way for fulfilling His laws, by the exercise of this love (now we can understand how *'love is the fulfillment of the law'?*). It is different from the first call of love mentioned above, for here the ball is in our court; the expectations are from us; it is we who must set the pace. And if everyone fulfills this commandment, then will any problem remain? Love will abound all around, in every relation.

The third call of love surpasses the other two. It is a call of *self-giving* love. It takes love to a different dimension, to a different plane. The call to love requires you to put others before yourself. It is a new command of love that has been introduced to mankind for the very first time. *It is the law of Christ.* It is seen in dying to self so as to live for others. In this love you lose your life in order to save it. This is what Christianity is all about: Love expressed in self-less service to others.

It is where you empty yourself for others. This is a call, where the level of love is not resting on our expectations from others, and also not on our expectations from our own self, but on God's expectations from us. And God's expectations have their expression in the life of Jesus and his sacrificial death for mankind. God's love is *'agape'* love; the highest and purest form of love, and the call to us is to have the same kind of love for others.

The call is made when Jesus says: *"My command is this: Love each other as I have loved you. Greater love has no-one than this, that he lay down his life for his friends. You are my friends if you do what I command."* [18] Our Lord showed this love and his disciples are to show the same love. *"This is how we know what love is: Jesus Christ laid down his life for us. And we ought to lay down our lives for our brothers."* [19] This is the extent to which this love must be willing to go. And not only for friends or brothers; Jesus died for the whole world, even for his enemies. But I believe friends and brothers are specified in these verses, so as to refer to all those who would believe and put their faith in Jesus, and thus make his sacrifice the sacrifice of love.

Is there to be a difference in our love for our Christian brothers (the family of believers) and our love for our neighbors, that is the world at large? In essence love is love, and Christian loves makes no distinction whether the recipient is a believer or not. The much popular and much recited verse of the Bible: *"For God so loved the world that He gave His only begotten Son ......,"* [20] reveals God's love for the entire world and not a select few. This is His *general* love. But those who accept His love and His grace given in His Son Jesus Christ, enter into a special love relationship with Him. They become part of His family and are brothers and sisters of Christ. That love is *special* love. In essence the same but now expressed differently and I would say more closely and uninhibitedly (for example here we are prompted to call God as *Abba,* Father).

In the same way our love towards everyone will remain the same, irrespective whether the other person is in the family of believers or not. The Christian hospitals give same treatment to Christians and non-Christians. The Christian educational institutes likewise. The

Missionaries of Charity sisters are not selective when picking up the needy from the streets. The famous surgeon Paul Brand did not ask the lepers to convert before he was to treat them. You don't change the extent or the quality of your assistance subject to the identity of the recipient or the beneficiary of your aid. So at the core, love remains the same. It cannot be different.

But in expression it can be. Jesus said, *"Love one another. As I have loved you, so you must love one another. By this all men will know that you are my disciples, if you love one another."* [21] By this all men will know that you are my disciples! Mark that! Love one another in such a way that the Christian community will stand out in the world. The distinguishing mark for the family of believers is the love they have amongst themselves. Love will be a witness to the world that we as a community are different and such will be the beauty of this love that people will want to become part of our community and thus come to Christ.

The early church stood out in this manner because of this Christ-like love (which love the world had never seen before) they had in the community. They gained the reputation of being different from anything else in the world, as being set apart from this world; and believers acquired the name Christians – Christ ones – which became their distinguishing mark. Does the Christian community stand out in a similar manner in today's world or has it been assimilated into this world to such an extent that no differentiation remains? The answer to this would not be encouraging. But in small pockets and groups, I believe, the Christian community still stands out in this age. Wherever there is seen a revival of the Spirit; a return to the early church of the first generation of disciples is also seen, to a large if not to the full extent. But unfortunately this 'return to the first century church' movement is not on a wider scale so as to make a global impact or have a broader visibility.

What was so special in the early church of the time of the apostles? It was love; love which resulted in the sharing of resources amongst the believers. *"All the believers were one in heart and mind. No one claimed that any of his possessions was his own, but they shared everything they had."* [22] They fulfilled the law of Christ by carrying each other's burdens.

Love was seen in action, as what John writes: *"Dear children, let us not love with words or tongue but with actions and in truth."* [23] Faith has to be expressed in love and love has to be seen in action. Dag Hammarskjold said, *"The road to holiness necessarily passes through the world of action."* And James was particular in pointing to this in his epistle: *"What good is it, my brothers, if a man claims to have faith but has no deeds? Can such faith save him?"* [24]

For the early believers their love and action were entwined. And the same is expected from us – believers of this age. We have to show that we are God's family, and that we are different, and that the difference is our love for one another, and that love is seen in action. Then is fulfilled the desire of Jesus: *"By this all men will know that you are my disciples."* Then that love will be like a beacon drawing the people to the community, as they too will desire to taste the love of Christ.

Mother Teresa, the apostle of love, once said: *"I have found the paradox that if I love until it hurts, then there is no hurt, but only more love."*

Christ lives in such self-giving love, changing the hurt to love. I wonder if we can love such.

We must. For Christ's sake!

1.  *1 Corinthians 13:13*
2.  *Mark 12:30.*
3.  *1 John 4:19*
4.  *1 John 4:12*
5.  *1 John 4:20-21*
6.  *Romans 13:10*
7.  *Romans 13:8*
8.  *Galatians 6:2*
9.  *1 Peter 4:8*
10. *Luke 23:34*
11. *Matthew 5:44*
12. *Galatians 5:6*
13. *Matthew 7:12*
14. *James 2:8*
15. *Leviticus 19:18*
16. *Matthew 22:37-40*
17. *Romans 13:9-10*
18. *John 15:12-14*
19. *1 John 3:16*
20. *John 3:16*
21. *John 13:34-35*
22. *Acts 4:32*
23. *1 John 3:18*
24. *James 2:14*

# Chapter ~ 36

# DIFFERENT SEASONS: GOOD TIMES - BAD TIMES

*"There is a time for everything, and a season for every activity under heaven: a time to weep and a time to laugh...."* [1]

Christian life is not all bed of roses, as some would like to believe. Many Christian groups and sects promise a life full of prosperity, health, and happiness for the believers. No derailment, no crash, no periods of downswing; but life that will always be on a smooth linear track after we accept Christ, they say. I am afraid that is a lie and they do disservice to the Lord by promoting him as a 'god of good times'. They promote him no different from how many other religions do with their gods. It becomes a contract faith, and the one who enters the Christian faith on this basis, is in for a rude shock. His belief will not last long.

"*God's purpose for us is always what will contribute most to our good,*" wrote Jean Pierre de Cassuade. This is the key! The Scripture express the same in the verse: "*And we know that in all things God works for the good of those who love Him, who have been called according to His purpose."*[2] God is able to use all things and all times, whether good or bad, to work out His purposes for our lives. He can use even the bad for our ultimate good. If we are willing to accept this, then we will be able to understand that God has in no way promised only good times in our lives. Why should Christians be an exception? Why should God suspend the laws of nature and the laws with which He runs the universe, so as to save us from calamity, disease, or tragedy?

Well sometimes He does. He intervenes in many cases (and we call them miracles) where it fits His purpose. However these are exceptions and not the rule. We believers, like non-believers, are subject to the laws and constraints of this world. That means we will go through pain and suffering caused by any of these factors: - financial problems, death of a near one, a major illness or injury, a natural or man-made calamity, career failure, troubled relationships and others such. A different sun will not shine on us. On the contrary we have been warned by the Lord himself that: *"In this world you will have trouble."* [3]

Though a Christian life will not be devoid of disappointments and pain, but one thing we have been promised; that during the periods when we are down, when going is tough and life is collapsing around us, we will be given strength to endure. His power will hold us, so that though we may stumble, we will not fall; we will bend, but will not break. The Lord will be strongly present with us in these periods; more so than in the periods of upswing. He will be carrying us in his arms so that we would be puzzled to see only one set of foot prints on the sand. They would be the footprints of the Lord. And then this realization will dawn on us: *"You will never know that Jesus is all you need, until Jesus is all you have."*

When we are going through a bad phase, when misfortune strikes us; we cry out, 'God why me'? Do we ask the same question of God when the going is good, when fortune is smiling on us? I am sure very few ask the question then; 'why me'? (Many of course do remember to thank God). I consider that most of us take it as our birthright (as Christians) to have the Lord send us only the good things in life. We argue 'aren't we the children of God'? As said before this is a fallacious view of our faith and it soon gets busted and leads to disappointment and maybe even 'walking out'.

There is another thing that we see. During the good times we do not have much time for God. We give Him only lip service and our worship becomes superficial. We go through the motions of observing our faith. But in bad times we have all the time for Him. Our prayers get fervent and become more often. Our worship gets passionate and heartfelt. Our heart yearns for God's presence. Strangely then, God does not have time for us; for so it appears to us. God seems to go into a silent mode. He seems to withdraw from us.

Point is why can't we take both good and bad times as one, as same? Why do they cause a different response, a different state in us? Why should a time be considered good or bad at all? *These are but different seasons and God is present in all the seasons.* Why can't or shouldn't we give Him; the same primacy in attention, the same intensity in worship, the same fervor in prayer, the same steadiness of focus, and the same amount of time in all the seasons – good or bad. I am sure He wants us to do precisely that. Someone said, *"You give God time and He will give you eternity."* But somehow during the good times we are just too preoccupied with the present, so as to give any thought to eternity. But good times don't last, just as the bad ones don't. Only God remains the one constant in our lives.

Let us look at the account of Job again. We have done it before, but his is such a fascinating case study that we can draw many lessons and much inspiration from this ancient tale. Job had all the good things in life – wealth, livestock, family, health, and a reputation of a God fearing and righteous man. Then things turned upside down. His life was hit by a spate of calamities in quick succession, so that he was left with nothing. His wealth and livestock were lost. His children died. His health was severely affected as he suffered from sores all over his body. His reputation took a nosedive as people, even his close friends, concluded that Job must have sinned and so had been punished by God.

What was Job's response when the bad times came so rudely in his life? He fell to the ground in worship and said, *"The LORD gave and the LORD has taken away; may the name of the LORD be praised."* [4] Though he underwent immense suffering, Job did not accuse God of any wrongdoing though he was prodded to *'curse God and die!'* [5] He still kept faith in the goodness and fairness of God. He held on strongly to his faith when he should have chucked his faith. In fact faith became his one and only lifeline during the time of his tragedy. His determination could be seen, when he said to his friends, referring to God: *"Though He slay me, yet will I hope in Him."* [6] In holding firm, in persevering, in still trusting and hoping in God, despite God allowing his life to crumble completely, Job showed exemplary faith.

It was Job's response to his sufferings which pleased God. Job showed that one must still keep faith when there is no reason to keep faith. He showed that one must still hope even when the situation has become completely hopeless. He showed that one must still trust God even when He has left no reason to justify our trust. That is why God has kept the Book of Job in the Bible. Job proved to be a man who had faith for all seasons, and thus stands as an inspiration for us; as how to face the good times and the bad times of our lives. The bad times will surely come, but it will be our response during that time that will matter, that will be crucial. Someone has aptly said that experience is not what happens to you, but is what you make out of what happens to you.

While we must face the good and the harsh times squarely, but all the same they do give rise to different feelings in us. The hard times will bring out feelings of helplessness, hopelessness, worthlessness, desperation, grief, dejection, anger, despair, shame, fear, guilt. All these are negative emotions which flood our inner selves when the going is bad. They create a dark cover over our souls. These feelings find their expression in the Book of Psalms. The Psalms is a fantastic book of human emotions. It wonderfully mirrors the soul. The psalms cover the entire spectrum of our emotions; from joy, exultation, happiness to despair, grief, anger. It is interesting to note that more than half of the psalms in the Bible are those which cover negative moods. Sample these: *"How long will you assault a man? Would all of you throw him down – this leaning wall, this tottering fence?"* [7] and, *"What gain is there in my* destruction, in my going down into the pit? Will the dust praise you? Will it proclaim your faithfulness?" *8* and, "From the ends of the earth I call you, I call as my heart grows faint." *9*

These are the 'dark' or 'uncomfortable' psalms for they give expression to the negative emotions in us. But God has included them in His Book, for like the feelings of joy and praise, these feelings are also real. God can accept all our feelings as long as they are an honest expression of our state of being. There is a psalm for every season and it is so because we will undergo different seasons in our lives, which will bring out different moods or emotions in us. So if you wish to give expression to the mood that you are in, which may have been caused by your circumstances; look up the Book of Psalms. You will surely find a psalm which will fit the mood. However the point that is being underlined is - that we will surely pass through different phases in our lives. The Bible says so and has kept the psalms ready for us.

Knowing that we will have our share of bad times, the questions we ask are: Whether any purpose is served in our facing them? Is there any intention behind making us go through them? Does God have a design or are these periods just incidental? Does God bring them about?

Well He does, but not always. But all the same, whether He engineers them or allows them in our lives, He sure does use them to build us up. There is only one thing that we will take with us when we leave this world. And that is our character. God uses the rough times, especially the rough times, to build our character Christlike. Paul explains, *"....but we also rejoice in our sufferings, because we know that suffering produces perseverance; perseverance, character; and character, hope."*[10] James says the same, *"Consider it pure joy, my brothers, whenever you face trials of many kinds, because you know that the testing of your faith develops perseverance. Perseverance must finish its work so that you may be mature and complete, not lacking anything."* [11] That is not lacking in any aspect of your character.

The founding fathers of our faith stressed this vital point forcefully and repeatedly; that trials and suffering will come to produce good in us and we must rejoice even during the times when we are going through them. Our deepest strengths only emerge through testing, and spiritual growth is only possible in the crucible of suffering. *"It is the fire of suffering that brings forth the gold of godliness,"* wrote Madame Guyon. God is more concerned in our godliness, in our character, than in anything else in our lives. *"Endure hardship as discipline; God is treating you as sons. For what son is not disciplined by his father? Our fathers disciplined us for a little while as they thought best; but God disciplines us for our good, that we may share in his holiness."* [12] This should give us enough encouragement as to the meaning of the trials and hardships, and the testing and troubled times, in our lives. God is not punishing us, as some may feel, but He is disciplining us for our own good, by these rough patches, even though it may not seem so at the time we are going through them.

Another reason for the bad times coming in our lives is to bring us closer to God. We can wander off and this is God's way of bringing us back; to even a closer walk with Him. *"Pain is God's megaphone,"* wrote C.S. Lewis, and sometimes that is the only way for God to get our attention. Pain makes us slow down and examine what could be wrong in our lives. God wants us to have a close relationship with Him; to know Him most intimately and not just superficially. And it is in the bad times of our life, when we realize the most, our dependence on God and our need to know Him and His ways. *"I have known more of God in times of struggle and suffering,"* said the English writer Malcolm Muggeridge.

And strange though it may seem, but it makes sense with experience; bad times do help us appreciate the good times more. They help us to count our blessings and to be grateful for them. We are then able to see more clearly, how good God has been to us. George Wald wrote, *"When you have no experience of pain it is rather hard to experience joy."* In a sense, joy becomes more joyous when we have experienced pain. While we are on the upswing, we do not fully value God's blessings to us; it is only when we are bereft of them, do we long for them.

God also brings around bad times to test and strengthen our faith; as He did in Job's case. The depth and maturity of our faith come out only when we go through trials and hardships. Peter writes, *"In this you greatly rejoice, though now for a little while you may have had to suffer grief in all kinds of trials. These have come so that your faith—of greater worth than gold, which perishes even though refined by fire—may be proved genuine and may result in praise, glory and honor when Jesus Christ is revealed."* [13] Faith is easy to come by when the going is smooth, life is in order, everything is in place, and God is in heaven. It is difficult to come by when it is most needed.

But faith is known for what it is during the storms of life, and is also build up by these very storms. C.S. Lewis wrote, *"You never know how much you believe something till its truth becomes a matter of life and death."* It is in those testing periods that we come to know how much faith we have, as also how much faith we need. Faith requires crisis in life and in our relationship with God, to mature; to become bedrock. And only a mature faith can accept that it could well be God's will to give us deliverance *in* the situation and not *from* the situation, that which we may be wishing for.

Sometimes suffering can come because of our faith. We can be persecuted because we bear the name of Jesus. Not all will go through such suffering; but still even today in many parts of the world, Christians do face persecution for their faith. We can feel for those who go through such suffering. Peter writes, *"However, if you suffer as a Christian, do not be ashamed, but praise God that you bear that name."* [14] In a peculiar way you are blessed if you suffer for Christ, because you bear his name. You are sharing in his suffering. Jesus had a special word for those who will suffer for his sake: *"Blessed are those who are persecuted because of righteousness, for theirs is the kingdom of heaven. Blessed are you when people insult you, persecute you and falsely say all kinds of evil against you because of me. Rejoice and be glad, because great is your reward in heaven, for in the same way they persecuted the prophets who were before you."* [15]

The time of testing can be extremely harsh. It is one thing to write or talk about it, but to those who are undergoing the phase it can be very painful – mentally, spiritually and physically. You wish it would be over. You understand everything; that it is for your good, that God would not have permitted it if it was not as per His purpose for you, that God is still in control and He is fair and loving, that He is disciplining and not punishing you. All this you know, but all the same you want the phase to end.

But sometimes the phase can be of an extremely long duration and you start wondering if God has forgotten you. Why doesn't He act? As the psalmist puts it, *"Why do you hold back your hand, your right hand? Take it from the folds of your garment....."* [16] You find God stretching your patience and your perseverance to the breaking point. But remember no matter how long your suffering turns out to be and how intense your pain, God will bring the phase to an end only when His purpose has been fulfilled. He cannot stop in the middle of the surgery and leave you on the operation table! But rest assured the phase will end. *"The future has a way of arriving unannounced,"* said George Will. Jeremiah in the midst of his lamentations holds out this lantern of hope: *"For men are not cast off by the Lord forever."* [17] God will not forget you nor will He forsake you. Selwyn Hughes puts it this way: *"Behind every cross lies an Easter morning."*

That morning will come; and when it comes, the joy that will fill you, will be immeasurable and unimaginable. Then these words of Augustine will appear to make sense: *"Everywhere a greater joy is preceded by a greater suffering."* You will be able to look back, to the painful time that you have endured, with understanding. And then when you go into the next trough in your life, you will do well to remember these words of A. W. Tozer: *"Always learn to judge the future by the past."* Just remember how God had delivered you previously. If He had done it then; He will do it again. The psalmist comforted himself with these words: *"I will remember the deeds of the LORD; yes, I will remember your miracles of long ago. I will meditate on all your works and consider all your mighty deeds."* [18] Just hold on. Have confidence. Keep trusting.

Tough times will come for sure in your life. It is how you handle them, is that what counts. You may not be responsible for what happens to you, but you are responsible for how you respond to what happens to you. You can either fall apart or get stronger. You can either fall away from your faith or you can grow in your faith. Just be sure that - *"No storm can sink the ship in which Christ is riding"* (quoting Selwyn Hughes). No matter how tough the time and how terrible the pain that you have to go through, you can endure it and come out a better person. *"What does not destroy me makes me stronger,"* said Nietzsche. This is provided you keep holding on to Christ and do not take your eyes off him. Peter could keep walking on the water as long as his eyes were on Jesus. The moment he took his eyes off him, he became conscious of the wind and began to sink. The same is with our lives.

When we look back to those phases where we had a tough time, and one day even at our entire life, we will find that they were necessary and that they were worth the pain that we had to suffer. *"From heaven the most miserable life will look like one bad night in an inconvenient hotel,"* wrote Teresa of Avila. Then we will be happy that we had endured, that we had stood the test, for:

*"Blessed is the man who perseveres under trial, because when he has stood the test, he will receive the crown of life that God has promised to those who love him."* [19]

Crown of life! That is too valuable a prize to miss out on. It will be worth everything.

1.  *Ecclesiastes 3:1,4*
2.  *Romans 8:28*
3.  *John 16:33*
4.  *Job 1:21*
5.  *Job 2:9*
6.  *Job 13:15*
7.  *Psalm 62:3*
8.  *Psalm 30:9*
9.  *Psalm 61:2*
10. *Romans 5:3-4*
11. *James 1:2-4*
12. *Hebrews 12:7,10*
13. *1 Peter 1:6-7*
14. *1 Peter 4:16*
15. *Matthew 5:10-12*
16. *Psalm 74:11*
17. *Lamentations 3:31*
18. *Psalm 77:11-12*
19. *James 1:12*

# Chapter ~ 37

# THE HEART OF THE MATTER

*"Create in me a pure heart, O God...."* [1]

The heart of the matter is the matter of the heart. The heart of Christian faith is the matter of the heart. Externals count, but compared to what goes on in the heart, they are less important. Christianity is the journey of the heart requiring the mind, and not the other way around.

The commandment to love God, which is the foremost commandment, includes both the heart and mind: *"Love the Lord your God with all your heart and with all your soul and with all your mind and with all your strength."* [2] You first love with your heart and supplement it with your mind. God wants us to love Him with our minds too, because He is ready to stand up to close and full scrutiny. He wants our faith to be fully rounded. *"Taste and see that the LORD is good,"* [3] is an invitation to experience Him with all our senses; and He sure will not be found wanting.

Although we have to love Him with all our faculties, but the love has to first begin with the heart, and only after that, we are able to love Him with our minds also. In the Bible, unbelief has been attributed to the *'hardening of heart'*, which then shuts our mind, so that: *"Though seeing, they do not see; though hearing, they do not hear or understand."* [4] When the heart is not right towards God, the reasoning faculty gets deadened and stops functioning.

*"Blessed are the pure in heart, for they will see God."* [5] Jesus in this Beatitude gave us the condition for seeing God; the state of our heart for us to enter His presence. Anyone who wishes to see God has to attain the level of purity necessary to welcome Him, who is holiness personified. *"Impurity separates us from God. Purity is the condition for a higher love – for a possession superior to all possessions: that of God,"* wrote Francois Mauriac. That is why David prayed, *"Create in me a pure heart, O God...."* He knew that was the prerequisite for the resumption of his communion with God, which had been disrupted by his sin of adultery with Bathsheba.

This coming from a man whom God called, *"a man after my own heart,"* [6] is somewhat astonishing. But if we look at the heroes of the Bible, we find that almost all of them were basically flawed and lacking in one or more essential character traits. They were not perfect. In David's case he was an adulterer and murderer. And over the course of his life he committed many sins. Then what was so special about these characters that God chose them and used them so wonderfully in fulfilling His purposes; that they eventually became known as men and women of God.

The one thing common to them, and to which God clearly gave more importance than anything else, was that their hearts were right with God (David sought God passionately with all his heart, right through his life). That was what God sought and found in them. No matter what happened in their lives, their hearts remained aligned with God. And God was pleased with them and used them as instruments of His glory. God searches the hearts of men, to see if there is a thirst for Him, the burning desire to be consumed with Him, to see if it aches for Him.

Why is so much importance given to the heart in the Bible, both in the Old and the New Testament, that there are many references to it? Why is God so much particular on what goes on in our hearts, and as David prayed, *"I know, my God, that you test the heart and are pleased with integrity"?* [7] Why is it that the sacrifice pleasing to God is, *'a broken and contrite heart'?* [8]

The heart is the barometer of the spiritual health of a person. If the heart is healthy than that person is spiritually alive. But we need to understand here what the Bible means by the heart. The heart is the seat of emotion, will, conscience, and intellect, in a person. It is the fulcrum of the morality of a person. Simply put heart as used in the Bible refers to the *inner man*.

Jesus pointed out that the heart is the repository of good and evil in a man, and that a person can only bring out what is in his heart. He said, *"The good man brings good things out of the good stored up in his heart, and the evil man brings evil things out of the evil stored up in his heart. For out of the overflow of his heart his mouth speaks."* [9] What is inside of you is what will come out. The inner man is revealed in the process. Just as a tree is known by its fruits; a man will be known by what he produces, which will depend on what is in his heart. You can argue that people are skillful in masking what is in their hearts, and their words and actions could deceptively hide what they really are. It could be true sometimes and for a while; but ultimately good or evil will come out. The real you would break out.

And Jesus declared that what goes in us – from outside to inside – cannot make us unclean or unholy; it is what comes out from us – from inside to outside - which does. *"What comes out of a man is what makes him 'unclean'. For from within, out of men's hearts, come evil thoughts, sexual immorality, theft, murder, adultery, greed, malice, deceit, lewdness, envy, slander, arrogance and folly. All these evils come from inside and make a man 'unclean'."* [10] These are the fruits of the evil that is stored in our hearts. By our fruits we will be known!

The heart is thus the center of our spiritual life. And it is the heart which God works on, to bring the transformation in us. For transformation to be lasting, it has to be from inside out. The inner man has to change. The heart has to change to be able to see the light of Christ. The heart has to change for the word of God to find its roots in us. If there is no change in the heart then there will be no new creation in Christ. God thus goes about reconstructing the heart. Everything else will follow once the heart has been made right.

The teachings contained in the Sermon on the Mount are directed to the inner man. They aim to create inner purity in a person rather than outer legalism. Jesus wrote the law on the hearts of men and women, as was promised long ago through Jeremiah: *"This is the covenant that I will make with the house of Israel after that time,"* declares the LORD. *"I will put my law in their minds and write it on their hearts. I will be their God, and they will be my people. No longer will a man teach his neighbor, or a man his brother, saying, 'Know the LORD,' because they will all know me from the least of them to the greatest,"* declares the LORD." [11] When the law is written on the heart, its reconstruction begins.

*"Here I am! I stand at the door and knock. If anyone hears my voice and opens the door, I will come in and eat with him, and he with me."* [12] It is the door of our hearts that Jesus is knocking upon.

Open it.

1. *Psalm 51:10*
2. *Mark 12:30.*
3. *Psalm 34:8*
4. *Matthew 13:13*
5. *Matthew 5:8*
6. *Act 13:22*
7. *1 Chronicles 29:17*
8. *Psalm 51:17*
9. *Luke 6:45.*
10. *Mark 7:20-23*
11. *Jeremiah 31:33-34*
12. *Revelation 3:20*

# Chapter ~ 38

# CENTER OF YOUR LIFE

*"Whom have I in heaven but you?*
*And earth has nothing I desire besides you."* [1]

**W**ho is the center of your life? This is a vital question; in fact the most important question of your life. For whoever or whatever is the center of your life will define you and control you. If it is Jesus (here in this chapter God and Jesus are used interchangeably) who is the center of your life then you have chosen well. If it is not Jesus but someone or something else; like a person, an ideology, a philosophy, a hobby, a fascination, material things, money, career, and even *yourself;* then you are off center. The truth is; man's life was created by God in such a way that it can function properly only if it is centered on Christ. If it is not, then it goes against the laws of nature, against the very structure of the universe. That life will not work – from God's perspective. Sadly there are even many Christians (used in the wider sense of the term) who do not have Christ as the center of their lives.

The center is the main reason for your existence. It is the pivotal point of your universe. Your life is structured around it and revolves around it. You every decision, your every act, is taken keeping the center in view. If God is the center, then as C. S. Lewis puts it: *"Every single act and feeling, every experience, whether pleasant or unpleasant, must be referred to God."* Awake or sleeping, consciously or unconsciously, God would pervade your every thought, feeling, and action. God would become the center of gravity of your life and all things would gravitate around Him. The center of your life is the focus of your attention. Some believe that if you keep your focus constantly on somebody, you will start developing his characteristics; you will begin imbibing his nature so that you become his image. Keep you focus on Christ and you will become increasingly Christlike.

God wants to be the center of our lives. Not because He wishes to dominate us, but in love He wants to guide and lead us through this life. He knows that without Him we are nothing and our lives will not work. Our life could have all the outward appearance and trappings of success, and may appear to be going smoothly in every aspect; but if it is not rooted in Christ, it would only be a bubble waiting to burst. It is a chimera in which most of the world lives and labels it as 'life is beautiful'. We can remain entrapped in it all our lives. To put it bluntly - life in which Christ is not there, will not work. It is only a mirage which is meant to fool us and keep us away from the true life. We attempt to create 'our heavens on earth' rather than take hold of *'the life that is truly life'.* [2]

We have a tree in front of our house which we had planted when the construction of the house was being done. So it is as old as the house. From a sapling that had been planted it had grown into a tall majestic tree. It had a wide cover and people enjoyed a good rest under its shade. For the past three years it had been budding beautiful red flowers. The tree was a blessing; for us and for the many who enjoyed its beauty and the comfort it provided. Sometime ago there was a big storm. The force of the gale was so strong that it yanked the tree from its roots. Like a fallen giant it lay on its side. We were dismayed at the sight and so were the people of the neighborhood. I wondered how a nine year old tree with quite a big trunk could get uprooted. Its external appearance gave the impression of solidity.

We had the fallen tree stripped of its branches and when only the portion of the trunk remained we set about planting it back; for we loved the tree and wanted to restore it. We then discovered what had been the reason for its fall. The advance of its roots had been blocked by a concrete sewage pipe and therefore they had not gone deep enough into the soil to support such a big tree. Clearly we had not taken enough care when planting it the first time. Now we wanted to make sure that we plant it back in such a way that its roots would be able to go deep into the soil and thus stand to the storms in the future.

The incident of the tree gave me a life lesson. The center of your life is what you are rooted in. And if Christ is not the center and your life is not rooted deep in him, then you would not survive the first real storm that comes your way. Your life externally may give the impression of solidity and well-being, but it will come crashing down if its roots are in any other center than Christ. Paul exhorts us to: *"Let your roots grow down into Christ and draw up nourishment from him. See that you go on growing in the Lord, and become strong and vigorous in the truth."* [3] And Jesus asked us to be like the wise man who built his house (your life) on the rock (on him). Then no matter how violent the weather (how severe the tribulation), your house will not fall; for its foundation is on the rock. The center of your life has to be firm and unchanging; otherwise your life will never be stable and will be ever shaky. Know that everything else can change, but Christ will not. *"Jesus Christ is the same yesterday and today and forever."* [4] This is the certainty we have in the unchanging and reliable nature of our center, who is Christ.

We must lead God intoxicated lives. Just as David lived his life. Here was a man, scoundrel in many ways, committing one sin after another including murder and adultery, and yet he pleased God so much that God called him, *"a man after my own heart."* [5] What was it in David that was different, that pleased God so much despite his many flaws and transgressions? *David led a God intoxicated life.* For him to live was God. He breathed God. He was consumed by his hunger for God. Read the psalms of David and you will see how passionate he was in his relationship with God. You may even get the impression that David was perhaps mad. Yes he was; mad about God and in love with Him. He danced himself to frenzy in front of the procession carrying the Ark of God to Jerusalem, and became oblivious that in the process he, the King of Israel, had become near naked in front of his people. For him that didn't matter; he was dancing before the Lord and only that mattered.

David's entire life revolved around God. *"On my bed I remember you; I think of you through the watches of the night."* [6] Anytime was a good time for David to remember his God, to think of Him, to praise Him, to break out in a psalm to Him. For him worship was not at set times. Every time was a worship time. He was in a constant state of worshipping. And such love pleased God, pleased Him no end, that He made an everlasting covenant with David; that his throne would be established for ever.

That is what God seeks in all of us. He is our first love; the most important person in our lives. Let us not give Him a reason to ever say to us, as He did to the church in Ephesus, *"You have forsaken your first love."* [7] He does not like to be pushed to the periphery or the margins. He has to be at His rightful place, which is the center. *He wants our everything, for He has given us His everything.* We have to saturate our lives with Him, with His love. We will know that Christ is the center of our lives, when we believe and claim just as Paul did: *"If we live, we live to the Lord; and if we die, we die to the Lord. So, whether we live or die, we belong to the Lord,"* [8] and also, *"For to me, to live is Christ and to die is gain."* [9]

Our God is a jealous God. He will not be content with any other billing than the number one in our lives. *"Do not worship any other god, for the LORD, whose name is Jealous, is a jealous God."* [10] So be careful; He does not like to be taken for granted. I believe this is what Jesus meant, when he said: *"If anyone comes to me and does not hate his father and mother, his wife and children, his brothers and sisters – yes, even his own life – he cannot be my disciple."* [11] That is you can't put anyone before me. I am either all or nothing to you. God can handle anything but our ignoring Him, our being indifferent to Him, our turning our backs to

Him. It hurts Him when we do that. He does not want to be shut out from any part of our lives, but wants to be part of our entire life.

I am much impressed by this statement of Fyodor Dostoevsky: *"If anyone proved to me that Christ was outside the truth then I would prefer to remain with Christ than with the truth."* This says it all; what Christ meant to this Russian writer.

God does not ask much from us. *He only asks us of us!*

Let us give Him.

1.  *Psalm 73:25*
2.  *1 Timothy 6:19*
3.  *Colossians 2:7 (LB)*
4.  *Hebrews 13:8.*
5.  *Acts 13:22*
6.  *Psalm 63:6.*
7.  *Revelation 2:4.*
8.  *Romans 14:8*
9.  *Philippians 1:21*
10. *Exodus 34:14*
11. *Luke 14:26*

# Chapter ~ 39

# SHARING IN HIS WORK

*"For we are God's fellow-workers ....."* [1]

**I** meet people who are involved in Christian ministries. Some work on voluntary basis and some earn their livelihood from it. More often than not, I get to hear from them that: *they work for the Lord.* That may be true but something about this statement doesn't sound quite right. I would rather that we say: *we do the Lord's work.* A subtle difference in the two but I believe an important one nevertheless.

You see, it is our Lord's mission that we are furthering in this world. Whatever be the Christian ministry, it is serving the mission that Jesus Christ had on earth; and which we, his disciples, have been entrusted with to carry it forward. His mission of establishing the kingdom of God, and bringing people to the true knowledge of God and acceptance of the salvation God has given to mankind in him (Jesus). All the works towards this are his, and in fact he works through us. We have to appreciate, that it is all about him and nothing about us. In fact it is essential that it be nothing about us.

Let us understand this clearly: Christian service or as some may call 'kingdom work', is not about us working for him but him working through us. We are just the agents, the vessels, the conduits, which are used by the Lord to accomplish his work. Christ continues to work on earth, even after he left the earth two thousand years ago. He has been at work in and through his disciples; who collectively are his Body on earth, the Church. We have the status of co-workers with him in the kingdom; people who lend their bodies, willingly, for him to advance his works on earth. He wants our surrendered bodies and our willing hearts; and then he can do great works through us.

As Christian life is dependent on God (His grace), Christian service is also dependent on Him. Human effort will not make the mustard seed grow into a big tree. It is God alone who will make our efforts fruitful. We have to offer ourselves as perfect offerings to be used by Him for His purposes. The more we surrender ourselves, the more He is able to work in us and through us. The more we decrease, that is rely less on our resources and strength, the more will He increase in us and His power will be able to work through us. Augustine confessed to God: *"I can do nothing without You."* God did not dispute that but was gracious to say to him: *"And I will do nothing without you."* That is how it works. God was giving Augustine the fundamentals of His working in association with human beings. 'You provide a willing spirit and the body, and I will provide the power. The results you leave to Me; you take the backseat'.

See to it that all glory is given to God. The danger is that you can become bigger than the work you are doing. The spotlight is on you, and if remains on you, it then means that you relish it. Then God is pushed into the background. You may still give Him lip service but the focus is directed on you and not on God. You may start harboring the notion that you are indispensable and that God is fortunate to have you working for His kingdom; that without you the ministry will not work. Beware and make sure that day does not come. For if God is not the prime focus, the center of the ministry, the reason for that Christian enterprise; then that work is of no worth to the kingdom of God. The ministry may expand, your enterprise may grow (like any commercial enterprise would that is run by sound business acumen) but it could well be that the Lord is not in it. Despite your service to the Lord, he may at the end say to you, *"I never knew you"* [2]; even though you may vehemently put up your defense and list all your accomplishments for him.

Christian service can well lead to spiritual pride and one must be constantly on his guard and make sure that God remains the focus, and that all glory is given only to Him – for everything is by Him and for Him. Only He should occupy center stage. You must efface yourself, and as John the Baptist declared, *"He must become greater; I must become less"* [3]; you also need to become nothing in the service of Christ, so that he remains in the forefront of all activity. It is his show and the spotlight has to be on the bridegroom and not on the friends of the bridegroom. The Master's glory is the joy of the servant; for only in his Master's glory is the glory of the servant. *"I tell you the truth, no servant is greater than his master ....,"* [4] Jesus said.

Sometimes the outcome may not be what you expected. Jonah was angry that ultimately God forgave the people of Nineveh and did not destroy the city as He had told Jonah that He would do. Remember it is God's work. He alone can decide what outcome is proper.

Sometimes you may be left out of the outcome or would not be there to see God's glory. Moses did not cross the Jordan river to the Promised Land, even though for 40 years he had led the Israelites in the desert towards this goal. It was not he but Joshua and Caleb who were in God's plan to lead the Israelites across the final and climactic stretch, while Moses just had the consolation of surveying the land from the top of Mount Nebo. Remember it is God's work. He can decide or alter His plans as He wishes. You are just a servant. Just do your job.

Sometimes the waiting can be unbearably long. You may be called by God for some purpose but then there would be a period of silence. You are left alone, in a limbo. You keep waiting for His guidance on the next step; what He wants you to do, how He wants it to be done. The wait can be excruciating (you keep asking, 'what now Lord? what for you called me, plucked me out of a comfortable situation'?) and can throw up doubts in your mind about your calling. Moses spent 40 years in the desert tending to the sheep of Jethro in Midian, before God gave him the details of his mission. David spent years hiding in the caves of the Judean desert before the time came for him to become king; for which he had been anointed much earlier. Remember it is God's work. He has His own timetable. You cannot tell Him when to do, as you cannot tell Him what and how to do. The time of waiting is the time of preparation; readying you mentally, spiritually, and even physically for the task He has chosen you for. He is making you suitable for the job ahead. For once you are thrown into the cauldron, He cannot risk your failure.

And sometimes be prepared to be overruled by God. There have been some who were reluctant to accept their commission from God. But God persisted with them. He wanted them for that mission. Moses tried his best to wriggle out of the mission to be God's deliverer to the Israelites, to take them out of slavery from the land of Egypt. The prospects of going to Egypt, a land from where he had run away as a murderer, and facing the mighty Pharaoh, the most powerful man on earth at that time, and putting before him the suicidal demand of letting the Israelites go; all these must have filled Moses with dread. He gave one excuse after another to escape the assignment, but God would have none of it. When he had stretched God's patience a bit too much, God became angry and told him plainly that he was the chosen one and he will have to do it. So get moving Moses!

Same was the case with Jonah. He was reluctant to take up the mission of going to the people of Nineveh and prophesying to them of their impending doom. Such announcements are likely to be met by lethal beatings. Jonah ran away from God, thinking that by this way he would escape the task. God pursued him, and after an adventurous journey in which Jonah found himself in the belly of a fish for three days, Jonah finally gave up and accepted the task. The point is: if God wants you for a particular work (for whatever reason He may have chosen you of all the people), He will be after you till you relent and accept. Of course this will be up to a point. If you become obstinate and do not budge, God may finally give up and go away. Then whose loss will it be? Undoubtedly yours. God will surely pick someone else.

His work will go on. Only you will have no part in it. And you would likely regret it at a later date.

But while we have seen that God is patient, up to point that is, there are times when He wants an immediate answer, a spontaneous response from us, when He calls. We read the accounts of Jesus calling his disciples. His saying only the words, *"follow me,"* evoked a spontaneous response from the disciples. Peter, James, John, and Andrew left their fishing nets and followed him; and Matthew just got up from his seat at the tax collection booth and followed the Master, when the call came. Such response displays willingness to trust and putting your confidence in the Lord. But to the one who wanted to first go and say goodbye to his family and then follow him, the Lord said, *"No-one who puts his hand to the plough and looks back is fit for service in the kingdom of God."* [5] Tough it may appear, but the Lord expects implicit and immediate obedience.

*"Often the work of God comes with two edges, great joy and great pain,"* commented Philip Yancey. That is true. It can demand a lot from you. Life is not easy from the point the call comes. Your whole life may require to be organized differently. Look at the prophets of old. Did any one of them have an easy life after God called him into His service? In fact from the worldly viewpoint their lives would appear to be condemned. And John the Baptist – what life was his? Living in the desert, camel hair for clothing, food of locusts and honey – in no way appealing. Paul faced all the hardships one can think of, when he shed off the name Saul and went about teaching and preaching the good news. He writes, *"For I am already being poured out like a drink offering ....."* [6] This apostle of Christ was emptying himself in his work for the Lord. So great was his effort and so difficult his life in Christ, that one can just sit back and admire the faith of this man, who was formerly an avowed enemy of Christ and the persecutor of his followers.

For all of them there was great pain in their lives but it was accompanied by great joy. Joy of serving the Lord and of the privilege of being chosen for his work. And that joy was worth all the pain of the world. Life indeed gets tough. It may not happen with all who are called into service, but it can happen to anyone.

While the outcome of any work of God is not because of you (so that there is no boasting), but nevertheless your efforts do matter; and therefore God expects you to give your all to it. It is God's work, so you must give your very best, more than your hundred percent. Your service is your offering and your offering has to be perfect. How can it be less? Our God is a perfect God and when Jesus wants us to be perfect like our Father in heaven, we have to strive for that perfection also in the work that we do in His service. The parable of the minas illustrates that. The servants gave different returns for the one mina each that was given to them. The master was pleased with those who had put the mina to good use and multiplied his wealth. His final comments gave his judgment: *"I tell you that to everyone who has, more will be given, but as for the one who has nothing, even what he has will be taken away."* [7]

God has given us many talents and skills; and when He calls us unto His service, He expects us to put them into full and effective use. Serve with excellence. Let your work be like worship that pleases the Lord. But I will put in a word of caution here. While we must serve the Lord with passion and with all our heart, leaving no stone unturned in our service of Him; at the same time we must not become possessive. Remember it is God's work. By Him and for Him. So let there be no boasting (I, me, mine) but instead thanksgiving and gratitude that He made us worthy by using us. God did not choose us because we were special; He made us special because He chose us. Take heed that the Bible says, *"...out of these stones God can raise up children for Abraham,"*[8] and remain humble and every grateful to God.

Our service on earth will determine our rewards in heaven. But our works do not work out our salvation. Only our faith does. We are saved by faith and not by works. We serve with gratitude *because* we are saved. Our work will define the position we serve God, in the world to come.

In a way all Christians (all those who are disciples of Jesus Christ) are in God's service, whether in full time ministry or otherwise. For the Great Commission which the Lord gave, is to ALL the believers and not to a select group. So each and every Christian is a foot soldier of Christ and in his life, in his sphere of work and influence, a witness to the Lord. We are told: *"And whatever you do, whether in word or deed, do it all in the name of the Lord Jesus, giving thanks to God the Father through him."* [9] Thus in our own ways, big or small, but as per God's will for us, we work for the advancement of His kingdom. But here too we need to be careful. It is very possible that while we may be bringing many to the kingdom of God and may be doing great works in His name, we may find that we ourselves are not in the race. Paul kept reminding himself of precisely this: *"....so that after I have preached to others, I myself will not be disqualified for the prize."* [10] We need to do the same.

Please note God is more concerned in what we become for Him (are we becoming like Jesus?) rather than what we do for Him. So in our enthusiasm for serving the Lord, we should not lose sight of what is more important to Him i.e. our relationship with Him and our development into Christlikeness. *"Many Christians are so intent on doing something for God that they forget that God's main work is to make something of them,"* said Jim Elliot. Our service is important, but our walk with God is more important.

*"I cry out to God Most High, to God, who fulfills His purpose for me."*[11] Every Christian, without exception, needs to know the purpose that God has for his life. And after knowing that, he must offer to God a willing spirit, a surrendered self, and the humble attitude of a servant, so that God may fulfill that purpose.

Then he will work in the kingdom of God in the same way as his Lord Jesus did.

1.  *1 Corinthians 3:9*
2.  *Matthew 7:23*
3.  *John 3:30*
4.  *John 13:16*
5.  *Luke 9:62*
6.  *2 Timothy 4:6*
7.  *Luke 19:26*
8.  *Matthew 3:9*
9.  *Colossians 3:17*
10. *1 Corinthians 9:27*
11. *Psalm 57:2*

# Chapter ~ 40

# IN THE IMAGE OF THE MASTER

*"Christ accepts us as we are but when he accepts us
we cannot remain as we are."*

— *Walter Trobisch*

**W**e have been called to be like Christ. The disciple has to be like his Master. Not a clone but the image of his Master. The image of Christ, the Christlikeness, has to be seen in the Christian, so that he can be identified as belonging to Christ. God loves his Son so much that He wants to make all of us, his followers, like him. It is too wonderful a thought that God should want us to be like Jesus; but the process towards it is long and painful.

*'The disciples of Jesus were called Christians for the first time at Antioch'*[1]; a few years after this new faith took birth in Jerusalem. Till then they had been known as belonging to the sect called *'the Way'*. The name Christians - Christ ones - appropriately described those who followed Christ and reflected the image of Christ in the way they lived, related with each other, and behaved with those who were outside their community. Their entire perspective to life was different from that of

the world. It was the way of Christ and the disciples had the mark of the Lord on their lives, and it was seen as such by the world. We need to appreciate that it is an honor to be called Christian, a name which has Christ in it; and that we have to live our lives worthy of this name. *We have to be like Christ.*

"*Christianity in its purest form is nothing more than seeing Jesus. Christian service in its purest form is nothing more than imitating Him who we see. To see His Majesty and to imitate him, that is the sum of Christianity,*" wrote Max Lucado. That is true and no servant can be other than what his master is. "*He cannot be above his master, it is enough for him to be like him,*" [2] Jesus had told his twelve disciples when sending them out on a trial mission to preach the kingdom of God. We have to be like our Master and must imitate and follow him in everything till, "*Christ is all, and is in all,*" [3] in our lives.

"*Every call to conversion includes a call to discipleship, to Christlikeness,*" said Dietrich Bonhoeffer. Our following doesn't end with our accepting Christ in our lives. In fact it begins. After conversion, discipleship must begin. To accept Christ is not enough; to become his disciple - which is really to become like him - is what must follow, more importantly. And a call to be Christlike is a call for perfection and is part of our sanctification on earth. The Master was perfect in each and every way - as Son of Man and as Son of God. The disciple has also to move towards this perfection.

The journey to Christlikeness is a tough one. It is a process which continues right through our lives. "*Christian life is not a short dash to glory but a long distance race calling for endurance,*" wrote A.C. Purdy. God has a lot of work to do in carving out the image of Christ in us. He has to make us unlearn many things that are offensive, free us from the hold of evil habits which seem to have a vice like grip over us, remove the idols that we cling on to so desperately, subdue our ego which is often much larger than us, change our sinful nature that is so obdurate. He will do whatever it takes and use whatever means necessary to make us like His Son. God will keep on chipping the rough edges of our character, keep on pruning the thorns in our nature, keep on chiseling our soul, till He makes us what He intends us to be.

However there is this underlying assurance that He will continue the work till it is completed and will not leave it midway. Paul writes, *"He who began a good work in you will carry it on to completion until the day of Christ Jesus."* [4] Day of Christ Jesus? Does it mean that the work of making us perfect continues even after our physical death? I somehow believe it to be so. John writes in his epistle: *"But we know that when he appears, we shall be like him, for we shall see him as he is."* [5]

This is provided we continue to allow God to work in us, which will require our increasing surrender of ourselves. We have to be a willing partner in our transformation into God's handiwork, in the process of our perfection, in God carving out the image of Christ in us. It is God's power working through the Holy Spirit in us which combines with our willingness to open up and surrender everything to God. A collaborative undertaking that ever was one. And be prepared for a rough ride. It will not be a growth curve which goes up in a straight line but will fluctuate between peaks and troughs, between ups and downs, between highs and lows. It will have moments of ecstasy of spiritual triumphs and moments of despair of spiritual bottoms.

But we are not to give up. God will not give up on us. We also must not give up on ourselves. We have to keep moving. As Paul writes in the epistle to the Philippians: *"Not that I have already obtained all this, or have already been made perfect, but I press on to take hold of that for which Christ Jesus took hold of me. Brothers, I do not consider myself yet to have taken hold of it. But one thing I do: Forgetting what is behind and straining towards what is ahead, I press on towards the goal to win the prize for which God has called me heavenwards in Christ Jesus."* [6] Note these words of encouragement from St. Augustine: *"On earth we are wayfarers, always on the go. This means that we have to keep on moving forward. Therefore, be always unhappy about where you are if you want to reach where you are not. If you are pleased with what you are, you have stopped already. If you say 'it is enough' you are lost. Keep on walking, moving forward, trying for the goal."* And Martin Luther King also provides us strength in these words: *"If you can't fly, run. If you can't run, walk. If you can't walk, crawl, but by all means keep moving."*

God does not want us to stop – either by way of giving up or by way of thinking that we have 'arrived'. He wants us to continue to give ourselves to Him, for Him to work in us as long as He wants. Many a times we may feel discouraged and frustrated at the slow progress that we see in ourselves. Many a times we may feel defeated by the un-Christlike parts in us that are proving hard to change. In those moments we may wish that it would have been easier if God could have injected perfection in us or given us a concoction of perfection to drink. We would have become Christlike in an instant!

But God does not operate this way. He works from within the person. He brings the change inside out. For that is a lasting change and that change also involves us as an active partner. God refines us like silver or gold, removing our impurities in the process. In the Book of Malachi, it is described about God that: *"He will sit as a refiner and purifier of silver."* [7] The refiner continues heating the silver till he sees his image in the piece of metal, which indicates to him that the silver has become clear of its impurities. And for the refiner to see his image he has to be sitting close to the fire!

In the same way God will continue to refine us till He sees the image of His Son in us. So be prepared but also rest assured that God will not give up. And we also must not give up till the race is over, till the battle has ended. *"To achieve the perfection that drew us on the quest, we must wait until the race has ended, until death, and the waiting itself is an act of extraordinary faith and courage,"* writes Philip Yancey. *"But when perfection comes, the imperfect disappears. Now we see but a poor reflection as in a mirror; then we shall see face to face. Now I know in part; then I shall know fully, even as I am fully known,"* [8] Paul assures the believers in Corinth. Yes, when we will fully know, when we will fully see, we will be surprised how much like Christ, God has made us.

Why God wants us to be perfect? We have to be perfect because He is perfect: *"Be perfect, therefore, as your heavenly Father is perfect."* [9] We have to be holy because He is holy: *"Be holy because I, the LORD your God, am holy."* [10] There is no choice. It is non-negotiable. If we have to live with God in eternity, if we are to be part of His family, then we have to become like Him. For no unholy or unclean person will see God or can enter into His presence. *"Who may ascend the hill of the LORD? Who may stand in his holy place? He who has clean hands and a pure heart ...,"* [11] the psalmist provides the answer to his own question. God's family has to be like Him. It is *His* family.

We are also co-heirs with Christ and will inherit God's kingdom with him. We have to be therefore like Christ, so that we may share in his inheritance. We are also his Body on earth – the Church - of which he is the Head. Just as the Head is perfect, the rest of the body also has to be made perfect. And we are Christ's ambassadors in this world, his fragrance spreading in this world. People will look at us to see the Christ in us. *"Of one hundred men, one will read the Bible, the ninety nine will read the Christian,"* commented Dwight L. Moody. Many will have their first experience of Jesus through us. How we live? What standards we have? Do people see Christ in us? Has he made any visible impact in our lives? Do we reflect the image of Christ for the whole world to see? Do our lives proclaim the message of Christ?

When Sadhu Sundar Singh walked in the villages of Punjab seeking alms, people used to point at him and say: "Here comes Christ." And that must have been not only because of his physical resemblance to Christ (that is to the generally accepted portrayal in the paintings of what Jesus must have looked like) but also his demeanor. Can we say the same of ourselves, that people see Christ in us?

Paul exhorts us to, *"live a life worthy of the Lord,"* [12] and to, *"conduct yourselves in a manner worthy of the gospel of Christ."* [13] Christlikeness should be evident in our actions, in our speech, in our faith, in our behavior, and in our character. Christlikeness should also be seen in our thoughts and attitude: *"Your attitude should be the same as that of Christ Jesus."* [14] For I need to accept that it is no longer me who is living in my body but Christ who is living in me and should be seen as such. Paul writes, *"For you died, and your life is now hidden with Christ in God,"*[15] and, *"for all of you who were baptized into Christ have clothed yourselves with Christ."* [16] We now wear Christ and it should be seen by all.

God made His Son like us to save us; and now that we are saved, He makes us like His Son.

Amazing isn't it?

1. *Acts 11:26 (modified)*
2. *Matthew 10:24-25 (paraphrased)*
3. *Colossians 3:11.*
4. *Philippians 1:6*
5. *1 John 3:2*
6. *Philippians 3:12-14*
7. *Malachi 3:3*
8. *1 Corinthians 13:10, 12*
9. *Matthew 5:48*
10. *Leviticus 19.2*
11. *Psalm 24:3-4*
12. *Colossians 1:10*
13. *Philippians 1:27*
14. *Philippians 2:5*
15. *Colossians 3:3*
16. *Galatians 3:27*